VACANT

A MINDSPACE INVESTIGATIONS NOVEL

Alex Hughes

A ROC BOOK

ROC
Published by the Penguin Group
Penguin Group (USA) LLC, 375 Hudson Street,
New York, New York 10014

USA | Canada | UK | Ireland | Australia | New Zealand | India | South Africa | China
penguin.com
A Penguin Random House Company

First published by Roc, an imprint of New American Library,
a division of Penguin Group (USA) LLC

First Printing, December 2014

ISBN 978-0-451-46694-5

Printed in the United States of America
10 9 8 7 6 5 4 3 2 1

To Ann, Tanith, Karen, the Even Odders, and Jeane,
to Kerry, Amanda, James, and Danielle,
to Jesse and Rebecca,
and all the rest who've helped me make
the series what it is.
Thank you.

And to the Millards
for being extraordinary on no notice.

CHAPTER 1

A sea of thoughts crashed into me like a tsunami, chaos given form with impossible force. I focused on the back of Isabella's sweatshirt as I followed her through the crowds, past the food on the outside rim of Phillips Arena.

She finally moved into one of the alcoves with the big sign—a something and a number. My eyes were in slits, focused only on her to block out all those damn minds. She stopped against the concrete wall, pulling me out of the way. The crowd pushed against my shoulder periodically anyway, bursts of particular minds striking mine as their bodies ran into my shoulder.

She said something.

"What?"

"This was a terrible idea," Isabella said, in the tone of someone repeating herself. "You're not—"

"It's fine," I said, through gritted teeth. "You paid all the money for the tickets. You begged me to come. We're here. Let's see the show."

"But—" Isabella waffled. Isabella Cherabino was a senior homicide detective for the DeKalb County Police Department, and as such was normally decisive. She must have had strong emotions about this concert, which I'd know if I wasn't spending every spare bit of my energy shielding against the crush of minds all around me. There were times when telepathy was more of a curse than a blessing.

"It's okay," I said. It wasn't, of course, but I was here, damn it. Might as well get through this.

She pulled me farther down the hall and waved our tickets again at new people, who pointed her down a set of stairs. I followed behind her, entire vision focused on the back of her shirt.

The ancient twice-remodeled stadium hosted hockey games, so it wasn't exactly gorgeous, and the floating screens overhead looked like they'd fall down at any time. The whole place smelled like fried food and beer—old beer—but that wasn't the worst part. The worst part was the people. Maybe a hundred thousand people were jostling and yelling and talking and *thinking* around me, loudly. Their mental waves in Mindspace—groups upon groups of thin, normal mind-waves—added up to an ocean of force that overwhelmed all of my senses.

She found our seats and pushed me into mine. I gripped the ancient wooden armrests with shaking hands.

I had no idea how she'd talked me into this. Telepaths did *not* like crowds. I hadn't had to deal with this level of overwhelming mental force since my final testing, more than twenty years ago now, and I strained under the pressure like a piano suspended over a cartoon character's head. I swallowed, forcing myself against it.

My old teacher's voice in my head reminded me that strength didn't always get the job done, no matter how manly it felt at the time. Sometimes you had to be the duck, swimming with the current while the rain slipped off your back. I tried that, focusing on moving through the pressure cleanly rather than blocking it. A surfer on the edge of the sea, pushed along but not fighting. It helped, but only some.

Then Isabella reached over and took my hand, and warm feelings leavened with a little guilt rolled up my arm.

"Thank you for coming, Adam," she said quietly. With the physical connection, I could feel her even through my shielding.

And I looked over and remembered why I'd come. I was with her.

Isabella was a beautiful woman with strong Italian features, thick, slightly curly hair she usually wore up, and a curvy body well worth a second look. She was in her late thirties, had a black belt in something Asian and deadly, and was one of the smartest people I knew. Her sense of justice in working with the police had been one of the things that had kept me on the wagon these last four years. Her strength of character and huge work ethic had been an inspiration for far longer.

It was impossible for me to believe that she was willing to date me; I'd been in love with her for years, and even though I couldn't say it out loud yet, *and* even though we hadn't had sex—she hadn't been willing to make the nearly permanent commitment that sex with a telepath implied— we were dating. Four months and change now. And she'd been falling asleep in my arms nearly as long. She'd even filled out the official relationship form with the department, calling me boyfriend in plain text where anyone could read it. It was a miracle, as far as I was concerned.

So if I had to stand in the middle of the worst press of minds in my life, I would. I'd do nearly anything for her.

After ten minutes or so, the lights dimmed and the crowd roared. The minds roared too, pressing against my consciousness like a hand squeezing a tube of toothpaste with the lid still on. Like that lid, I felt under pressure, impossibly strained. I wondered whether I'd really be able to survive this.

The screens came on, and the image of the aging rock musician Cherabino liked came on in a still photograph. Then the image fractured to be replaced by the concert logo. The crowd roared, and Mindspace trembled with pressure and interacting minds. Only two hours until it was over. She'd spent a fortune on the tickets, I told myself.

A manufactured smell—of volcanic gas, engine oil, and ozone—flooded the stadium, and the roaring of the crowd grew louder. Then the lights dimmed, and green spotlights flooded the empty stage floor in front of us. The smell of deep woods added to the mix in the air, growing things and moss and sunlight cutting through the darker smells of civilization. The smell came back to me from the minds around me, lessening the pressure with pure sensation.

A trapdoor opened in the middle of the stage, and a figure was slowly raised into the green light. The rocker's peaked hair caught the light with glitter and phantom holograms, and the clothes were not much better, tight-fitting to a fault, glittering. She slung her spiky guitar in front of her body and strummed.

The noise filled the stadium and every mind in it, shaking our seats with pure sound. Isabella next to me was transfixed, her focus coming through our psychic Link.

The minds around me echoed the sound of the opening bars of the song, echoed the lights now turning red as the rocker screamed about dropping bombs, about bursting minds in the sixty-years-ago Tech Wars. And as she quieted and sang intense notes about a child growing up in a shattered city, every mind in the place cried with her.

I dropped my shields, dropped them entirely, and pulled my hand away from Isabella.

"What?" she said.

"Shh," I said. The band was rising up at the back of the

stage on more platforms from the floor, the lights ramping up, but I didn't care. I closed my eyes.

The music swelled in screams again, drums coming in, and the beat fell into the minds of the crowd. The vision of what was happening onstage came through a thousand minds, an overlapping kaleidoscope vision of one idea, one experience, one moment. And it continued. It continued.

No one was here who didn't love this band. No one paid who didn't live for this moment. And here, in the middle of all of it, I felt like a feather flying in the wind, a glider sailing on the sea of emotional high. The music swelled again, and my heart with it. Sound and vision and fury and a thousand happy minds crashed into me, and I breathed them in.

Sometime later, the world dissipated into a sea of clapping, and I came back to myself. I built shields, slowly, to block out the Mindspace now fracturing into chaos. The pressure, the unpleasantness returned, and I returned to laboring against it, but left in my mind was that one, pure note, the note that had started it all.

Isabella poked me.

"What?" I said, reluctantly opening my eyes.

"I said, did you like it?"

"That was . . . that was great," I said. It was the understatement of the century.

"Are you okay?" she asked. Then she wondered if she needed to call Swartz, my Narcotics Anonymous sponsor. "You look . . . high."

"Just the concert," I said. I stood then; someone pushed by on their way to the aisle. "Can we hang around until most of the people are gone?" I asked. I'd rather not deal with all those minds wanting so desperately to get out of here; I was already feeling the edge of that flight response and didn't want it intensified.

"Sure," she said, but she looked at me suspiciously.

As another couple moved out of the row, squeezing in front of us, I realized I had to make an effort at conversation now. I really wanted to sit down and process what I'd just experienced—something I'd never, in my forty years, even dreamed of—but this was Isabella.

"What did you think of the ballad about the miniature giraffe?" I asked her.

"That was hilarious," she said, still looking suspicious. But she sat down, and I sat down, and as people moved out of the old stadium like ants and strange smells moved through the concert system in front of us, we talked.

After a while she was even smiling.

I'd done well tonight, I thought to myself. But at the back of my brain, I wondered. Did I really need something else in my life that was that . . . addictive?

We waited over an hour, until the majority of the minds were long gone. When we walked out of the arena building, it was dark, and the street was nearly deserted, just a few clusters of people here and there. Our breath fogged in the late-February air, the winter on its last greedy weeks of cold. Bioengineered trees with luminescent glowing orbs illuminated the sidewalk in dim blue light, which stretched farther than you thought it should, beautiful and simple, feeling artificial and natural all at once. They held up well to the cold, I noticed, as I huddled in my jacket a little deeper.

A small group of guys stood about a hundred feet away, their body language tense and confrontational. Cherabino's hand moved toward the gun on her waist she wasn't carrying.

Then one guy yelled, and the group turned inward. The dull *slap* of repeated fist blows hit the air.

Cherabino considered whether to get involved.

I turned—but it was too late. A man stood there, at least fifty-five and thin. He was short, balding, with dark skin that caught up blue highlights from the bioluminescent streetlight. In Mindspace, his presence had wiry strength and desperation mixed. He held a pole as tall as himself, maybe fifty T-shirts hooked into loops on the pole, shirts with a cheaply copied logo of the band we'd just seen.

"Buy a shirt. Just ten ROCs," he said, but his tone was angry.

"No, thanks," I said.

"Keep moving, sir," Cherabino said, a little of her cop voice leaking into her speech, moving toward a defensive stance.

Another guy came up, behind us, one of the ones from the group who'd been fighting. The others held back, working out their aggression, close to leaving. I moved around to look at him.

"Buy a shirt or my buddy and I have something to say."

"No way those are official shirts," I said. "You're stealing from the artist."

I felt the first guy's decision, but Cherabino was already moving.

Pain from behind me. Cherabino in judo mode.

The buddy charged me. I went to get a grip on his mind—and failed.

He punched me in the jaw. I saw stars, and my legs went out from underneath me.

I blinked up, trying to get my bearings, but he kicked me. I whimpered. Not the most manly moment, but it hurt, damn it. I pushed back up.

Cherabino was over me then, badge out in the guy's face. "Police," she said.

She went flying and somebody kicked me back down again. I put my hands over my head to protect it and tried to get a grip on the guy's mind one more time. Slippery fellow—we had bad valence, terrible valence, and I couldn't get a grip.

I went for the first one—and him I could grip. I hit the center of his mind, knocking him out. He slumped down, landing on top of the abandoned T-shirt rack.

I got up to my knees just in time to watch Cherabino punch the buddy in the face. "Police," she said, standing over him. "Don't ever let me see you around here again."

"Shouldn't you arrest them?" I asked.

She considered it, then gave me a hand up.

The buddy took off running, and she let him go. "Not worth interrupting my date over," she said. She glanced back at the guy I'd knocked out. Then sighed. "Is there a way to wake him up? Leaving him unconscious probably isn't the best of ideas."

I took a look at my handiwork in Mindspace. "If I wake him right now he'll have the world's worst headache."

"Serve him right. Do it. Then let's get out of here."

We walked back to the parking garage across the street, her feet moving faster than I preferred. Her anger was still in play. Mine too. We shouldn't have gotten involved in a stupid fight outside Phillips.

She found her car, an old beat-up sedan, where she'd left it on the fourth floor. Her parking job was crooked, which was typical for her. She unlocked the car and let us in.

"You sure we shouldn't have arrested them?" I asked as I swung myself down into the seat.

"We're in Fulton County and off-duty. More trouble than it's worth," she said, but wasn't exactly happy about it. She turned on the fusion engine, it slowly warming up with a whine.

I closed the door. My body was calm by now, my heartbeat

more settled, but I still felt jumpy, still felt too sensitive. I was open to Mindspace, monitoring what was going on, which was why I felt it.

All at once, I felt a shift in the world, a collapsing in, a hole disappearing into the fabric of Mindspace. A cold wind across my sense of the future, itching and then gone. A mile away, perhaps, just at the edge of my senses for even the strongest signal. A mile away behind us.

My stomach sank. "Someone just died."

"What?" she said.

"Someone just died behind us. Violently, to be that strong."

"Murder?" she asked.

"Or they fell off a building and impacted the ground. Strong, violent stuff."

She sighed. I felt her considering.

"Go ahead and turn around," I said. She was a workaholic and obligated to the department. Getting in the way of her job wasn't going to get me anywhere. And the feeling of that death bothered me. I wanted to know what was going on.

"But—"

"It's fine," I said. "Let's find out who died."

"Okay." So she turned the car around.

CHAPTER 2

I gave her directions, eyes closed, a macro game of hot and cold as we got closer to what I'd felt, back and forth along streets.

"Right," I said, and a few moments later she turned right.

"I see it," she said, and slowed the car.

We parked a few hundred feet away, engine settling and then turning off. On the sidewalk was a scatter of T-shirts like molted feathers, a metal pole with cloth loops now dark with blood, and a man who had clearly been beaten to death. Beyond it, a pay phone under one of the arena's lights.

"Is that . . . ?" I asked into the silence of the car.

"Yeah," she said, staring at the steering wheel. "Yeah, it is."

She got out of the car, walking past the body while I sat there, in shock. What had happened in ten minutes? Why hadn't I felt anything but the death? Why hadn't my future-sense kicked in a little? We might have saved his life by arresting him.

Cherabino picked up the pay phone, and I closed the car door behind me gently.

"I need to report a murder in Fulton County," she said as I stood over the man. She added her police number and additional identifying information.

His face was dented, actually dented in a couple of areas,

while swelling around his eyes made him look . . . inhuman, like clay formed by a child sculptor, only an approximation of a man. His body looked worse, arm out of socket, clothes dark with blood. His leg was clearly broken, half out of place.

I'd touched his mind, just a few minutes ago. And now the absence, the hole in Mindspace that signified his death, was like a fresh wound in the world.

She hung up the phone and walked back over to me, hands deep in her coat pockets.

"Are we . . . ?" I asked.

"They'll look at us for a little while, but the forensics won't match up and they'll let it go," she said. Her mind added that we might have to spend the night in Fulton County Lockup. Maybe. But running would get us far worse, and professional courtesy should extend somewhat.

Distantly, sirens wailed. I shivered in my jacket.

It was a sad and unfortunate truth that the person to report the crime was often the first suspect. In this case, that meant that Cherabino and I, out of our jurisdiction, were suspects. I wasn't entirely surprised when they bundled us up and took us into the station. I was surprised when they kept us for hours.

I found myself on the opposite side of the interview table, in a strange room, with yet another stranger asking me questions. She was a fortysomething woman with strong features and a hard personality, what my father would have called a battle-ax when I was growing up—and he would have meant it as a compliment. Unfortunately, after three interviewers, I was less than pleased with her on principle.

"You lost your job with the DeKalb County Police Department recently," she began, after the usual softening-up questions. "Tell me about that."

"My job at the DeKalb County Police Department changed focus and hours," I replied as precisely as possible. "I'm a consultant. I consult. Unfortunately one of the consulting jobs I took outside the department last year made Paulsen—my supervisor—uncomfortable. It was decided to move me more directly to the homicide and robbery squads to work with Branen and his team, who do not have the same concerns about other consulting." I'd had a few hours to figure out how to phrase that by now. Plus, Swartz and I had discussed the best way to say it for job interviews.

"What was the consulting job that made your superior uncomfortable?" the interrogator asked.

"I'm sorry. What was your name?" I asked, tired of being played like a civilian. After the second interviewer, they'd already left me alone for an hour and a half with bad coffee and no bathroom; I'd spurned the one because I'd planned for the other, but it had to be two a.m. and I wanted a nap. Another nap, I should say. She'd woken me up once already. Or her predecessor had. I was losing track.

"Officer Malone," the woman said, after a moment of consideration. "I'll repeat, what was the consulting job that made your superior uncomfortable?"

"Officer Malone. Thank you." I made myself relax my body language a little more . . . more "open," less defensive. "The consulting job that made my superiors uncomfortable was one with the Telepaths' Guild. I can't go into details."

Her whole demeanor changed then, her body drawing back, her lip curling under. "The Guild? You worked for the Guild?"

I nodded.

Any professional courtesy she'd given me up until that point vanished like a mirage. She peppered me with question after question, hostility mixing with her fear at being alone with a "traitor telepath" until finally she brought in another stubborn-minded male interrogator.

I held on to my temper with both hands and answered the questions as honestly as possible, going over what I'd seen outside the concert over and over again. Finally, after two hours, I said, "Are we done?"

"For now," she said, anger in every line. Then they left me alone.

Great. It was going to be one of those nights, wasn't it?

About four in the morning, I slept. And, miracle of miracles, they actually let me sleep for long enough to count as real sleep.

Sleeping outside my apartment was always a risk, since the lack of my specialty telepathic wave cancellation machine meant I felt Mindspace fully even while unconscious. Sometimes that meant I slept badly. Sometimes that meant I saw other minds, or other futures, without control.

This time the dream came back, the dream that was a variant on the vision I'd had two months ago.

I saw a boy, a boy who was a growing telepath, a boy who felt familiar in some indefinable way.

We were in a barn with old, musty hay. Beams of sunlight dropped through rotting boards, leaving spaces in the barn's walls. The air danced with motes of dust and the smell of fear.

A man stood against a wooden beam, holding a long cord. The boy didn't know who the man was but was terrified of him. I, knowing, was even more terrified; the man's name was Sibley, and he was a professional hit man. He'd taken the boy for some unknown reason, and he knew I was connected to him.

Don't be afraid, I told the boy. *Don't be afraid. We're coming.*

A phone rang. I picked it up.

"You shouldn't have invaded my home," Fiske's voice said.

A chill of fear ran down my spine, and I knew the boy was going to die.

Then the vision disappeared, and I found myself back in the real world. Someone hit my ankle, again, with a booted foot.

"Wha—?"

"Get up," Malone said. "Your sergeant is here to collect you."

"What—?"

"Get up," she repeated.

So I got up, preceding her and her hostility into the cramped quarters that was this particular precinct of Fulton County Police.

But, as we passed more desks for cops, I couldn't shake the fear. That fear, and a boy who was about to die, and that it was my fault. My P-factor was seventy-eight percent, which meant that my visions of the future—when they decided to work—were right about three-quarters of the time. When they came to my personal safety, they were even more accurate, unfortunately. Unless I could figure out how to stop it, this vision would likely come to pass, and a boy would die. My gut felt empty, all too empty.

At the front of the station, I saw Cherabino with deep circles under her eyes, looking haunted. And there, behind her, was Sergeant Branen.

I'd never been so happy to see the bastard in my life.

But I was also cold now, cold and afraid for a boy I didn't know.

Branen greeted me, clearly unhappy, while a precinct full of strangers stared and judged.

I returned the greeting. "Sir."

"You okay?" Cherabino asked.

I felt like crap, and the vision worried me. But I also didn't want to stay any longer than we had to, so I said, "Yeah. For now."

"Follow me out," Branen barked.

Cherabino glanced at me, then away. She was very aware of Branen's body language right now, and I didn't blame her. It wasn't a good situation for her boss to be dragged out to another precinct to pick us up. I didn't know what to do, frankly. I hoped she did.

Outside, street taxis whirred by in front of the Fulton County Police Building, the dirty road with puddles of unnamed substances. The skyscrapers towered overhead with shining glory of anti-grav-assisted supermaterials, pristine and beautiful above, the dirt and disuse below beneath their notice. The police building seemed an angry troll in comparison, dirty and old, squatting on land that it jealously guarded. The air was warming up a little, at least, and the pollution didn't seem too bad today.

Branen moved to a police car with the DeKalb County logo, currently parked illegally in a loading zone near a neighboring building. He pointed to the back, where I went with a sigh. I didn't like being treated like a criminal.

"You too, Cherabino," he said.

A spike of anger from her, but she complied. I watched the thoughts bubble up in her head like a lava lamp roiling, but none stuck. None turned into words; the car was oddly, starkly silent.

Branen drove in silence, pulling out onto the busy street cautiously, working his way through the one-way streets and limited skylane on-ramps with concentration until he settled on the Freedom Parkway airlanes. Behind us, the early-morning commuters in their flyers stretched out like ribbons above the major interstate, ribbons between sky-scrapers on all sides. Ahead, the early-morning sun edged above the horizon, soft, beautiful light that promised a new day. It was lying, of course. The vision—and the treatment from the Fulton County cops—still lingered. "They have witnesses that saw you beating up both citizens," Branen said finally, voice dangerously low.

"They started the fight," I said.

"Not you, Ward. I don't want to hear from you at all if I can help it. You were down on the ground according to witnesses. I'm talking about Cherabino. They said she flashed her badge, apparently, then said some very harsh threats. Threw more than one punch—a few kicks—started the fight and then ended it with excessive force. One of the guys ran away, the other she knocked out and kicked. Then, maybe fifteen minutes later, you both find a body of the same man. On the two-year anniversary of the Neil Bennett beating. Your timing could not have been worse if you'd planned it." That was right; Bennett had been beaten by three officers in one of the southern metro counties after he talked back to one of them. He'd lost the use of a lung and nearly his life. I'd completely forgotten about it; it hadn't been my county. Branen had to know, though. Branen was political.

He added, "Did you plan it?"

Cherabino protested, "No, sir. And I didn't—"

Branen cut her off. "This is a political time bomb. On the two-year anniversary of the Bennett beating. With officer brutality already on every media channel in the city."

Wow. That sounded terrible. But she hadn't done anything wrong. The witnesses had clearly screwed up their memories of who had done what.

I told him, "Sir, that wasn't what—"

Cherabino protested, "I didn't—"

"I have your side of the story in copious notes from Fulton County," Branen said. "I'm not interested in hearing it again. I'm interested in handling this time bomb."

"Seriously, I was with her the whole time. She threw a couple punches and a kick after they started it, and then they continued after she told them she was police. It was—"

"Ward, if I hear one more word from you I will fire you," Branen said. "You can't testify in court and with your background your testimony isn't admissible into Internal Affairs hearings except as a courtesy. Even then, I won't put you on the stand because the two of you are dating. You have no credibility, and there are three citizens with excellent credibility against you. It's a train wreck waiting to happen, and I'm not going to play that game. I'd suggest you shut up about now and be grateful you aren't being brought up on your own charges."

"Ch-charges?" Cherabino asked, for the first time losing her cool confidence.

"This department has a zero-tolerance policy for police brutality, and the witnesses say you crossed that line many times over. Your hand-to-hand training—especially the judo—means you have the skills, and you did punch out the rookie last year. And on the anniversary, with the media already involved . . ." He sighed. "Cherabino, you're one of my best officers, but I can't play favorites, and I can't assume your innocence, not under these circumstances. I have my own career to worry about. I can't be seen to tolerate excessive violence from you or anyone else. Not at all after the Bennett incident, and especially not on its anniversary." Bennett had gone to every media outlet he could find, and his battered body had played very well on the national news. I'd seen something about that in the paper yesterday.

I swallowed. We were really in trouble, weren't we?

"Sir?" Cherabino said, hurt emanating from her in sad waves.

Branen flipped on the lights and sirens and changed lanes nearly on top of another car, which moved out of the way with a bob of the antigravity engine.

I swallowed my stomach as we fell another five feet in the air, just in time to join the ground traffic below. I could see where Cherabino had gotten her driving skills.

"Sir?" Cherabino repeated. "I didn't do anything wrong."

"The hearing will determine that, not me," Branen said. "Considering what Internal Affairs already has on the docket, this one is getting fast-tracked. You'll face both issues together—the trip to Fiske's house a few months ago and this incident—and you'll do it this week. I'd suggest your lawyer and you have a long, hard conversation. If your job survives the process, I'll be stepping up my supervision. You might have the highest close rate in the department, Cherabino, but you are not above the rules. Not for a bad kill. Not for police brutality. Not now." The last was said with such certainty that she reared back like she'd been hit. He was sure she'd done this, and his disgust at the fact was obvious even to her.

She'd never said she was above the rules, her mind leaked into mine. She was overcome with shame that Branen, the supervisor who'd believed in her and been there for her during her husband's funeral and after, would think she'd beaten a guy to death. That anyone would believe that of her . . .

I don't believe it, I said quietly, with the flavor of my mind so she'd know it was me.

Shock and horror. Then: "Stay out of my head," she spat out loud, and her mind became a wall against me.

They left me on the main floor of the police department, Branen telling me to go home.

"She really didn't do anything wrong. And I was there too. Why aren't I being accused of anything?"

Branen stared me down. "Ward, you have to understand. I have three witnesses saying she was involved, and none for you. You got lucky. Right now the less I see you, the better; you understand?" He was worried about possible murder charges, about the family suing the department. He would do everything in his power to keep those two things from happening, but he had only so much control.

The police brutality charges—those he believed. Isabella had always had a temper, and he absolutely believed she'd done this thing.

Shocked, I stayed behind as they walked into the department. Crap.

CHAPTER 3

Tuesday morning and I was, two days early, in the old coffee shop to meet Swartz. He was there at our regular (rescheduled) meeting for the first time since his heart attack months ago, and when I walked in and saw him—five minutes before the appointed time—it was like a small miracle, a return to what was and had always been.

Swartz had been my Narcotics Anonymous sponsor for years now, and was a good guy and a good friend. He'd also been an early riser for the entirety of the time I'd known him, and seeing him here now was like a return to normalcy. The last of the puffiness in his face from the procedures had finally left, and his color was coming back.

A few months ago he'd had a heart attack, a bad one, that had damaged the vessels around his heart bad enough to keep him from being eligible for an artificial heart. He'd come very close to dying. How close still bothered me. I'd made a deal with the Telepaths' Guild for one of their medics to heal the damage. I'd spent all the money I'd had, and owed a great deal more besides, but it had been worth it. Swartz had been worth it. Even if I was terrified he'd never fully recover, and that I'd be in debt to the Guild for the rest of my life.

Here now, he was looking good. He'd gotten a pot of

licorice coffee for me and a pot of herbal tea for him, which already sat on the worn wooden table, ready to go.

I said hello to the bartender and folded into the leather booth, pulling off my scarf and gloves. I was smiling, really smiling, for the first time in a long time.

"You look good," I said. It was true, and it had the pleasant additional effect of distracting me from the events of earlier.

"I'm doing better than they expected. Should be back to teaching by summer."

"Just in time for summer school," I said. "And all the really difficult kids." I set my scarf down in the booth and took one of the ugly coffee cups off the tray, pouring a cup of that licorice coffee I associated so strongly with our meetings.

"The kids just need a little attention."

"I'm sure," I said.

The vision from earlier still haunted me. I'd seen it over and over, and now we were talking about some of his kids. Worse, Cherabino was in the middle of a political train wreck, and I couldn't help. I couldn't help. Even so, something about being around Swartz made the world make more sense. Just sitting next to him made it less overwhelming.

I poured the coffee, the strong smell of licorice normal and comforting in context. Today, for once, I had my three things picked out and ready to go, not that it made me feel better about the vision. "I know what I'm grateful for this week."

"Already?" His amusement leaked into Mindspace very clearly.

"One, Cherabino took me to visit her grandmother again, and this time she didn't hate me." Unlike the last time.

"That turned out well, then," Swartz said, with a nod. "Good."

I wished everything with Cherabino went that well, that easily. I wished the conversation yesterday had gone better. I didn't know what to do. Often, I didn't know what to do at all, like now, with Branen so . . . something.

But this morning, this moment, was supposed to be about gratefulness. I nodded in acknowledgment. "The second thing I'm grateful for. Having control over my own money again, even if it's going out faster than it's coming in while I'm on part-time hours." I sighed. "I'm getting nervous." And with the department not wanting me there right now, it was only going to get worse. I was worried about Cherabino too.

Swartz held his cup of herbal tea loosely, not sipping, like it was more for the warmth than anything else. "Stay humble. Work the problem. You have a PI license now," he observed.

"I guess I could try to freelance some with that," I said cautiously. "I wouldn't know how to start, and anyway, you said the structure of a real job was good for me."

"Sometimes a man needs to make his own way. Seems like this is a chance for you to prove you can," Swartz said. "It's good for a man to test his mettle."

"I may not have a choice. I need to do something," I said cautiously. "My savings is okay for another month or two—maybe three if I'm careful and they give me more hours—but it won't last forever. I've been working for the police department for years. I don't know how to do anything else. And if my hours are down . . ."

"Didn't you work for the social work office for a while?"

"Cherabino got me the job after I helped her with the case, after I got out of that rehab she recommended me to.

I can't say I loved the job, but I did okay there until she came looking for me again."

"You've known Cherabino a long time," Swartz said.

I nodded, then sipped the licorice coffee again. "We're still together." It still seemed surreal that we were dating. I kept expecting her to end it. She had a long-standing fear of people getting too close, and while I understood it—her husband had died in her arms at a particularly bad time—I kept expecting it to come bite me in the butt.

"Don't borrow trouble. Enjoy what you have now."

"Yeah." For a man who couldn't read minds, Swartz had a nasty habit of reading mine. He knew me too well.

"What's wrong, kid?"

I found it hilarious these days that Swartz called me kid. I'd turned forty recently. I suppose to Swartz I was a kid, though. He'd been born old, and oddly, that was comforting.

"Isabella . . . well, she's getting blamed for a murder she had nothing to do with. And since we—" I stopped. Took a breath. "Remember how I told you we dropped in on Fiske's house after I had that vision a few months ago? Well, it was kinda worse than I told you."

"Worse?"

"Well. Um, we shouldn't have done it, but Cherabino thought he was threatening Jacob or something and she didn't stop to ask questions. So she rides in like a cowboy with nonlethal guns blazing, and I follow her in, because as dumb as this is I'm not going to leave her to get injured. I knocked out, like, six, eight people with telepathy and one of them ends up hitting her head. I . . . I might have killed her, maybe. Maybe just a concussion. Either way, by the time we get to Fiske and Cherabino threatens him, I know it's going very bad. I mean, Fiske is the organized crime boss of half the Southeast, and there we are in his living room. Cherabino's on the task force. She knows how bad this guy is—there's a literal file six inches thick of crimes she's sure he's masterminded. Violent stuff."

Swartz glanced around the room carefully, then back to me. "Should you be talking about this kind of case information in a public place?"

"Probably not," I said, and sighed.

"You appear to be alive. Why did he let you go?"

"I don't know. That's the thing. We pissed him off, royally. He did manage to set up a situation that invalidated most of her evidence against him, but there's still the task force. Which Cherabino isn't on anymore. She was supposed to have a hearing to discuss the stupidity of it all, but now . . . well, they're grouping those actions with the murder we found. I get why we're suspects, or at least she is. I mean we found the body, but you'd think we'd get a little professional courtesy and, you know, them not assuming she did this thing. But they're making it seem like it's a pattern, and it's getting political. It happened on the wrong day apparently. I'm worried."

Swartz looked at me and blinked.

I laughed. Had I really found a situation that Swartz didn't have a wise answer for immediately? Just my luck.

After a few minutes, I said, "I'm worried about her." I wanted Swartz to tell me what to do.

Swartz replied with a thoughtful "You think that this Fiske man is influencing the murder charge?"

"No," I said immediately. "No, that's stupid. He's not like that."

"So, what are you saying?"

I'd answered quickly, but now I was starting to wonder. Cherabino thought he had a few judges in his pocket here in Atlanta. . . . "I don't know what I'm saying. She has half a dozen enemies anyway, but nobody knew we were going to be at that concert. The odds of this being a deliberate thing . . ." I trailed off. "The brass is smart. They'll give her a slap on the wrist and then go find the real killer. They have to, right?" I had to believe that, regardless of the political stuff. The department stood by their officers. They always had, right?

After a short pause, Swartz said, "The truth has a funny way of coming out, even if you don't want it to."

"Yeah." My brain flashed fuzzily through the interrogation last night and the vision. That vision. I forced myself back. "It feels like I need to do something, but I don't know what to do. It's Cherabino."

"If she needs you, she'll ask for help," Swartz said calmly.

"This is Cherabino," I said. "You've met her, right? She'd say she was fine lit on fire and covered in supercancer. And then she'd work a fourteen-hour shift and close two cases and then complain nothing got done. It's not me here. I swear."

Swartz thought about that for a moment. "Pushing your way into the situation isn't going to help anything if she doesn't want you there."

"It would make me feel better."

He took a sip of his tea. "Even so. What's the third thing?"

"The third thing I'm grateful for? You know, I don't remember."

"I'll wait."

I sipped at the coffee and thought. And thought. "I wish I didn't have the visions," I said finally, unable to think about anything else.

"That's not something you're grateful for."

"I know."

Swartz waited, patiently, and after ten minutes of silence he pulled out the NA Big Book, the collection of readings we did for Narcotics Anonymous.

February was Higher Power month, where we came to believe in a higher power and being restored to sanity. This time, the sanity seemed a bigger miracle than the God stuff. The powerlessness I felt, could feel all over again. The surrender—and the sanity—were harder.

I caught a bus back to the DeKalb County Police Department, which took forever. Worse, the mood of the bus passengers was particularly grim today. Traffic was heavy, and I felt the sadness, despair, and frustration of a dozen strangers like they were my own. They worked all day and still couldn't pay the bills. They despaired. I despaired too, actually, some reflected emotion and some a lack of sleep and a lack of knowing what to do about Cherabino.

The ancient stone steps of the department felt almost restful in comparison, despite the officers bustling to and fro inside. Their minds moved in preset patterns like an insect colony in progress, a dance seen a hundred times before. Booking had some particularly loud suspects screaming at each other while the arresting officer tried to keep them apart, but otherwise everything was normal.

Cherabino was on the ground floor, unexpectedly, deep circles under her eyes. She spoke with one of the secretaries, the one who handled human resource forms.

How are you? I asked her quietly as I approached. She didn't look good.

She flinched and looked up in my direction. "Adam."

The secretary, an older woman with a twin sweater-set, looked between us with full attention, just ready to collect the latest gossip. Since I'd been sitting in the pool here, they thought they knew everything about me, but were always looking for more information. The straightforwardness of that motivation was surprisingly calming, at least on the days when I wasn't feeling self-conscious.

"What's going on?" I asked Cherabino, ignoring the audience.

I saw her close down, her face taking on the blank cop look. "I can't talk," she said in that tone that brooked no argument. Her mind was also pulled in, closed, with a sense of urgency.

I waited, concerned.

"I'm sorry, but I really can't talk right now," she said. She thought that it would be a few hours before she got enough sorted out that she could come find me. Her head hurt, the beginnings of a migraine.

I realized she had deliberately opened up enough for me to read her so that I'd accept her answer. That was a big moment of trust for her.

"Sure," I said, much to the disappointment of the secretary, who was trying to figure out what extreme thing had happened between us. I turned and went back to my almost-desk. But I watched Cherabino, in Mindspace, for the next ten minutes, until she went back up the elevator and I made myself let her mind go.

I sat at my borrowed desk in the secretaries' pool for another fifteen minutes or more, staring at the phone, trying to decide whether I could handle going home on my own right now or whether I needed to call Swartz. I wanted my drug. Nearly four years clean, and I wanted my drug desperately in that moment.

I felt Cherabino's headache moving across the Link into my head, and I was exhausted. And lonely. And worried. Talking to Swartz might be a good idea before I did something stupid.

The phone on the desk rang.

"Yes?" I answered.

"This is your watcher, Edgar Stone," came a man's voice on the other end of the line. Great. Stone worked for the Guild, and while he wasn't a bad guy, among other things it was now his job to make sure I paid back my debt on time. That made me not like him.

I sat back in the chair and rubbed my eyes. Looked like the secretaries would get some gossip this morning after all. "Your timing is terrible."

"I've called you three times. Don't you check your messages?"

"I've been busy."

"Listen, I'm sorry to tell you, but the Council has changed their mind about the terms of your debt."

I blinked ahead. "What? I don't think they can do that."

"You haven't been working your hours consistently. I warned you that could be an issue."

I'd worked out a system to pay back the Guild with labor over time. "I just did that mental hospital job for you."

"That was three weeks ago. You're supposed to put in hours every week."

"That was over a week all at once. What had to be several thousand ROCs' worth of labor, even with my Structure training out of date. Don't I get some leeway? On average, I'm still on track."

There was silence over the line for a moment. "Adam, you have to understand that the Guild isn't as lenient with subordinate telepaths as it is with its members. I understand that you haven't dealt with us in a number of years. I've tried to work with you. But this can't go on."

"I paid half of the debt in cash when we arranged for the medic to visit Swartz—on time, I might add. And I've been chipping at it when I have time. I have work for the police to do too. I'll get to the hours when I can, okay?"

"Let me be completely plain with you, Adam. The Guild expects their money, and while I'm personally very grateful for the work you did in November—"

"As you should be," I interrupted. "I solved a major case

for you at considerable personal risk. Not to mention—
well, other things." I didn't want to go into too much detail
in the department.

"Yes, well. You have to stay current on your debt or
there will be consequences."

"You used to be nicer to me," I said.

"I'm sorry, Adam. This is policy from the highest levels
and I will enforce it. I'll send you a list of jobs. Pick something or pay the cash. But do it soon."

A chill ran down my spine. He was serious.

I made the minimum necessary polite words to get off
the phone and then hung up. Crap, what was I going to do?
Did I go home, or did I stay here? This was a crap day
already, and it wasn't even ten o'clock yet.

I finally settled in with paperwork, stupid stuff left over
from a previous case with Cherabino, transcribing her stupid half-sentence scrawl into a reasonable approximation of
a real report. I squinted at the latest note, written on the side
of a napkin in what had to be a crayon. The handwriting
was abysmal.

The phone next to me rang, again. I put down my pen.
Seriously, I didn't know who was giving out this number.
The desk wasn't even technically mine.

"Hello?"

"This is Special Agent Jarrod of the FBI," a deep man's
voice replied.

"Thanks for calling me back," I said. I'd called just last
week asking about work. Jarrod had tried to recruit me a few
months ago and said there might be consultant jobs available, jobs with real money. Real money sounded fantastic
about now, but the timing with this morning and Cherabino
was terrible. I probably couldn't leave town right now. "What
can I do for you, Special Agent?"

"Our usual telepath consultant has recently been involved in a car accident," Jarrod said.

"Not serious, I hope," I said, what I hoped was the correct response to bad news. Did this mean . . . ?

"Unfortunately so, but it seems to be a completely normal accident and the doctors say she'll make a full recovery in time. I was calling to see if you'd still be willing to consult on a case or two. We have an urgent need a few hours south of you." He paused. "You are aware . . . we work under the Center for the Analysis of Violent Crime. We don't get the easy cases. This one's odd."

"I understand," I said, but I didn't.

"I'll need you to be at an address in Savannah no later than four o'clock this afternoon," Jarrod said.

I looked at the clock. It was ten thirty now. Savannah was maybe four hours away by groundcar, and with my felony drug record a groundcar was all I could rent, even with cash in hand. Assuming I could get the cash in hand that quickly. "This is not a good time for me," I said. Cherabino might be avoiding me right now, but that didn't mean I didn't need to be here when she surfaced from whatever she was doing.

"I'm out of alternates right now and I'm willing to pay for the inconvenience," Jarrod said, and then named a number for payment that made my head swim. A number that would let me buy off the Guild for at least a few months, and put me back in the black in my finances otherwise.

I winced. There was no way I could turn that down, not with the Guild breathing down my neck. But I'd never worked for the FBI before, or anybody in law enforcement other than the county police department. And I knew that Cherabino would need me. It would hurt—it would really hurt—to turn that down. To keep from doing it for just one more moment, I asked, "What would I be doing, and how long should I expect to be there? Any special considerations?"

"It's an attempted kidnapping of a ten-year-old boy," Jarrod said flatly. "With threats and every likelihood, they'll try again. I've got every physical guard in place and more than a few equipment safeguards. But I don't have anybody that can guard him mentally, or anyone else for that matter. Like I said, I'm willing to pay extra if you can be here by four."

I closed my eyes. A ten-year-old boy. My vision played back through my eyes, a ten-year-old boy being threatened by my old nemesis, Sibley, a man who worked for the horrible Fiske. "Is the boy blond?" I asked.

"Why do you ask?" His voice was suspicious.

"Let me ask another question. Is there any way this case has a connection to Garrett Fiske or Blair Sibley?"

A long, long pause. "There was a note on your record that you can do some kind of future-sensing thing. Have you already heard me call you?"

"Is that a yes?"

"Yes. On the first count. And very likely on the second."

Crap. Crap. Crap. "Give me an hour. I need approval and a chance to get my stuff together. Even assuming I get both, making your deadline will be hard. Also, you should know. I'm not a Minder. That's not my specialty, and what training I've had is years old. You want somebody to protect your crowd, you really need a specialist. The Guild has somebody for a lot less who can show up in ninety minutes." I'd try to show up anyway, help out somehow. If this was the kid—if this was the vision—I would never, never forgive myself if I didn't try. "I will absolutely help you in whatever way I can, but you may need to spend your money on the professional here." I'd do this one for free if I had to. I didn't get a vision without it being critically important, and this was a kid.

He made a frustrated sound. "I can't do that. The new appropriations rules say I can't hire anybody who works for the Guild for federal work. We've got a judge here with a very sensitive case going on now, and the Irish Telepath Guild won't be able to send someone for over two days. I've got nos from everybody else on the list, and this is not an optional assignment. You're not attached. I'll take sloppy over nothing, if you can be here now."

I sighed. If this was what I'd seen, this was going to get bad, and quickly. "How long should I pack for?"

"Pack for a week or more in multiple layers. Show up in a suit, and get galoshes. You'll need them if we end up in the marshes. Also, bring whatever supplies you need to do your magic, get approval, do whatever the hell you need to do, but get on the road. I can't be vulnerable like this."

"Understood," I said, but my nerves were itchy. Attempted kidnapping? Something that wouldn't stay attempted for long, if my vision was any indication. "A judge—?" I started.

He cut me off. "We'll go over the details when you get here. Let me give you the address. Call me back if—and only if—you can't make it by four. And call quickly."

We took care of the details, and then he hung up the phone.

I stood there, staring at the phone. Had I just agreed to scramble halfway across the state on no notice to work for the FBI on one of my weakest mental skills? Was there any chance in hell Branen would approve it? (Probably, my brain chimed in. He wasn't happy with me right now anyway, and being elsewhere might be helpful.)

Worse, was I really going to leave Cherabino right now? In the middle of whatever the hell was going down?

Yeah, I guess I was. If I wanted to look myself in the mirror ever again, I couldn't see what I'd seen and do nothing. I'd had that vision over and over again. With a boy, dying, dead if I didn't do something. I'd thought the ten-year-old kid was possibly Jacob, Cherabino's nephew, but nothing had happened and the vision kept coming. I didn't know this was it. But if there was any chance in hell I could save a kid's life, I needed to get on the road.

I set the phone down on its cradle and walked upstairs.

CHAPTER 4

"**Where's Cherabino?**" I asked Michael. He was the junior detective currently working with her, a nice guy. I didn't know what to do with nice.

He looked up. "You don't know? She dropped by earlier, then left. She looked upset. Said she wouldn't be available for a few hours. I don't think she's in the building."

How in hell had she left without me noticing? She must have gone out the courtyard door just to avoid me. I made a frustrated sound.

"Can I use the phone?" I asked.

He shrugged. "Be my guest."

I picked up the phone in the cubicle and dialed her home number, but it just rang and rang. Finally I hung up. Either she wasn't at home or she wasn't taking calls, and it wasn't like I could burn a couple of hours getting there by bus, damn it. She shouldn't do this to me with all of this going on. But I couldn't wait either, not if there was a chance.

"Everything okay?" Michael asked.

"It looks like I'm out of town for at least a week on a consulting job," I said. "I need to get it approved with Branen, but that's where I'm going. If you see Isabella, tell her I'll call her at home tonight, okay?"

"Sure," Michael said.

I left, frustrated, and went down to Branen's office. The

door was open. I took my life in my hands and knocked on the doorframe.

"What in the hell are you doing here right now?" Branen barked. "I thought I made it clear I didn't want to see you in the station for a few days." A stack of paperwork was in front of him and he was scowling.

"I've gotten a call from the FBI for consulting work for the next week," I said. "Last time we discussed this you said I should take it."

"Good," Branen barked. "I don't want to see you any-where close to here for the hearing, you understand me?"

"I do," I said.

His eyes narrowed as he made a decision. "You're a bad influence on Cherabino. Now that you're in my depart-ment, I don't want you here during the hearing." He was angry at me, irrationally angry, blaming me for what had happened even though it made no sense. "I'll throw you out if I have to. If I throw you out you won't be coming back for work, regardless of your close rate."

"I understood that," I said. I didn't know what he was talking about with the close rate, and he seemed to think it was important. Also, he was far more angry with me than was typical for him. He was close to Cherabino, I knew, and this whole situation had to be hard for him.

I reached over and read off the top of his mind. Every detective I'd worked with had had a jump in his or her case close rate, some as high as an extra forty percent. He dis-liked me, even more today, but under their current budget and work crisis he needed the close rates. But he'd been a lot happier when Paulsen was handling my headaches. She actually liked me, and could get me to do things without screwing up his department.

I'd let the thoughts about me go, but I had to stick up for Cherabino, on principle. "She really didn't do anything but defend herself. Do an investigation. She never touched that pole. Her fingerprints won't be there."

"I just got off the phone with Fulton County, and the pole was wiped clean."

"Well, there you go."

"Take the job with the feds. When you get back, come and see me. You won't be working with Cherabino again, but I'll give you other work if you stay out of the way. I can't stop you dating her, but I can stop the influence on the work." He was angry again, very angry, and concerned about his career and the future of the department with this case in the news.

"I'm not a bad influence," I protested out of habit.

His face settled. "That's what my son's friends say. And yet he comes home drunk anytime I'm not there to stop it. Go take your job with the FBI."

He turned his back to me, a dismissal.

I turned and left, at double time. I knew his anger and his assumptions were irrational, but they still hurt.

It had been years since I'd driven more than a few miles at a time, and longer than that since I'd driven with no one else in the car with me. An odd, echoey feeling, as my mind got wisps of Mindspace emotions cast out by other drivers onto the space above the road.

The section of I-16 I drove through could have passed for hell. Endless road and sky and trees in one long stretch, so that no matter how long you drove it seemed you never got anywhere. Eternal motion without progress, surrounded by land without a single defining landmark, so that the mind grew bored and numb, left with nothing to think about but its failures. Its failures and that vision, the one with the boy who was being strangled. A boy that perhaps I could save.

I probably shouldn't have left without saying good-bye to Cherabino. I was worried about her already, terribly worried, and if Branen didn't want me at the department and I couldn't testify, well, there had to be something I could do.

It was lonely in this stretch of road, lonely with guilt and hard choices on every side.

But—that vision—if I could save a child's life, if there was any chance, I had to try. And I was committed now, committed and driving all too fast to make the deadline.

The future was changeable. It had to be. I had to believe it, and I had to believe Cherabino would be okay.

As I drove into town, the air smelled . . . different through the cracked car window. Saltier, flatter almost. Plus mold and sand, and something else I couldn't identify. Pollution, maybe. Savannah had to have nearly as much of it left over in the air as Atlanta did. More, if you counted the oceans. Enough to make you sick if you weren't careful, though this time of year it wasn't nearly as toxic as it would have been in summer.

The sky was wider, somehow, in this area of the country, the sun brighter, the land flatter, and the sidewalks actually had people walking on them. Parks were everywhere. It was beautiful to look at, but the ambient feeling in Mindspace was quiet, a heavy quiet full of sadness and generations of unchanging days.

I began to pass under huge oak trees, several stories high with branches reaching like arms of some monster overhead, long streamers of moss hanging like hair beneath their branches. The closer I got to the address, the more of them there were, on either side of the road in front of houses and dominating parks. Their upper branches were twisted, post-Tech-Wars damage perhaps, but the trees themselves looked okay. The occasional bioengineered bush dotted the parks as well, blooming out of season in blue flowers. Only on this side of town, though; the parks earlier hadn't had any of those winter flowers.

The stoplights hung low here, and as I waited at one of them, I noticed an ancient, tall orange metal post with a circular thing on top. It said Bus Stop on the circle, its paint cracking away but still legible.

Isabella would like this place, I thought, and the thought hurt.

I turned onto Washington Avenue, the huge oaks now stretching over the street on both sides to make a sort of tunnel of branches and dripping moss. It was beautiful, the sunlight mottling the divided street and the cars parked on the sides. Maybe it was just as well that I'd only brought a groundcar; with all these trees everywhere, I hadn't seen a skylane for antigravity flying cars since the interstate. Everyone grounded to come into the city, taking it by wheels and steps as their ancestors had done.

The houses here were old, really old, much deeper than they were wide, and no two looked alike. I drove slowly, looking at addresses. I was on the wrong side of the street, and the numbers started moving in the wrong direction past another park on the left. I moved into the left lane at the next stoplight and did a careful U-turn, uncertain if it was allowed.

I found the place and pulled into a small side street across from a park so beautiful I could hardly believe it was real, one small pay phone sitting at its corner, next to a statue. I parked the car and looked up.

The house was charming, with solid redbrick and two levels of blue-shingled roof. There was a wraparound porch and tall windows with small panes at their tops, windows designed for a world without air-conditioning, a world now centuries past. While some of the wood had been replaced in places and thick coats of paint sat all around it on all sides, those high-up small panes remained, ready to open and create a cross breeze in a hot house.

Three minds stood around that porch, one in plain sight above the stairs, one just behind the window to the far right, and one out of sight on the other side of the house. Other minds were farther on in the house, more faint. None seemed to have the order I associated with a trained telepath. There were always surprises—fire-starting, microkinesis, and other rare Abilities didn't show up the same in Mindspace as telepathy and so frequently got overlooked. Even so, I was confident I was the biggest fish mentally for half a mile in any direction, the outside of my mental range for normal thoughts.

All of that was good if I was really going to try Minding again. There were plenty of people here for the physical bodyguarding, and assuming open minds and some cooperation I'd be able to coordinate with them if a mental attack came up. But the rest . . . I'd had my training, and made good marks, but that had been years ago.

The guy in plain sight on the porch had a suit jacket on as well as an unbuttoned trench coat. If you looked carefully, there was a slit in the trench coat and a bulky spot beneath it, probably a gun, the slit there to make it easier to draw under duress. That and his mental signature made me think ex-military, ex–Special Forces, maybe. He was focused, bored, and twitchy all at the same time, with the kind of twitchy that made me think he was an adrenaline junkie and hadn't seen action for too long.

As I approached the front steps, I kept my gloved hands where he could see them, away from my coat. Don't startle the twitchy guy. It was a long-term survival motto of mine.

"I'm Adam Ward, the consultant that Special Agent Jarrod

called in," I said before he could challenge me. "I'd like to talk to him if he's around, before I go in."

"Telepath?" the man asked. He was tall, I saw, as I reached the bottom of the steps, tall with a faint, diffuse scar like an old shrapnel wound down the side of his face. "You're Ruth's replacement?"

I climbed the stairs, slowly, so he could see me. *That's right,* I said, directly into his mind, loud enough and with enough texture he'd know it was me.

"No need to shout." He was thinking he liked Ruth a hell of a lot better. Also, that I was an ass for just stomping in and that Jarrod had better know was he was doing. "Give me a minute and I'll get Jarrod for you," he said, no self-consciousness about the negative thoughts at all.

"Okay," I said.

He gestured to the guy behind the window I couldn't see clearly from this angle, and a woman came out of the door, watching me as he went in. She scanned the surroundings, and I noticed a bulge in her jacket as well, right where a gun would be. She was short with some mass to her, mass I got the impression she used for weight lifting or fighting; there was a strength to her mind, to her presence you didn't get from someone who sat at a desk. Her shoes were athletic shoes, her clothes were office wear, and her scowl was all business. She thought in Spanish; or at least the language portion of her thoughts right now was Spanish, which I didn't really speak. Then she switched over in her brain to proto-English structure. I watched, interested; very few people were truly bilingual at that level, and it was interesting every time.

"Mendez," she said finally, identifying herself.

"Adam Ward."

She nodded, looked back out behind me. "The attempt

was this morning. We got here about noon—her usual security detail is down to one man, and we've got the rest to cover for the next week. We've got some help from the sheriff's office, which in this county handles court security, but they're concentrating on the courthouse. It's a high-profile case."

"What case?" I asked.

She stared at me in disbelief. "The Pappadakis case. It's been all over the news."

"Wait. She's trying the Pappadakis case?" I asked. That was in the Atlanta papers. George Pappadakis, manufacturing tycoon with ties to restricted technology in Canada and Greece, had supposedly beaten his mistress to death. "Didn't a witness recently disappear?" I asked her.

"The only one who saw him there with the woman, yes. She was a licensed prostitute and had expressed concern for her safety several times according to the local PD. They're trying to determine whether she left town on her own or someone did something. Jarrod has us helping when we can."

"I thought this was an attempted kidnapping case," I said.

She made a frustrated sound. "It is. The judge's son was attacked this morning. We assume it's related to the high-profile Pappadakis case she's trying, considering his reputation and the death threats she's been receiving, but we don't know this for certain. Investigation is definitely still in process."

I wondered what the connection was to Fiske. Maybe he and Pappadakis were buddies, maybe there had been another trial against one of his henchmen, or maybe Jarrod had just said what he thought would get me here.

"Are you even paying attention?" Mendez asked. She was kinda touchy, but honestly, after Cherabino that was just making me feel at home.

"Yes, mostly."

"You need to talk to Jarrod for any other briefing," she said. "It's not my job, but honestly, it's all over the news."

"Thanks," I said, a little awkwardly. "If I understand, I'm here to Mind, to mental bodyguard. I may need to get familiar with your mind so I can rule you out. Coordinate if anything happens."

"I suppose that's true." She took a step forward, still watching the surroundings behind me. Then she met my eyes. "You do what you have to do, you monitor whatever, but if you say one word about what I'm thinking—ever—even to me—we're going to have a problem. Understand?"

"Perfectly." I stood up under her glare the way she was expecting.

She thought I was a loose-lipped bastard and probably incompetent.

I smiled.

She flashed a strong sexual image of herself and someone else. A female someone.

I blinked, lost the smile, but after a second regained my aplomb. Women didn't usually play that particular card, at least not that quickly. Still, clearly a test. "How long will Jarrod take to get here?" I asked.

After a moment, she nodded. I'd earned a "possibly trustworthy" label in her head.

Just then the door opened, and the man I presumed to be Special Agent Jarrod walked through. He was a man of average height, swarthy, with craggy features, in a very well-fitting suit with a thin tie in a perfect knot, an American flag tiepin holding the tie to his starched white shirt. His thinning hair was cut in a perfect copy of the G-men haircut of the FBI under Hoover, like a blast from the buttoned-up scary past. While he was at least fifty, he had the feel of a man just beginning the prime of his career, confident and decisive, ready to take over the world.

"Ward," he said, greeting me.

"Sir," I said automatically. For some reason he reminded me of my father, who was a distant man in my childhood, a buttoned-up lawyer, and a man who hadn't spoken with me in over a decade. I could see that this would be a problem if I let it be; I'd have to aggressively fight against this first impression if I wanted to do a good job. So I took the initiative. "I'm here by deadline. What do you need?"

Jarrod took a few steps forward, blinking. Probably surprised to see me in a suit. Heck, *I* was surprised to see me in a suit. "Good. I need you to go interview the guard who fought off the attack—make sure you get any details you can possibly get from her—and then meet up with the boy. You'll be Minding him—the judge too, if you can manage her, but she has court security and the boy is your focus. He's Tommy, age ten, and he likes boats. I'd recommend you start with that. After you interview the bodyguard. I need a second opinion there."

"Um, normally people give me more information than that." I glanced at Mendez, next to me, who was eavesdropping on the conversation without shame. Another mind was coming up around the side of the porch, but the mood didn't seem threatening, so I let it go with some monitoring. "What happened exactly?" I asked. "Who are the major players? What's the bodyguard's background? What exactly am I trying to learn here?"

Jarrod frowned. "I realize you're coming from a background in interrogation, Ward, but our priority is the boy's safety. I want anything and everything we can get about the situation as it relates to that." His mind told me that he expected me to realize this already.

"That's fine," I said. "Specifically what kind of Ability

threat do I need to focus on? Teleportation, for example, is a hell of a lot different from telepathy."

Jarrod's mind spiked with irritation, and he said, "Let's take this aside for a moment." He looked at Mendez, who shrugged and went back through the door into the house. The guy coming around the house paused, turning around with a clear "oh, look, I have an errand" attitude.

It said a lot about Jarrod that his people would move so quickly over something so trivial. Either he was a badass, or his people really respected him.

"Ward, I realize you're new here, so let me explain how things are going to go. As a rule we're going to do things my way. I like questions. I like input. I like somebody who thinks. At a certain point, though, I've hired you because you solve problems for me. In a crisis situation, you take orders, just like the police officers you've worked with before. You bring up problems, fine, but I want solutions too, or at the very minimum the beginnings of them. And if I tell you to do something, you do it. Your job is to handle the mental gymnastics. I don't want to be bothered with those details unless something unusual has happened."

"Understood," I said.

"Bodyguard first. You'll want to get up to speed on the judge's high-profile case as well, but only after you meet Tommy and get your Minding magic set up. I'm afraid we're a day late and a dollar short right now, and you're coming in late, but we need to catch up. I'll start bringing you personnel to get familiar with later today."

"Okay," I said, for lack of anything better. I was starting to get the impression their old telepath worked with the team very, very well. Trying to jump in on no notice, on something that wasn't my specialty . . . well, it could get very bad very quickly. And Jarrod didn't seem patient with a learning curve.

"The guard is in the front parlor," Jarrod supplied. "Near the kitchen. Send Loyola out here please."

I took that as a dismissal, and worried though I was, after a quick glance to identify another suited agent behind me where the extra mind had been, I went forward into the house.

CHAPTER 5

The inside had been renovated in surprisingly modern colors and furniture. Ugly, in my opinion. The entryway opened into two rooms to the left and right, with another longer hall farther on. To be honest, I hated the house immediately from the inside; it was all art and artistic texture in contrasting colors like a designer had been allowed to work freely. Even the furniture was in unconventional, odd shapes. The couch in the right room looked like a praying mantis hunched over. It had to be custom, and expensive, but it just looked strange. The old wooden floors and the ancient crown molding were the only parts of the room I liked at all; the rest was a riot of texture and color and planning that just seemed . . . busy. Like it was trying too hard. Pretentious, but not in an interesting way.

In the center of the rightward room was the man I'd met first, the ex-military guy who'd asked me if I was a telepath. He stood about four feet from a woman perched precariously on a chair shaped like a tilted cereal bowl. She was at least thirty, with pretty microbraids, practical but professional clothes, and a statement necklace I suspected held a hidden weapon. Her arm was in a makeshift sling, and she sat, slumped a little, with a cloud of frustration and grief hanging over her in Mindspace. For all that her appearance was not what I was expecting, this was clearly the bodyguard.

"What's your name, one more time?" I asked the ex-military guy as I got closer.

"Special Agent Loyola."

"Like the saint?"

"That's right," he said in a tone that dared me to make something of it.

"I didn't think the FBI normally did protection duty," I said, the detail suddenly bothering me.

"We do a hell of a lot of weird stuff in this unit," he said. He was thinking that some of it was because, unlike a lot of people in the FBI, they didn't mind working with telepaths and other unusual talent.

"Um, Jarrod wants you at the porch," I said.

Loyola nodded and moved back out through the front door. It closed behind him.

I went back to the front parlor, where a vase perched on a coffee table, a flat slab of what had probably once been an industrial sign of some kind. It seemed the most normal sitting surface in the room, and with the sunlight pouring in through the large window behind me, its metal surface was warm and inviting. This was probably a lie—the only surface and the only moment in the whole experience that was the least bit inviting. I shouldn't take it seriously. But it did seem the only flat surface, so I sat down.

I introduced myself to the bodyguard, who I could see now that I was closer, was clearly fighting off guilt. I decided to treat this like any other interrogation, a gentle one, aimed at a witness and not an immediate suspect, but an interrogation all the same.

The vision and my urgency were pulling at me to find the kid, to meet the kid. I had a chance to make that vision not happen and I needed to take it. I also needed to call Cherabino, make sure she was okay, and make a good impression here and now, and figure out a way to survive as a Minder on old lessons over the next few days.

But not now. Now I needed to focus on the bodyguard. I took a breath, and then another, forcing calm. I'd had plenty of time to settle in the car on the way over here, I reminded myself. Plenty of time. Now I had to handle this, another interrogation. I was good at interrogations.

There was usually something I'd say in the beginning, something that would make the interviewee feel comfortable and want to open up. I couldn't quite find what to say, and I finally settled on "I'm here to help the family figure out what happened so it doesn't happen again."

She nodded, almost too sharply, and that guilt-sense intensified. Not that it proved anything at this point; she'd be a lousy bodyguard if she didn't feel it when bad things happened on her watch. Her arm was also hurting her, a lot; it felt like a gunshot wound only partially patched up, and she'd likely need a doctor soon. Her gut also hurt, what felt like bad bruising. It said a lot about her that she sat here waiting anyway. Either that same false guilt was driving her to make sure the boy—and the family—were okay, or real guilt was preventing her from leaving the scene. Too early to tell. But I needed to decide. Soon.

"What's your name?" I asked, gently, in case it was the former possibility. "How long have you been employed by the judge?"

"I'm Tanya," she said, very slow. "It's been about six months now."

"What happened to make the judge decide to hire you?" I asked.

"I wasn't there. What I was told when she hired Jason and me—"

"Jason?" I interrupted. I hadn't expected the judge to be female, so that much was news to me, though I probably should have read it off Mendez. The bigger news was a partner who wasn't present—they'd mentioned, I thought, that he was in bad shape somewhere.

She nodded, jerkily, and the grief-sense intensified. "We're partners with a private security firm. The sheriff's department hired us to supplement after she started getting threats. Jason . . . he got shot, bad. He's out of surgery in the critical care unit. They're not allowing visitors, not unless you're biologically related. I couldn't just . . . I couldn't sit there, doing nothing. So I came back here as soon as they'd let me go. Sooner, probably." She met my eyes. "I want to help. I need to *do* something."

"I understand," I said, the old mainstay in interrogations, but in this case, I actually did understand. I had that feeling eating at me too, especially right now.

"The hospital has this number if anything changes," she said hurriedly, without prompting.

"I'm sure they'll let you know the second you can do something there," I said in as kind a voice as I could manage. "Right now you can help me understand what happened. Let's go back to the judge. What did she say when she hired you and Jason?"

She took a breath and settled, getting that focus I associated with cops on duty. "She said she'd been getting death threats for years, but usually the threats were generic and handwritten. But the new ones were very specific, cut out of newspaper like an old movie, and threatened her son. And she had the case on her docket in a month. The media was already going crazy. So she hired us, but we're getting paid through the sheriff's department."

Interesting. There were no images attached to her description of the letters. "Have you seen the newspaper letter threats?" I asked.

"No, and I didn't ask."

I didn't know exactly what that meant, but I made a mental note. "Have there been any incidents prior to today?"

She took a breath and looked up, like consulting a reel of mental footage. "Nothing . . . nothing I would have called significant until today. A few minor scuffles, one disturbed man who charged our car—we called the police on him—and a small, badly made explosive we caught and disarmed at the courthouse. A few yelled threats. Amateur stuff. I'm not sure the explosive would even have gone off; when they analyzed it, the chemical makeup was missing an ingredient. Someone was angry, but that someone didn't have the knowledge or the resources to really make good on that anger. Plus, he left his fingerprints on the casing."

She paused, thinking hard for a moment.

I had a policy that if an interviewee was talking freely with good detail, I didn't interrupt the inevitable pauses unless the person was clearly assembling a lie. Even then, I might guide the talk into more details rather than stop him. Over time, anyone who's talking freely long enough will give you something you can use. But the time was eating at me here. Staying quiet was hard. Staying quiet and focused was very hard.

"I did notice someone tailing us on the way to Tommy's school a few times," she said. "Or I thought I did. Tommy is at Savannah Christian, across the city, and I tried to vary the route just in case. Jason wasn't there that morning—usually one of us goes with the judge and one with Tommy—but I'm better at countersurveillance than he is. It was only the same car twice, and then different cars. I changed our route and it seemed to stop, though . . ."

"Though what?" I asked. "What else did you see?"

"Jason thought we were jumping to conclusions, maybe, but even when he was there he saw a woman and then a man in front of the school a few times who didn't look like teachers to him. So we doubled up on security for Tommy and brought in the sheriff's department more formally for a day or two, just in case. We were just being paranoid," she said, then looked green. "Obviously not that paranoid."

According to the police I usually worked with, the trouble with good situational awareness was that you often read details as suspicious when they weren't necessarily. With so many false positives, if you were in a neighborhood you didn't patrol regularly, sometimes you made mistakes. In this case, though, obviously she hadn't.

"Let's move to this morning. Tell me what happened, slowly," I said. "From the beginning. Any detail you can remember might help us prevent another attempt from succeeding."

"We got up at the usual time—for the family, that's about seven, but I'm up at four so we have some coverage overnight. Jason's up late," she explained. "With two of us in a nonemergency situation, we don't do the whole night, and even so we have to nap during the day sometimes, but it's something. I keep telling Marissa to get a dog, but she says she works too much."

"Marissa?" I asked.

She gave me a strange look. "The judge. Marissa Parson. She's a superior court judge for Chatham County. We travel with her these days to the courthouse. Sometimes Tommy comes too, to keep his schedule as unpredictable as possible. Marissa got him a tutor and special permission to take his tests outside school if he misses. It's what I told her when she hired us, that she'd get the most bang for her buck if we had one target instead of two, and if that target was moving in as unpredictable a schedule as we could manage. But he's got to go to school sometimes."

"That morning," I prompted.

"Yes. That morning. The family got up. Tommy had forgotten to tell his mother she was supposed to bake cupcakes, which with the nanny gone would mean I was supposed to bake cupcakes, so there was some discussion about stopping at a local bakery before the judge decided Tommy should have to tell his class himself why he was empty-handed. Um, let's see—the police escort came about eight, and then Marissa left first. Tommy's cupcakes battle meant we were running late."

"The nanny is gone?" I asked.

"Um, yes. For about four weeks now. Marissa didn't like to discuss it, but I got the impression that she and the nanny had had a strong disagreement over Tommy that couldn't be resolved. Marissa has strong opinions. I know she was annoyed with the woman, and probably she fired her rather than the nanny quitting. I wasn't there, though. With Jason and me as extra adults in the household, Marissa hasn't felt a pressing need to hire another nanny. She's interviewed a few but hasn't found one she was happy with. Like I said, Marissa has strong opinions."

"I assume you drove Tommy to school that morning?" I asked, after I'd had a chance to process that information. "When did the kidnapping attempt begin?"

Her demeanor changed then, and her shoulders tensed. As I'd suspected, she'd been avoiding the topic, sliding away from it subconsciously, and didn't like the reminder of the flight. Her grief returned, along with that guilt. "Jason drove," she began, and paused. Then, more slowly: "Jason drove, and I sat in the back with Tommy. He was talkative that morning, and I had to split my attention between what he was saying and the road."

She shifted in the chair. "Well, this van comes out of nowhere, around some corner behind us, coming way too fast. We're stopped at the railroad tracks, the blinkers going like nuts, and there's nowhere to go 'cause we don't know how tall the train's going to be or how fast it'll go."

I nodded, seeing a flash of the scene in her mind. Anti-grav-assisted trains on dedicated tracks could carry up to two extra stories, several tons each, and at speeds that made the air currents around them dangerous for a vehicle in the air anywhere near. They weren't exactly safe even for a grounded vehicle, but they'd been well enough back and in the air shadow of a couple of brick buildings. The van had come around one of the buildings behind them while they were pinned against the barrier of the tracks. It sounded preplanned to me.

"Anyways, I yell at Tommy to get down like we prac-ticed and Jason pulls the car sideways, yanking it around while I struggle for the gun. They open fire then, and Jason gets hit twice before he can deploy the car's protective plates. High-caliber stuff. Tommy's down, in the foot well, and I'm stretched out on the seat, gun out and firing through the slit in the plates. Tommy makes this sound—I find out later he's gotten burned from the plate engine deploying too hard, too hot—but he stays down, and he says he's okay when I yell at him.

"I'm firing at what little I can see, and I can hear Jason doing the same, though he's hurt—it's clear he's hurt—and the plates are getting hit with this awful sound. The whole car's shaking with the air from the train. Then it goes quiet. Tommy's jacket is flashing that red light—he's pulled the emergency tab and it's screaming through the police radio channels like it's supposed to. I'm breathing too hard. I'm worried about Jason.

"Then this horrible screeching. They have something to breach the plates, like an old Jaws of Life hydraulic or some-thing. I'm screaming at Tommy, 'Get out the back, run, run,' and he's not moving so I push him back into the other foot well, but then I hear a pop and I turn back around and I know it's all over. This guy in armor and a helmet like the military or something—standing there with the hydraulic thing. The door's gone. The plates are gone, and he throws the thing down and pulls up a rifle toward my head. I throw myself in front of Tommy, hoping maybe I can buy some time. And then I hear a bullet go off from the driver's side. The eye of the helmet goes out and the rifle drops, and I'm picking me and Tommy up and getting the hell out of the back."

She went silent then, and shivered. She'd run on foot, carrying the kid, at her maximum speed, thinking the whole time that Jason had saved her but was going to die in the process.

"The train zoomed out, but the blinkers were flashing and I could see the next one coming maybe a mile or two away. It was a stupid thing to do," she said, looking down. "My trainers will scream murder over it, but I jumped the tracks. I carried Tommy all the way across, another guy coming after us the whole way. We made it clear but he didn't." She looked back at me, almost defiant. "He didn't make it, and when the air wave knocked us down, I got Tommy down without even a bruise. I walked him a mile or more before we heard the sirens."

I made a mental note to track down a man's body on one of the large trains coming through—it would have been found at the next stop, Charleston perhaps, or a smaller town in between. But in the meantime, I needed to know. "This is very important, Tanya. Think carefully. In the time between when you were running away from the car—from the time you exited until you crossed the train tracks—did they shoot? At you or at anyone else?"

She thought about that one carefully, and I shifted, my butt having gone numb on the hard coffee table. I forced myself to sit up straight, though, for the appearance of authority even if not the reality of it.

"No," she finally said. "When I had Tommy, they didn't shoot at all. My gun was back in the car—I had a knife, but they didn't know that. Maybe they thought they'd get him more easily. They did start shooting once the train passed again, but I don't think it was at me."

So two important facts: the assailants had likely wanted Tommy alive, based on their actions, and there was possibly another group or a set of cops without sirens involved at the end. "One last question," I said. "You keep saying 'they,' but you've only described two men—the first in the armor and the helmet, and the second on foot chasing you. Who were the others? How many were there?"

Tanya closed her eyes, mind flashing through images quickly in reverse and forward, picking through the jumble of her memories of a stressful time for any clues. "I saw four," she finally said. "At least four."

And of the four she'd seen, none were Sibley. "At least?" I prompted.

"There might have been one more. Maybe behind the driver's seat of that van. The door was open and there was a figure with a large-caliber gun, I saw it for less than a second through the slit, but I noticed the gun. I had to. I tried to throw bullets that way, but I don't know how successfully. The other one was behind the man in the armor; he had a flak jacket on, I think." She frowned. "Yes, a jacket. My trainer has been running drills on those lately." Her heartbeat sped up as she remembered the situation and the danger she'd been in. I noticed she took deep, deliberate breaths to get that back under control, almost without thinking about it.

"Your trainer?" I asked.

She nodded. "The company has us do two hours a week of skills training to keep us sharp, usually one with guns, one without. I skipped this week because of the high alert, but last week was identifying backup. They try to run us through high stress so we don't freeze up. Guess it worked this time."

Part of that last statement was a lie, or she was hiding something, but I couldn't tell what, or even if it meant anything. Sometimes being a telepath was frustrating.

She looked back up at the clock on the wall.

"Go ahead and call the hospital," I said, responding to her thought without meaning to.

A frisson of fear ran up her spine, but she controlled it. Crap, another normal spooked by a telepath. I took an extra moment to examine that fear up close, to make sure she wasn't going to go out of her way to hurt me to stop the fear.

No, she wasn't one of those.

I let her go as she got up to make the call. I, in the meantime, had other priorities.

CHAPTER 6

I **entered an** old room, ancient floorboards covered with a large rectangular rug in bright colors, an antique small bed topped with a cheerful bedspread with a pattern of cartoon boats. A boy sat in the middle of the rug, on the floor, watching a bright blue toy boat float like an anti-grav car, *whirring* around and around a path at eye level.

He moved his hand, adjusting one of the floating yellow guide markers, and the boat's path adjusted too, a cheerful *beep* sounding with the change.

I cleared my throat and the boy turned, too quickly, like he was on edge. He backed up, his knee pulling a cord from the wall. The boat fell, all at once, along with the floating markers, hitting the floor on top of a red-and-green mat with a *crunch*. "Stupid boat." He backed up a little farther and yelled, "Mom! Somebody's here!"

"I'm Adam," I said as gently as possible. "I didn't mean to startle you." I stayed by the door, giving him space until his mom arrived. More likely, the FBI agents, but I wasn't going to be picky either way.

Tommy was ten years old, just under five feet tall, blond and tan, with a round face and deep brown eyes that seemed to catch everything. His khakis and blue polo shirt might have been a school uniform, might not, but both were wrinkled, the shirt with a small stain near the collar.

Behind me, Special Agent Loyola came down the hall-way, a female presence not far behind. The judge, most likely.

I turned. "Response time is a little slow," I said to Loyola.

He took the comment personally. "Perimeter is sealed off. A mouse couldn't get in or out without either us or the sheriff's department knowing about it." He stuck his head in the room as I moved to give a bit more room. "You okay, kid?"

"Yeah, I guess," I heard from the room. Not exactly happy, but he'd had a big day.

I nodded to the woman, who was wearing some kind of dark pantsuit with a wide collar and more than her share of expensive jewelry. Her dark-blond hair was noticeably fixed, sprayed down into an almost helmetlike rigidity. She was examining me critically.

I kept my hands where everyone could see them. "I'm the new telepath," I said. "Introducing myself as requested. I'll need a good view of your son's mind so I can stop any threats before they get through in Mindspace. It'll take about ten minutes."

She looked at me critically, the full weight of countless hours dealing with criminals riding on her now. She didn't seem comfortable.

I opened up a little in Mindspace. As suspected, she didn't like a grown man wanting to get up close with her son right now, no matter how good the reason. This would have been easier with the female telepath Jarrod usually worked with, just for her comfort level, but the fact was, I was all we had. Media frenzy aside, being male did not make you inherently dangerous to children; there were far more trustworthy, good people out there of both genders than there were criminals of either. But you couldn't exactly tell that to a woman whose son had almost been kidnapped today. Her reservations seemed normal to me, if big.

"You're welcome to be there the whole time," I said. "In fact, it would probably help things."

"What exactly will you be doing with my son?" she asked finally.

Loyola came out in the hall and shut the door. "Ma'am, Ward checks out. He was specifically recruited by the FBI agent in charge of this situation because he can do the job in front of us. We've worked with telepaths many, many times before. There's a level of coordination and early warning you just can't get any other way, and I'd highly recommend you cooperate fully with the process. It will keep your son much safer."

I was surprised. I hadn't expected him to go along with this that easily.

It didn't mean he liked me, his mind added loudly enough that I'd be sure to pick it up. But united front and successful assignments and all that.

"What exactly are you going to do to my son?" the judge asked again.

That was the question, wasn't it? I pulled on very old school lessons in Minding and best practices for Minding children. "I need—with his permission—to make a light connection with your son's mind for the next few days, or until whoever it is that is threatening you both is caught. And I need to stay within about a hundred feet of him during that time, night and day, no matter what else is happening."

"You want to be in the same room as my son while he's sleeping," the judge said, not happy.

"It's best practices. We've worked with telepaths many times before and they're trained to a very high standard,"

Loyola said. "I've had them in and out of my own head multiple times."

"Next room is fine," I said.

"You can stay with your son yourself if it would make you more comfortable," Loyola said. "But starting tomorrow morning the majority of the FBI will be tracking active leads, and you've requested the security to be at the courthouse, not here. A telepath and a physical guard—meaning, me—are pretty much all we're going to have to work with, other than local PD drive-bys. I'd suggest you let us do our jobs. I'm still happy to move everyone to the safe house," he added, with a spot of hopefulness.

"We're staying here," the judge said, with steel, like they'd had this conversation before. "If you won't let us go to my mother's in Washington State, we'll stay in the house. Thanks. Tommy's had a horrible day, and taking him out of familiar surroundings is not how we take care of my son. I told you. You either work with my decision or you leave."

"Do you have any specific questions?" I asked. Then, to assuage her understandable fear: "I'm happy to demonstrate what I'll be doing on you first, if it will make you more comfortable."

She swallowed, and I felt a burst of nerves. Ah, looked like what was driving her reluctance was an underlying fear of telepaths. Looked like the kind of low-level fear half the normal population had as a result of horrible news stories and endless telepath villains in movies. Great. Another one.

She shook her head. "If the feds say it's necessary, and they've done this before, I have no reason to object. But be aware both I and the other agents will be checking in at unpredictable intervals."

I blinked. I had been expecting an outright no, or a demand to experience the properties of the thing herself. "That's fine," I said.

The kid in the other room was getting impatient, I noticed. He'd get up in a moment to see what was going on. I had a sudden attack of nerves myself. I needed to be here. But for what, I didn't know. The universe thought I could make a difference, save this kid, I told myself, or I never would have seen the vision in the first place.

The judge was still hesitating.

Just then, her son opened the door on the other side of Loyola.

He came out and after a small hesitation went over to hug his mom.

She looked at me over the top of his head. In that moment, I had her. She'd go along with it. Which was good, because I had to figure out a hell of a lot of other details, and soon, if was going to head off this vision.

Tommy pulled away. "What's going on, Mom?" He tried to figure out how to ask about the danger returning, about what had happened to Jason, and couldn't . . . couldn't quite get his brain to settle on the tangle of what had happened in a way that would give him words.

"Do you know what a telepath is?" I asked him.

He looked up and nodded, slowly, still a lot closer to his mom than he would have stood under any other circumstances. I had the feeling he was a tough guy, usually. But the events of this morning would bother grown men, and he deserved truth, not babying.

"I'm here to help stop this morning from happening again," I said, addressing his unspoken fear. "Agent Loyola and I are going to be making sure you don't get hurt."

His anger flared. "Like those punks could have hurt me." All bravado, hiding fear.

Fear I understood. "Would you take my hand for just a minute?" I asked. "You'll feel a tickle in your head for a bit. I'll be able to find you anywhere."

I held out a hand.

He looked at me, then at Mom. The judge nodded. She wasn't happy, but she was going along with this.

Tommy reached out and took my hand.

Three things happened at once. I reached out my mind and enveloped his carefully. It was instinct. It was something I'd rehearsed in my mind so that the fulfillment of it took little thought. My mind settled like a blanket around him.

The second thing, he reacted like a prototelepath, like a boy who'd develop significant, reliable Ability—empathy, perhaps, or telepathy—in just a year or two. He moved away from the contact, and then, suddenly, unpredictably, toward it. Our minds merged around the edges.

And three, my mind recognized him. On the deepest, most visceral level, I recognized his mind. This—this was the boy from my vision. The boy who would be tied up in the barn. The boy whom I'd seen killed in the vision months ago. I was certain. I knew him.

Before I could suppress the information, it traveled between us. I saw the moment it registered—and fear, real fear, blossomed.

"We have a problem," I told Jarrod. Tommy was back in his room, unwilling to speak to anyone, and his mom was with him. I had no idea if anyone would let me near him, not after the hysterics he'd thrown. But at least he was calmer—I knew that much through our light link. Unfortunately I had the impression the calm was the calm before the storm, the suppressed disbelief that would wear off over time to lead to more hysterics.

"Special Agent Jarrod," I said. I felt beat up, and guilty. I'd screwed this up already.

"One second." Jarrod was fidgeted with some kind of electronics board with his left hand, his right holding up

one side of a large set of headphones to one ear as he listened to something. One of the household phones was off
the hook, its cord plugged into his board.

I probably should have been concerned; there was a reason normals (and Guild) feared computer technology since
the Tech Wars had used the computers to bring the world to
its knees. For that matter, I probably should have been more
upset that this particular machine was powerful enough,
had enough electromagnetic field to it, to change the waves
in Mindspace in subtle ways. It would affect my concentration, my ability to see trouble coming. I should probably be
campaigning for him to turn whatever it was way down or
off so I could do my job.

But instead I was focused on damage control right now.
I had a hell of a lot more to worry about.

"This is important," I said.

He did something that made it *whine* in a perhaps-
Mindspace-perhaps-reality frequency I wasn't sure anyone
else could hear. It bothered me like nails on a chalkboard.

Stop, I said into his mind. *That hurts.*

He looked up with an annoyed burst, and hit a switch
that turned off that sound. "What is it, Ward?"

"We have a problem," I said. If working with Paulsen
had taught me anything at all, it was that bad news got
worse with time. Even worse if someone other than yourself delivered it to your supervisor.

He set down the handset and turned all the way around.
"Exactly what kind of problem?" His voice was low, and
cold.

I filled him in, hitting the vision only lightly, focused on
the fact that I'd probably scared the living daylights out of
a kid who was already scared. "A completely amateur mistake, and I'm not excusing it," I said. "But there's no way I
could have predicted his telepathy, or this connection. His

mind did not react in a way it should have, and the information traveled without me being able to control it. As far as the vision goes—this is the guy we talked about on the phone. Sibley. At least I think it is."

He frowned. "Blair Sibley?"

"You know him?"

A burst of frustration, quickly brought into check. "Yes, Ward. I know Sibley. I was the one who gave you the damn file in the first place."

"Isn't he supposed to be in jail?" I asked. "A lot of us worked very hard to put him there." Cherabino would be furious, I thought, if he got out in time for the vision. Then I worried about her and her hearing. I'd have to call her soon.

Jarrod didn't stop for my worry. "That's the first phone call I'm going to make after I talk to you. If we have an ex–British Special Forces on the loose mucking up my case, I want to know why. There's been a loose connection between Fiske and Pappadakis established, like I said, but this turns it to a completely different level. We've been investigating old cases and this changes priorities. Assuming your visions are accurate." He regarded me.

At least that I had an answer for. "My precognition doesn't work as often as the standard, but when it does, the Guild has clocked me at a 78P. I'm accurate over three-quarters of the time, and I'm sure of this one. If we don't do something, that's where we're going to end up."

He nodded, thoughts moving in a slow dance, like freshly caught fireflies in a jar.

After a moment, I asked, "How have Fiske and your guy been connected?"

Jarrod glanced around, saw that no one was within eaves-dropping distance. Then he looked back at me. "Unofficially we're pretty sure that he's been supplying Fiske with parts for the illegal Tech trade. It's across state lines, so the Tech Control Organization has brought us in for our transportation expertise. Thus far no one has been able to prove anything. I'm here to monitor the murder investigation. The case is largely circumstantial, but if they can get a conviction, it's the first one we'll get on this guy. The rest of the team is here to monitor the judge and make sure everyone is protected and the guys behind it are found, but my focus is on the trial. Pappadakis has been under federal surveillance for over a year, and this is our first real chance to take him down."

"Oh," I said. People weren't usually this open with me. Even homicide detectives in the DeKalb Police Department weren't this open with me after they'd known me for a while.

"Sibley is dangerous. If he's involved at all . . ." I trailed off.

I thought about the machine, the small cube Sibley had carried the last time I'd run into him. With that cube in hand, any mind around him was highly suggestible. But it was an illegal thing, a thing based on Guild technology, and I didn't know what would happen—to them or to me— if the normals discovered such things were possible.

"I'm familiar with the file. I'll get more information."

Jarrod looked at me. This talk about visions made him nervous, and the situation was a great deal worse if Fiske was involved, if that was credible. Still, whether or not it was, he needed a telepath.

"Why do you think the attack is related to the Pappadakis case?" I asked him. "Since you've been investigating other cases as well?"

"It's the most current, the most high-profile in the media, and the threats escalated during the weeks of the indictment and so on. I'm hoping that if there is a connection, we'll find it and build a much less circumstantial case than the one being tried now. I'd like to cut the head off this trade. Thanks."

"Is the illegal Tech trade so bad?" I asked, and then realized that I'd run into a large section of it earlier in the year, with some items involved that had scared even me.

Jarrod nodded. It would be even better if the threads here would lead back to somebody senior, like Fiske, but he was here for what he could get. "How bad is the situation with the boy?" he asked me.

A long pause.

"Well, it's not good," I said.

"Walk me through exactly what he saw and what the consequences are. Give me a solution."

I replied, carefully, going back through the vision in a bit more detail, and then—reluctantly—emphasized that we'd made some kind of strange connection. All the while his body language, his feel in Mindspace was getting more and more closed, more and more tense and steady.

I ended with "I can probably downplay the memory the next time I interact with him, assuming he'll let me once he's calmed down sufficiently. He's a prototelepath, though, which makes things trickier. I think I can fix this." I had to fix this. I had to be here, to ward off the vision.

He was silent so long I thought he'd caught a message from outer space or something. Finally: "I expect you to do just that. You need to get him comfortable with you."

"Understood," I said. I was worried, but . . . I had to tell him, right? He was my current boss. "There are complications now that you need to know about."

He shook his head. "I need more complications like I need a kick in the head, but fine. Walk me through the bottom line and what you're going to do about it."

"I . . . I don't think I can leave him, not more than a

couple hundred feet away, not without screwing up the Minding for a good while. I'd rather stay within a hundred feet. If I go outside the distance, it'll hurt him, likely, or at least me, and I may not be able to get a good connection after this one is broken. I've never run into this situation before and I've only read about it once, in a book. If we stay within that distance, everything should be fine for now. If anything, I'll have an advantage in monitoring him. Should. A lot of this is new to me, like I told you when you called."

He thought about that. "You don't have a supervisor you can call for advice—is that right?"

I nodded reluctantly. "That's part of the deal when you get someone not-Guild."

It bothered me that I'd screwed up with Tommy, and it bothered me more that now I couldn't leave him. I felt overwhelmed, and worried about what would happen to Cherabino now. Would she be okay? I was getting more and more committed to this by the moment, and while I wanted to save Tommy's life if I could—I had to—I felt torn. A part of me felt like I should be in Atlanta, with her. If she lost her job, I was pretty sure she'd do something stupid, like leave town with no forwarding address, or beat someone up badly. She already had the mark on her record, after all.

Jarrod frowned, and my attention returned to him. "Well, then. You're going to have to figure it out. I expect a report on the situation—with, again, bottom lines in a bulleted list—by the end of the day. With solutions, and whatever you've already implemented. Whatever we need to implement."

I was over my head and I knew it. "I'm supposed to tell you what to do?"

"Make recommendations, Ward. You're the closest thing I've got to an expert, and I expect to use that expertise. I also expect to keep the Parsons safe and stable, and I'll work with you on methods if we remain at that goal."

It all felt big, in that moment, big and overwhelming. A kid's life—and some good agents' lives—might depend on me if Sibley came calling. And Jarrod was just . . . just trusting I'd get it done. Just taking me on as part of the team, no hostility, no yelling, no dismay at what had happened. I didn't know what to do with that. Finally I settled on usefulness, the one thing that had kept me employed in Atlanta, and prayed it would be enough. "Understood. You'll have some version of that before tomorrow morning. Also, I'm willing to help with the investigation," I said. "That's far more my specialty than Minding anyway." That I could do. Hopefully.

"Your specialty is interrogations."

"And crime scenes in Mindspace. You get emotions, context, and the occasional case breaker that way."

He didn't know how he'd get me to the crime scene if I couldn't be more than a hundred feet from Tommy Parson, he was thinking.

"I understand that Tommy is my primary responsibility, though," I said into the silence.

"That's right."

There was a long pause.

"I suppose you're waiting to make that touchstone on my mind. Ruth did it in the first hour. Go ahead."

I hadn't heard the word "touchstone" before, but it made sense. In a stressful situation, as a Minder I'd be communication and protection for the group, so I needed to be able to keep track of the group members. I forced calm. "You don't have any telepathy I should know about, do you?"

He shook his head, irony leaking from him. "Not a bit. I think I test negative on the scale." He paused, then added slowly, "Ruth said she had to scream at me if I'm not paying attention."

I nodded. I reached out, breathed in the feel and shape of his mind—indeed, mind-deaf as a doorpost—and placed a small, light tag that would fade out over the next week or so. I'd be able to find him with it. There had to be better ways to do that, but I wasn't a Minder and had said so repeatedly. This would work, which was all that mattered.

I disengaged, and the tag reacted exactly like I expected. No odd connections. Nothing. Maybe I could do this.

"Done?" Jarrod asked, attention already returning to his board of technology.

"Yes, sir," I said.

"Get going, then. And fix things with Parson's kid. I need you on good terms with him."

"Yes, sir."

Back into the main front room, right and left. The body-guard was slumped over some papers, her body language defeated, a slow sense of guilt and pain coming from her. I kept moving, feeling like a fire was lit under me.

In the hallway, Loyola was standing outside the kid's door.

"You going to tell me what happened earlier?" he asked me.

"Later," I said. "Right now I have orders from Jarrod."

Oddly enough, he accepted that.

What would Cherabino do in this situation? I didn't know, but in the interrogation rooms, if you couldn't get a kid to talk, you talked to the parent. I asked Jarrod, "Where is the kid's mother? I need her help."

He looked at me. "She's working. She's been very ada-mant that we're not to disturb her and that you're not to upset her son again. That isn't normal operating procedure for you, is it?" He was trying to be generous, but right now I seemed very incompetent.

Well, it looked like I was going to have to tell him as it was. "He's a prototelepath. The kid. He's a lot more powerful than expected, and his mind's not stable. He got a look at a vision of the future I had . . . and, well, he's in danger in it. Would scare the living shit out of me if I saw that and wasn't used to visions." I felt . . . itchy, impatient, under too much pressure.

"A vision?" He lifted an eyebrow. Clearly he didn't believe in such things.

"Yeah, well, it was a scary image," I said. "You going to tell me where the mother is?"

He regarded me, and I didn't know what he saw right then. Finally he said, "Last door on the right, all the way down. Looks like a linen closet."

"Thanks," I said.

CHAPTER 7

I knocked on the door firmly. It did indeed look like an ancient linen closet door, native to the building of the old house.

"Come in," Marissa's voice said.

I took my courage in my hands and opened the door. I walked through a narrow space of about two feet, entering into a full-sized room with a slanting low ceiling and a large window on the left. I hunched, even though my frame at a few inches shy of six feet wouldn't actually brush the ceiling at this point. It felt like it would.

Marissa sat at an antique wooden desk, turned toward the wall. One side of the desk was covered in piles of legal-sized folders, legitimately three feet deep at one point. A child's-painted ceramic jug held pens to the right, and legal pads and notes fanned out around her on the right of the desk. "One minute," she said, writing something to finish her thought, then closing the file open in front of her. A typewriter perched on a smaller table to the right, with typed pages scattered beneath it, and a large lamp illuminated everything.

She rotated in her modern office chair to look at me. Irritation came from her mind when she saw it was me.

"I'm working," she said. "I've already had to put off

three hearings. Some of these cases have been on the docket for months. Is this urgent?"

I was surprised. "No. Don't you want to be involved in the decisions about your son's safety?"

She closed a file and sighed. I noticed then how tired she felt, how frazzled. "I don't really want to be involved in the decisions about my safety."

"Didn't you call the FBI?" I asked, just to fill in a hole. I wasn't not sure how Jarrod knew about her case.

"That was the staff attorney. I made the mistake of showing her the threatening note I was worried about, and she called the FBI. She thought, for some reason, the threat against my son was their jurisdiction. She reads too many crime novels. Then the attack . . . happened, and they had you here within the day." Her emotions were mixed, worry and self-consciousness and fear and irritation and things I couldn't quite name. "I'd rather none of this had happened."

"Marissa—"

She held up a hand. "Judge Parson." Her voice was gentle but firm.

Fine. "Judge Parson, where is the staff attorney now?"

"At the courthouse, filling in at another judge's courtroom. Then she'll be doing research for me until I can get back." She thought she should have cleared the schedule entirely and driven with Tommy to her mother's in Washington for the duration. It would have been easier if she could somehow make it happen. But with the FBI here that wasn't really an option. And the caseload was never-ending. "I missed four hours this morning that we had scheduled for the Pappadakis case, and a case hearing this afternoon. The longer things pile up, the harder it's going to be to get them sorted again."

I recognized the thought patterns of a workaholic; Cherabino had given me plenty of experience with those. Parson was worried, not really facing what had almost happened to her son this morning. So I'd be gentle, let her have her bubble as long as she could.

"Was there a reason you came to see me?"

"I just wanted to make sure you were comfortable with me Minding Tommy for the next few days. I'm still happy to demonstrate the mental connection, or to walk you through what I do. Or answer questions. You're his mom. You need to be comfortable with this."

"I'm not going to be comfortable with this," she said to me. "I've got strangers coming into my home without an invitation or by-your-leave, and I'm not going to be comfortable with the need for protection against these threats. I really don't like it, and I'm not going to."

"You're his mom, and I want you to be comfortable," I repeated, forcing down irritation. I'd give her the benefit of the doubt and assume it was just me, for now. I had made her son go into hysterics. It was understandable.

"I trust that you will learn from your mistake earlier and *not* upset my son again. I do understand that this is the situation we've got and we're going to deal with it. What do you need?"

I needed the vision not to be true. I needed the responsibility of everything not to be falling on my shoulders like it was. I needed Cherabino to be okay, to keep her job and her sanity even without me there. But when it came to the judge? That was simpler. "I need you to back me up. I'm going to do whatever the hell you need me to do to be comfortable, and then we're going to go in and say hello to Tommy and you're going to tell him it's okay to trust me. I'll need you guys to listen to me when I say there's a threat, and I need your permission to monitor his mind—and to a lesser degree—your mind."

A frisson of nerves and drawing back came from her. I reminded myself she hated telepaths. Or maybe it was just me. A lot of people hated me, and at this point her feelings didn't really matter. The job did.

I continued. "I know you don't like this. But there's at least one known threat out there, and I can't do my job without your cooperation."

What known threat? her thoughts asked, all too strongly. That was right—whoever I thought had attacked her son. She stood, slowly, and breathed deeply. "I am a court judge for arguably the largest and most important media trial of a magnate that has ever happened in this city. I have at least a dozen other cases waiting for my office to schedule and adjudicate. I am getting death threats. I can't do your job for you."

I reared back, forcing myself to stay calm. "If you want to stay alive, you'll make time for this. I need one touch point to your mind and I need you to stay reasonably close."

She shook her head. There again was that nervousness.

"I can't make you accept any more monitoring than you'll allow," I said finally. "But don't let your fear get in the way of your son's safety. The threat to his life is very real—as you saw this morning. Go in there with me now. Please."

"I am *not* afraid," she said with anger, but she was. After a moment, she said, "Fine. Take care of Tommy. I'll even introduce you. But let me work. Let me have this."

"Thank you."

"You upset him again like that and you won't like what happens," she said, a real threat couched in flat words.

"I understand," I said. Finally some emotion I understood. Different people dealt with grief in different ways, and her being detached and angry at me, specifically, was probably easier than facing the real situation about her son. I'd give her some more room, if she'd help me.

I paused. She should probably know, even if she wasn't likely to react well. "Your son is a prototelepath," I said. "In a few years, he's going to be strong enough to need Guild training."

A look of disgust passed over her face. "I know. I blame his father," she said, and stood, clearly trying to move the conversation along. "Let's get this over with."

Parson knocked on her son's door, gently. "It's your mother," she called, and with no more ado she opened the door and walked in.

Tommy looked up from a comic book, his eyes red. He was startled and defensive, but he didn't want to show it. "What is it?" he asked, sitting up, leaving the comic book up, a picture of a woman in 1940s costume fighting a darkly shaded guy with gears on his arm.

"This is Adam Ward," she said. "He's a telepathic bodyguard, like the other bodyguards. He's promised not to scare you again—and if he does, you come find me, okay? But otherwise you're to let him guard you, at least until this situation is over. I need to work now."

Tommy's face went through dismay and fear before settling on something I couldn't quite read . . . his blank face perhaps. "Can't you just stay with me for a while?" he asked quietly.

"Not right now, honey. I need to work," she said. Then, without any other explanation, she left.

Which left me and Tommy a few feet from each other, neither one of us precisely happy with the situation.

I didn't know how to handle this. I had been counting on

Parson to help me get on Tommy's good side. I had to get on Tommy's good side. The vision . . . well, it just couldn't happen.

Tommy looked back out the door, after his mother, and I felt his loneliness. I couldn't just keep standing here, so I tried the one thing in front of me.

"Why don't you tell me about the comic book?"

"It's the tenth one in the series," he said, like I was an idiot for not knowing. "*The Cat Avenger.*"

"Well, I've never read *The Cat Avengers,*" I said. "Is it good?"

"*The Cat Avenger,*" he repeated.

"Is it good?" I repeated.

He nodded, but I could feel his loneliness again. He really wanted his mom. It had been a terrible day and he wasn't sure it was over yet. He didn't know—and I didn't either—why she couldn't come sit with him.

I walled up my worries, all of them, into a small area in the back of my head. If I spent too much time thinking about them in front of Tommy, it wouldn't be good for either of us. I needed to be the guy he could trust if everything went wrong. That was what a Minder did, and that was what I needed to do now.

I sat down on a chair not too far from the bed, close enough to be there, far enough not to crowd him. "Look, I'm sorry about earlier." I hated apologizing, but in this case, he deserved an apology. "I should have done a better job with that. I didn't mean for—well. You're going to be a telepath, in a few years, and that changes things. I should have been more careful."

Now I had his attention. "I'm going to be a telepath?"

I nodded. "Your brain has already got the beginnings of a good Ability going. Give it a few years and you'll be Guild, probably." I wasn't sure why they hadn't found him through the school screenings already, but probably he'd been absent that day.

"Like on TV?"

"A little bit like on TV," I said. "But real telepaths aren't the big guys you see on TV. They look like everybody else. But they can do cool things."

Tommy thought about that. I moved in a little closer in Mindspace and found him surprisingly open, sharing his thoughts with no filter—at least for this moment. He was thinking about some movies he'd seen and the comic book character he was reading. It would be pretty cool to have powers like that. "If I'm Guild, I'll have lot of friends and people around all the time, right?" he asked.

"Most Guild people do," I said. "But you have to be a friend to make a friend too. It's not guaranteed."

"Oh," he said.

He probably knew that from school already, but I didn't want to hand him a blank check. The bigger question was what he'd seen from my head. "You want to talk about what you saw?" I asked.

"Not really," he said, and stared at me.

Okay. I tried it a different way. "Look, what you saw is just one possible future. I'm here to make sure it doesn't happen that way. We're all here to make sure it doesn't happen that way."

"Okay," he said.

"You want me to leave the room now, don't you?"

"Maybe." He looked down.

I sighed. "I need to be within a hundred feet of you to make sure nothing bad happens, like your other bodyguard. If you want me to go into the hallway, I will, but if there's some kind of alarm I'll need to come back until the problem goes away."

I expected him to tell me to go, but instead I got a sense

of fear and danger from him then, a wobbly memory of the morning. "You're really a bodyguard?" he said, very quietly.

"For your mind, yes. And there're three agents out there who'll jump in to help if I can't." Four, maybe? Plus other minds around the house? I'd have to meet everybody eventually to sort them out.

"And you're really going to protect me?" Tommy asked.

"I am." I meant it as a promise, a real promise, the kind you didn't break without bleeding.

He thought about that for a long while. "Okay," he finally said.

"Okay?" I asked.

"You can stay around for now," he said.

"Thanks." It wasn't the rousing endorsement I'd expected, but it would work. As I sat there, I monitored the situation around me and tried not to watch the clock. I also worked— hard—not to worry about Cherabino or about the vision in front of Tommy. But it was work.

Half an hour and some talking later, Tommy had settled down with the next comic book in the series and I couldn't stand it anymore. I had to use the restroom, so I went outside into the hall.

I found Loyola outside waiting for me.

"How is Tommy holding up?" he asked.

I looked behind me, to make sure the old wooden bedroom door was closed behind me, and then lowered my voice anyway. How was I supposed to know? "I don't think the attack's hit him yet. I don't know if it will. His mom's not being very supportive." And I had my own issues, which I was sure were communicating their own tension to Tommy.

"I've noticed that too," Loyola said, and then visibly held back another sentence. I was curious, so I peeked. He thought the judge treated her son more like a pet than a child, and violently disapproved. It wasn't his place to say anything, though.

His eyes narrowed, as he guessed I was looking at his mind. "Best thing you can do for Tommy is to be there and be consistent. As much as possible anyway. Neither one of us is his mom, but worst thing in the world is to be alone at a time like this."

"Yeah," I said. I was most concerned with his safety, and again, I had to pee. I needed to wrap this up.

"Tell me what happened. Earlier. When he freaked out."

I pushed down irritation. I was still new, and I still had to explain myself. Hell, I always had to explain myself. "I made a mistake," I said. I caught him up on roughly what I had told Jarrod. It wasn't a secret, exactly, though it didn't make me look good either. "You have questions?" I asked.

He asked a couple, and I answered them.

I summed up, in the hope of ending the conversation: "It's just additional information at this point, something for us to take seriously but not to worry about much. We're already on protective duty. It's not like this information changes any of that."

His thoughts about that were cautious, like someone placing his feet carefully in a darkened room. "How likely is it that we're dealing with the events of the vision?" he asked. "How much can we plan in advance and head this off?"

That was the question, wasn't it? I damped down impatience and decided on honesty. "I have no idea. The future is mutable, or it usually is. I think it's likely . . . judging from my previous experience here, we're much better off taking slow moves to change things than aggressive action. Aggressive action can backfire."

He huffed. I waited, but he said nothing else, and his

brain was just churning over what I'd said from a few directions, discomfort and speculation mixing with my words. And I needed to go.

But I'd also been gone from Tommy for several minutes now, and I was supposed to be the Minder. So I took a quick look at Mindspace, behind me, to check on Tommy.

I got a much clearer view, much faster, than I would otherwise expect. Probably the connection between us meant I could monitor his mind more easily than the average. Tommy was facedown on his bed, working through the comic book, engrossed in the story. He didn't notice I was there, which was both good and bad.

Since I was open to the house anyway, I took a look at the surroundings, making sure I could account for all the minds. Everything seemed normal, so far as I knew—but then, in the front room behind me, I felt the bodyguard's mind shimmer in and out of reality.

"Crap," I said.

"What?" Loyola asked, annoyed, but I was already moving down the hall in her direction. I entered the main room.

Yeah, she was slumped over on the left in that bowl-shaped chair, hand drooping to the floor, color ashen. The bandage on her arm was covered in blood. But it was her mind that bothered me. Did she have internal bleeding?

"Jarrod," I said to him. *Jarrod,* I said into his mind directly.

"What?" He looked up, frowning at me from the board over on the right.

I gestured. "Tanya's going into shock. Somebody's going to have to drive her to the hospital. If that's me, we need to pack up the kid and go now. She can't wait."

I added a little strength to her mind, not enough to stabilize her, but enough to help her last a little longer. It would buy us another few minutes.

Jarrod sighed and got up. "One thing after another," he muttered under his breath. He headed out to the porch, me following.

I blinked in the light of the setting sun.

"Mendez," Jarrod said, and she turned around.

"What?"

"I need you to get Tanya to the hospital, ASAP," Jarrod said. "Check on the other bodyguard while you're there. Take Sridarin with you."

Mendez thought dark thoughts about the woman being the one on hospital duty, but out loud she just said, "Yes, sir. Emergency?"

"Looks like it."

The other mind I'd felt came up the front steps. He was a young guy, maybe twenty-one, of Indian descent, and he moved with the quick-footed grace I associated with soccer players. He and Mendez pushed past me immediately; they had Tanya up before I was back in the room.

"I'm fine," Tanya mumbled as they half carried her out of the house. I felt her mind fade in and out again, and I added another shored-up piece to her mind. Then I opened up to the house again. Loyola was joining the others up front, the judge was on the phone in her office upstairs, and Tommy was out of his room and looking for me.

I checked in and then locked myself in the bathroom to take care of my bladder. And worry, a little, where Tommy wouldn't hear me.

A few minutes later, I met Tommy in the hallway, barely in the front room, senses fully open. His feet creaked on the old wooden floors, as did mine, as did everyone else's who was moving all too quickly to respond. A chorus of creaks everywhere; it was distracting.

I needed to pay attention to the mental space, not the physical noise. With everybody involved with the emergency at the front of the house, I needed to pay attention to every single fluctuation in Mindspace in case this was a setup. How anyone could predict that Tanya would go into shock at this exact moment, I didn't know. But it was my job to be paranoid. And I was worried, more worried than ever, and feeling very paranoid.

"Is Tanya okay?" Tommy said.

"Let's go to your room," I told him, "away from the windows." My tone was probably too intense, and I didn't try to hide my concern for Tanya, but I added a determination to prevent any problems well before they started.

I reached out and touched his shoulder, pushing him gently in the direction of his room.

He was scared, suddenly, horribly scared, his mind flashing back to the attack this morning all too vividly. I pushed the images down. I was scared too. It wouldn't hurt anything to move through a defensive posture—even if nothing was wrong now, it might make him feel safer and me feel more practiced if anything else really did go wrong.

Inside the room, I closed the door and turned to the window, which seemed too low and too vulnerable. "Here, help me move the dresser in front of the window," I said. So we did that.

Huffing and puffing, I stood back. Better, maybe. More warning. With the images of his attack echoing in my head with all his strong emotions, the danger seemed all too real to me now. I opened up my senses wide, and watched the car taking the bodyguard to the hospital leave the property.

"Is Tanya okay?" Tommy repeated in a small, worried voice.

"Tanya is in shock." I turned to him. "They're taking her to the hospital now. She should be okay."

"The hospital?"

I thought about how to explain it. "When you lose a lot of blood or telepathic energy all at once, it throws your whole body out of whack. You can die." Old lessons paraded through my head: the mental signatures of someone in Stage 2, where intervention was most effective, which Tanya perhaps had passed. Chemical charts of sodium, potassium, and acidity of the blood, which I'd been forced to learn as part of my teacher-training, both for blood loss and for Ability overwork. I was more familiar with the internal feeling that I'd reached my limits. They pushed you in advanced training, over and over again, for that reason. So you knew when pushing harder would hurt, but be okay, and you knew when pushing meant you could likely die. There were limits to the human mind and body, and while you could train for more endurance, for more strength, all humans eventually hit a wall beyond which they could not go. I wasn't as familiar with blood loss, with physical damage, but in those cases it had to be the same. Beyond a certain point, you had to have help to survive. "She'll be fine," I said, as if by a force of will.

"She's not a telepath," Tommy responded to me.

I blinked, and paid attention again. I really had spent too much time around normals not to be expecting to be read at any moment. "No, she's not. She had to have some bleeding inside. I don't think the arm injury was enough on its own." I tried to consider whether I could have spotted it earlier. "The hospital isn't far. She seemed like she'll do okay with IV fluids. Odds are she should be okay." I didn't know whether I was trying to convince him or me. I'd seen too many fellow students—and myself—come back from telepathic shock with a full recovery. But blood loss was different, and she hadn't felt good.

"Will Jason die?" Tommy asked, quietly, after a moment.

"I don't know," I said. I looked around and finally settled for sitting on the floor. My knees creaked, but I made it. "There're a lot of things I don't know. I'll try to claim them. But the folks at the hospital have this as their job. They see it every day, and they're as good as anyone is at making people get better."

"That's not an answer," he said.

"No, it's not, I guess." I cast about for something to talk about. I'd already struck out on the comic books, and I didn't need to worry about Cherabino more, not right now. There—over there, the floating anti-grav boats I'd seen once before. "You going to show me the boats there?"

He sat down, in that boneless way only children had, like his joints were made of rubber. "They're just boats." He was actually trying to read me now, and I let him.

I felt Loyola coming down the hall. *Come in slowly,* I told him. *He's going to spook easily.*

I got a general feeling of agreement from him.

"Speaking of, we'll have to make contingency plans sometime today," I said. Then, in response to his thought: "Contingency means something that you don't think will probably happen but you want to plan for it anyway, just to be safe."

"Like Tanya did with the car," he said, flashing to drills he'd done to drop out of sight. In the emergency he'd done it. He was proud of that. But he'd been so scared. And although he was calming down now, he was still scared. Everyone else was moving so quickly, and they said Jason might die.

"I don't know what's going to happen to Jason," I told him. "But he wanted more than anything in the world for you to be safe. That's something I want, and Loyola wants, and all the agents are here to make sure of. It's better to see the danger coming. In the meantime, we're just going to have to do some drills like you did with Tanya, just in case. It probably won't happen," I said again, trying to reassure him.

He seemed dubious, and I felt his low-level fear. I didn't know how to help.

A soft knock came on the door, and then it opened slowly. Loyola stuck his head in. "Is there a reason the dresser is blocking the window?" he asked after a moment.

"It made me feel better," I said.

He came in. "Short of a robot army invading the area, I don't think a dresser is going to make much difference."

"Robot army?" I asked.

He shrugged. "I like B movies." He thought moving the dresser didn't hurt anything either, and reacting to everyone else's distraction was a good habit to be in. Maybe I was competent after all.

I suppressed a sarcastic comment.

"B movies are awesome!" Tommy said. "Jason lets me watch . . ." He trailed off.

"Well, we'll watch a few together, then. I'll even make popcorn," Loyola said, then paused. "If there's nothing critical going on right now, how about you get started on your homework?"

"Aw, do I have to?"

"Just because you're not going to school doesn't mean you don't have to keep up," Loyola said.

"But what about Adam? He said we had to do preparedness drills. Like in case something happens. Isn't that better than homework?" Tommy's mind wasn't nearly as afraid now that the adults were acting normal.

Loyola looked at me, thinking really, why was I scaring the kid even more?

"Homework sounds like a good idea. We'll do drills later. Life goes on, right?"

Tommy pouted and then sighed, all drama. "I don't want to do homework. You don't have to do homework."

"Kid, I do homework all the time."

Loyola laughed.

CHAPTER 8

I **sat at** the kitchen table, paging through a two-year-old magazine on art that I didn't really care about while Tommy sat and drank orange juice and ignored his home-work. He was watching me, and I let him. As much as I wanted to be rattled by the connection I'd accidentally made between us, I was the adult and the professional at the table and I needed to be calm. Regardless of how his mom had treated me, or how uncertain I was about this connection I hadn't seen coming, or how over my head I felt in dealing with a ten-year-old. Or even the vision weighing down on me, or the worry about Cherabino's job. I had to handle this. I had to be the strong one.

I forced calm, calm and openness like I'd do for another telepath I liked. As expected, after a few minutes he started poking around in my mind. I let him. Another telepath would have a much "louder" mind than a normal and would be easier to hear, not to mention the connection between our minds, which would probably let him see me even when his Ability wasn't stable, which would happen at his age, where he was in the development curve.

I let him look, and stayed calm. Certain things got bot-tled up, filed, and locked away, but that would be the same for any telepath.

He drank orange juice and poked around some more.

"Having fun?" I asked finally.

"What's the . . . the . . . itchy. . . . thing in your head?" he finally asked, making a flailing motion with his hands like words were failing him. He'd been looking at me very seriously for minutes at a time, so even in the absence of good words I'd happily answer questions. He meant the thing in my head that he could see getting twitchy; at least I thought he did.

"I want a cigarette," I said, which was true, if incomplete. I wanted my drug, Satin, my addiction. But the cigarette would do for now. "Don't ever start smoking if you can help it. Even when you're not smoking you'll spend half your life thinking about the stupid things. Plus, they're expensive." Even so, I couldn't see myself giving them up anytime soon; if I stayed around here, I'd probably have to get some of the stupid plastic-tasting gum to keep myself from going crazy or smoking in front of the kid. Not happy either way, but there it was.

"Oh," he said, but settled. He had a name for what ailed me, which actually was helping me too. Something to focus on.

"You'll be a telepath. It'll take a couple of years for your Ability to stabilize, but you'll get there," I said after a minute, in answer to his unspoken question.

He blinked and went back to his orange juice. Unnamed fears and hopes and the memories of this morning all jumbled up together in his head, getting stuck, rubbing up against each other.

I went back to the magazine. He'd work through it on his own, or I—or more likely, his mother or Tanya—would be able to ask questions that would help. But pushing him to talk before he was ready didn't seem useful, not at this stage.

Besides, I was out of my league and I knew it. He was far younger than I was used to dealing with in students, the structure of his mind seemed fine, and there was nothing I could investigate right this instant. His bodyguard was likely to have seen more significant details than he would have, considering her training, and the laws about mind-reading and consent in kids were tricky. I still felt a bit helpless, though. And worried about what was to come. Could I really keep him safe? Could I really not worry in front of him?

I turned another page in the magazine, and came across an article with a star drawn by it. A Savannah artist and art professor at the design college, showing in a New York gallery. There were pictures of his work, intricate 3-D things set on top of canvases, not quite paintings, not quite sculpture, with many gears and brightly colored paint so that your eye was drawn to them and you half expected the whole thing to move.

"Do you guys know this guy?" I asked.

He leaned over to see what I was looking at, then straightened. "He's a friend of the art teacher at school. The school went to the opening." A vague sense of wanting to be there too. "Mom said I couldn't go, not since we're going to be traveling soon and I don't get to go to school much as it is." His mind informed me that this was stupid. "I'm not in school anyway. They're doing a field trip to the courthouse and River Street this week. I really wanted to go, but she said no again. She says no a lot."

Then he started thinking about this morning again, raw red thoughts full of fear and confusion.

I tried to figure out how to tell him we'd do everything in our power to keep that from happening again. His body-guards were good; they'd protected him once. And the FBI and the sheriff's department would do their jobs too. That was why I was here. Because the universe believed I could make a difference. I had to believe that.

He settled a little, from my thoughts or emotions or not, I didn't know, and a question started to rise to the top.

I felt an anxious mind approaching the house at a very fast clip, and I clamped down mind-protection shields around both of us, moving around to right next to him, between him and the door.

Tommy descended into fear, outright fear, at my actions. I reached out, grabbed his hand, and emanated calm, as much calm as I could manage. "I'm right here," I said.

My attention was at the front door, where the mind was headed.

Two minutes later the sound of moving feet on old floors, then the minds up at the front in high, instant alert, guns up and ready.

After a moment, the alert settled down two notches, and I heard the door opening. I braced; if there was a threat from a telepath, there might be every reason to suspect he'd get past the guards.

I settled Tommy's mind behind mine, wearing it like a mental backpack connected to me and shielded by me, but not taking up any mental hands.

He struggled—*Still and quiet,* I told him. *Still and quiet until we know what's wrong. Like you did for Tanya this morning.*

That made him even more afraid, his heart beating like a drum in his chest, but he stilled.

I extended out mentally, preparing myself to fight a possibly superior enemy long enough for the others to come. It had been years since I'd done this for anyone but myself—years.

Another burst of fear from Tommy.

Stay right there, behind me, and we'll be fine, I said, and forced myself to believe it. *I've survived a number of these fights in the last months, and you're coming with me too.*

He settled, somewhat comforted but still afraid, into that backpacklike place behind my mind, waiting.

I waited too, but the new mind stayed put in the front room, the others around him and suspicious.

In the real world, Loyola moved, gun in hand, down the hall past us. "Ma'am," he said to the judge; then I didn't catch the rest. A minute later, she followed him back past us.

A man's voice murmuring in the front room, perhaps Jarrod's, another replying. Then the judge's higher voice, in rough anger.

Then another voice, in a calm tone I didn't quite understand.

Tommy's mind relaxed then, and he got up from the chair and pulled his hand away. "That's Dad," he told me seriously. I got a brief picture of a tall man with bruises on his face.

Another half-heard comment.

I double-checked the surroundings. I didn't know all the fed minds yet, damn it, but nobody seemed all that new.

"Are you sure?" I asked. I was already nervous.

He nodded. "I'm going to see him now." And he was down the hall. I trotted to keep up.

Assuming he was right, it was more or less safe, and nobody else seemed worried. Even so, I took a mental note that Tommy was the kind to make his own decisions, and quickly, when it suited him. I'd have to keep an eye on him.

In the main room, a circle of FBI agents and sheriff's department guys stood around a tall man in a suit and a haircut that reminded me of Fred Astaire, very old-school indeed. He had a few bruises on his hands, and one on his neck that was already multicolored in the healing process. I got the impression he was a partier, a hard partier, earlier in life, but his mind when I checked seemed completely sober.

It lit up when he saw his son. "Tommy, good to see you. I trust you're well."

"What are you doing here, Dad?" Tommy asked, holding back. "You're making everybody nervous, and you're supposed to call first anyway."

The man made a show of looking around, the boxes perched on his palm moving with the motion. "As I said, I heard what happened and ran right over. I brought you all some donuts as a thank-you for keeping my son safe. Am I right that our law enforcement professionals love pastries?"

Every cop in the place responded to the comment emotionally, most irritated, a few amused.

"Quentin, you're doing it again," the judge said.

"Doing what, my dear?" Quentin flashed a bright smile and set the two flat donut boxes on a nearby surface, the coffee table. "Am I not allowed to visit my son when the mood suits me?"

"You know very well you're supposed to call before you come over," the judge said. She sighed. "And you know your charm doesn't work on me. Not anymore."

"I'm wounded, truly."

"I'm sure you are."

"Don't I get a hug?" Quentin asked Tommy. "I brought your favorite kind of donut."

Tommy just looked at him.

Loyola, the closest to the coffee table, opened the box. "There're some cream-filled ones here."

"No one eats the donuts until I have more information," Jarrod said. "Who exactly are you?"

Quentin stood even straighter, turning toward Jarrod. "Quentin D. Alexander, at your service, sir."

"What relationship do you have with the Parsons?"

"Dear Marissa and I were married at one time, or didn't she tell you? She does leave that detail out occasionally. Tommy is my son, of course. A widely acknowledged fact, for all she doesn't like to claim it."

The judge crossed her arms over her chest. "Quentin is a con man. A good one, but just a con man."

He tipped an imaginary hat. "Glad to hear you appreciate my skills. Though of course I admit to no such thing. Now." Again he addressed Jarrod. "I've heard you fine gentleman are in town with the FBI. Is there a particular reason that federal agents should involve themselves in an attack on a county superior judge? You don't have jurisdiction here, unless I am mistaken."

Jarrod reluctantly introduced himself. He took Quentin's hand, and shook it just a little too hard; my mind registered discomfort from Quentin. Jarrod let go. He was thinking very hard, trying to figure out how the judge had come to marry a con man and have a child with him without stopping her career in its tracks.

After all the thoughts swirling in his head, Jarrod merely said, "This is an investigation in progress. I cannot comment on details."

Quentin smiled, like he suddenly knew a lot more than he did before. He nodded at me, particularly, picking me out of the crowd with no trouble. "And you also have a telepath. How delightful. What interesting and unusual details this day is bringing about."

I hadn't told him I was a telepath, and I didn't wear a Guild patch. I'd gotten out of the habit of being recognized. Was this where the boy got his Ability? It seemed likely.

I didn't really trust this guy, though.

"I think it's time for you to leave, Mr. Alexander," Jarrod said. "Unless you have additional information to add to our investigation."

"Didn't you see the donuts? I'm told sugar is brain food, the breakfast of champions." He held up a hand. "Sincerely, though, I appreciate your diligence in helping to keep my son safe. What happened this morning—I cannot think about what might have happened. If there's anything I can do—anything at all—you call me at once. I will leave you my number."

"How can you possibly help, Quentin, really?" The judge shook her head, looking tired.

"You know that I know people. Quite a lot of people. Some of whom won't talk with the police. Surely you remember."

"I was never involved with your friends, Quentin, and I resent the implication that I was, in front of federal agents."

"Why should we believe anything you say?" Loyola said, tone dismissive.

"We'll take that number," Jarrod said. Next to him, Mendez glanced at him, like this response was unexpected. But she looked back at Quentin.

"You're offering to speak with these friends in exchange for what exactly?" Mendez asked him.

"Out of the goodness of my heart, naturally."

Jarrod went from conflicted to certain then. "Thank you for your offer, Mr. Alexander, but we can take it from here. You'll understand if we have any questions we'll be interviewing you. In detail."

Quentin smiled.

Everyone else just stood there, waiting.

"That means you need to leave now, Dad," Tommy said.

"I know, nugget." Quentin reached over and ruffled his son's hair.

Tommy reached out and hugged him, quickly, like he was embarrassed to be caught.

"Where were you this morning, by the way?" Mendez asked.

Quentin's mind, stronger than the others in the room, flashed a surprisingly clear picture of a poker game at a seedy club back room. "Sadly I spent the morning at the veterinarian's having my poor doglet treated for her cancer. She's been a brave soul, but it doesn't look good. It's very sad."

"Uh-huh," the judge said loudly. "Quentin, leave your number with the agents and leave. Tommy's okay, and you'll see him on your weekend. You'll ask him all the questions then."

"If my presence is no longer needed," Quentin said, "I will make my way out."

He did stop to write down a number on the top of the donut box, producing a pen from a pocket with a flourish and writing in a large loopy scrawl. Then he tipped his imaginary hat again and left.

"You okay?" I asked Tommy.

"Yeah," he said in a small voice, and turned around, moving toward his room.

Jarrod caught my eye before I could follow. "Alibi?"

"He wasn't at the veterinarian's," I said. "But he wasn't anywhere close to the attack either. He seems genuinely wanting to help find whoever it was that attacked his son. I think you can let him go if you want to. He's not meaning any harm, at least not to us."

Jarrod nodded, dismissing me, and I went back to find Tommy.

That was fast. I guess I wasn't used to cops taking my word seriously. It was kinda nice actually.

If it wasn't for the weight of the vision and my worry about Cherabino's job hanging over me like anvils, this might actually be a good day. I wished I could believe it would continue.

It was dark outside and I was hungry. Very hungry. Out of desperation and nothing more, I was now standing over a hot stove with a cardboard box in my hands, puzzling out the directions for a dried soup. I'd stayed with Tommy the whole time, and had mostly avoided any major lapses in conversation. But with the day going on and my fuel tank getting low, that would change if I didn't eat.

I needed to call Cherabino, to check up on her and ask how the hearing was going, but I didn't want Tommy to overhear. I didn't want to scare him. The conflict between the two feelings was making it much harder to puzzle out the directions on the soup box.

"You need water," Tommy said. He was perched on a tall stool in front of the raised counter, a breakfast bar or some such.

I looked back at the mix. "Yeah, that makes sense," I said, and located the sink. Check. Now for measuring. Eight cups of water, exactly?

"That's not a very good soup," Tommy said as I opened cabinets in the overly modern kitchen. Measuring cups, measuring cups . . .

"Third cabinet on the right, below the counter," he said, with the dismissive tone of a kid stating the obvious.

I counted cabinets and opened the third one on the right.

"The other right," he said.

I moved to the other cabinet. *Kid thinks he knows everything.* "Aha!" I said, then under my breath: "Jackpot."

"Can't you make macaroni?" Tommy asked. He swung his legs forward so they hit the counter in front of him. *Thump-thumpity. Thumpity-thump.*

"Not unless it's dead easy," I said. "Rehydrating dehydrated food is about the extent of what I can manage. Unless you want to take a shot, this is what we have. Unless you have peanut butter. I can do peanut butter," I said hopefully.

"Mom says peanut butter is fattening," Tommy said.

Of course she did.

"Why isn't anyone else cooking?" he asked me.

"They're doing rounds of the property and calling their contacts for research and talking to your dad's contacts," I said. "It's just you and me. They'll probably have some food later, but I wouldn't count on it." Most cops I knew carried around bar-shaped meals in small packages to tide them over, and I'd been known to do the same but had left Atlanta in too much of a hurry.

"Mom says Dad lies a lot so he can get what he wants," Tommy said, still thumping the front of the counter.

"That's usually why people lie," I replied, and got the water level right in the cup after the third try. I poured it into the pan, which sizzled and spat steam at me. I stepped back.

"I don't like liars," Tommy said.

"You don't like a lot of people, then," I said. I'd spent years in the interrogation room separating out truth from lies; even the innocent people lied about something under that kind of pressure. The trick was to figure out what the lie was and why they were doing it. Why in hell were those witnesses lying against Cherabino? It made no sense. It got them nowhere.

"Do you really talk to so many people? Like in the movies? You're a police officer, right?"

I got the last of the water in without burning myself and opened the box of dried soup. I threw it in, most of it ending up in the pot and not on the stove. I should probably have had a bigger reaction to him reading me—he seemed awfully consistent for someone his age—but I'd just spent a bunch of time at the Guild. He was doing surface thoughts only, what the Guild considered public space, and if I kept a lid on the worst of what was going through my head, that was okay. But I had to be careful.

"Can you do all the stuff telepaths do on TV?"

"What?" I turned around, stirring the soup. "What was the question?" He asked a lot of questions, but I guessed that was okay. Questions were better than terror, and at least they meant I knew where he was.

"Like disappear, and make people do things, and lift things with your mind, and make people see things that aren't there. And make fire. The fire part was cool." His mind, now that I was paying attention, flashed a B-movie version of a pyrokinetic holding fire in his hand. "If I'm really going to be a telepath, can I make fire too?" He was thinking the kids at school who made fun of him would run from fire, and it would make them like him.

"Um, I can't make fire—except with a match—and I doubt you'll be able to either," I said. "That's a pyro, and the Ability is pretty rare. And the disappearing part is usually a teleporter. I know some of them, but that doesn't mean I can do it. I have to walk everywhere, but then again that keeps you in shape. Honestly? Right now you're probably not going to be able to do much but see what people are thinking sometimes, and that's not going to be super stable. Give it a year or two, though, and you'll be able to train and get more control. If you have one of the secondary Abilities, either you'll discover it on your own or it will come out in training." I considered testing him, or doing a deep-scan to determine, but with the strange connection that had established itself earlier, I wasn't sure I could control the situation well enough. The only other person around his age I'd ever spent any time with was Jacob, and thus far Tommy hadn't reacted at all the same way.

"Who's Jacob?" the kid asked.

"My . . . the woman I'm dating and work with, her nephew," I said awkwardly. "Girlfriend" didn't seem quite right in context, too small and too large a term for the present discussion, but we weren't quite police partners anymore either. Even though I missed her input on this case and her presence. I took a breath. "Anyway, he has a health issue and a very strong Ability that's pretty stable right now. He's getting training, but he's ready for it too. You'll get there, and honestly, you'll probably do better in the Guild system when they come around recruiting. The Guild's not a bad life, not if you're one of them."

He thought about that. "Will I still get to see my mom?"

"You'll spend a couple of weeks with her three times a year. More if there's a good reason and you go through the approval process." I stirred the soup again, looked at the clock, and called it done. I located the bowls in an upper cabinet. "If you'll remind me later, I'll teach you how to separate yourself from other people's thoughts. It takes a little bit to get good at, but that way school won't be so loud and distracting." And I might get away with more worries in front of him if he could shield better.

I missed Cherabino. I really did, but I pushed that to the back of my head and focused on the soup. And Tommy.

He blinked at me.

"Really," I said. Then handed him the bowl of soup. "Now eat up."

He watched me over the rim of his bowl while he ate.

"Ward." Jarrod stuck his head in the kitchen.

I looked up from the donuts we'd found for dessert. "Yes?"

"Ward's a funny name," Tommy observed. If that was the worst he was saying about me, it was a good day.

Jarrod ignored him. "We need your talents in the main room for a moment."

"You going to be okay on your own?" I asked Tommy. "You won't go wandering off?" Suddenly even being a few feet from him seemed dangerous. That vision was coming whether I liked it or not.

"Don't be stupid," he said.

"Um, okay." I looked at Jarrod, who then turned around and left, a clear expectation that I'd follow. Reluctantly, glancing back at Tommy, I did, but I kept mental tabs on him. I'd know if he moved a foot.

There was a card table set up in the corner of the main room, one of those supermaterial tables that would fold up into the size of a pack of cards and then fold out into a lightweight table with a nice pattern of cracks on the top (and hinges on the bottom) to make it look decorative. Of course the lightweight table would hold up the weight of a small car without buckling, so as expensive as it was, it was a good choice for them. Normally people would put a tablecloth over it to make the surface more even, but Jarrod hadn't. With all the electronic equipment he'd set up on another, similar table next to it, perhaps he hadn't had the time. It seemed like they should be watching the electronics more closely, more carefully. Dangerous stuff there—nothing rated for a civilian—and they were treating it casually, like it didn't matter. This bothered me. Didn't they know how dangerous computers could be after the Tech Wars? Weren't they worried a supervirus would attack their equipment and destroy everything?

Mendez stood next to Jarrod, a thick sheaf of papers in hand. She set them down on the table, starting to fan them out over its surface. I forced myself to calm down. Being a bundle of nerves and worry wasn't going to help anyone.

"What's going on?" I asked. Why had they asked me here, away from Tommy?

"We just got the judge's letters back from the local crime lab," Mendez said. "Analysis of the physicals will take another few hours, but I thought we'd give you a look."

"What?" I walked closer to the table.

The letters overlapped like the blades of a folding fan, a few faceup, the rest spread out with edges showing only. Some of the letters were handwritten, others typed, but the ones on the stack to the right, the ones that bothered me, looked like something you'd see in a movie. Large and mostly brightly colored letters cut out of magazines and newspapers spelled out things like YOU KNOW WHAT YOU HAVE TO DO, and LET HIM GO OR IT'S OVER. A shiver went up my spine.

"The newspaper letters look ominous," I said. Like the kind of thing a movie villain sent, right before somebody died. If the judge had been getting these for weeks and months . . . I understood then on a deep level why she'd hired the bodyguards.

Who, now that I thought about it, were dead or severely injured. This wasn't a safe job I'd taken on. This wasn't a safe job at all.

Jarrod moved next to me. "The lab says those are more recent, and created by only one person or a single group working together. The rest are from several individuals over a matter of years. Please take a look."

I swallowed. "Can I touch the letters?"

"Go ahead."

I picked up one, looked at it sideways in the light. The magazine and newspaper letters weren't attached with glue; they weren't rippled enough. I poked one of the cutout squares. It was solidly connected to the lined notebook paper page, like the two materials had fused. "Paper-weld bonder?" I asked. "Those are usually owned by businesses, not individuals, because of the cost, right?" Maybe we could find him that way, and take the danger out of the situation before it escalated. Nothing would make me happier.

"Yes," Jarrod said slowly.

"We can probably track those and get an idea of who's sending them. Legwork, but I don't mind calling around." I'd do the most menial tasks if it would keep Tommy safe without me having to go toe-to-toe with Sibley like I did in that vision.

Mendez looked at me in surprise. "Aren't you going to read the letters?"

I looked at her, confused. I was new here and clearly wasn't doing what they expected, though what they expected wasn't clear. It didn't hurt anything to read the things out loud. "You aren't listening. Do the thing or I will destroy—"

"No," Jarrod said. "That's not what she meant."

Mendez frowned at me. "Read them. Like, read them."

"Ruth could get a vibe off an object and tell us more about who it belonged to," Jarrod said. "I take it that's not part of your skill set."

I blinked at him. "No . . . not really. Um, I can try to do something like that, but even when that works, it's not usually paper for me. Especially if it's been handled a lot by other people, there's usually nothing left in Mindspace. But—" I forestalled an objection. "Really I will try."

The note in my hand felt like nothing, a completely neutral object with no emotion to it at all. I picked up another sheet, the YOU KNOW WHAT YOU HAVE TO DO missive, in the hopes that this one would be better. The letters looked darker, more crooked, and it looked angry and disturbing and urgently wrong. But in my hand, in Mindspace, in any way I could think to look at it, even this one was just paper. I didn't have a clairvoyant gift, even though perhaps Ruth had had a slight one. I couldn't see anything. The man—or woman, I supposed—who'd created this had probably spent less than an hour with it, and while I could imagine a disgust and threat coming from them, that was all it was, an imagination.

I shook my head and put the paper down. "I assume

Ruth had a clairvoyant gift, but it's not something I have. It's just an object to me." The only times I got anything from an object was if it was with its owner for years upon years of constant use, and even then I didn't get a lot of information. I didn't understand clairvoyants, not at all. Their gifts didn't seem to obey the laws of Mindspace physics, at least not easily.

"You're getting nothing?" Jarrod asked.

"No. If it was there at one point, it's worn off by now." I made a frustrated sound. "Look, you bring me to a crime scene, a place where somebody had an altercation or a death in the last few days, I'm your guy. I'll get you several layers of information on what happened. But I need a place. The place. Most telepaths do, to be honest."

"Oh." Mendez's mind leaked dull frustration, mixed with embarrassment turned to anger.

Now I was embarrassed too and worried I wasn't doing what I needed to do.

Jarrod shifted, his spine going a little straighter. "It's good to know limitations. It's getting late. Why don't you make sure Tommy is settled and feeling okay?"

"I can be a help to you," I said, wanting to believe it, needing to believe it. "I'm good at my job with the police, which is a hell of a lot of investigation and no bodyguarding at all." I'd proven myself there. Cherabino—and Michael, and Branen, though he protested otherwise—had seen me in action. They'd seen me be successful. I worried that these guys wouldn't. And even the last people to see me successful hadn't given me a full-time job.

I wished Cherabino was here. She'd know what to do.

"I'll keep that in mind," Jarrod said, but his voice was flat and I couldn't tell whether I'd pissed him off or not.

So I did the thing they expected me to do. "I'll check on Tommy now," I said.

"You do that."

Mendez poked at the letters, a mix of emotions in her. Death threats had a weight to them in her mind, I thought as I left. I wondered what that was about.

And I wondered, all over again, if Cherabino was okay. She had to keep her job. Witnesses and politics and everything else, she just had to keep her job. It was who she was.

CHAPTER 9

Tommy came up to me a while later. I was seated in a low oddly shaped chair near the back of the house, close enough to the hallway to get to Tommy if needed, having pulled a reading lamp down to a pad of paper to work on my report after I'd called Cherabino's house and she hadn't picked up. I felt him approaching, but as his mind didn't seem agitated, I kept working. Working kept me from worrying.

He stood there in front of me for a while.

I kept working.

He continued to stare.

I finally put the paper and pencil down on the ground. "Something I can do for you, Tommy?"

"You're a telepath." His face was scrunched up.

"Yes."

"And you say I'm going to be a telepath."

"Um, yes." I wasn't sure where this was going.

"You said you could teach me." He stood straight, waiting, like obviously I was going to teach him right now on one prompt.

I stood up. Actually I might. I liked the calm pushy Tommy, and I'd been a teacher—for older kids—for a number of years. I wasn't familiar with teaching anyone his age the basics, but considering the situation, having him with more skills would only help us. And it might get my mind off things, which I needed very much right now. I kept seeing the vision, and my death, and Cherabino's job, on the line, none of which were probably like I worried they were. No, taking some time to teach Tommy, to do something I was good at, would only help me. And him, hopefully.

"What do you want to learn?"

He frowned deeper, then gave it up. "I don't know. What is there to learn? I've never been a telepath before."

I laughed.

"What?"

"Just the way you said that was funny to me. I'd be happy to teach you. We should probably start at the beginning." I tried to remember what the beginning was. It had been a very long time since I'd either learned or taught that beginning.

He stood there expectantly.

"Why don't we move to the kitchen where there're stools enough for both of us?" I asked to buy time.

He turned around and went in that direction. No lack of action in this kid; it was corralling the action into something useful that was going to take all the effort.

I turned around and switched off the reading light. Then I found Jarrod's gaze to make sure he'd paid attention. He'd been sitting well across the open room, working on his own set of paperwork, and his head was up now, and he nodded. He didn't seem pissed at me, which was good, but I knew I hadn't helped all that much with the investigation, not yet.

I followed Tommy into the kitchen. Of the whole ridiculously designed house, I liked this kitchen the best. They'd put in simple cabinets and kept the original trim on the top of the room, and a butcher-block counter. Small lights illuminated the area this late, small lights that felt soothing.

Tommy turned on the overhead light, and it got a lot brighter.

My ideas got a lot brighter too as I joined him on the stool next to him. He was waiting patiently as I managed to focus.

"Let's start with the basics. Imagine your mind is a house," I said. "Like this one. In fact, if you like this one, you can picture this one."

"I liked our last house better," he said.

"Great, picture that one," I said, feeling my way through the analogy. "Or your dream house. There are a couple of stories, lots of rooms, and doors between some of the rooms. You get to walk anywhere in your house you like, and you get to invite people to visit you, but you also get to close off some of the rooms and not let people into them. There's a main floor, where you have your kitchen and your living area, and it's a good space for people to walk about. You have stairs up to the top floor, where you keep the stuff that's personal, that's just for you."

"That sounds . . ." Tommy trailed off.

I felt his spot of loneliness. Sometimes his mom left him in his room, "space just for him," and left him alone for hours.

I felt for him. I really did. I felt my own loneliness too, and my guilt at not being there for Cherabino when her world was falling apart. I took a breath and continued on with the lesson, because if I stopped, I probably wouldn't pick it up again, as much as we had going on. And it wasn't a bad time for lessons, and it wasn't a bad time to earn Tommy's trust. "The house is everything you need it to be, when you need it to be that," I said. "That's the great part about this mind-house. Let's say upstairs is for you, is yours. You can have as many ideas and things in your head to keep you company as you like. Sometimes you might even invite somebody very special to some of those rooms. But they're yours and you get to decide what happens to them. You might have a dog up there to bark and play with toys if you want, for example. But you don't invite people in, not upstairs."

He thought about that. He'd always wanted a dog.

I thought about mentioning the basement of the house, something you generally did with someone older. The basement was where you kept the horrors, the secrets, the things you didn't want with you but couldn't let go. But Tommy was likely too young.

Of course he'd heard part of that, and was thinking his mom had a basement. A big basement.

Hmm. I couldn't go rummaging for more information right now—it wasn't ethical, especially in a teaching situation—but I'd ask him about it later.

"Let's start with something simple," I said. "Most people when they're your age or they're just starting out, their house is leaky." I held up a hand at his protest and offered a strong mental image. "The walls have big holes in them, so the air comes and goes and all the weather comes into the house whether it's good weather or bad."

"That doesn't sound very fun," he said. Maybe his mind was a bit like that, he thought. Especially at school, or around his mom. Things came in and he couldn't stop them.

"On a good day, when the sun is shining and people are happy, it can be very fun," I said. "But a large part of what the Guild does in its entry classes is teach people how to seal up the walls, put siding in and a little armor, and put in big doors and windows that are strong enough to let the world in when you want and shut it out when you want. It can be a lot of work. But it puts you more in charge of your own space, your own head, your own mind. And it lets you understand the world better if all you're hearing isn't noise."

He thought about that. I let him. It was a big idea, a big model on which to view the world.

"Other people have houses too?" he asked.

I nodded, trying to decide how much to ask.

"Sometimes they don't lock their doors."

I nodded again. "And you see in without meaning to."

"Yeah."

I waited for him to ask whatever question was wandering around in his head.

"My mom thinks about stuff a lot," he said quietly, but in the tone of voice like something was wrong.

"Does she?" I asked quietly. His mind was turned inward, closed, so unless I wanted to go rummaging around—not ethical in a kid that age even as a Minder—I had no way of knowing what he was thinking. Had I been so worried about myself and my problems that I'd missed something major? A stab of guilt hit me then.

"Yeah," he said. "She has a lot of—of things I'm not supposed to talk about."

"Like what?" I asked as casually as I possibly could.

He looked up and focused then. "I'm not supposed to talk about them."

"Is she hurting you?" I ventured. I wasn't one to push, but if there was abuse or danger going on and I'd missed it . . .

I got a flash of hurt then, from him. "No." She didn't hit him or anything, not like Michelle at school, whose parents hit her. "She says work stuff . . . she says I'm not supposed to know about that stuff and she could get in trouble if people knew that I knew."

"Knew what?" I asked.

"Dead bodies and stuff," he said, in the matter-of-fact voice nobody but a ten-year-old could pull off. "And stuff for her cases, and stuff about bad guys and cops and . . .

stuff." He waved his hand. "She is under a lot of pressure. I'm not supposed to worry people." This last was said in the tone of voice of someone repeating something another had said a million times.

"I see." I waited patiently for him to talk more. Often people would tell you anything you wanted to know, just to fill the silence. Or adults would anyway. I'd never seen evidence kids were all that different.

He sat there for a long moment and said nothing. Then: "Are you going to teach me the house thing or not?"

"Sure," I said, and clamped down on my concern so he'd feel that I was normal again. I was worried about him, though. There was something not right here, something . . . off. And I hadn't spent enough time with him to figure out what it was.

I took a breath. He'd have to come to trust me on his own, I guessed. I hoped. In the meantime, a lesson cost me nothing, and it made me more present in his life.

"Let's start with building you a sliding door," I said. "Something really basic that gives you control over who comes in your house."

He nodded.

"With your permission, I'd like to walk into your mind— just the beginning, just the little foyer area. It's easier to show you what to do than to try to describe it in words," I said.

"You knock first," he said.

I shrugged, and pictured a doorframe on the outside of his mind, and me standing there with a fist upraised. I knocked, gently, the sound pictured strongly enough he'd be able to experience it clearly.

Come in, he said in a happy tone. He'd gotten what he wanted the first time just by asking. He was vaguely smug about it.

I stepped in, just in, as I'd promised. His mind was a

tangle of thoughts laid about the edges of an open clear space, boxes and bales of thoughts in no apparent order, but all tied up with twine. I'd never seen so many disorganized piles in my life. Still, I was here to show him something specific.

And earn his trust.

Now, I started, *the most important thing about telepathy is picturing something very clearly, so clearly you believe it. Let's start with a floor for your house.*

Okay . . . , he said.

In the next twenty minutes, we built mental models over and over, letting him find the pictures that would communicate best to him. And below the surface, I monitored the structure of the changes he was actually making, and I corrected, gently, when something was wrong.

At the twenty-first minute, I put a stop to it. He was sweating in the real world, and starting to tire in the mental one. I helped him surface back to reality.

"Time for bed," I said. "It's going to be an early morning tomorrow."

"Aw, do we have to? I was just getting good at the house thing."

"They'll be plenty of time for more lessons later," I said, and ushered him toward his room.

As I moved back out into the house to check in for the night with everyone else, my body was tired but my mind was wide awake. I didn't know what secrets the judge held, but whatever they were, they bothered Tommy. And that made me worried, in a whole new way.

It was after ten p.m., very dark, with the outside streetlight pooling stripes of light on the ancient wooden floor of the back hallway. I sat on a thick cushion on the floor, staring at the phone. I'd grabbed one of the handsets from the main room—there were no fewer than three—when it had become obvious the rest of the household was going to bed. I was looking at the phone, oddly scared of it, oddly nervous about calling Cherabino after all this time of not knowing. She'd be okay, right? They had to see the truth and let her keep her job. It was the only possible reality that made sense, but I knew with a horrible certainty that politics wasn't about making sense. I didn't know what she'd do without her job. I just didn't know.

Tommy was asleep in the room behind me, the door shut to protect against noise. I was out in the hallway with a small pallet set up. Not ideal, but doable, at least for tonight.

At least I could do my job. I closed my eyes and scanned the area around the house, getting to know every mind, every current of Mindspace, within my range. Jarrod was asleep in a guest bedroom, the judge in the room next door. Loyola sat, cleaning a gun, in the front room, thinking tired thoughts and trying to plan. Two more minds, one outside curled up in a car seat, the other inside, sleeping underneath a basement window they'd considered one of their biggest security risks. Plenty of people around. Tommy would be fine, I told myself. But that vision still haunted me.

I widened my senses, as far as they would go, and looked carefully at the space around the house, as far as I could sense. The neighbors next door were fighting, quietly, over money. A hungry dog poked through an overturned trash bin across the street. A man stood, smoking, in the cold at the end of my range. Odd to smoke outside this time of night; I moved in carefully for a better look.

I pulled back after a moment. He was worried about losing his job, and unwilling to talk to his wife about it. There was no threat; he wouldn't be moving from that general area, and might hit up a donut shop in an hour or so.

After that, I moved back to check on Tommy, whose mind was dreaming disturbed dreams about trains and crashing thunder and a monster made out of shoes. He was deeply asleep, though; I nudged his mental pattern toward calm and called that good enough. It would either stick or it wouldn't, and I was unwilling to do more. We were connected too much as it was.

I opened my eyes in the hallway, which seemed even darker for the time away. The phone was there, staring at me. My body and my Ability were exhausted; I wasn't used to this, and I was short on sleep anyway. I sat there, looking at the phone but not calling, for a long time.

The vision stuck in the back of my head, the smell of the moldy straw, the scream of terror. I hadn't known Tommy long, but the more I talked to him, the worse that fear sounded, the worse my own fear of the vision became.

Swartz said the only way to deal with fear was to face it head-on. I picked up the phone. It rang.

I left a message on Stone's voice mail, telling him where I was and that they could expect another payment in the next few weeks from me. Gave a number.

Then I hung up and stared at the phone again, and couldn't quite bring myself to call her. I shook my head and pulled out the file on Sibley, the guy who'd almost killed me a few months ago. He was every bit as dangerous as I remembered, with a penchant for killing for hire with an odd serrated cord he had special-made. When, of course, the client didn't want the death to look natural.

He was a cold killer, a sharp killer, someone who enjoyed the control of the death. I'd felt his leavings in Mindspace on several crime scenes, and I'd met him in person. He'd strangled me, cutting off my air just to play with me, just to play with his prey. If things had been different, I would be dead now, by his hand, seeing that intensely controlled face as my last sight. Even now, when I thought about him coming after me, I felt a chill go down my spine. I was afraid of him, legitimately afraid of him, and getting involved with this case and putting myself in the line of danger was idiotic.

But on the other side of that wall was a kid, a perfectly normal prototelepathic kid, who didn't deserve to face him alone. Unfortunately I hadn't figured out yet how to stop that vision from happening, and odds were, I was running out of time. It was a knot in my gut that never let go, a tension that didn't leave me.

I got up and put on a coat, going out to the back stoop for a cigarette of my own, watching the drizzle of the day fall slowly to earth and the smoke billow in the cold air. It was strange not to be in Atlanta. It was strange to smell the faint salt of ocean in the air, and see gnats in clouds. It was strange to feel the ancient oaks, almost minds, settled into Mindspace. And most of all, it was strange to be without Cherabino. She would know what to do right now, I thought. She would have something for me to do, some lead to trace down, some possibility to keep this thing from happening. She'd tell me we could handle it, and we would. We always did.

But I wasn't there for her now. I wasn't there to help her handle whatever it was, and that ate at me. It hurt. And worse than that was the absence I felt, the missing piece she left in my life, not being beside me.

There were days I spent every waking moment with her, and slept near her at night. There were days we passed each other in the department with a nod, too busy running from one thing to another to even speak. But mostly, even before she'd agreed to date me, even before Swartz had told me to ask, it was her. She was part of the warp and weft of every day, or she had been. Even recently, when I'd been doing so much volunteer work with Narcotics Anonymous, she'd been there nearly every day. For her to be gone now— Well, I felt alone. Adrift.

I'd have to handle this one myself, and that terrified me.

I stubbed out the cigarette in a planter already full of butts and went back into the house. I could ask, at least.

I settled on the cushion and dialed. It rang three times, and I prayed she hadn't left her home phone off the hook completely. I couldn't take that. I wouldn't be able to hear her voice, and the silence would be the worst, the confirmation that whatever was going on was destroying her. Cherabino only took her phone off the hook when it had been a train wreck of a day, a bad day on the level of not just deaths, but bad deaths. Deaths of kids, or worse. She always seemed so strong—she had to—but the closer I'd gotten, the more I'd discovered it was an act. She cared deeply, and sometimes that caring hurt. Even so, she'd do anything for her job, for justice. It was one of the things I admired about her. The phone rang, again, and it hurt me I wasn't there.

She picked up. "Hello?" Her voice was irritated. It was like heaven.

"It's me," I said.

"I was starting to think you'd fallen down a well. Do they not have phones down there? I almost went to bed already twice."

I blinked. A year ago that tone would have put me off, or made me go on the offensive. But not now. I understood her too well, and I was too relieved to hear from her. "This is the first time I've been able to get away," I lied. Simpler than listing the times I'd tried to call her. Then, cautiously: "I'm sorry I left without saying good-bye."

She made a *hmrph* noise. "Work comes first. It always does. You left a message. How's the FBI treating you? Can you talk about the case?"

"You're not mad at me?"

"Why would I be mad at you?" she asked, in a reasonable tone of voice.

I paused. This was not at all how I'd expected her reaction to go. "Um, I have no idea."

"Well, then."

A silence came over the line, and my worry came back.

After a moment, I offered, "The FBI seems a lot like the police department, without all the red tape. Or, at least, if there's red tape I'm not the one dealing with it. At the moment I'm watching someone."

"Watching?" she asked, with a frown to her voice.

"Minding." I paused. That wouldn't help. I tried to figure out how to explain it. She got grumpy sometimes until she understood something. "Remember when we had that threat against you in the Bradley case? How I followed you around so nobody could attack you telepathically?"

"Of course I remember you following me around. I still don't know what Minding is, though."

"Um. Well . . ."

"Does it work with the fishbowl analogy?" she asked, into the pause.

"Sort of. More of a spider at the center of the web, maybe. I sit at the center of the web, and if I feel a vibration on the edges, I go out to see what it was. If it's a threat, I either shut it down myself or call for reinforcements. That's what I did, guarding you then."

"Oh." Another pause. I could hear her breathing, lightly, something surprisingly comforting in the dark hallway. Just having her here, even over the phone, meant the world.

I tried to figure out how to ask for help, which Swartz said I needed to do more of. How did I put what I needed into words?

But before I could, she said, "I'm glad you called. It's been a hard day. A terrible day."

"What happened?" I asked. It was something to say to keep the conversation going. And I'd been so worried about her. "Are you okay?"

"Well." She sighed. I could almost see her shaking her head. "It . . . they're escalating my inquiry. It starts tomorrow. I said I almost went to bed . . . the truth is, I can't sleep."

"That's fast."

"I know."

"You didn't do anything. You don't have anything to worry about. Plus, your lawyer said she had a plan." I said it quickly, forcefully, like I believed it. I had to believe it. But I couldn't see her, I couldn't read her, I couldn't tell how she was, not really.

"That's what she says. But they're lumping together the incident from early in the week in with the visit to Fiske's house. They're calling it a pattern. They're calling in the captain and Internal Affairs and now they're bringing in the county commissioner. Branen was right. This whole thing happening on the anniversary . . . well, it's bad. They're leaping to conclusions. It's in the paper."

Crap, that was bad. "Are you okay?" I asked.

"No," she said, a syllable that just sat between us. "No, they're saying I beat a guy to death. Of course I'm not okay. And for me to end up as the poster child for police brutality . . . well, it's ludicrous. The lawyer agrees with me, and she thinks the truth will come out. It'll be bad, but the truth will come out."

"It has to," I said. "You need me to testify, you say the word."

"You can't leave Savannah."

"Yeah," I said. It was a sad sound, a sound of regret.

"I'd really like you to be here," she said quietly.

I closed my eyes, guilt hitting me. "I can't. I . . . want to be there, I promise you." But the vision and Tommy and all the rest . . . I couldn't live with myself if I left and then he died.

"I understand work," she said, but her voice was hurt.

"Whatever you need, you tell me," I said. "I'll find a way to do it from here."

"I need Branen not to believe I did this thing. I need this stupid hearing not to be happening."

She might as well have asked for me to grab the moon out of the sky and hand it to her. In some ways, that would be easier. I literally had no influence on any of that.

So, not knowing what to say, I said nothing. And neither did she. The silence lasted what felt like forever.

"I'm sorry." Apologizing hurt, but for her, I'd walk over glass. "I really am."

She sighed again. "Me too. Me too, okay? But I'll figure it out. The lawyer doesn't want you at the hearing anyway."

"What's her plan?" I asked.

After a long pause, she said slowly, "She's pushing for an extension, and turning their character voucher requirement on its head. She's got twelve people willing to testify that I make good decisions in the field." Her voice was stronger now. "Not just Michael. Some of the other detectives, the beat guys. My training officer's even coming out from retirement to be there. And she's going to be ripping through their nonevidence and their witnesses like crazy."

"So the department's taking it personally. That's good for you," I said, though what the hell did I know? "You've got the highest close rate in the department, and everybody knows you're doing three jobs for the salary. You prove that, with the budget crunch, they can't afford to lose you."

"Maybe. We've still got the issue with Fiske. And the rookie."

"No maybe about it. You're a good cop, Isabella. You know that, I know that, and the department knows that. Plus, you're cost-effective, and you get the job done. With Michael helping out, if anything your close rate has gone up. I'd bring up all of that too. Enough stories, the money going the right way, you become the poster child for a well-run police department. They have to understand that. They will." I added the last firmly, trying to get myself to believe it.

After a pause: "I hate politics, Adam."

"I know."

"They're . . . this brutality thing, if it sticks . . ."

"You didn't do anything wrong," I protested, into the silence in the dark hallway. "Nothing wrong!"

"If it sticks, I'll never live it down."

And there was my worst fear made reality. She was scared. Given enough time, in person, she'd probably tell me that directly—I was a telepath, after all, and could reasonably be expected to know already. A lifetime in the cop world meant it wouldn't be easy for her to admit, though, not even to herself. I felt like I had to say something, anything, to make it better.

"You know how Swartz has another wise thing to say in pretty much every situation?" I asked her, desperate.

"He has a saying for when you're called up in front of Internal Affairs?" Clear disbelief was in her tone.

"Well, no. But remember the last time I lost my job with the department?"

"You mean two months ago?"

"Not November, before that. Three years ago."

"Oh. Yeah. You're lucky Paulsen likes you or I never would have gotten you rehired after you fell off the wagon

again. Even if you did get through rehab with a recommendation."

Ouch. "I got through rehab with a recommendation
from the center director to the captain. Personally."

"I still had to beg," she said.

She was in a royal mood today, clearly. But with what
was happening to her, maybe that was okay. "The point is
that I didn't know what was going to happen, and it all
seemed like it was going to fall apart. Swartz sat me down
and waited with me. Do you know what he said?"

I waited.

Finally: "No. What did he say?"

"He said courage is not the absence of fear, but doing it
past the fear. And that faith was stepping out when things
were uncertain. 'Builds character,' he said. 'Do it anyway.'
And I did."

After a moment: "Easy to say when you know the ending."

"Yeah," I said, and realized I'd just given myself part of
the answer I needed, completely by accident. Maybe. I still
felt uncertain, and afraid, and was facing things I didn't
really know how to face. Sibley scared me, and the thought
of him threatening Tommy too . . .

"I'm nervous," she said, meaning she was scared. I
hated hearing her scared, and I hated not knowing what
would happen, or how she'd react to the worst, if it came out.

"You know I'd do anything if I could take the blame for
this one, right?"

"They've already cut you back to part-time and docked
your pay twice after the rehire," she said. "But they can't
blame a teep for having a vision. They can't do anything
else to you."

She knew I hated the derogatory term for telepath, and
her using it felt personal. I swallowed my protest. Instead I
repeated, "You didn't do anything wrong, and they'll figure

that out. I have faith." And I'd find a way to have faith in my own situation. I had to. It wasn't like Cherabino could really tell me how to deal with a vision. It wasn't her specialty any more than canvassing a neighborhood was mine.

"That makes one of us," she said.

"You're not alone," I said, one of the first things they teach you to say in the Twelve Steps program. But I felt alone, and I'm sure she did too.

"Thanks," she said.

"You're welcome." I thought about whether to tell her about Sibley, and then decided I had to. "There's a connection in this case to one of our old nemeses," I said.

"What?"

"Sibley. Remember him?"

"It's not like I could forget that guy. It's just weird. No one uses the word 'nemesis.' Isn't he still in jail?" she asked.

"Obviously not," I said.

She made a frustrated sound. "We worked our asses off to get him in jail. Hell, some good cops bled to get him there. I'll ask Michael to track it down. I'm not supposed to be working active cases right now, but—"

"You're getting Michael to keep working them anyway," I finished for her. "He probably needs the experience in working something on his own anyway."

I could almost see her blink, shifting gears all of a sudden. "Well, yes. And I'm not letting that son of a bitch walk around without me having something to say about it."

"I just . . ."

"What?"

I had to talk to someone. I had to. "You know the thing I didn't put in the report with Sibley?"

"Yeah. . . ." She seemed cautious.

I hadn't put Sibley's device in the report because I knew that kind of mind-control thing was not only illegal, but might start an active panic with the normals. I'd reported it to the Guild like I was supposed to, but there was no way of knowing how far they'd gotten. Sibley hadn't had it when he was taken into custody. I didn't know where the thing was.

"Well, if it happens again—and I don't know whether it will—I'm not sure whether I can do my job here. He almost killed me last time, Cherabino."

"Oh." She seemed tired all of a sudden; I couldn't tell if that was whatever Link between our minds finally letting her emotions echo, or whether I was dreaming that emotion up, or projecting it from my own experience. "Yeah. I'm sorry. Do you have a knife or something?" It was illegal for me to carry a gun and we both knew it.

"No," I said, "there wasn't time when I left Atlanta."

"Well, see if they'll get you one, okay? Having a holdout weapon has saved my life more than once."

I'd been there for one of those times. "I'll ask," I said, even though it would hurt to admit I needed a weapon. My mind was normally all the weapon I needed, but I'd do whatever it took to protect Tommy and get us both out of this. I'd rather have her here, though. I'd rather she be here to carry the weapons. I missed her.

She yawned, loudly.

I wanted so much then to lean on her, to talk about the case. I wanted to lean on her, to involve her, just to be with her. But she was under one of the worst stresses in the world right now, and I couldn't add to that. No matter how much it hurt.

I did the noble thing then. "I've got an early morning," I said. "I need to go."

"Okay," she said, and yawned again.

I hung up, but it took every ounce of strength I had, and it left me alone. I wanted the drug then. I wanted it, but I couldn't have it. And that hurt too.

The next morning I was woken by a ringing phone. I lifted my head from the cushion, and my whole body creaked.

"Wha?" I said.

Tommy stood over me. "The phone's ringing," he said.

I mumbled something. I felt like I'd hardly slept at all.

"Aren't you going to get it?" he asked.

"Get what?"

"The phone." He sighed and went over to pick it up himself, but it stopped ringing on its own before he touched it. He frowned at it.

I sat up, bones hurting against the hardwood floor, and ran my hands through my hair. A pile of files were fanned out in a messy pile next to the phone. My late-night reading.

"Well, go get him!" a bellow came from down the hallway.

Mendez, the female FBI agent who'd gone with Tanya to the hospital, trotted down the hallway. "What are you doing with a phone in the hallway?" she asked me, then: "You know what? Never mind, go ahead and pick up. Jarrod's irritated. Who's calling you anyway?"

"Let's find out," I said, and sat up. I picked up the phone, conscious of her standing there and staring at me. Tommy was doing the same from another angle. Observation in stereo, with me having just woken up, my hair doubtlessly cowlicked to perfection. I reminded myself I'd had perfect strangers watch me do far more personal things than talk on the phone.

"Hello?" a man's voice said on the other side of the line.

I introduced myself. "Who is this?"

"It's Stone," he said. "You left a message."

"Yeah, just letting you know I'm out of town and unavailable for work," I said, choosing my words carefully with the audience. "It's unavoidable."

"You're out of town. Where?"

I looked at my audience. The city was large enough to make it difficult to find me, and it wasn't a secret. I hazarded the truth. "Savannah."

Mendez shook her head.

I shrugged.

"I can find some work for you to do there," Stone said. "There's a school—"

I cut him off. "I'm consulting, and will be for the whole week. You asked me to call you when I'll be out of touch and I did."

"There's no need to be rude about it," he said.

I frowned into the phone. "I'm not being rude. I'm telling you what you asked me to tell you. I'll call you next week, okay?"

"You still owe the Guild a significant debt," he said.

Great. Probably the stupid call was being recorded, and certainly I was being watched by Mendez and Tommy. Oh, what the hell? "I'm making payments. You know where to find me. What's the issue?"

"Debt collector?" Mendez asked, an eyebrow up.

I rolled my eyes and nodded. "I'm making payments," I said. "Honestly, you're out of line."

I felt Stone poke at the tag he'd left in my head.

I forced myself to tolerate it. I didn't like having someone in my head I hadn't invited, and between him and the boy and the half-faded Link with Cherabino, my head was getting to be a well-traveled place. "You done?" I finally asked.

"You're not under duress," he said quietly.

I was surprised. "No. No, not at all."

A general sense of acceptance. "If you run into trouble, you can call me," he said. And then he hung up.

Wait. I could call him? And why would he say so? I was very confused.

"What was that about?" Tommy asked.

"Ask Mendez," I said. "I need a shower." I creaked up onto my feet, clothes mussed, and grabbed my bag next to the pallet.

Then I stopped. I could feel his hurt. I sighed and went back to him. "I'm sorry. I'm groggy in the mornings. I don't feel good. But I shouldn't have snapped at you." I looked over at Mendez. Oh, what the hell. He was a kid, and the rest of his world was falling apart. The least I could do was tell him the truth. I turned only to Tommy, ignoring her. "I made a deal with the medical part of the Guild to save my friend's life when he couldn't afford it," I told him. "It's a source of ongoing stress, because they want to be paid faster than I can pay them. But my friend is okay now, and I'm making payments."

"You saved your friend's life?" the kid asked in a small, awed voice.

I sat on my irritation. "I asked for help," I said. "Sometimes you have to do that. Now, can I take a shower in the bathroom at the end of the hall?"

"Sure," Tommy said, still in a little of that awed tone.

As I passed Mendez, she was thinking maybe I wasn't so bad after all. That and intimate details about her latest girlfriend that I would rather not have known.

CHAPTER 10

When I got out of the shower, freshly shaved and dressed in clean clothes, I felt better. I'd kept tabs on Tommy's mind from a distance, ready to dash out and handle something if necessary, but the spiderweb I'd set up hadn't vibrated with any new minds, and everyone seemed calm. Not that I was good at this, mind you, but my old skills were tolerable. I thought.

I stuck my head in Tommy's room, only to find him playing with the antigravity boats again.

"Where's my mom?" he asked.

"I'll find out," I said. "You okay?"

"Yeah."

"Good." I waited, but he went back to his boats and said nothing else. But I couldn't exactly strap him to a chair because I didn't feel comfortable right now, and getting a little distance—briefly—might help me settle without scaring him. I went back out to the main room, deciding to check in with Jarrod on the way.

Jarrod was waiting for me. He looked grim.

"I was just about to do that report," I said. "Really. Tommy is fine, and there are no apparent threats."

"It's not that. Tanya died this morning in the hospital," he said. "Seat belt syndrome, they said. Jason is pulling through and was just moved out of intensive care."

"Oh," I said. My stomach dropped into my guts. "Oh." I looked around for a chair to sit in, finally settling for a footstool in front of a table. At least I thought it was a footstool; it was oblong in shape with a flat top. It seemed like a stupid thing to focus on right now.

I'd just met Tanya the day before, but I could have sworn . . . "I didn't notice the shock in time, did I?" Guilt crawled all over me. She shouldn't have died. Not for something like that. Not after saving Tommy.

Jarrod looked grim. "None of us did. She was sitting right here, in the room with me, while I was doing technical checks. None of us are happy about this, Ward." He took a breath. "I will want a full report from you—it's overdue—but some new information has changed our threat assessments. I need your help."

I looked up. "What do you need?"

"You were the last person to talk to Tanya, and to be honest the only one of my team to get her full account of what happened. Jason is still unconscious. You are the closest thing we have to an adult eyewitness. Ideally . . . if you're serious about your investigation on the scene, I want you to walk the area with me." He paused, and I could feel calculations going on behind his eyes. A lot of them. Finally he said, "We're due in court shortly. Make sure you're ready."

"Court?" I asked.

"The courthouse anyway. I want to keep an eye on the judge, and the locals aren't taking things as seriously as I would like," Jarrod said. "I have a strong feeling that if this is all connected to the murder trial as we assume, the best and first place to find out where the threats are coming from is that courthouse."

"I can't leave Tommy," I said. "Not more than a hundred feet. Two hundred, maybe, in an emergency, but I wouldn't

recommend it." I ran my hands through my hair, uncomfortable. It was still wet from the shower. "I don't like separating the two of us from the main group." I was still new
enough at this Minding thing not to be sure I could handle
things completely on my own. I hadn't been completely on
my own in years. At minimum, there had always been
Cherabino and her gun available. I hoped she was okay
today, the first day of her hearing. I wished I could be there.

"We'll bring Tommy along," Jarrod said. "And if I can
get away, we'll bring him to the crime scene anyway. With
any luck, he'll be able to tell us more than Tanya did."

I paused. "Don't you think this all is putting a lot of
pressure on him? He's just a kid. I mean, he should be at
school, right?"

Jarrod shook his head. "Not with the permissions the
judge has already for independent study. Like you said, we
can't split up the group. He's going to have to be brave.
You're going to have to figure out how to make him brave."

I swallowed. That seemed like such a huge responsibility on top of the other half dozen things Jarrod wanted
from me. I suddenly understood why this job was paying so
much.

"Anything else?" Jarrod asked me. "We need to leave in
twenty, so make it quick."

"Tommy wants to know where his mom is."

"The sheriff's team has already escorted her to the
courthouse. She wanted to be there extremely early, and
they failed to inform me. We'll be discussing that later. In
either case, they're more responsible for her safety than
we are."

I thought about that and then finally ventured, "We're
going to have to tell Tommy about the bodyguard."

"I'd rather not."

"We've established that he can get to information from

me without me necessarily controlling it," I said. "If I know, he needs to know. I don't imagine anybody—much less a kid—is going to take that information well as a secret."

Jarrod took a deep breath, then let it out. "I'll do it, but I'll do it in the car, en route, where we can control things better. Now get yourself and Tommy ready. Like I said, we leave in twenty."

The phone rang next to me in the hallway, and without thinking about it, I leaned down to pick up the receiver.

"Hello?" I said while all three FBI agents around me froze, one gesturing wildly.

"Who is this?" a man's voice said on the other side of the line.

Special Agent Jarrod mouthed something at me. I didn't understand, but I pulled the information from his mind— *this could be a call from the person behind the attack today, and it could be dangerous to say FBI. Also dangerous to hang up too quickly.*

"I'm Adam Ward," I said before the silence got too long, lacking any better answer.

"Adam Ward?" a man's voice said, a voice that sounded all too familiar.

"That's right. Who is this?"

"You have to be a few hundred miles from where you're supposed to be." He laughed, but the sound was ugly. "What a coincidence. Well, you were next on my list in any case."

"What do you mean?" I asked slowly, looking at Jarrod.

"You'll find out soon enough," the man said, still in that familiar voice that made me feel like a mouse in a trap. "Now put the judge on the phone."

It was Sibley, the man who'd nearly killed me. The man who was threatening Tommy in the vision. He was out of jail, obviously, and focused on the judge, exactly like I'd feared. Adrenaline dumped into my system.

"Put the phone down," Special Agent Jarrod hissed.

"I can't do that," I said to them both. My heart beat too quickly.

"Fine," Sibley said. "But be aware, if you're tangled up in this I will treat you accordingly. Tell the judge if she doesn't do what my boss has told her to do, and soon, we will follow through on his threat."

"What threat was that?" I asked quickly. Around me the agents were scrambling, turning on the electronics, but I knew it would be too late. My stomach was sinking. None of this would be recorded, would it?

"It's simple. He'll destroy the thing she loves the most if she doesn't do what was agreed."

Crap. That sounded ominous. But I had to keep pushing, had to keep getting more information. "That attack on her son today, that was you, wasn't it?"

"What an idiotic question. You'll have to get smarter if you want to survive this game with my boss. And by the way, he's not forgotten your trip to his home. Don't think you'll be able to forget it either."

Across the room, the red light on the electronics setup finally went on.

Jarrod held out his hand for the receiver, and I handed it over. But I could hear the dial tone even as I did so.

I sat down, the pit in my stomach vacant, painfully vacant.

Mendez looked up from the electronics panel with a burst of frustration I could feel. "No," she said to Jarrod. He hung up the phone.

"What just happened?" he asked both of us in an intense tone. Loyola sat down in a chair with a frown.

"Sibley just called," I told the floor. "He just called, and it looks like my vision will come true."

"Nonsense," Jarrod said. "You said yourself we can head this off. We'll do just that. Stay close, take steps, and we'll do the same."

Loyola shifted. "At least we know the major threat now."

"But we can't prove it," Mendez said quietly. "We still have to make the connections."

Jarrod straightened his posture and looked directly at me. "I expect a detailed report. Go find yourself some paper and pencil and write down the conversation word for word. I expect it done in the next ten minutes."

"Um, okay," I said. The adrenaline was still coursing through my system, my hands shaking, my body wanting to run. I wanted my drug, or at least a cigarette. I wanted to lock myself into a small closet and call Cherabino.

But I didn't get to do that today. Today I had to make sure Tommy was safe, and that the vision didn't happen. Right now that seemed an incredibly tall order.

"And you," Jarrod said to Loyola. "Make sure Tommy is ready to leave on time. Mendez and I will be figuring out why we didn't record this. Ward?" he prompted when I didn't respond.

"Yes, sir," I said, and stood. "I'll get you the information." But inside, I was shaking.

Tommy finally came outside to the car, bringing four different bags. I accepted the rebellion, carried the stupid bags, and loaded the car. My Ability to defend myself wasn't dependent on me having hands free, and that wasn't true of anyone else here. Since I was still jumping at the smallest sounds, the smallest changes in Mindspace, it was probably good to give me something to do. Too much adrenaline was as bad for focus as too little.

When I noticed Tommy looking at me funny, I sat down hard on the roiling emotions. I had to be in control. I had to. Otherwise it would scare him, and I'd done that one too many times already for comfort. *Control, Adam. Control. You're a highly trained telepath—you can do this.*

We piled into an armored limousine, the only car Loyola could find on short notice, and went. Jarrod sat in the back with Tommy, me next to him. The boy had his arms crossed, and he was looking at me like he knew I was holding something back.

Finally, halfway there, Jarrod told him about Tanya's death. But he told him like you'd tell a cop—all matter-of-fact and *I'm sorry*—and it didn't go over well at all.

Overwhelming anger and grief poured out of that child like water from a faucet, flooding the Mindspace all around. I braced myself against it. Holy crap, that kid could be strong as a telepath in a few years. But he just sat there, controlled. His eyes watered, and he stared, shocked, but nothing happened for a long moment.

Then he broke down, and yelled, and screamed, and Mendez almost drove off the road it was so sudden.

"You said she would be okay!" he yelled at me. "You said! You said!"

"I know," I said, it killing me. "I know. I'm sorry." I said it over and over again.

But it was like the relief of pressure from a valve; I rode it out, knowing that he needed this moment. Hell, I needed this moment. Jarrod seemed discomfited.

Then the emotion got weaker, and weaker, until a general low sense of despair passed between us.

Tommy turned around and buried his head in my armpit, and I held him, awkwardly. His small back shook as he reached out mentally—and asked if it was all true. I confirmed that to him, mind to mind, with regret, and patted his back. He cried, and he cried. I might have joined him, a little, in the backlash of all that emotion. Coming down from all that adrenaline was hard enough on its own, and I got it. I really did.

Death was horrible. And it didn't get better with time; it got worse, especially as you got older. Death made you feel small, and helpless, and aching with the unfairness of it all. I hadn't known Tanya well, so her death was an abstract still, though it would hit me later. But there were other deaths. Dane had died, my best friend at the Guild. My mother had died, in a slow, horrible slide through illness to death, until at last the death was a relief and her absence a piece forever missing. Last year, Bellury had died because I'd been an idiot to go in without backup. Death was horrible, and if Tommy was crashing into it, I crashed too.

I held him, and I was there, but that was all I could do. I felt helpless. I had nothing to offer him, except the kinds of things Swartz said about heaven and justice in the next life, things I wanted to believe, and on my best days, kinda did. I had nothing to offer him, except that I was there. He and I, ten and forty, both caught in the grief and railing against the unfairness of it all. I got it. I got it all too well.

Jarrod, like a cop, had kept his eyes averted. After maybe ten minutes he couldn't take the silence, and so he spoke. "None of us thought this would happen. Sometimes you just . . . sometimes things happen. I'm sorry."

Tommy sniffed and pulled away from me. "You didn't even care about her at all," he said to Jarrod. "I want my mom."

"It was her job," Jarrod said. "It was her job and she did a good job." He regretted all of this messiness.

Now I was on Tommy's side. A good woman had died today, had died because we were too stupid to get her to the hospital earlier. Had died because . . . because someone had attacked Tommy, and it wasn't fair, and it wasn't right.

And I was here to make sure this kid lived. It was a huge responsibility, a nearly impossible weight on my shoulders.

I wondered how I'd pull it off. I worried I wouldn't be able to.

"Be angry," Loyola said to Tommy from the front seat, after being silent the whole trip. "You be angry. You cry and be angry and do what you have to do. But you don't forget, she chose this. She chose to do her job and keep you safe over everything else. Remember she chose you. Remember her for doing that."

Something Swartz had said to me during his God moments kept echoed in my head, *"Greater love hath no man than this, that a man lay down his life for his friends."* Tanya had done what all bodyguards hope they never have to, literally had given up her life to protect her charge. Maybe that was the key. Maybe Loyola was right; we should remember her for this and nothing else. Maybe she'd earned the right.

But it was terrifying, because if things went badly these next few days, this next week, maybe that could be me too. I'd have to find a way to wrestle with that. I'd have to find a way to deal with it, or at least to push through like the cops did, and look into the face of death and assume I was immortal despite all evidence to the contrary. Despite seeing and hearing Sibley, the face of my almost-death. Because I couldn't give up, I couldn't leave. I had committed and I had to stop what would happen, or die trying. Maybe literally, as terrifying as that was.

Tommy sniffed, his anger turning to confusion, and he slouched in the seat. "I want to go home," he said. He wanted to be alone, and play with the toys that were his and not be caught up in all of this.

"I know," I said. I also wanted this to be over. But, unlike him, I had the perspective to know it wouldn't be over for a good long time. I was worried, all over again, about us, about me, about him. About Cherabino.

"We're about to arrive at the courthouse," Jarrod said, and found a box of tissues from some unknown spot. "We'll need to walk in." He handed me the tissues.

The clear subtext was that we needed to pull it together. I closed off as much as I could, but I was furious, honestly. A bit of human decency wouldn't be uncalled for.

I scrubbed at my face, handing the tissues to Tommy to do it himself.

Mendez met my eyes in the rearview mirror while she was driving. I dipped into her head. She'd gotten permission for us to set up in the judge's chambers, and for her and Jarrod to end up in a file room, where they could set up and give the kid some space. She had information about the investigation from the home office that everyone would need to talk about, though, and if I wasn't at the meeting, she'd catch me up.

Thanks, I dropped in her head, cautiously. She nodded slowly and returned her attention to the road.

It bothered me, oddly, that the people in this unit were so accepting of telepaths.

It bothered me more that Jarrod was pushing all of this through so quickly—it was like he had threat information I didn't.

The courthouse was a squarish building made of concrete with thin blocks of windows cutting through in horizontal stripes that reminded me of the old black-and-white prison garb you saw in the movies. Two palm trees sat like crows overlooking the walkway in front of the building, and to the left of the two double doors in front burned a memorial torch. The front had a looping driveway thing, to give space, and a grass divider in front of the regular street. Other large buildings of several stories boxed in the court-house on several sides.

Mendez pulled the car around the building to a large parking deck, spiraling up narrow paths, up and up to the highest floor. The concrete was ancient, and the narrow paths up creaked as we drove over them. Mendez went on high alert, ready to turn on the anti-grav at any moment. But it held. We parked in a small space out of the way, maybe a hundred feet from the elevator.

We all moved out of the car as a unit, to protect Tommy. As we moved, though, I noticed his anger and disgust. Disgust in particular was a red flag; disgust was the emotion most often preceding actual violence, and while he was ten, under this kind of pressure cooker he might explode.

As we got to the elevator he pushed the button five times, emotions going crazy in him, and waited impatiently. When the elevator got there, he was the first in, fidgeting madly with the button panel as everyone got in.

As soon as the doors were open on the ground floor, he made a dash for it.

"Hold up," I yelled, huffing as I fast-walked in his direction. He was already on the crosswalk, moving toward the guard on the front door. My cigarette-poached lungs were never very happy with running, and running and talking at the same time just wasn't going to happen. *Hold up,* I said in his mind, much more insistently.

Loyola outpaced me, loping past to catch up with Tommy. He flashed his badge just in time to keep the security guard from going for his gun. "FBI," he said, in explanation, as he walked.

Tommy just kept going. The movement was freeing for him—he wanted out—but he hadn't taken any of his bags with him. At least he was moving toward the side entrance for the courthouse, but there was another armed guard there. Fortunately Loyola was a runner. I doubted the kid could outpace him.

In the meantime, I slowed, watching the world and minds around me for trouble, opening my eyes and all my senses as wide as they would go. The bodyguard dying made all of this real somehow. I was responsible to make sure nothing happened to Tommy. Would I be able to do it?

Mendez was behind me, with Jarrod, in that tone of mind I associate with a conversation about details. Loyola was very aware of his surroundings, and Tommy's running was helping him. No one else in the area seemed to be paying overt attention.

The armed guard to the courthouse wasn't taking Tommy as a threat, even at a fast pace, and he'd heard the edge of Loyola's loud declaration.

"I need to see ID," he said as Tommy slowed. I heard him through Tommy's mind, a weird kaleidoscope effect that I'd only had happen previously with Kara and Cherabino, legitimate Links between our minds. It was strange, and even stranger, I felt a . . . pull as he got farther away. I'd have to stay close; I had no idea what would happen if I did not. Nothing good, I was sure.

My formal shoes clattered against the concrete walkway as I got closer. People at the front of the building had stopped, all in the formal wear of people going for a day at court. One lone journalist carried a camera with a ridiculously large flashbulb, but his regard was more about curiosity than anything else.

"I'm Tommy Parson," the kid said, pulling out a school ID. "Judge Parson is my mom. I've been here before. This dweeb is following me for the FBI."

The guard took the ID, glanced at it, and handed it back. "Sorry. No one told me to expect you." He was a tall guy, and bored, and his wife had just left him; all information readily available to my senses on first meeting.

He handed the ID back and spent more time on Loyola,

who handed over an FBI badge. I caught up and waited behind Loyola, scanning the surroundings. There were plenty of minds in the hallway just inside, but none were paying attention in this direction. I was already beginning to get a headache behind my eyes from all of the emotion earlier; combined with the relentless information from all the minds around me—and the need to pay attention—the headache was only going to get worse.

"Who are you?" the guard said, in the tone of voice of someone repeating himself and very irritated about it.

"He's with us," Loyola said in a firm tone of voice before I could say anything. "Also, my colleagues behind us—the woman, and the thin guy in the suit. Now, are you going to let us in or not?"

The guard stared at me and tried to figure out how far he could push this. He didn't like me, and I suspected it was because he had just enough Ability to detect another telepath, without any additional information. He knew I was a big fish and wanted to watch me.

This was both gratifying and frustrating, of course.

"Now, please," Loyola said.

Tommy read the guard's decision before he acted, and the kid was already pushing through the door. Fortunately I'd read the same decision and was moving myself.

He was going to be a handful, wasn't he?

In the crowded hallway beyond, Tommy stopped in front of a fortysomething man with a small scar on his right eyebrow and a pair of wire-framed glasses, currently standing in the security screening line. Next to the man, another guy, clearly a lawyer, stood.

"Did you send the bad guys to kill me yesterday?" Tommy asked. "Tell me to my face."

"You can't . . . ," the lawyer said, then trailed off.

"Who are you?" the man asked—but he asked me.

"This is Tommy Parson and entourage," I said, coming up behind him, still puffing.

Something about the man read like a shark to me, a predator, someone used to being the top thing in the eco-system, able to do whatever the hell he wanted, whenever the hell he wanted it. I moved up behind Tommy, just in case, ready to move if anything were to happen.

"You shouldn't be talking to Pappadakis," Loyola said, now right there as well. "Come on, let's wait for them to move through." The entire hallway had quieted, and every-one was now looking at us. Jarrod was still talking to the guard outside, and Mendez was torn between. We were on our own.

"This is Pappadakis?" I asked quietly.

"Did you?" Tommy demanded, angry and grief-stricken.

The lawyer glanced at the screening guards, just to make sure they were paying attention. "My client will not answer any of your questions."

"No," Pappadakis said anyway. "No, I didn't," he said, and I believed him. His mind had the ring of settled fact, but he was not surprised. Either he was the world's best liar—which I would not put beyond him—or he'd known about the attack from other sources.

"You'll leave my client alone," the lawyer said.

"Seriously, Tommy, let's go back outside for a second," Loyola said. "Excuse us."

I followed, watching the minds around us for disgust, for strong decisions, for anything that felt threatening or personal. It was like three music tapes played all too loud, all at once, so that you couldn't quite sort everything out, much less enjoy it. I vaguely saw the back of Loyola's suit, saw his hand on Tommy's shoulder, steering him, saw the door again.

Fifteen minutes later we were up on the fifth floor,

ancient carpeted gray hallway lined with benches and the occasional solid door, signs everywhere. More people sat in the benches, and a sign said CHILD SUPPORT HEARINGS THIS WAY. The buzz of all the upset minds was intense.

I was a terrible Minder, maybe, but the kid was in legitimate danger and I had to step up.

Finally we were led through a secure area, a quieter hallway that smelled different, passing through another door into a small room—a judge's chambers, according to the door. Judge Marissa Parson. She wasn't there.

CHAPTER 11

There was a surprisingly large amount of waiting involved in bodyguarding. Well, more than I was expecting, or was used to; Cherabino was an impatient cop, and she'd long since figured out a way to bribe others into doing the real time-consuming work while she powered on to the next thing. It meant working with her gave you whiplash sometimes, and you drowned in the paperwork she handed you, but you didn't often get bored.

We'd settled in, me on a chair, Tommy on the floor almost rebelliously, though I didn't tell him he couldn't. He was making complicated paper boats, cutting file folders into pieces and folding them into shapes he then assembled with tape into boats. Since the file folders appeared to be empty, I didn't protest.

I sat in an overstuffed armchair to the right of the room and Tommy, under a reading lamp next to a big bookshelf. I was monitoring the surroundings in Mindspace, sure, but in this part of the courthouse the minds might as well be on a loop. They did the same things, thought variants of the same things, over and over.

I was thinking about Cherabino a lot lately. Not only because of this trial—though it killed me not to be there and I was desperate to know what was going on—but because I missed her. I missed her as a person. And now, when I

was worried about nearly everything, I missed her compe-
tence, her experience. There was very little in the world she
hadn't seen at least once, or could find someone who had
on two minutes' notice.

I picked up the phone on the large desk and dialed Cherabino's office number from memory. It rang three times.

"Hello?" Michael's voice picked up.

"It's me," I said, glancing at Tommy still on the floor.
"Is Cherabino around?"

The tone of his voice changed to something more careful. "No. She's at the hearing right now and will be for a
few hours. Something I can do for you?"

I considered hanging up but decided we really did need
more information. And Tommy still seemed happy with
his homework. "I'm in Savannah, and the case we're dealing with . . . um, it's been linked to Sibley, the killer for
hire Cherabino's been tracking for a while. I was hoping to
get a copy of her files on him overnighted down here."
Maybe seeing his information in black-and-white would
help me sort out what was real and what I was imagining.

A long pause, which wasn't characteristic of Michael.
"I'm not technically supposed to be sharing information
with you at this time. Since you're working for an outside
agency."

I made a frustrated sound. "Ask Branen. He approved it,
and as near as I can tell he's a fan of interagency cooperation to start with. The FBI will spring for the cost of the
shipping." At least, I hoped they would.

"Adam?"

"Yes."

A pause. "Strictly between you and me, she's not doing
well. If you can come up here today, I'd recommend it."

My stomach sank, and my guilt returned tenfold. "What's
going on?"

"They've got another two days of hearings, but it's bad. I've never seen the powers that be mobilize like this, not this quickly. The union reps are protesting, and they just sent in Chou and his team. It's turning into a witch-hunt."

One of the foremost lawyers that worked with the department, Chou was good but he was expensive. For the union to hire him, it felt that Cherabino's hearing was crossing some essential line on principle. Considering what Branen had said, that wasn't out of line, and in fact it was probably a good thing. But I wasn't there.

"That's . . . that's rough," I said. My stomach sank. "I can't leave," I said. "I want to be there, but I can't leave. There's a ten-year-old whose safety depends on me being here." I couldn't even imagine what would happen to Tommy if I left. "I can't leave him."

Tommy looked up at me then, and frowned. He didn't like being talked about like he was helpless.

"You do what you have to do," Michael said, but in the tone of voice of someone who thought I was in the wrong.

I took a breath. Speaking of Sibley . . . "Did Cherabino have you look up the jail records for Sibley? She said she would."

"Yes. Give me a second." There was a long pause while I listened to the sound of papers rustling. "Okay. I talked to the warden this morning. He was released on a special order sometime early in the week. Cherabino has a flag on his case, so we're entitled to notifications. I'm not sure why they didn't go through in this case."

"What in hell is a special order? Do you have any idea where he went? Damn it, you put people in jail, you expect them to stay there."

"Hold on, I had nothing to do with this. There's no need to yell. And I don't know who ordered it. The records are sealed . . . or at least not easily shared. It's not any of the people that Cherabino suspects of being on Fiske's payroll, but the DA's office has been looking for that kind of evidence for a year now. No luck."

"What's a special order?" I asked. I felt like beating my head against the wall.

"It's a rule from post–Tech Wars. Nobody uses it anymore, and they hardly used it then. If somebody with enough power wants somebody out for a time period, they can order it. They're supposed to go back to jail when they're done with whatever the special mission is. It's like a governor's pardon, only temporary. This one's for six weeks."

Strange. I'd never heard of the rule, but then again a Guild education didn't emphasize normal laws and I'd had to pick up police rules as I went. "You don't know who gave the order?"

"No. That's what I've been trying to tell you. It's been redacted, and the warden didn't approve it personally. It's the strangest damn thing. I'll see if I can't figure out more for you, but it looks like a dead end. I'll turn it over to the Fiske task force. Maybe they can prove the connection."

I took a breath. "If he's pulling strings on that level, the task force has bigger problems."

"Yeah. He destroyed the last case they built against him. If this is him, I'd say he's moving on some kind of plan he needs Sibley for. Maybe the task force can piece it together."

A plan with Sibley lined up with my vision perfectly. "Thanks," I said in a bitter tone. I didn't think that the task force would be able to do anything, not fast enough.

"Thank you for bringing it up. The department spent a hell of a lot of money and effort getting this guy behind bars, and we put a flag on his record. We should have been informed when this happened. The captain isn't happy. I'll . . . I'll see what I can do about sharing the rest of the information. I don't think anyone's going to have a problem with it, especially if you guys are suspecting him in a case down there."

"Thanks."

"You're welcome."

There was another long pause.

Finally I said, "Tell her she can reach me after seven at this number." I gave him the judge's house number, ignoring all protocol. If Cherabino needed me, I'd do whatever it took. I would. Even if it was too little, too late.

Tommy's safety was worth it. It had to be.

"I'll tell her," Michael said.

"Thanks." I waited, realized there was nothing more to say, and hung up.

After an hour, I was literally hurting for a cigarette, so I pulled Loyola into the room with Tommy and went outside to smoke near the side door of the courthouse. I saw the guard again, and he harassed me for ID again. Neither one of us felt entirely happy with the results of that one, but I made it out the building and moved to the corner of the building to smoke where I wouldn't get in anyone else's way and was still—barely—close enough to Tommy.

That connection was tight, though, stretched like a tense rubber band in the back of my head. I poked at it as I smoked. The information on this from the book I'd read was sparse, and that was ten years ago. I didn't have a lot of details on this kind of connection. The human mind—especially the pubescent and prepubescent human mind—was inherently unpredictable. Probably there was something in Guild records with a full write-up, but that did me no good right now, and right now was critical.

I worried about it as I smoked and watched the cars go by in front of the courthouse, people walking up the front steps, people being belched out of the front door in large groups. The minds were a cacophony of sound outside, so I shielded up to my gills. I told myself I needed a break, and the truth was that I wouldn't do Tommy much good from out here anyway.

I was almost done with a too-fast cigarette when I saw him. My heart nearly stopped.

Sibley was standing across the street, next to a tall kiosk full of soy-print newspapers and degradable magazines, paying the teenager in charge of the kiosk in cash. Pale and bald, average height with a muscular frame, he was dressed to blend into the crowd, a quiet suit that would have fit in anywhere in the world, but with shoes meant to run in. I knew that face despite the sunglasses. I'd know it anywhere.

A car passed along the street between us and I took a step forward, then another. When the street cleared, Sibley was looking up—and directly at me.

He smiled and gave me a two-fingered lazy man's salute, fingers to forehead, and another car passed between us.

I trotted toward him, still unable to believe what I was seeing—and then the connection with Tommy choked me like an invisible collar, tight. I could keep going, maybe. I could push through and break that connection—but I had no way of knowing what it would do to me, or to Tommy. And my priority had to be Tommy.

His hands were empty, and I didn't see either the device or the gun or any other suspicious lumps on his person. But there was no way to be sure this far away. No way to be sure.

Sibley took his paper and walked away. I hesitated. But then I turned back, hustling toward the security guard to put him on alert. Then to Jarrod, to stir up whatever security we could.

I tried to connect to Jarrod via Mindspace as I walked,

but he didn't hear me. Deaf as a doorpost, I guessed. I let Mendez know, though, and moved as quickly as I could.

This was getting all too real.

Jarrod agreed with my assessment, and I left him scrambling half the city and three departments. It was my job to find Tommy and stay with him. It should have been my job in the first place, Jarrod had said.

I passed Pappadakis's lawyer in the hallway outside the courtroom, who apparently had stepped out of his client's trial to take a phone call in the otherwise empty hallway. He stopped talking when I got within sight distance, and put his hand over the phone. "Do you mind?" he said, and glared at me.

I frowned, wondering if this was Sibley he was talking to, but it felt like paranoia. When I tried to read him, all I got was a sense of fuzzy wariness. He and I had poor valence; our minds meshed badly, so that while another telepath might be able to read him perfectly well, I could not.

But I didn't have the time to stand here and drag it out of him. My senses were already back in Minding mode, tracking every mind in the vicinity. Hopefully it would be enough.

I hustled back to the judge's chambers, worried.

At a time like this, I wished I had a physical weapon of some kind—a knife perhaps, or a Taser, or even pepper spray in a pinch. The cops would make fun of me to no end if I got caught with pepper spray—or even a Taser, to be honest—but if it gave me a chance to walk away or to overcome an attacker with my telepathy, I'd take the ribbing. I didn't normally carry a weapon; my mind was a weapon all on its own. But it had already proven useless against Sibley, and like I'd said, he'd almost killed me. And maybe he was there, and was a threat. Maybe.

Needless to say, I was jumpy when I closed the door behind me.

Tommy was on his feet already, Loyola with gun ready.

"You might knock," Loyola said, lowering the gun. His heart was beating too fast, the decision not to shoot too fresh.

"Next time I will," I promised.

"What's wrong?" Tommy said. I could feel his panic, his reaction to my own worry.

Crap. Now I was scaring the kid. I pulled on years of intensive training, and forced calm. Deep breath in, deep breath out, calm down the limbic system. "I saw a threat outside, but I reported it and we're fine," I said, and then forced myself to believe it. "If anything, it's good news. You can't shut down a threat you didn't see."

Loyola met my eyes, question in his body language.

No, not good news at all, I told him mind-to-mind. *I'd appreciate you sticking around.*

He nodded significantly.

"You're lying to me," Tommy said, sounding hurt.

Crap, again. I stood closer to him. "I'm not lying to you. I just don't want you to worry more than you have to. We've seen the problem. We're dealing with it. Right here is probably one of the safer places in the world right now—local police are on their way on top of the usual security system, and the bailiffs are all armed as a matter of course." I said this firmly, making myself believe it. Sibley had rattled me, though. Sibley had rattled me a lot, and my heart was still beating all too fast.

"You saw the bad man, didn't you?" he said. "The one from the vision."

Great. Teach me not to think too loudly around Tommy. I took a breath and responded, "I told you I'd stick around and keep you safe. I intend to keep that promise."

There was a silence as I looked at Tommy and Tommy looked at me.

"Don't die, okay?" he asked in a small voice.

Loyola put a hand on Tommy's shoulder then. "No one's dying today. Now, don't you have more math homework to do? Nothing calms me down when I'm tense like math homework."

"Really?" I asked. "Math stresses me out."

"I'll help you with the homework," Loyola said. "No sense in letting the teep do it."

"Telepathic expert," I corrected.

"Teep," he said.

Tommy looked back and forth between us, but his panic had faded.

"Fine, teep," I said, just to keep that panic out of his eyes.

But my own heart beat too fast, and I jumped at every change in air pressure, waiting for the threat to hit.

Tommy sprawled out on the floor, pencil in hand while he did his homework against the floor. Math, judging from the rows of numbers and letters. He had a set of headphones on, listening to the radio; pricey things, those, to be so small and yet properly analog and therefore not Tech-law-restricted. His head bopped in time with a beat I couldn't hear as his pencil slowly leaked numbers and formulas onto the page. Algebra, of course; I had no idea whether that was advanced or behind in the normal world for his age. It didn't really matter, I guessed. I had no similar work, and I was still strung tighter than an overtuned guitar.

Loyola was on a chair not far from him, checking a previous page of work for progress. I noticed his gun was out, set on a low table within easy arm's reach with the gun pointed toward the door. His body language was relaxed, but it was a sham; he was seated forward, at the edge of the chair. For all of his slumping, he could be up and moving within a few seconds. I was about the same in Mindspace.

I sat back in the armchair, trying to read an FBI procedures manual and not having a lot of luck. I'd need the information eventually, but right now it was too dry. Every time someone walked past in the hall outside I'd look up. But I couldn't just worry either; I didn't want Tommy getting any more scared than necessary, and considering our strange connection, that meant I needed to be legitimately calm, not just acting like it. I had to.

I looked up. Someone was walking down the hallway in our direction again. This time they had a sense of specific purpose, if I could trust my senses. I didn't recognize the mind from earlier in the day. It wasn't Sibley, I didn't think, but at this point that didn't mean anything to me.

"Heads up," I said.

Loyola was on his feet, gun ready, and I was moving toward Tommy, my own attention on the door as the mind got closer and closer.

Tommy got to his feet and said, "That's Dad again," with the kind of dismissive attitude only a kid could really pull off. "Don't shoot him."

I reluctantly let go of the defense I'd been building for us both and pulled more of my attention into the real world.

Tommy opened the door, and we saw the bruised face and classic pre–Tech Wars haircut of Quentin Parrish, who had his hands in the air and his mind pulled into as small a profile as he could make it. He had a hat in hand.

Loyola lowered the gun, slowly, but did not put it up.

"Apologies for startling you, gentlemen," Quentin said. Then when he saw the words had registered, he smiled the large smile of a man who was used to charming his way into anything he wanted. "Not that I don't appreciate you watching my son with that kind of hair trigger, but what do you say I lower my hands, you lower your gun and mind, and we have a nice conversation, huh?"

"Fine." I took a deep breath, intentionally trying to lower my adrenaline level and heart rate, and eased away from Tommy in Mindspace.

Tommy glanced back at me, I nodded, and he threw himself at his dad, who caught him up in a bone-crushing hug.

"Excellent to see you, boy," Quentin said. "You been doing your homework?"

"Yeah," Tommy said, and pulled away.

"You realize you just walked into a building full of lawyers and cops," I said to Quentin. "And then into a judge's private chambers without so much as a by-your-leave."

"Oh, they know me here," Quentin said.

"You're a con man and you're showing up to a courthouse, where they know you," I said, slowly, trying to get my head around the concept.

"And why shouldn't they?" he asked me. "I'm not guilty of anything at the moment."

I paused. Really?

"Tanya died," Tommy put in, and then I noticed that low-level sense of grief that had just intensified. "And Adam saw the bad man across the street."

Both my and Quentin's attention immediately turned to Tommy.

"Who is the bad man?" Quentin asked me then.

I debated how much to tell him.

After I said nothing, he turned back to Tommy. "Tanya was the woman taking care of you?" Quentin asked.

Tommy nodded. "The guard. She was nice."

"I see." He dropped his bag on the floor and took his son in his arms. His mind was moving with questions, but he didn't ask them. Instead he said, "We're going to figure this out, nugget. You stay close to the new guards, okay?"

Tommy broke down then and cried for a moment before just holding on. After his tears slowed to sniffs, Quentin looked back at me.

Complications from the attack, I mouthed.

He nodded and pulled Tommy over to the oversized chair. He knelt down on the floor next to it, leaning toward his son. He seemed . . . more present today. Less here for a show.

Tommy sniffed again and rubbed at his face. I gave him a handful of tissues, which he took with a little bit of irritation, but he blew his nose.

"Now. You going to tell me what happened yesterday morning?" Quentin asked the kid gently. "The only thing I know is what I heard on the news." And from the questions he'd asked his criminal contacts, his mind supplied. But nothing near enough to understand fully what had happened. And he didn't like that I was spotting somebody close by. If something was going down, he should have heard about it.

"Mom says talking about bad things doesn't make it better," Tommy said reluctantly.

"Your mother thinks things will go away if she ignores them. It doesn't work like that. Why don't you tell us what happened? I'll pinkie-swear not to tell your mother you told me."

Tommy stopped, thoughts dripping across his mind like a faucet turned far too low. He was tired, and I felt like I could say something, but from what I could tell Quentin was plenty strong enough to tell this himself.

He started, "They pulled over the car and Tanya pushed me to the floor like we practiced. There were a lot of loud bangs, and Jason got hurt—like really bad. It was—a lot of things happened really fast, and it was a lot in my head." His thoughts replayed the day, a more jumbled and colorful version of what I'd heard from the bodyguard earlier, with the intense sensory overload of intense emotions to a tele-path. "The bad guys . . . they got closer and there were these bangs on the car. I got burned on the floor, but Tanya was so worried I didn't say anything and then she wanted us to run. We almost got hit by a train." His memories spi-raled backward, to the beginning, through the picture he'd gotten of the criminals behind him in the brief moment before they ran, a guilt-anger thing from the criminal, and a panic feeling when they crossed the train tracks. He hadn't liked leaving the other bodyguard behind in the front of the car. He'd lost a shoe on the walk afterward, and Tanya was hurt too. The sole of his foot had gotten a piece of glass in it and she'd taken it out for him. How could she be . . . dead? How could she not be okay?

And Tommy descended back into grief.

I realized that Tommy was more mentally open around his father, and his father around him, than either was on his own. Whatever Quentin had done or not done, it was a hell of a lot more warmth than I'd seen from the judge.

Quentin patted his shoulder. "That's a hard thing, nug-get. Thanks for telling me."

He turned to me and very, very quietly and awkwardly asked me mind-to-mind, *Did you get that?*

What? I asked, confused. Also, how in the hell had the Guild missed Quentin? This was not one but two strong telepaths who'd apparently escaped being recruited. It made me nervous.

A pause, like he had to remember how to speak mind-to-mind all over again. *You're a hell of a lot stronger than anyone I've seen in this mind thing. I assume you got a picture of his memories? See if there's anything we can use. Right now I'm hearing only rumors on the street, and none of them agree.* His mental tone was flat, intentional, with none of the bravado I associated with his outside presence. This internal feeling was actually similar to the judge's.

Tommy sniffed, and Quentin pulled him back up for a hug. The tears intensified, but they seemed healing. Having his father here was making a difference, which I hadn't expected.

I backed up, taking a seat in the chair behind the desk and thinking. Quentin was a con man, sure, but he might have a point. And telepathy. And he was clearly willing to use his own connections to track down what was going on. That guilt-anger feeling from the criminal . . . it was the guy who'd approached the car. Perhaps a low-level telepath himself, as their brains tended to leak a louder signal in Mindspace for Tommy's prototelepath brain to pick up under pressure. The odd thing was, the guilt-anger wasn't directed at anyone in Tommy's vicinity; it was a reaction to something related to someone behind him, one of the other bad guys.

I wished I could go back to the scene and see the residue from the guy's mind directly, maybe get a feel for who he was in Mindspace. Jarrod had said that he'd take me there later, but thus far nothing had seemed to go as planned.

I was trying to figure out how to make that trip happen when the door opened again, and Marissa, the judge, came through the door.

I blinked, and suppressed a too-extreme reaction. I was going to have to get a lot better at reaction times and monitoring if this Minding thing was going to work.

Loyola, now standing, lowered his gun. "Once again," he said in a too-controlled voice. "People need to *knock*."

"It's my chambers. I'll walk into my own chambers without knocking. Thank you," Parson said. I *felt* more than saw the second when she saw her ex-husband. "Quentin," she said. "What in hell are you doing here?"

He got to his feet. "Darling. So good to see you. As you can observe with your own eyes, I'm spending time with my son. He's had a wretched day. Several of them, in fact."

"Our son," she said in a biting tone.

"Certainly. He is your son too."

Tommy stood up on shaking feet, squared his chin, and said, "Mom, don't fight. Dad will leave in just a minute." He looked at his dad, who sighed and nodded.

"Of course, nugget. You call me if you need anything. I'll check the answering service several times a day. Don't hesitate to call, all right?"

"Could I have a copy of that number?" I asked, not sure why I asked but figuring it wouldn't hurt.

He looked at me, surprised. Behind him, Parson tapped her foot impatiently. Like, literally tapped her foot. I hadn't seen anyone actually tap their foot in impatience in years.

Quentin wrote down the number for me.

"Thanks," I said.

"Don't mention it." And then Quentin got his hat. His charming exterior broke, and I saw clearly the irritated, worried guy underneath. I watched him carefully as he left.

"I suppose if you people are going to overreact every time I walk in the door I'll stay in another set of chambers this afternoon—Judge Darwin is off today, I believe." Parson looked at me in particular there. Again, I got the distinct impression she was avoiding me. The question was whether she hated telepaths, or just me. I might never get the answer to that one.

"There's room here," I said. I had questions I wanted to ask her anyway.

"I have twenty minutes to eat lunch and gather my thoughts before the case continues. I'll go elsewhere. Thank you."

"It's no trouble for us to move, ma'am," Loyola said, but I could feel his disquiet too.

"No," she said. "No, thank you."

She turned and left, and I worried again. I wanted my poison, my drug, at least until Tommy looked at me. Then I made myself go back to the FBI procedures manual. It was boring, but it was something that wouldn't hurt him to overhear.

Despite this, I spent most of my mental energy monitoring for danger.

CHAPTER 12

An hour later, Loyola had gone out to coordinate with Jarrod, and I was reluctantly chewing on a meal bar: one of my least favorite things in the world. I much preferred rehydrated dehydrated vegetable noodles to this crap; at least the noodle stuff was warm, and you could add red pepper things for taste. The bar was just a heavy block of might-be food. But I was hungry, and I'd need fuel to be able to stay at a high alert. I also wanted Satin, and a cigarette, and not to be here, but I'd have to settle for the food.

I worried about Cherabino again, and Sibley. I worried about a lot of things as I finished the meal bar.

The sound of the old doorknob came then, a *click* from across the room. I looked up. Tommy had just left.

I cursed. I yelled at him mentally to come back here, but it was like yelling at the wind.

I dropped the wrapper in the trash can and took off after him, huffing and puffing after just a few steps (cigarettes are not good for the lungs), and finally caught up to him in the hallway. He hadn't even been moving that fast.

I caught his shoulder. "Hold up. Where are you going?"

"I'm bored," Tommy said. "I want to see the murder trial. We're surrounded by the good guys. I won't be in any trouble." He turned around, shrugged off the hand casually as

Mendez behind me stopped just in the hallway, mind alert. "Look, you can come with me."

And he started walking.

I followed him, uncertain. Relieved, though, that he was intending to stay in the building. Not sure what to do. "It's a murder trial," I told him. "It's likely to be pretty violent." I'd dealt with enough dead bodies in the course of the job that I wasn't likely to throw up anymore, but that didn't mean I liked it. Even pictures weren't very appropriate for a kid.

"Oh, Mom lets me look at crime scene pictures all the time," Tommy said, deadpan, and oddly I couldn't tell if he was lying or telling the truth. I wasn't used to an out-loud conversation that skipped ahead either. "I'm bored," he said. "And if that trial is what everyone's worried about, I want to see it."

To be honest, I wanted to see it too.

He smiled. "Let's get a good seat in the back."

I didn't fight as much as I should have. Mendez followed us.

"You know this isn't a good idea," she said.

"Yeah," I said. "I know." Court security was everywhere, I told myself. I couldn't stay in that small room and not think about certain things for much longer. The courtroom might be safer, or not safer, but at least it would be different. I needed different right now.

The courtroom was smaller than I expected, the judge's raised seat and witness stand looking out onto the jury box to the right, currently filled with twelve serious-looking citizens whose major emotion was boredom and overwhelming responsibility, like a set of cops doing critical paperwork.

The back of the room, where we sat, had three ancient wooden pews that reminded me of Cherabino's family's church. The darkly stained wood was worn blond in the centers of the benches with the pressure of a thousand seated butts, the backs rubbed lighter from a thousand nervous hands.

A row of media sat impatiently in the second row, pads of paper and pens out, not a camera in sight. Immediately in front of the front bench was a low wall and then two tables for defendant and lawyer and assistant district attorney and her police detective helper. All in all, a quiet, cramped day in mayhem with Judge Parson sitting over all of it like a forbidding crow.

I noticed that Pappadakis sat back, body language relaxed like he hadn't a care in the world. His lawyer was back as if I'd never seen him outside, but the man was both nervous and resolute. They were planning something.

Parson said, "Court is now in session," and hit her desk with the little judge mallet thing. The crack of it echoed through the courtroom as all assembled went quiet. The jury's attention focused like a light on a lens.

The DA stood. "Your Honor, thank you for the recess. We'd like to call our next witness, Mrs. Marcia Josepha Garces, domestic employee for the defendant."

The judge nodded, and a small woman in a long coat stood up from the front row of benches, a woman whose nerves were getting ever larger as she made the few steps up to the witness stand. She was pretty at first glance, in that classic Hollywood Cuban way, with just enough wrinkles and silver hairs to make her seem authentic at midfifties without taking away from the prettiness. But on second glance you could see her life hadn't been easy. She stooped, moving slowly from too many heavy loads, and her hands were rough and older than the rest of her. She'd still styled her hair, though, and worn pearls to the courtroom along with practical shoes.

Garces was sworn in, hand on a battered Bible, and took

her seat carefully. She clasped her purse in her lap, knuckles going white from their pressure around the purse's straps.

"Mrs. Garces," the DA said.

"Yes?"

"Mrs. Garces, explain your relationship to the defendant."

"Mr. Pappadakis? I am his housekeeper. I clean and cook simple things and manage the other employees. There's a part-time fancy cook and a landscaper and other people sometimes when he throws parties. Mr. Pappadakis likes the house perfect so that his guests will be impressed." She looked down, as if ashamed of something, and her nerves increased.

The DA went back over to his table and brought up a large picture that he placed on an easel, a picture of a thirtysomething woman with a face beautiful enough for sculpture and a smile that spoke of sex. "You knew this woman, Lolly Gilman?"

Mrs. Garces nodded. "She and Mr. Pappadakis . . . they are lovers. She is often at the house when his wife is gone."

I looked around the courtroom, but I didn't see a wife here. I could be missing her in the crowd, I supposed, but if she really wasn't here, that didn't spell good things for whatever relationship they had left after all of the cheating.

"You okay?" I asked Tommy.

"Yep." He leaned forward, apparently fascinated by the trial so far. I sat back and got comfortable.

The assistant district attorney had left the picture up, as if by accident, but I'd been to enough of my father's trials as a teenager that I knew very little in a courtroom was truly by accident. He was paused, halfway back to the witness stand, at the angle best suited to show his handsome profile to the jury. He had the kind of physique that lifters worked hard on but never looked right in a suit—except, of course, that he'd spent the money to have his suits custom-tailored to show the bulk of his shoulders to best advantage.

After a moment to let his reluctance to ask the question fully sink into the jury, the ADA said, "But she was not the only woman Mr. Pappadakis had at the house when his wife is gone, was that correct?"

Mrs. Garces nodded, still looking down. "He has paid to put my children through college," she said finally. "It is not right to say bad things about a man who does such things."

The ADA paused. "You've sworn to tell the whole truth, Mrs. Garces. How often did your employer have women other than his mistress and his wife over to the house?"

"I try not to see," Mrs. Garces said. "I go to the little house he gives me and I try not to come out. But there is always a mess in the morning, and I must clean. Often they are still there. There are many."

"How many, would you say, over the last year?"

"Many," she said, her quiet voice seeming to echo through the whole courtyard. "Many, many. They are prostitutes, many of them. Some show me their license so I will help them get the payment they were promised. Some just want to leave. Lolly, she is there most often, but never when one of the others is there."

"Were there any unlicensed prostitutes?" the ADA asked.

Next to me, Tommy squirmed a bit and I wondered if the content was going to get too intense for him. I was hooked into the interrogation, wanting to see where this was going, but I also knew I had a responsibility to make sure he was okay. I had no idea what was appropriate or inappropriate for his age when it came to court cases.

"We need to leave?" I whispered to him quietly.

"Nope," he said.

"It's no big deal if you want to go back to the chambers."

"No way. I want to see what happens." He was thinking

that if Pappadakis was really the guy who'd sent the bad men, he wanted to know why.

In a way I thought he had a right to know, so we stayed.

Up at the front of the room, the lawyer asked again, "Any unlicensed prostitutes?"

She nodded, still looking down as if ashamed. "These try to leave before I am up, but sometimes they do not. They . . ." She trailed off and shook her head again.

"What were you going to say?" the ADA prompted.

"They most often have bruises on their skin. Sometimes a black eye. They have no agency to call and complain."

Tommy had a small burst of anger from next to me, and a picture of some kind of superhero fighting against the bruises. I only felt disgust at the kind of guy who could do that. It fit very well with the picture of a man accused of killing his mistress.

"Objection, speculation," the defense lawyer said from the front.

"Sustained," the judge said.

The ADA waited a moment for that to sink in with the jury anyway. "Did you ever see one of them get their bruises?"

She reluctantly said, "They have no bruises when they arrive. They have many when they leave. I do not hit them. Bron, the gardener, he does not hit them."

The ADA glanced toward the judge, then back at her. "Have you ever seen your employer hit them?"

Mrs. Garces took in a shaky breath. "Yes, I see him hit them. I try not to see, but I see. It happens. But when they have visited, he no longer hits me or his wife. So I am grateful. Sometimes it is better when they come often."

"He hits you?" the ADA asked.

She nodded and held on to the straps of her purse tightly. "It is good money. And it is not often."

"So Mr. Pappadakis has a history of violence with

women," the ADA said, pausing again with his good side toward the jury.

"Objection," the defense lawyer said. Next to him, Pappadakis was getting angry—his body language hadn't changed much, but the anger was nearly pulsing off him in Mindspace.

"In your experience," the ADA said to Mrs. Garces.

"I'll allow it," the judge said.

"Yes," Mrs. Garces said, very quietly, but it was like a bullet went off from a gun—Pappadakis's reaction was so big. "Yes, he has much history with violence to women."

"Thank you, Mrs. Garces," the ADA said, with a big smile for the jury. "No more questions."

The defense lawyer, sweating a little, got up and asked a few obligatory questions about exactly when and where she'd seen evidence of things, trying to discredit her testimony in various ways. Unfortunately for him, Mrs. Garces stuck to her story and provided relevant details of enough different occasions that he ended up weakening his own case.

He ended with "But you did not see what happened on the night of December the fourth, the night in question, when Miss Gilman arrived?"

"No," Mrs. Garces said in a clear voice. "No, I went to bed early with a sleeping pill. When I woke up the next morning, Bron had already found her. The gardener. She was dead. She had been beaten to death. They say to me she was beaten to death with a lamp. It is a horrible thing."

Beaten to death with a lamp, huh? I hadn't liked Pappadakis on sight, but if he was the kind of guy who'd beat his mistress to death with a lamp, I liked him even less. Of course, he was on trial, not convicted, not yet.

"Please stick to your direct knowledge," Judge Parson instructed her. "Did you see her get beaten?"

"No. No, I did not. As I said, I was asleep."

"So you do not know if he was involved in the crime," the defense lawyer said. "The gardener could already have covered up the crime by the time you arrived, and then asked you to corroborate his story."

Mrs. Garces drew herself up to her short height and said clearly, "Bron Jones is a good man and very loyal to Mr. Pappadakis. He would never have hurt Ms. Gilman. Never. If anything, he would have defended her as he did us. He kept Lila, the cook—he defended her more than once. He did the same for me. That is the kind of man he is."

Well, that didn't go as you'd planned, I thought, watching the defense lawyer try to recover from that. A low blow to go after the hired help for potential killers to get your client off, but it wouldn't be the first time.

I wondered how bad the beating really was. We'd clearly missed most of the critical testimony about it, but they didn't have a clear connection to Pappadakis or they wouldn't have bothered to ask Mrs. Garces about his history. Looking over at him sitting in the defense stand, however, I had no problem whatsoever imagining him beating his mistress to death. His suit was nice, but he had that shark vibe and plenty of strength in his blunt hands.

And Fiske, with all he'd done and set up, wouldn't have a single problem getting this guy off from a murder like that. He'd probably been the one to make their one and only witness disappear.

It scared me, because if he had been willing to go that far, and maybe now help Pappadakis put pressure on the judge, what chance did I have?

Loyola's mind came toward mine down the hall behind us as the defense lawyer asked another few questions designed to put doubt on Bron, the landscaper, or Mrs. Garces. Apparently they'd already heard Bron's testimony yesterday and he was trying hard to make it suspicious. I had no idea how it was coming off to the jury, but I could feel the lawyer's calculated lies from across the room; he was doing everything in his power to pull attention off his client. The ethical lawyer thing to do, of course, but it didn't make me like him all that much.

The ADA had an objection that had the judge pull both lawyers up to the stand then.

I felt Loyola's mind enter the courtroom and come toward me. He sat down next to me, the wooden benches creaking. He had a small canvas bag, slightly open, that he set on the floor.

I nodded at him; he nodded at me.

"Hi," Tommy said.

"Hi," Loyola returned. "What are you doing in here?"

"I wanted to see what's going on," Tommy said.

Loyola thought about that and then let it go.

"What's going on?" I asked him quietly.

He pulled his bag to the bench next to himself. "I have news," he said.

After a glance at the action in the front of the courtroom, then back at Tommy, I nodded. Something I needed to know, I assumed, or he wouldn't be interrupting.

Loyola handed me a paper, one labeled PHONE TRANSCRIPT, a wiretap number, and then a date and time under the letterhead of the ATF, the Alcohol, Tobacco, and Firearms Federal Department, the group that Jarrod had said he was coordinating with.

The transcript had someone calling a "special" number at a gun shop and ordering a set of very specific guns three days ago. It was a woman's voice, they said. And the ATF official had written in on the margins that the guns they were ordering were at least five decades old, with restricted parts, and the codes they were using weren't actually matches to the gun names, though they sounded right. The gun shop hadn't asked for a name or explained the paper-work process to buy a gun, something that legally would take longer than three days. Instead they'd promised to have the order by the end of the week, asked about a silencer, and then quoted an obscene amount of money. "The junior rate," they'd said. "Partial." And then they'd set up a meet-ing place about half an hour outside the city. They'd had to get directions twice.

At the end of the page, a scrawling set of handwriting guessed *Hit? Work for hire of some kind. Flagged too late to tail.*

The timing was right for it to be the attack on Tommy. And judging from the military gear and the sloppiness of the attack, a gun shop was a good bet for where they found their customers.

"We'll need you to talk to the gun store owner tonight," Loyola said to me, very quietly.

I nodded, significantly, a promise. Loyola took the papers back and folded them into his bag.

Jarrod stopped by a small diner to get food, bringing back messy sacks of Reubens and fries. We ate in the car. Tommy was tired but was talking about the trial in a way I thought was probably healthy, considering. He ate more fries than sandwich, but I wasn't his mother and at least it was food. I was tired too, my head hurting from a long, long day trying to monitor far too many minds moving in far too many directions.

"Ready to visit the gun shop?" Jarrod asked me.

I swallowed my bite of the Reuben after chewing a moment. "It's seven o'clock," I said. "Don't we need to get the kid home?"

"I'm not a kindergartener," Tommy said. And he was thinking his mom hadn't been in a good mood today in court. He wasn't looking forward to going home.

"It'll be a short trip. He can stay in the car. We've got his comic books," Jarrod said flatly. "If you're serious about helping with the investigation, I need you to talk to this gun store owner. Thus far the ATF has gotten nothing out of him and I need information."

I paused, trying to get a feel for whether Tommy was really okay with this. Whether I was really okay with this. A streetlight cast small squares of light onto the inside of the car. It was the only light around, the shadows deep.

"We're leaving now," Jarrod said, and motioned for Loyola to pull the car out. I took a last bite of the sandwich and packed up the wrappers, mine and Tommy's, in the bag. I cleaned my hands on a napkin and watched the buildings and lights of the city flow past.

You okay? I asked Tommy.

I'm okay, he said back awkwardly. It was one of the first times he'd sent a thought to me directly mind-to-mind, without me prompting him. He was coming a long way in a short time, I thought. I was still surprised the Guild hadn't recruited him already. He was new, though, and couldn't hide his exhaustion and overall fear from me.

We moved down a street without streetlights then, and it got dark in the car for a moment.

If you'll follow us and stand around quietly, I'll give you another telepathy lesson tonight, I told Tommy mind-to-mind.

He lit up like a lightbulb, happiness and excitement spilling all over everything. I wished I shared his excitement.

Why did I feel like I was lying to him? I intended to do the lesson and everything. I really did. Maybe Cherabino would have known what was wrong, but I didn't. I'd have to figure all of this out totally on my own.

We drove through several streets in Savannah until we ended up at a long concrete box with bars on the window, which looked rougher than the one (and only) gun shop and range Cherabino had taken me to a few months ago. One lone streetlight sputtered overhead, a half-dead bioluminescent bush in a median in the cracked parking lot looking like it hadn't had any water in years.

The sign above the concrete front said HARD KNOCKS in harsh lettering, with a single painted gunshot hole, with a ragged edge.

Mendez and Jarrod went ahead, to introduce themselves to the gun shop owner; I collected myself, finally getting out once I was sure there were no minds around likely to be an issue for Tommy. The surroundings felt . . . too empty actually. Much too empty, though I couldn't put my finger on any particular reason why.

My feet weren't used to dress shoes, and so the blisters of the day rubbed as I walked across the parking lot, low-level distracting pain. I'd had to learn to ignore much worse as part of my Guild training, so it wasn't a deal breaker. I'd have to peel off the socks and treat the things so they didn't get infected later. But the pain was a useful focuser, a useful distraction to keep me thinking about everything in my life that could go wrong.

I felt Tommy's impatience a step behind me. And a sudden burst of emotion from Jarrod in Mindspace ahead, tamped down all too suddenly. I walked in the front door, which they'd already opened, and saw why.

Lying on the floor was someone I presumed was the gun shop owner, shot in the chest at least twice, the blooming blood on his shirt already drying into that funny brown-red, limbs already stiffening in rigor mortis.

"I take it you did not expect a crime scene in here?" I asked Jarrod, blocking Tommy's view of the scene with my body. Just in time, felt like.

"Hey, I want to see," he said.

"No, you don't," I said.

Jarrod sighed, and walked over to the wall, where a phone hung.

CHAPTER 13

Once I got Loyola to watch Tommy in the car, just a few feet away from the gun shop, I convinced Jarrod to let me read the scene.

I dived into Mindspace, stupidly, completely blind, and without an anchor. Cherabino should have been there, should have provided the real-world anchor for me, should have held out that mental hand to keep me grounded and finding my way back. I missed her again suddenly. I missed her being here.

But I was too embarrassed, too self-conscious to ask my new boss—or worse, Loyola—for help in all of this. I'd manage. I'd manage if it killed me. And it might. Mind-space wasn't the safest place in the world.

Swartz would disapprove of foolish risks if asked. He'd also understand the need to feel strong, or at least I hoped he would. We'd doubtlessly be talking about it at length at our next morning coffee meeting.

I took deep breaths, forcing myself to focus. Scattered thoughts were dangerous enough in the real world; in Mind-space, you ran the risk of losing your way or losing yourself, worse still without an anchor. I could do this. I must.

The world grayed out, disappearing into the not-quite sight of a world without light, like the depths of the ocean, or the world of a bat, all reflected waves and heard realities.

I sank deeper, until I saw the rapidly filling in hole where a mind used to be. The death, sitting in the middle of the room above the body. He'd been killed here, but then again I think we'd known that.

I approached the area where I thought the killer should have been standing, the angle of the gun having shot from this end of the space. There—there. I knew that mind.

Sibley.

A frisson of fear overcame me, but I pushed it back. All too easy to get lost in your own fears in Mindspace; Mindspace was receptive, after all, and all too often would help you along the way, would echo your own fears until the feedback loop shut you down. If you let it. If you were powerful enough, and sadly I was just that powerful.

I breathed, deeply, in and out, letting the real world of my body and my lungs intrude here until I calmed.

A small spot here. Near the satisfied mind brimming over with the gunshots, with the violent control. With the win. But there—there—was that small spot. An aberration. A fuzzy blob where, like the water around a rock in a stream, Mindspace had moved around something here.

Sibley had his gadget, the thing that had controlled me the last time I'd seen him. He had it now, and all my worries would be for nothing if he brought it and I couldn't counter its influence. I'd stayed up late several nights trying to figure it out, trying to come up with a counter. I was out of time.

I surfaced, fear trailing after me like smoke in air.

Last time we met, he'd almost killed me. And worse, that thing—that sphere he held, taken from the research of a Guild girl who'd thrown her lot in with Fiske—had made him able to control me. He'd tell me to jump and I jumped, literally, unable to keep my mind, my body from obeying. It was crude, suggestibility only, nothing specific, but if I couldn't counter it, he could come right up to me on the street and tell me to give him Tommy, and maybe I would.

I'd have to figure out a way to stop this thing in its tracks, and soon.

My heart sped up, and I surfaced out of Mindspace only just, only barely escaping my own fear.

I told Jarrod what I'd found, holding back the machine but telling him about Sibley. Jarrod made a thoughtful face. A face, and some floating diffuse thoughts, and nothing else. "I need to make some more phone calls," he said. "We need to be able to track this guy's movements."

"Do you think you really can?" I asked.

"I don't know. The ATF's guy tracked him back to a meeting with three local toughs he's apparently hired. They've got something in the works, but right now we're a step behind."

"Oh," I said. I didn't know what to add, or how to add it. I didn't know if I could even talk about the device without starting a major incident with the Guild or worse.

But I knew what I was going to do. I knew what I had to do, to stop the vision from happening and have some chance to get back to Cherabino in time. I knew what I had to do to survive this.

My priority was Tommy and his safety, so Loyola and I were sent from the crime scene back to the house along with Sridarin, who worked for the sheriff and whom I hadn't spent much time with, since he was guarding the judge.

After we checked in with all the major players and his mom said hello, Tommy asked me about the lesson.

"In a little while," I said.

"You said tonight. My bedtime's in an hour," he said.

"I know. I'll hurry," I said. "I have to work."

He made a nasty face then and slunk down to his room, thinking I was just like all the other stupid grown-ups.

It hurt, not only the reflected emotional thing from him, but it hurt me to be put in a category with all the adults in his life who had failed him. I wasn't that guy. I didn't want to be that guy. But if I had a snowball's chance in hell of keeping the vision from happening, there were certain things I had to do.

I dialed the number to the Guild's public relations office by heart. Kara's number. Kara was my ex-fiancée, currently married to someone else. She was one of the few people in the world in a position to get me what I needed—if she would. She also owed me from a few months ago.

She picked up. "Hello?"

"You work too many hours," I said, "and this is coming from someone who works with workaholics."

Kara made that clicking sound with her teeth I found so annoying. "No one asked you to criticize me. If you're calling about the debt, I swear there's nothing I can do. The Guild is changing its credit policies to increase cash reserves. That's applying to everyone—including the rank and file. If anything, you're getting a better deal than most."

I paused. Wait. This wasn't just a specific attack against me? "What in the world does the Guild need a ton of cash for?" I asked, a chill going down my spine. Probably another Guild First warmonger position; I'd run into their radical ideas a few months ago when I worked for the Guild to pay off a large portion of my debt working a murder case. At Kara's request.

She sighed. "You know I can't comment on that."

It bothered the crap out of me. Whatever was going on could not bode well for the normals, or probably for me. The Guild amassing cash reserves—on top of all the other

Guild First crap—wasn't good for anyone. But I had a hell of a lot on my plate already without adding that to the mix.

"Was there anything else, Adam?"

"Yeah," I said. "Yeah, I was calling out of the goodness of my heart to let you know about a potential problem the Guild should be dealing with."

"What's going on?"

I looked around the darkened house. No one was here immediately to overhear, and I was pretty sure they weren't recording outgoing conversations, not with the conversation we'd had the other day, and not with the judge so resentful of their presence anyway. But still . . . "I'm not on a secure line."

"Okay . . ." She trailed off. "You asking me to Jump somewhere?" She sounded tired. Teleportation across distance took up a lot of energy, and she hadn't been a courier in years, I knew. Plus, it was late.

"Not necessarily," I said. "You remember when we were talking about boxes back in August?" That was the code we'd used to talk about some Guild technology that was missing from their storage, technology too illegal and politically dangerous to be discussed directly. Sibley's device was a different technology from a different batch, but I was hoping she would understand the code anyway.

A pause while she thought about it. "The boxes that were missing from the vault?"

"Exactly," I said. "And then there was the very tiny box that you showed me in that holding cell, with Stone there, remember?"

"Um, the one that they made after telling me they wouldn't? The one the family got very upset over?"

"Upset" was an understatement; there had nearly been a Guild war over the device she'd shown me then, that device and the lack of communication on the highest levels of the Guild Council. Not that I rated Council access now.

"That's the one," I said. "I think I told you about a similar box that Sibley had?"

"Who's Sibley?" she asked.

"Remember when I almost got strangled to death?"

"No."

"Anyway, he works for Fiske, who I know you know about. The box . . . well, it's one of those trick puzzle boxes. You press a button and it . . . well, it 'marnififes.'"

She paused. "As in . . . ?"

"Yes." Marnifife wasn't an actual word; it was the verb form of a guy's name, Marny Fife, who at the beginning of the Guild was famous for influencing other people's thoughts and behaviors with coercive thought waves. It was against everything the Cooperist ethical system believed in, but it was still taught to schoolchildren as an example of what not to do. It was cheating, and coercive, and did not treat other minds with the respect due them as human beings. But it was effective, at least when Marny Fife did it. Kara and I and our school friends had used the term for anyone outside the ethical lines, but it still had enough of its old meaning, hopefully for her to understand.

"The box itself marnififes? And the people around it . . . ?"

"Yes," I said. "Yes, exactly."

"Oh." The word dropped like a bomb. She understood.

"I need you to look up the plans for the one you have in custody and get me the combination that will keep it from working," I said. "I'm not against a physical intervention to break the thing, but I really need a counter to it, or something to gum up the works. I'm in a situation . . . I can't be marnisifed," I said awkwardly. "I swear I won't share the information any further, but you guys can't afford to have these things on the loose any more than I can."

"Enforcement will want to get involved."

"We're in the middle of a high-profile case all over the media," I said. "In my opinion, sending a bunch of goons in Guild uniforms will cause more harm than good."

"You could be right. But here's the thing. If I send you a counter, certain parties here won't be happy. It makes the box in question useless. And you know I can't stall on this kind of information forever. It will come out, and I will have to answer to my superiors."

"I won't spread the information. You know me well enough to know that. And honestly, Kara, you've never liked this tactic anyway. It's not Cooperist. It's not Cooperist at all, and considering who has their hands on it right now, the Guild would be better off lopping off the head of this thing completely."

"Are you suggesting we take steps against normal criminals?" she said in a very flat tone.

"No, I'm suggesting nothing of the kind. That would be a Koshna violation," I said. It would violate the treaty that gave the Guild the right to rule itself, and considering the level of fear in the normals against the Guild right now, it might erupt into war. I'd been against this level of mind-technology ever since I found out about it; it violated the letter and the spirit of that treaty. But exposing the Guild wouldn't get me anywhere either, and I had the feeling if the Guild showed up in force I'd lose the FBI job, which I needed.

I sighed. "Hold off on the force, okay? I'm trying to play this as well as I can. I'm giving you the information and my best impression on how to resolve this to both our best interests. I will likely come face-to-face with this on my own; best-case scenario is that I take care of it quietly and either destroy the thing or return it to you. But you have to give me the ability to do that. I promise I will coordinate with you when this all is over with my best information about where to find it if it gets away."

She clicked her teeth again and made a little frustrated sound. "You keep putting me in impossible situations."

"Considering the recent adventures at the Guild, I really wouldn't complain," I said. Her request had put me in a series of ever-escalating situations that had nearly cost me my Ability and my life. It was over now, but I wasn't exactly happy over the cost. "Whether you acknowledge a debt or not, I did you a favor, a big favor that nearly cost me everything. I'd suggest you find a way to help me now."

I felt bad as soon as the words were out of my mouth. I didn't want to be that guy, the guy who played hardball to get anything done. I didn't want to be my father, who didn't care who he had to hurt as long as he won his court case and his client succeeded. I didn't want to be that guy. But apparently right now I had to be.

Kara didn't seem to respond as well to niceness, not now, not when her agenda for the Guild and all its complicated layers won out over me and my favors every time.

She was silent.

"I'm not asking this time," I said. "I'm telling you, get me the counter to this thing. It does neither one of us any good if it takes me out and the case goes bad in public. Worse if some idiot figures out why. That benefits the Guild not at all."

After a moment, she said, "I don't like it when you're like this."

It hurt me, but I said nothing. It would maybe save my life, and Tommy's life, to get this thing. So her hurt feelings didn't matter, couldn't matter, in that grand scheme.

She sighed. "I'll call you back tomorrow with a counter. Give me a number."

I did, and hung up, feeling guilty. But I'd gotten what I'd picked up the phone to get.

I found Tommy in his room. Guilt still hung around me like atomized cologne, and probably would for a week yet, but I'd do what I had to do to keep that vision from happening. To keep my promises. Starting with this one.

Not to mention, forward motion felt good.

"You wanted me to teach you stuff," I said. *About telepathy,* I added.

"Yeah," Tommy said. His voice was disengaged, but he was interested. He'd sat up and was paying a lot more attention.

I'd watched him in action, and he didn't seem to have any gift other than the common send-receive of telepathy. He hadn't been able to light a fire, teleport, lift things with his mind, or any of the other less common Abilities, not that I could see. And there was no way to test for precognition; it was something that developed in your teens, that woke you up in the middle of the night shivering in terror, or it wasn't. The brain had had thousands of years to develop a warning sense of danger, and some minds took that to the extreme.

So Tommy was a regular, plain, unleavened telepath. But from everything I could sense, he'd be a strong one—and strength made up for a lot of limitations, if you trained it right. And for whatever reason, his brain was still settling, still working itself into consistent telepathy. Otherwise he'd have been recruited by the Guild already. I had no doubt that would happen soon, though, and the more I could give him in the meantime, the better. Not to mention the more we'd have to work with if something really did go horribly wrong.

"You serious about the lesson?" I asked.

"Sure," he said, but he wasn't. He was tired, and distracted, and mad at me and everyone else a little. And I wasn't exactly at my best either.

"We'll do it another time," I said.

"You promised tonight," he said. He was slouched on a chair, and that wasn't a terrible position. You wanted to be comfortable, more than anything. But he wasn't taking it seriously right now, and sometimes posture led to a change in attitude. If we were going to do this, we would do it correctly.

"Fine. Grab a pillow and come sit down on the floor with me," I said, pulling a folded blanket to the floor. "You might try cross-legged. You want a straight back, though. That's the important part." I sat down, legs outstretched awkwardly in front of me. Cross-legged hurt my knees on a bad day, and I'd long since come to terms with that. I opened up my mind enough to let him read the information if he wanted to.

"Now, let's talk about what I do when I Mind," I said. It was as good a place to start as any, and he'd had plenty of opportunity to watch the action so far. It would also ground me in this job and this reality strongly, which I needed right now. "I keep track of the minds and the emotions in the surroundings. My range is maybe half a mile in all directions, more if the emotions are strong. I've seen folks with larger ranges, and I've seen folks with shorter ones. It has to do with how sensitive your brain is to the fluctuations in Mindspace."

I shifted and straightened my back, and Tommy settled himself across from me. He was cross-legged, of course, no pain. Kids were like that.

"What's Mindspace?" he asked.

"Mindspace is the space in which minds interact with the world, through a medium no one really understands."

Tommy made a face, not getting it, so I switched to "Imagine water, right? If you're in the bathtub and you move your hand through the water, the water makes these waves that run into the side of the tub, right? You move your hand faster, the waves hit the tub harder. There's more energy. Well, telepaths are like your hand—well, let's say they're goldfish in the water."

"Ew, goldfish?" Tommy made a face, picturing a bathtub full of him and goldfish equally.

"Let's say an aquarium full of goldfish and we're standing outside," I said.

"Okay . . ." The word dragged out of him. I was starting to lose his attention. Crap, it had been a long time since I'd worked with the younger ones.

"Okay," I said. "Imagine you're a goldfish, I'm a goldfish, your mom's a goldfish, and Special Agent Jarrod is a goldfish."

"Why are we all goldfish?"

"Because we're swimming around and the water moves," I said, holding back annoyance. "Like in the tub example. When you see in Mindspace, you feel the waters move and it tells you a lot about the mind whose emotions are moving things. When you're a telepath, you make stronger waves. Usually you're also more sensitive to the movements."

"I'm confused," he said, frowning.

I sighed. "Let me show you an example."

He looked at me. I looked at him.

You going to let me show you? I asked quietly, mind-to-mind.

"What do you want me to do?"

"Remember the sliding door I showed you how to make earlier? You'll need to push that aside for now."

"Oh. How do I do that?"

"Just think about pushing it aside and letting me walk into your foyer for a moment. Don't think too hard about it—it should happen on its own."

He frowned and did it.

"Good. Very good."

"Now what?" he asked, the words echoing in the foyer of his mind.

I knocked.

He told me to come in, which I did.

I stepped in and worked on increasing the detail of our shared house-picture. This wasn't a bad image for him to start with, and while it had its limitations, it wouldn't teach him too many bad habits. I solidified the walls, giving them texture and paint and wainscoting, adding pictures and a low table with flowers to the space. The entryway would be a dark wooden floor.

Tommy insisted it should be carpet.

Fine, carpet. I had him add some layers and texture to that, until it felt real. Until he could smell the space, which was always daytime, and be comfortable and happy here. And then I cheated.

I formed a thought the size and shape of a marble, or at least it would look like that from the outside. I showed him the thought, a shining marble sphere of light.

You ready? I asked.

He settled in, bringing a picture of his own body into the space as a stand-in for his mental self. Good, very good. Having a strong sense of self was everything, and he was already ahead of the game.

I dropped the shining marble, and it fell, slower than you'd expect from gravity, falling, falling until it hit the carpeted floor. It sank in, like a rock in a pond.

The carpeted floor fell too, then rebounded like the surface of that pond. Ripples spread out through the floor, hitting our feet and shifting shape, hitting the walls and making the walls ripple too like the smoke in a mirage, like the world with waves.

Cool, Tommy said. *Cool!* The projection he had of his body rippled and shimmered too, before disappearing. He was still here, just more diffuse. *Do it again.*

Come on back, I said. *Get yourself nice and present here, and go stand at the far side of the room.*

He struggled with that for a moment and then complied, an approximation of his body appearing again, until he walked over to the other side of the room. He was standing in front of the small table. The flowers, I noticed, had lost all their color, fading out once his and my attention had moved from them. I put some attention back and the petals sharpened, the color brightening. I re-added some detail to the shared world.

Now this time I want you to focus on what you feel in the corner, at that particular point in the room. I held up a "hand" to forestall his objection. *Yes, it's all in your head here. But if you can stay really conscious of that one spot in particular, it will make it easier to understand what I'm talking about. You can do it. I have faith.*

I formed a thought again, this one a little bigger, a shining sphere with internal moving clouds. Tommy was ready in his corner.

I dropped the marble, and it fell even slower, its mind-mass picking up momentum very slowly.

It hit the carpet, a larger stone in a smaller pond, and the world rippled. Deep waves emanated from the meet point, along the carpet, at the table, through the walls. Tommy's self rippled too, but he stayed present enough to feel the shape of the world moving through him.

I gave him a minute to be excited and to think about what he'd felt; then I said:

It's different when you're looking at the whole of the world. I'll show you that in a minute. But we started here, where you can feel the energy moving, on purpose. Most everything in the world moves in waves—like that—and while your brain tends to read the waves like listening to sound—you aren't always aware of the shapes of the information coming at you—it's always there. This is how Mindspace and the world in your mind and other people's minds really works. Knowing that can let you manipulate things to get some cool effects.

The room around us was slowly diffusing, slipping away into more and more vague pictures. It would disappear in a minute; Tommy was focused on what he'd just experienced and I wasn't spending a lot of energy to maintain the picture either. I kept just enough for the feeling of a three-dimensional room with carpet, and let the rest go.

Can you surf the Mindspace thing?

I laughed, startled. What an incredible image. *Maybe,* I said. My old mentor, Jamie, could move Mindspace in a virtual tsunami, could make the world crash in on you. Mindspace moved just that big, and if you could ride that energy somehow . . . *Maybe one day you'll figure out how,* I said. *Telepathy and all the rest are still young sciences. There's still a lot of corners to explore and things to figure out from scratch.*

He thought about that, and the edges of the room moved away still farther, until we stood in a white box with diffuse light.

Not everybody can see Mindspace for themselves, and it's probably too early to know for sure whether you can or not, I said. *We can try to build you up to that later. But for now, want to see what I see when I Mind?*

Sure!

I let the projection go, and settled him in an observer

position, strapping him in like the second seat on an impossibly big hang glider. I went slow, letting us transition out of his mind, out of him in control, and back to the wider world with me driving. Then, once he and I were both comfortable, I opened up my mental eyes and drifted down into Mindspace.

The world became the depths, a place where light did not exist and was not needed. But I could still see, still perceive like a bat echolocating through the night. His mind was behind mine, tucked up on my back like a set of wings, blind and unaware.

I invited him in to see with my eyes, feel with my senses. I was slow, and awkward, not having done this in years. There had been a time when I could do it with an entire classful of students at once, a gift that had made me rare and valuable beyond price to the Guild. I couldn't anymore, and that hurt. But there wasn't time for guilt, or regret, or anything else in the moment. This moment was for teaching.

Where are we? Tommy's voice came as he stared through my eyes.

Mindspace, I said. *Mindspace at your house. This can be dangerous, realize that. But it's wondrous too. Don't go looking on your own; promise? And I'll show you what I see.*

Sure.

I got the impression he'd have agreed to anything at that point, just to see more.

I broke down the world into its eddies and swirls, and surfaced enough to see the minds around us. Loyola, asleep in a chair at the front of the house, his mind like a rock in a lake, largely weight and no interaction. Mendez, like a water bug skimming along the surface, very aware of her surroundings as she paced the property line outside, hand on her gun, looking for an excuse to use it. Jarrod, deep in structured thought like lists of numerical values in some color-coded chart, as he weighed pros and cons of some decision.

The judge upstairs, worrying about the FBI and the situation she was in. I skimmed over her quickly, making a mental note to return later, to ask her the questions that had been brewing awhile. But now was not for that. Now was to show Tommy what was possible.

I moved out, to the street, to the edge of my range, careful to go slow and not to lose him or disorient him in this new space.

There are so many of them, Tommy said. *So many.*

Minds dotted the street, up and down in the houses, some sleeping, some not. A cluster of school-aged girls in the closer house, watching some kind of scary movie as a group. A couple having an argument farther down the road. Mind after mind lined up like eggs in an endless carton, disappearing at the edge of my range. And closer, a man walking his dog, the dog's simple thought shapes popping off him like cartoon bubbles.

Maybe Tommy could see Mindspace after all; those cartoon bubbles certainly weren't how my mind interpreted the world.

I could feel him tiring, already; you worked for years to develop the endurance to stay here long, to control your telepathy for any length of time, and I'd had to work like heck to get mine back when I'd lost it. I may never get it all back. But what I had I was grateful for.

I'd have to tell Swartz that, at our next meeting. I was grateful for the control I was getting back.

Ready to go back? I asked Tommy.

Yeah.

I left slowly, quietly, pulling us both back to the real

world and our bodies with the utmost of gentleness. His
wonder and sorrow at leaving mixed with all the emotions
bubbling up inside me, until we surfaced, and I let him go.

He took a minute to wake up, and yawned.

"Let's get you ready for bed," I said.

I'd forgotten how much I'd missed teaching. I'd forgotten . . . Tommy was going to be special one day, and I
wouldn't be here to see him grow into it.

Not that it would matter if Sibley got ahold of him.

A few minutes later I went to the kitchen to get a glass of
water and found Judge Parson sitting there, in a thick robe
over flannel pajamas buttoned all the way up to her neck.
Her hands circled a chunky mug full of tea on the kitchen
table. She looked at me when I came in, like she was daring
me to challenge her right to pajamas in her own house. I
declined.

Instead I fixed myself a glass of water and came and sat
down next to her. Her body language stiffened when I sat,
but I stayed anyway. I was getting more and more concerned about Tommy, about the vision, and since he'd gone
to bed it was only getting worse. If Cherabino had been
here, she would have said the judge was one of the apexes
around which this whole case turned, and yet the judge was
avoiding me. The fact that I had seen her hardly at all in
two days was like a red flashing light.

"Tommy and I watched part of the trial today," I told
her, after a moment of silence.

Parson shook her head. She really didn't like having me
here. "He should be doing homework."

"He did that already," I said. "He wanted to know what
you were working on. Especially if it was important enough
that he was attacked to stop it."

"It was a bad idea. Yesterday's testimonies would have

been entirely inappropriate for a child. Today was better, but you should have checked with me about the content before you presumed to let him observe."

"You seem stressed," I said. In the interview rooms, this would be a real flag.

"Of course I'm stressed. I have a major media trial to preside over—one in which the ADA's star witness has disappeared—and letters containing death threats arriving at my office. Not to mention my child, whom you keep insisting on bringing into danger."

"The star witness has disappeared?" I asked her. That was right—I'd heard about it a week ago in the papers and again from Mendez. I refused to engage with her on the her-kid-in-danger topic—I was here to help, and if she couldn't see that, she wasn't paying attention.

She nodded. "She disappeared. She was a licensed prostitute, who was supposed to testify that she saw the defendant beating his mistress to within an inch of her life that night. The lady of the night left in a hurry, so she didn't see whatever the final blow was, but it establishes a timeline and puts a considerable weight of suspicion on the defendant. The ADA says she was very concerned at depositions about her safety—it's possible she went underground for her own protection."

"But you don't believe so," I said.

She shook her head again. "The kind of people that work with this man . . . he's been associated with more than one serious high-level criminal. If you believe the charges, he beat Savannah's premier escort to death, breaking her jaw and thirteen bones in her body before she died. The lady of the night may have been right to fear for her safety. I have the difficult decision of whether to admit her deposition as evidence now. Taylor has a right to it, so far as it goes, but if she's left town, it does cast her credibility into doubt and the defense will use that to full advantage."

"If someone else has made her leave town?" I asked, meaning, someone killed her.

"The police will track it down eventually. They always do. But I don't think they're going to do it in time for this trial, and I'd like to get it buttoned up enough that we're unlikely to get an appeal."

"You think he did it. You think he killed his mistress."

She paused for the critical moment that made me believe she did. But what she said was "I think he's entitled to a fair trial. And so will every newspaper and television station who's sent a reporter." She paused, discomfort sitting on her strongly. "Some of them are running the story of what happened to my son."

It felt like she was going to say something more, but then she didn't. "What are they saying?" I asked. I hadn't watched TV since I'd gotten here, but clearly the media were important to her. If they were escalating the situation with Fiske or whomever else, I probably needed to know about it.

"Some of them say I'm brave to stay around despite everything." She seemed uncomfortable with that, and shying away from something. "Some say I'm a villain for ruling so harshly against him at times. Pappadakis has quite a following, since he's active in charity circles. They run tape of him feeding the hungry, or visiting the orphanage, and he can do no wrong. Anyone who knows the truth knows he's involved in shady deals. Anyone who knows the truth will know I'm not the criminal here. He's accused of beating a woman to death, for crying out loud. The media is being unreasonable."

"Why are you getting attention and not District Attorney Taylor?" I asked her. "Seems strange. He's the prosecutor."

She shrugged. "It's the reality of the situation that a woman in my position is more remarkable than a black man in his, at least here in Savannah. Add in a child in danger, and the media will enjoy reporting."

"It bothers you."

"Yes, it bothers me. I preside over a jury trial! They decide innocence or guilt, not me. The ADA lays out all the damning evidence against this monster in sheep's clothing. And yet I get the time on the media with people questioning my every move. And the letters! I get death threats daily in the mail, and Taylor gets maybe one a week." The world was an unfair and unjust place, she thought, and her ex-husband and the FBI poking around were only making it more stressful for everyone. She didn't really believe another attack was imminent, and anyway, she'd much rather focus on the things she could control and get this trial done beyond reproach.

I took a moment to reflect, to let her reflect, but she dampened down her thoughts with all the suspicions of a cop in front of a telepath. No additional information there; she didn't trust me.

So I tried a different tactic. "You realize that in all of this, you've never talked about Tommy in terms of anything but his impact on you?"

"I'm doing the best I can," she said immediately, even though it was clear she wasn't. "I'm a single mom with a high-level critical job, and we both must adjust as best we can."

"Why take him out of school when things get rough?" I asked. "Why not just let his father pick him up and take him for a while?"

"Quentin is a criminal," she said, almost spitting the words. "He's a criminal and a manipulator and a liar. He'll tell you what he thinks you want to hear, and he'll use it to manipulate you, even if it doesn't make him money. Tommy will take on those qualities over my dead body. Nannies are the far better choice."

"You don't spend a lot of time with your son," I pushed, sensing a secret or a frustration here.

"I do the best I can!"

"You don't act like he's very important to you, and I don't understand why you would have married Quentin if you hate him so much."

"Tommy was an accident, okay?" she said, nearly spitting the words. "Quentin deceived me and married me, and then I was pregnant. There wasn't a choice. There were only decisions. There are always decisions. I'm a single mother, and I'm doing a decent job."

I didn't think she was, and it must have shown on my face, because she said, "You don't get to judge me. You don't get to judge me, not with your history."

"What history?" I said, just to see how far she was going to take this.

"You don't think I do research on the people I let around my son? Does the FBI know you're still in Narcotics Anonymous?"

She was lashing out, and while it still stung, none of this was a secret from anyone. I was far more interested in what she was deflecting attention from than my own stuff right now, though maybe that was because of my phone call with Kara. Either way, I was chasing this down. "Technically that's anonymous, thus the name. In my case it's not a secret. Every employer I've ever had has known about my history and my recovery. What I need you to tell me now is, what are you hiding?"

An overwhelming sense of fear, and then anger, anger like a tidal wave.

"I'm not hiding anything," she said, but even the most rookie interrogator in the world could have seen she was lying.

"You know I know that's a lie. Are you certain that Pappadakis is the one sending the death threats?"

I saw her consider whether to walk out, and finally settle for an angry "It's not him; it's the don, you idiot. He called me twice and as much as said who it was."

"What does he want?"

"There's some kind of trade going on. I recuse myself from this case, or I let in suspect evidence from the defense, neither one of which I'm going to do." A complicated set of feelings attached to all of that, and that overwhelming anger. "Because Pappadakis is under his protection or something stupid. So apparently he gets to get away with beating his mistress to death. The man thinks he's going to manipulate me into letting him throw the trial, but it's not going to work. I've got the jury sequestered, and the police are on board. Thus far we've blocked three attempts at influencing the jury members, and it's getting worse. It's a lot of pressure, but the pressure's not right. Nobody gets to flaunt the law just because of who they know. I shouldn't have to deal with this, but it's here and he's not going to flaunt the law on my watch. It's just not going to happen."

That was all true, so far as it went. But there was something she was holding back, something more complicated, and it was almost, almost there, but it slipped out of my mental fingers like sand.

"So, when you didn't do what they wanted, they attacked your son to make you?" I asked. "Why didn't you call the FBI yourself? Were you already working with the police?"

That created yet another round of anger and complex emotions. "If you have to ask me such ridiculous questions, you're clearly incompetent. Go guard something. I have other things to do with my limited time. Like actually adjudicate."

She stood up, sloshing her tea over the table, and walked out.

Interesting. I cleaned up the tea, trying to figure out what I'd learned, and trying to figure out if she'd try to get me fired—and if that would work. In Branen's department, the answer was probably no. Branen played politics well, but he generally played them for his own team, and she wouldn't count. Whether Jarrod played the same way or not was yet to be seen.

A lingering sense of guilt hit me, from Kara, from Parson twisting the knife. It did sting. I did feel guilty. But Judge Parson was just another interviewee, in a way. And whatever was going on with her, she was lying her ass off, and putting her son, Tommy, in potential danger along the way. She was hiding something, and she was lashing out to do it.

I wondered if she had a good reason, or if there was something deeper going on. Either way, if it got in the way of Tommy's safety, I had no patience for it. I had a kid to keep safe, and a vision to stop.

CHAPTER 14

I went out into the main area, pretty sure I was going to see the judge complaining to Jarrod, but no. It was quiet, darkened, with only a few lamps brightening the space. Jarrod was nowhere to be seen, and a quick scan of the surroundings placed his mind upstairs somewhere, asleep. The judge as well, though it took me a moment to think about it to identify her.

I worried about what was going to happen, and I worried about Cherabino's job and her sanity, with me not there for her if things went bad. Mostly I worried about me, and I tried not to think about my cravings for Satin, a cigarette, a way out.

I forced myself to be useful. I scanned the rest of the surroundings. I was here as a Minder, after all. Sridarin was out in a car across the street, along with the usual neighbors up and down it. Loyola was outside on the porch, feeling cold, bored, and watching for danger. I could see his outline faintly through the window in real space when I surfaced.

Mendez sat at the crosshatched thin folding table with a stack of paperwork. She looked up when my footsteps came within a few feet of her during the scan. Her angular face seemed more angular in the light, the lamp setting deep shadows into her face.

"Guess the paperwork never ends for most cops," I said. Maybe she'd let me stand here awhile. She was the closest thing I had to authority I understood, to someone like Cherabino or Paulsen, rather than Jarrod, with his more complicated old-school style. She felt more familiar, and I needed familiar right now.

"How's Tommy doing?" she asked me. She was tired, bone tired, and missing her girlfriend, which I understood but wasn't allowed to comment on.

"He's okay," I said. "Nervous. Can I ask you a question?"

"Sure, what is it?"

"Can you walk me through what you have with the case so far?" I asked. "Specifically with the death threats. I think I'm missing something with the judge." If I was going to be awake anyway, I might as well be working.

"The death threats were sent by US Mail, so we had jurisdiction when the senior staff attorney called us," Mendez said. She pushed her notebook aside and pulled over some of the stacked folders from next to her.

"Why haven't I seen the senior staff attorney?" I asked. "I've been in and out of her chambers and here at the house."

"She's at her mother's house until all of this blows over. She was very concerned about the attack," Mendez said. "Loyola talked to her, and all of our background checks held. She has alibis, and the judge didn't object to her being gone for the foreseeable future. If anything, they fought."

"They fought?" I asked.

She nodded.

"What did they fight about?"

"She didn't want her to call us, supposedly, but she said she'd talked to one of the bailiffs and they thought it would be best, considering how much coverage the case was already getting in the media. They didn't want it to turn into a conflict of interest, or the appearance of one, where the police and the prosecution are responsible for the life of the judge. Judge Parson has vigorously denied any such issues."

"She doesn't seem to want us here," I said. "Any idea why?"

Mendez shrugged. "She's said some things in passing, but I don't think it's as big an issue as you say it is. People don't always appreciate having federal agents around poking into their lives, and trust me, we did a lot of poking in the hours after the attack."

I was used to being extremely involved in a case, and sitting on the sidelines with imperfect information while other people did work was frustrating me. "What kind of poking?" I asked.

"The judge had been talking to the police about the case and the jury sequestration steadily until last week, when we get half the calls logged. There was an incoming call about then, and according to the staff attorney she reacted badly. As near as we can tell, it was another death threat of higher quality. She doubled the bodyguards she already had on her son and changed her routine."

"Which should have been enough," I said.

"Maybe. But the attack happened anyway. And she hasn't been steady since then."

"Do you think she's afraid for her life?" I asked.

"I don't know what I think. Jarrod's having us track down additional case details, so I'm working on that."

"Okay," I said. I was missing something; I knew I was missing something. "Where was Quentin in all of this? The boy's father?"

"We don't know," Mendez said. "A lot of what I'm doing is trying to track his movements."

"He seems genuinely loving of Tommy," I said.

"Doesn't mean he's not threatening his ex-wife," Mendez said. "Or behind some of these other things. A lot of times perpetrators like to hang out and watch the FBI work. I don't think it's likely, but it is one of the things we're looking at."

"So the letters are the key. They're why you guys were called, right? Walk me through the letters again."

She pulled them out. "As you can see, the ones we're concerned about all had that paper weld to them. Before you ask, no, that was a dead end. A library model and we couldn't get respectable fingerprints."

I thought about that. "How long do you think this case will take?" I asked.

"I don't know. This has been a pretty strange case. We don't normally work protection duty, and most all the time we get called in on kids' cases they've already been taken. I'm not complaining. It's just impossible to say what's normal. You might ask the sheriff's department, since they handle a lot of security locally."

"Did you ever get back a physical workup on the letters?" I asked.

She pulled another folder over. "Yes . . . yes. Assorted pollens consistent with the Southeast. The older ones seem to be from somewhere north of here, away from the ocean, some of them with Atlanta-consistent pollution markers, but the ones we're worried about change—the last one has a marsh-flower pollen on it."

"So whoever it was was here?" I asked.

"That's what it looks like. Assuming we can trust the pollens didn't cross-contaminate. The letters were stored together."

"Do you think we have a viable threat against the judge?" I asked. "Against her son?"

"Yes, I do," she said. "The local air force base had a storeroom with more than a pallet's worth of equipment missing since the last inventory. There are weapons out there, more than just the ones used in the attack. Enough weapons to be a viable threat even against all of us."

A chill went down my spine. "When was the last inventory?"

"Four months ago."

"So someone could have stolen the military gear we saw?"

"Yes. In fact, I think it's likely that it never left the city. ATF is tracing its sale through that gun shop we were investigating."

"You think they're going to be used against us. Whatever's left from what was stolen."

"Yes. I see no reason to think otherwise."

I processed that for a long moment. Just when I'd thought this situation couldn't get any worse . . .

"This case is turning into a snarl for you," I said finally.

She shrugged. "It wouldn't be the first time the FBI coordinated between a handful of departments. Whatever it takes to get the job done, or at least that's what Jarrod says. The ATF should find the weapons before they're used."

"Should?"

"Hopefully," she said. "But keep your eyes open."

After a night of very little restless sleep and a lot of worry, I woke up when the first ray of sunshine puddled down the wooden floor to land in my eyes. My bones hurt, again, from sleeping on a cot in the middle of a hallway. But either they didn't hurt as bad or I was more resigned to the pain; I got up and stretched, my knees protesting, before finding a stale pastry of some kind in the kitchen. I even found—and successfully made—a decent pot of simcoffee, so the day was already working out somewhat well. That is, if you ignored the danger hanging over my head and the general lack of sleep.

People were stirring, and Sridarin was outside keeping an eye on the street. Tommy was sleeping deeply two rooms away. But no one was in the kitchen, and there was a perfectly good phone there. It was also about seven, more or less when Cherabino usually started her day. Maybe I could check in on her, have one less thing to worry about for the next few hours.

I dialed her number. It rang twice, and she picked up.

"Mmrph?" she answered. It was kinda cute.

"How's the hearing going?" I asked, probably too quickly. "You okay?"

"No," she said, and sighed. I could hear the rustling of fabric, probably her sitting up. I could picture her rubbing her eyes.

"Did I wake you?" I asked.

She cleared her throat. "Well, I probably had to be up in fifteen minutes anyway. How's the case going in Savannah?"

"I'm making progress," I said. "It's a nontrivial threat level. The new boss is strict, but that's nothing new. I get the feeling they're not letting me in on all the case details, but I am the Minding consultant, not the detective consultant. But the threat's bothering me, worse the longer nothing happens."

"That's normal for any kind of protective duty," Cherabino said.

After a moment of silence, I offered, "Still, it's strange." I thought about mentioning that I'd seen Sibley again, but I didn't know what I would say.

She made an agreement sound, but I could tell her heart wasn't in it.

"Why aren't you okay?" I asked.

She blew out a breath. "So the lawyer called character witnesses for me. Like, half the department."

I nodded. "She said she was going to."

"Branen stood up for me. Boyles stood up for me. One of my ex-partners drove in from his retirement cottage on the beach just to speak up for me."

"That's great," I said.

"It was. It sounded good. And then . . . well, I told you they're putting it in the papers, right? Some kind of watershed police brutality charge."

"I thought your lawyer was getting that thrown out!" I half yelled, then lowered my voice and looked around the half-empty kitchen with chagrin. "That doesn't make any sense. You were clearly set up. The date was just a coincidence. They have to know that. And the union's on your side, isn't it?"

She made a frustrated noise. "Internal Affairs doesn't think so, and they're letting reporters in the room. They never do that. The union's on my side, sure, for now, but even it doesn't want to do too much to support 'police brutality.' Honestly I'm disgusted with the whole thing. This is everything I ever hated about politics, and if Chou wasn't there fighting for me, I'd be in a very bad place. He says at this point it's not even about me. It can't be, and he's saying . . . well, he was saying we'd beat it by getting people to speak for me. The politics are just politics, he said, and they'll blow over. But I'm not sure I believe that."

"Why not?" I asked. "I mean, they don't really have anything but the witness testimonies, right? And those have to be overcome by the folks speaking for you."

She took a deep breath. "Well, no. They've brought in some old things and some evidence. They pulled my file and are reading it to the whole room. They got that rookie I hit when Stephens picked the fight with me to say I started it. And they . . . they're bringing up what happened after Peter was killed. They say I was too harsh on the guys who killed him. Too harsh!" Her voice broke. "Bastards are still breathing and they say I'm too harsh. They have to be building a case for some kind of political reason."

"What else?"

"Isn't that enough?"

"You said evidence," I said, my stomach knotting more and more as we went. "You don't throw around words like that without a reason. What's the evidence?"

A long pause, with her breathing not exactly steady. "They found my fingerprints on the pole. I think I told you that. The angle . . . the angle, it's what they say you'd need to beat the guy to death."

Holy crap. I closed my eyes. I was there. It couldn't be true. It simply couldn't. Guilt and shame and hurt for her mixed up in my guts. "Could it be one left over from the fight?" I asked.

I could almost see her shaking her head. "No."

I took a breath. "It's not like you can't fake fingerprints. I'll drive up, I'll tell them what happened, and we'll go from there. Um, I may need to bring a ten-year-old with me. Do you think we can find him a spot at the department? Maybe get Andrew to watch him?" It would break every rule they had here, but she needed me. I couldn't not go.

"What are you doing with a ten-year-old?" she asked.

"Minding, I told you."

"You can't testify," Cherabino said.

"I have a record, but so what? I saw what happened, and that has to matter to someone."

"The lawyer said you can't testify. We're dating and you've already . . . it's not going to look good for me to be dating a felon. And a telepath. Okay? It's on the record, and they'll probably bring it up, but then the lawyer will bring up your records and your saving my life. I asked. Twice."

"What do you mean it's not going to look good with you dating a felon?" She'd never used that word before. Never. It hurt.

"It's the lawyer's concern, I'm sorry. I . . ." Her voice broke. "I need you to just be okay, okay? I'm doing the absolute best that I can right now. I need you to understand. I have to get through this, and the lawyer says he has a plan. I hope—it has to work. It has to."

"What was the third thing?" I asked, emotions tight like a guitar string with too much tension. One move would break it.

"Fiske is scheduled to testify today against me."

I stared straight ahead. "What?"

"Yeah. Garrett Fiske. The man who plays poker with the devil and who we know—but can't prove—is involved in half the nasty stuff in the city? Yeah, that guy. Apparently he and the mayor are friends and the mayor thinks he should tell everyone how violated he felt when you and I told him to back the hell off. Apparently it's fine to threaten my nephew and Lord knows what else, but the minute we—"

"Fiske?" I interrupted, still unable to believe it.

"Yeah."

"Garrett Fiske? How in hell is he testifying in a police building?" I asked, everything else disappearing in the face of that one central stupidity.

"And you want to know the worst part?"

"What?"

"The fingerprint is half-smudged, like I tried to wipe it off the thing after I was done. It's a bang-up job. The lab's sure the timeline fits exactly—apparently the oil and sweat were the right age. They wouldn't go into details even when I bribed them. It looks pretty damning." She huffed again.

"That's . . . that's. . . ." I didn't know what to say. How could they have found a fingerprint if she didn't leave one? I hadn't thought she'd touched the pole at all.

"Adam?"

"What?" I said.

"You were there, right? I didn't do more than rough him up a little, right? You're sure I didn't kill him?"

I closed my eyes. If she was doubting herself, it really was bad. "Yeah, I was there. He was alive when we left him. Alive with a few bruises and a headache. He was even awake."

I paused then. Had I hurt the guy? Was this my fault? "It wasn't an aneurism or a heart attack or anything like that, was it?"

"You were there," she said. "Half his face was caved in. Whoever killed him did it with their fists and that damn pole."

"Oh," I said. I remembered that now. It all felt so far away. It had been a long few days, a few days that had felt in some ways like months had gone by. I felt like reality was shifting underneath me as surely as it had shifted in Tommy's mind after the marble. "You didn't do anything wrong," I said. "You certainly didn't kill the guy." And I believed it. I did. But the whole thing made me very tired, and far more worried than I had been.

"I'm going to fight. I have to fight," she said, but she sounded tired too.

"Of course you will. You sure you don't want me there?" I said.

"You've got work, and you need the money. Plus, I've got to keep it together and I'm not sure you being here will help with that. If you can't speak for me, I'm not sure anything else is going to help." She paused as I tried to figure out whether she was lying. "Where are you anyway?"

"Savannah," I said. I thought I'd told her that, but who knew? I wasn't happy right now. I was worried for her and offended, still, a little. And I missed her, her absence like a sore tooth.

"I need to get ready for work now," she said, and added a good-bye in a tone of voice she knew I wouldn't argue with.

"Bye," I said to the empty dial tone. She was running away again, and this far away, there was nothing I could do about it.

I sat at the kitchen table, another cup of simcoffee and a stale piece of bread with butter in hand. I stared at the scarred wood tabletop while the coffee went cold and the bread got even staler. I tried to not feel offended, and to make connections. It was beyond belief that Fiske would be involved here in Savannah and be testifying against Cherabino and it all be unconnected. But for the life of me I couldn't see a common thread. It still felt like it was all falling apart, or would. I could see the vision coming now, and I didn't know how to stop it. The same for Cherabino, whose job I was now afraid was really, truly in jeopardy.

The phone had rung earlier, and they'd picked it up in the main room. Tommy was stirring in the other room, doubtlessly woken up by that phone, and me trying to get the energy to go check on him. The surroundings seemed clear in Mindspace; I'd checked while I drank the half a cup of simcoffee that I had. That didn't mean I wasn't still jumping at shadows, trying to get ahead of Sibley. It was only Friday. Or just Friday. We'd have the weekend after this, not have to go into the courthouse, maybe. Would that make things worse or better? I wished I knew.

Jarrod came into the kitchen then, saw the coffeepot, and grabbed a cup. He seemed . . . agitated. He also carried a crisp new file folder with some things in it.

"What is it?" I asked, pulled out of my own obsession only out of force of habit. In the other room, Tommy was getting more active and I'd have to deal with him soon. Jarrod looked at me while stirring the coffee. "Maybe I can help," I said. I needed to do something useful right now. A phone call to Swartz had only let me leave a message with his wife, not talk to him. Something useful and distracting would be great right now, pull me away from thinking about cigarettes or Satin or running away. "What's going on?"

"Maybe you can," Jarrod said. He came to the table, bringing the coffee and the file folder. "At least ask some questions from a new angle. So you know the team's been investigating the attack?" he said.

I nodded. "Something about working with your federal contacts?"

"Yes. The staff attorney called us because of the death threats via US Mail. That's our jurisdiction. Guarding witnesses technically is not, but since there's a telepathy angle here and we work with nonaffiliated telepaths, we've been given authorization to extend our responsibility. In any case, we've been asking questions through our existing contacts and comparing lists."

"Lists?" I asked.

"People with access to military resources, either in

surplus or off the air force base in town. People matching the loose description of the attackers you gave us. And, most recently, the list of people who've called the gun store in the last six months. If we get a hit on DNA from the scene there, even better."

"I'm pretty sure Sibley killed the gun store owner," I said.

He nodded. "You told me that."

I looked at him more closely then, feeling the edge of his exhaustion under the agitation. There were circles under his eyes, deep ones. Likely he hadn't slept much more than I had. It made me like him a little better.

"What's the issue now?" I asked. "Other than the fact that there's a hit man out there who easily wants us all dead and seems to be threatening the judge directly?" I still hadn't told him about Sibley's mind-control machine, and after my conversation with Kara last night I thought that unless he'd listened in on that conversation, I probably shouldn't tell him. I didn't want to be the start of a Guild-normals war. But I also didn't want the team to get blind-sided.

Jarrod laughed, a dark sound. "Other than serious danger and a ten-year-old? And the fact that the judge can't tell us anything useful? That should be enough. Even if we still can't connect Pappadakis or anyone in his company or staff to the killings yet. We've got locals tailing half a dozen people, trying to get ahead of the issue."

"But it's not enough," I said, my stomach sinking. "That's what you're saying. It's not enough."

"No. There're six names on our final list, suspects I wanted to track down today and have a talk with. I had the local police put out an all-points on them. Standard procedure so that somebody with more manpower brings them in if we can manage it. I got some notes on their usual habits from a detective who's dealt with them before at about two last night." He stopped, and his mind felt . . . shaky then.

"You've been busy," I said cautiously. "There're several of us who can get on the phone and help."

Jarrod nodded slowly. "We need to go down to the FBI lab today sometime and figure out what evidence they collected at the attack scene and if it can tell us anything."

"I don't mind going. Labs are educational," I said. I'd bring Tommy with me. "A moving target is harder to catch, right?"

"Depends," Jarrod said, and sighed. "Priorities have shifted, though. That last phone call? My APB came back. Four of the guys on the suspect list were found this morning."

I leaned forward. "Found where?" He meant "found dead," didn't he? That was what his mind was saying.

"Found in the marsh, by a conservationist working on a pollution-cleanse. Apparently the ties on one of their ankles came loose."

"Dead," I said.

He nodded. "Dead, with their throats cut in a thin line, in a pattern the detective who called me had never seen before. The conservationist goes to that section of the marsh twice a year at most. It's sheer luck he found them, much less that I got a response on my APB."

"Throats cut in a thin line, like a strangulation device?"

"Yes." He thought, as I did, that this was Sibley's work. "It's suspicious that the four most likely suspects for Tommy's attack all ended up dead."

"Okay, I don't get it," I said. "There's absolutely no reason for Fiske to want these people dead if they're working on behalf of his buddy Pappadakis."

"Assuming they are, in fact, working together as we

think they are," Jarrod said tiredly. "We keep hitting dead ends on this one. Honestly if that bodyguard hadn't gotten Tommy out of there that morning, I'm not sure we would have been able to find him so quickly. His father doesn't seem to have any involvement whatsoever. The letters are a dead end—"

"How hard is it to fake a fingerprint?" I asked him then.

He blinked at me. "It would take some knowledge and skill, but the materials are freely available. Why?"

"Would someone who knows what they're doing be able to make a partial with a smear?" I asked. "With oils that are the right age?"

"That's a whole other level of difficulty," Jarrod said. "It's highly unlikely anybody would go to that much trouble, in my opinion. Usually a complete fingerprint in the right place will get you anything you want. And, as I'm sure you've learned, people leave their natural fingerprints everywhere. Again, why?"

"Unrelated case," I said.

"I don't pay you to work other cases while you work for me," Jarrod said.

"It was one phone call with a homicide detective I work with all the time," I said. "It's not a big deal. She was just getting another perspective. It didn't affect this case at all."

He looked at me, unconvinced.

I looked back.

"You take a lot of phone calls while you're here."

I felt guilty, like I'd done something wrong. But I hadn't, I didn't think. "You wanted me to leave on three hours' notice, right? I'm here, but there's stuff I can't leave undone. I'm keeping it under control. I really am."

"See that you do."

I nodded, and then that thing that had been bothering

me about this conversation came back up. "I still don't get why Sibley would kill those guys, much less dump them somewhere where no one will find them. It's not like him, I don't think. As near as we can tell, Fiske pays his guys well. It's not good for his organization if he gets a reputation for killing contractors randomly."

"You've worked on a case against Fiske directly?" Jarrod asked. Now I had his full attention.

"That homicide detective I was talking to? She was a member of the task force against him. I'm not surprised that you can't connect Pappadakis with any wrongdoing; if he's taking lessons from Fiske, he's going to be good. In several years, they've never been able to make evidence stick against Fiske. Witnesses end up dead. Judges are paid off to exclude evidence. But if you talk to the guys on the street, the 'big boss' calls the shots. You do what he tells you, or you clear things through the organization, you're fine. You get paid. Everything is great. Fiske has a reputation for being ruthless in business, but he doesn't move without a reason. In his own way, to the guys he works with, he's one of the fairest organization leaders they've had in a long time. Not that he won't slit their throats in a heartbeat—or have his guys do it—if they cross him. It's why he's stayed in power so long, and why he's been able to expand his territory this far south in the last few years."

Jarrod thought about that. "So he only kills people that go against him, which makes sense. Let's take it a step further, though. Why were these guys going against him? Why kill them specifically, if they're good little soldiers?"

"All of this assumes Sibley is still working for Fiske. For all we know, Pappadakis or some third party could have hired him to do this work."

Jarrod shook his head. "Either way, I don't see the benefit of killing them unless it's to shut down our investigation. It's like someone is going through systematically and closing down every possible avenue we have of connecting A and B. It sounds to me like it's completely in line with what we know about this group anyway. Ruthless and self-serving."

"I don't buy it being all the same people, though," I said. "There have to be at least two—" I stopped midsentence, having just realized that Tommy was standing in the doorway with wide eyes. I'd known, on some level, that he was there. There weren't any threats anywhere in the area— both of those things I'd been monitoring steadily for hours. But I hadn't thought to keep him from overhearing things.

"Who is killing people now?" Tommy asked in a very small voice.

"No one is killing anyone," Jarrod said, like denying everything would put the genie back in the bottle.

Tommy's expression closed like someone had slammed a door. He turned to go.

I sighed and went after him.

In the hallway, I said, "Hold up."

He turned back, rebellion in his every line.

Probably I should lie to him, but I didn't see how that would help. And I didn't want things coming out later. So I tried. "The unfortunate truth about investigating bad people is that that they don't always do what you want them to do. Sometimes they do bad things before you can catch them."

"Who did they kill?" Tommy asked, unable to help himself. He wasn't happy, but he also wasn't shutting down.

"A gun store owner who may have brokered the deal, and now some of the people who we believe attacked you." He probably already mostly knew about the gun store owner, but telling him officially might as well happen now along with news about the other deaths.

"The guys who attacked me are dead?" Happiness and sadness mixed inside him like the ingredients to a grade-school papier-mâché volcano, ending with a burst of fear. "Does that mean I'm safe now?"

"I don't know," I said.

He looked up, and his mind wanted comfort, wanted a hug. It went against nearly every habit I had—telepaths don't touch as a rule, and I'd been working with the police for years, who were just as much against touch—but I reached out and hugged him, awkwardly.

He grabbed onto me, shivering, emotions still roiling inside him in ways he couldn't quite cope with. He was grabbing my clothes, at least, so the skin-to-skin telepathy increase was minimal. But those emotions were overwhelming, even from a distance, even from the outside.

I didn't change anything; I didn't manipulate or cause anything. But I stood there and let him shiver, and helped dampen down his emotions from the outside, small structural changes to help him feel more in control. Just at the point where he could think again, I stopped. He needed to feel what he felt.

"There's too much dead," he said then.

"I know," I said, feeling it too. He missed his bodyguard, and he was terribly, terribly afraid now that I would die just like her.

But he hadn't said it out loud, and I didn't want to lie and tell him that it couldn't happen.

Loyola knocked on the hallway side, a dull thud of fist impacting wall.

I looked up.

"We need to leave for the courthouse soon," Loyola said. "Sridarin and the judge left twenty minutes ago, and Jarrod doesn't want us separated for any longer than necessary."

Tommy pulled away from me then and rubbed his face. "Nobody can die today, okay?"

"Okay," I said. I hoped I could keep that promise.

And then he turned and went back to his room to get his toys together.

CHAPTER 15

I was still at the house. Tommy was moving slower than Jarrod wanted, and Loyola was back there trying to hurry him up. Even Mendez had asked for another ten minutes to pack equipment. Jarrod was in a mood, and I was spending time on the opposite side of the house so I couldn't feel it.

The phone in the kitchen rang, and I picked it up.

"Is this Adam?" Kara's voice asked.

"Yeah. Let me call you back on another number," I said.

"Um, okay. I'm at the office."

Ignoring Jarrod's impatience across the house, I grabbed a jacket and walked across the street to a pay phone and dialed. This was more important than a ten minutes' delay.

A woman walked her tiny bioengineered dino-lizard past me along the sidewalk. The thing hissed as it got near to me, its mantle rising and turning red-yellow. She glared at me like this was somehow my fault and pulled the lizard along forcefully. It went. Nasty thing, it was like a blazing sign of wrong priorities. Get a cat from the pound; cats were free.

Kara finally picked up the phone. "Guild Public Relations Office. Kara Chenoa."

"It's me."

"I want you to know we had to get an engineer and a Structure guy to work overnight."

"Huh?"

"For your stupid demand. For that influencer device. We had two pros work overnight on the thing on my request directly. My superiors aren't happy with me. But we have a solution. You aren't going to like it."

"That was fast," I said. Then, awkwardly: "Thank you."

"I didn't do it for you. Honestly the Guild needed this. That's what I told the departments, along with the request for discretion. If it's out there, we need to be able to counter it."

I tried to take that personally and just couldn't muster up the energy. Kara played for her own team, always had, and lately maybe it wasn't bothering me quite so much. At least not if I got what I wanted. "What's the solution?"

"Is the line secure?" she asked.

I turned around and scanned the surroundings. With the exception of the woman and her dino-lizard (currently peeing on a flower bed two hundred feet away), no one was around. "No. But it's a public phone I doubt is monitored. Say what you're comfortable with." It was chilly out here, but not outright cold; warmer today. Hopefully it would stay that way, though in late February even in the South I doubted it.

A pause. "We're not going to get any better?"

"No."

"I'll chance it, I guess. You remember your Structure basics?"

"I used to teach the stuff, Kara."

"With your history, I didn't want to assume."

Okay, that one hurt a little. Mostly how she said it, dismissive and judging, with hidden weights, more than the fact of my drug history. She'd been the one to turn me in to the Guild. Maybe it shouldn't surprise me. "You going to tell me or just string me along for another half hour?" I asked. "I'm running out of time here." I really was; Jarrod would be out looking for me at any moment.

"So, the mind has thirty-six set points for telepathic communication, yes?"

"Yes. Which are we changing and how?"

"You remember them by name, not just position still?" she asked.

I was irritated. "Yes, I do remember, Kara." It was a valid question; I'd had a lot more opportunity to do practical hands-on work than teaching in the last ten years. But I was tired of being asked the same stupid questions over and over again. "Give me the answer, okay?"

"The pro wanted me to be absolutely sure." The rustle of papers, and then her voice changed to read something. "A1, B5, B7 through 9, A13x, and C4 need to be closed, as fully closed as possible. HL7 spun up as much as you can hold. And . . . you're really not going to like this. Processor 4 muffled as much as you can stand."

I closed my eyes. "That one processes all the senses, not just telepathy, Kara! You screw with it too much the wrong way, and you're blind and deaf until somebody comes to bail you out. I don't have anybody to bail me out down here. And with those comm points closed, really, Kara?"

"I told you you wouldn't like it."

"Why in hell do you have to make so many changes? That's like spinning three plates on your head while you do the tap dance samba singing 'Yankee Doodle' over a pothole. There's no way I can do all that, not and Mind my charge."

"You're Minding now?" Kara asked. "You're not certified for that."

I could hear her disbelief, disbelief and judgment. "They cared more about non-Guild talent than credentials for this job. It's legit, and that's all I can say. I didn't misrepresent. And it's a good thing I am here, considering. Who else would have called you and put up a fuss? I need to know, though. Why so many mind-changes?"

She sighed, then offered resentfully, "They aren't exactly sure what part of the mind the interference waves are manipulating. It was trial and error, honestly, with the version we have. This was the first combination that worked. You want an answer quickly, you're going to have to put up with some fuzzy edges."

"The mind has plenty of fuzzy edges all on its own," I said.

"Yeah, well," she said, in that tone of voice you get when someone complains about the weather. "What are you going to do? I don't like you taking Minding jobs."

"It's not like you have a vote anymore," I said. "And you put pressure on me to get money. You can't get too particular about how I get it, now can you?"

"It doesn't have to be like this, Adam."

"You're the one who started it."

She sighed. "I got you your answer. Please keep your side of the bargain. I really need that device to not get out in the normal population."

"Don't we all," I said. "Tell me that group of sets again, slower this time, please."

"Try to listen this time." She repeated the numbers, and I paid close attention.

Then she hung up on me.

"Good-bye to you too," I said.

It started to drizzle, a cold, cold drizzle that interacted with the nasty gray fog in a way that made me think pollution, and nasty pollution at that. I wanted a shower, but there wasn't time.

Jarrod stood on the back porch of the house, tapping his watch. I nodded and moved faster.

I just prayed the information Kara had given me would be enough.

And then I went back in to deal with Jarrod. I was only ten seconds later than Mendez and got away with a single, frustrated wave to hurry up.

We made it to the courthouse with maximum alertness and minimum excitement. Then, after a long and careful procedure, Tommy and I settled into the judge's chambers for the morning. A long morning. Hours passed, hours during which I was on too-high alert and was fighting off worry—and a craving for my drug—only through sheer will, because Tommy was watching me.

About noon, I couldn't take it anymore. I was starving. And losing track of my emotions. A walk would do me a lot of good, but I couldn't leave him either. "Let's get lunch," I said to Tommy.

He sat up, thought he was hungry too, and started picking up the toys strewn everywhere.

"Leave them," I said.

Tommy looked up.

"Really. We'll clean them up when we get back. I'll help."

"Okay," he said. He was nervous about leaving stuff in his mom's office. She'd get mad.

"It'll be fine."

"If she gets mad, it's your fault." He stood up and got his coat.

"Fair enough."

We moved out into the now-crowded hallway at lunchtime. I could still feel his nerves over the general cacophony of the surroundings. Now that I was moving, mine were settling. A little. I still wanted . . . a lot of things I couldn't have.

"What do you feel like eating?" I asked him.

"Food," he said.

"Very funny." I pulled us to one side of the hallway, close to the benches. For security's sake, I should get Loyola or Mendez to escort us. When I went to locate their minds, both were halfway across the courthouse, busy in something mentally demanding. I looked around. There were a *lot* of people here, to the point it felt overwhelming in Mindspace. I couldn't see us being in a lot of danger in this kind of environment.

"What are you waiting on?" Tommy asked me, not happy.

I sighed. "Nothing, I guess. Let's go." We'd go to the busiest place, the one all the jurors were going to, close enough to the courthouse that everyone could get there immediately.

The deli across the street on the opposite corner from the courthouse was to the right of the newspaper kiosk I'd seen Sibley at earlier, but it was crammed with people, with no danger to be felt anywhere around. I remained alert but kept moving. Inside, it was standing room only, a line for the food all the way to the door. But a group of courthouse employees—led by a bailiff—just abandoned a table as we got near. I dashed forward and sat, hurriedly, uncaring of the abandoned plates.

An old lady gave me the stink eye, but I'd claimed the table fair and square. Tommy next to me leaked a little embarrassment, but he sat down.

Another group of three pulled the second small table away from ours and sat down too, talking steadily like a flock of geese. The old lady harrumphed at them.

I ignored Tommy's embarrassment and started collecting

up plates. "Let me clean, and then I'll get in line. You hold the table. What do you want?"

Ten minutes later—after watching Tommy like a hawk from ten feet away—I was back with a tray, two sandwiches and two flimsy veg-fiber cups, one with water for me, one with some sugary neon drink Tommy wanted. He perked up when he saw it, and I got the distinct impression his mom didn't let him drink the bright green stuff.

I settled the food and unwrapped my sub. Fluffy ciabatta two inches thick cradling a bounty of thick soy loaf, artisan lettuce, fresh tomato, two thin strips of grown bacon, and mustard so sharp it cleared your sinuses. Good stuff.

Tommy had half his drink gone already and his sandwich barely unwrapped. The surroundings were loud, constant chatter filling the space like the constant thoughts, raindrops falling on the surface of a lake. Tommy seemed distracted—very distracted. I realized I'd closed off my mind in self-defense.

I opened just enough to remind him mind-to-mind, *Remember the house? You need to slide your door closed and pull the curtains a little.* I paused, knocked on his mind, and when allowed, helped him build rudimentary defenses against the chatter.

When I settled back into the real world, the deep line in his forehead had disappeared. He opened up his own sandwich and tore into it.

"Thanks," he said, his mouth full.

"You're welcome."

"How many people have you saved?" he asked, after his next bite. I saw that tinge of hero worship again, and didn't know what to do with it.

"A couple," I said, a little uncomfortable. "I've only worked with the police for a few years, and mostly they have me doing interrogations and helping with crime scenes. There's nobody to save at a crime scene; you're there to figure out what happened."

"Oh," Tommy said. I expected him to ask me about crime scenes, since we'd been to one already and there'd been that display in the courtroom. Instead he asked, "What did you do before you worked with the police?"

I paused, putting the sandwich down. Questions about my past were always tricky, particularly in a context like this. "I was a professor at the Guild for a while," I said. "I taught the advanced students for Structure." It was true, so far as it went, and I was prepared to talk about it in depth, answer all his questions.

He ate the sandwich a little more, cut peppers falling out of it onto the tray.

I let him think; I could feel the thinking. He knew he'd be a telepath, and I'd answer whatever questions he had about telepathy in as much detail as he wanted.

But instead he asked, "Why'd you change jobs?"

I took a sip of the water, to buy time, and to try to decide what to do. My past wasn't a secret—everyone I'd worked for since rehab had known about it in advance. And the kid had a bad habit of pulling information out of me without being able to control it. Details coming out later under bad circumstances would be much worse than telling him now. As much as telling him now wasn't the best choice either.

I put the water glass down. "I changed jobs because I got addicted to a drug named Satin, something the Guild was experimenting with. I took it way too far, and I don't think they work with it anymore—but there we are. I had to put my life back together. I've been clean almost four years."

"You take drugs?" His voice was too loud. We were attracting attention.

"I've been clean almost four years," I said again, in as calm a voice as I could manage. "I didn't lie to you," I said, deeply embarrassed by all these strangers staring at me, judging me with thoughts that leaked through my shields. It would have been way easier to lie to him, and now I wished I had. "Look, let's talk about this."

"Whatever," he said in a tone of voice that didn't invite further discussion.

"No, seriously," I said.

But his attention had moved, across the street looking through the window at something I couldn't see. He was frustrated at me, that much I had felt, but now the feeling turned to something like . . . longing.

I turned. There was a school bus in traffic, pulling up in front of the courthouse.

He was on his feet now, putting his napkin down. "That's the field trip. They're doing the field trip to the courthouse." Flashes of friends from school shuffled through his mind like a pack of cards, and that frustration and longing coalesced into movement. He was walking out.

I left the paid-for food on the table and followed, dodging condemning thoughts from the old lady and all the others. So I hadn't picked up after myself. This was more important.

Wait up, I sent to Tommy as he moved to the crosswalk. That kid was slipperier than a fish on a line. Worse, because there was no line. *You know you need to stay close to me.*

"My friends are here," he said, words heard more with my mind than my ears. "You're a liar anyway."

I stayed a pace or two behind, my lungs struggling as I broke out into a half run. Tommy was already halfway across the street, headed straight for that school bus full of kids—it was his school district written on the side of the bus, and a teacher with Ability lead the way into the courthouse. Kids everywhere.

She greeted Tommy when he came up to her, and I stood impatiently on the side of the street waiting for another break in the traffic. I never should have told him. I never should have taken him out of the controlled situation in the courthouse, no matter how hungry and anxious I was. I should have tied him to the damn chair in the deli, something. A black sedan with tinted windows stopped in the middle of the street with a screech of tires, nearly getting hit by the car behind it, which reared up on its anti-grav to stop the collision; the sedan bounced back, then up, above the car behind it, before settling with the driver cursing up a storm. I threw myself to the side, away from it. What the hell?

The sedan crossed traffic—highly illegal—and screeched into a spot next to the school bus.

The teacher yelled at the kids to back up, but they all were staring, not moving.

Four men got out of the sedan. Four men in ski masks, one of whom had a mind I knew, a mind I'd been looking for in the crowd for days.

The kids yelled now, but it was too late. I was running, uncaring of the cars, thirty feet to go. Only thirty.

One of the guys was Sibley; I was sure of it. And he was here. I didn't how in the hell he was here, but he was. Everyone was reacting.

And worse, he had an object the size of his hand, and he was lifting it up. Crap! The device. I was in trouble. There was no way I could block the device, not here, not now. My heart spiked with fear, but I ran harder.

But—but—he dropped it like a stone on the ground, and a blinding flash came. A noise like immeasurable thunder.

And I was on the ground next to the bus, a hundred

minds around me overcome with confusion, my mind overcome with a kaleidoscope of pain. I couldn't think. I couldn't breathe. And distantly, I felt Tommy's mind panic, panic on a whole new level.

They were taking him, I thought, before I passed out. They were taking him and I'd failed. I'd failed.

CHAPTER 16

Pain flew across my cheekbone and I woke up. Mendez had her hand up to slap me again, but I grabbed it. Our minds half merged for an instant before she knocked me out, pulling her hand away with a shocked and nasty look on her face.

"That was unnecessary," she said.

"Your fault," I said, and struggled to sit up. "Touching a telepath with no warning is bad for everybody. How long was I out?" I demanded from a mostly seated position. The grit from the roadway was under my hands and I only saw cars forward and back, cars, Mendez, and two uniformed police officers.

There was a man darting across traffic coming toward us—my sluggish mind identified him as Quentin, Tommy's father.

I grabbed Mendez's sleeve—the sleeve, not her arm, and pulled her toward me. "Where is Tommy?" And what in hell had Sibley thrown on the ground? I hadn't been prepared for that. I hadn't understood that.

Her face went completely blank. "They got him." I'd fallen down on the job, she was thinking, but with that kind of coordination, the bad guys had been planning something for a long time. "They shot a security guard and the kids said they took him away. The guard shot one of them first, though. They left him behind."

I released her sleeve, stomach and head both feeling sick, and pushed myself swaying to my feet. The world wobbled, but I breathed deep and breathed through it. "I need to talk to the guy they left behind."

"He's out cold," Mendez said. "Jarrod wouldn't let him go to the hospital, but the paramedics are working now. He may not wake up."

I checked my body, checked my mind for damage. I wasn't good, but I was functional. The bad part, though— the connection I'd had with Tommy was torn, like a mostly unraveled rope in the back of my brain, just holding on by a thread. I didn't dare mess with it for fear even that would break.

It had happened. The thing I had been working against, fighting against, missing Cherabino to prevent—the thing had happened. The vision had happened or would happen. It was inevitable now, and every second I delayed in acting was one more chance Tommy would die.

Tommy—the kid—the interesting, slippery, fun proto-telepath I'd been guarding, he could die. He could truly die now if I didn't do something.

I was angry now, angry and guilty and worse. "I need to talk to the guy," I said. "I don't care what it costs us."

They'd taken the attacker into an internal room of the courthouse, what looked like the break room for the security personnel. Two of them stood at the front, defensive and ready to fight.

I told their minds I was okay and pushed through. Either they'd fight it or they wouldn't, and Mendez was less than a minute behind me. She could sort it out.

Inside, Jarrod and Loyola and two paramedics stood over a guy in a ski mask currently on a stretcher at hip level.

"He's going to bleed to death," the first of the uniformed paramedic hissed at Jarrod. "I've got one bag of blood in his type, and we're through that. You're costing a man his life."

"He doesn't—" Jarrod saw me then. His lips were in one thin line.

"I'm here," I said. "I can get the information. You want to know anything other than where they've taken Tommy? I'll have seconds, at most." I didn't add that I'd likely cause permanent damage to the guy—memory loss if he was lucky. Information retrieval from someone who was unconscious was a brute-force, cruel thing, but I'd had the training and right now I didn't give a shit whether I hurt him. Not if it would save Tommy's life.

"You can't talk to him right now," the other paramedic said, a woman this time, and calmer. "Not a chance in hell. You let us take him to the hospital and get him real care, you can talk to him in a few hours. Otherwise he's going to die for no good reason."

"Do it," Jarrod said. "Location is all I want."

I paused, conscience fighting with the desperation of the situation. "Be aware this is unethical," I told him.

"You get me the information in the next ten minutes, and I'll authorize any tactics you take," Jarrod said.

I didn't know whether to be grateful or irritated, or even to hate him. But I didn't have time to do any of those. Tommy's life was on the line, and it was my fault. I stepped up next to the stretcher. Loyola was looking at me differently, like I was a threat now. He didn't approve of torture, of any kind, and he was sure I was about to do something he would call torture. He wasn't wrong.

I met the woman paramedic's eyes. "You want your patient to survive, you will back up at least four feet. You do *not* approach until I give you the okay. That applies to everyone," I said louder. "Give me three minutes and then you can take him to the hospital."

The paramedic looked at Jarrod; Jarrod nodded, and everyone backed up. Loyola had his hand near his gun. He thought he was surreptitious, but I saw the decision in his mind.

It didn't matter. I took a deep breath, and regretted. I regretted this already, and under any other circumstances I'd kick myself in the ass before I'd even consider it. But Tommy had been terrified, and it was my fault. That vision—that horrible vision—was very likely to come to pass unless I moved now.

I forced absolute calm. Then, ruthlessly, I did something I'd only ever done once before, in a life-or-death situation directly authorized by the Guild. I dove directly in an unconscious man's mind, without permission. I wasn't gentle—I couldn't be—but I wasn't any more cruel than I had to be either.

I surfaced, feeling exhausted and dirty, exactly two minutes later. "Patient's yours," I told the paramedics, and sat down in one of the chairs on the outside of the room.

I would say this for them; they moved. In the space of two deep breaths, they had him prepped and out the door. It slammed behind them.

And I hated myself. I hated myself intensely in that moment, for crossing that ethical line. I'd have to live with it for the rest of my life, and it would hurt. But if I could save Tommy, I would take on that and more.

I looked up at Jarrod. "Keenan didn't know what the final destination was, but they're abandoning the car just outside River Street and moving on foot for a little over two miles until they hit the next transport."

Loyola scowled at me.

"Where on River Street?" Jarrod asked, his tone of voice urgent.

I shook my head, the bits of memory and discussions and decisions that weren't mine floating around like snow in a snow globe, refusing to settle into patterns despite my desperation. "I'm still sorting the images," I said. "Probably I'll get it on the way." I prayed I would get it on the way, or I'd crossed that line for nothing.

Jarrod nodded, then spoke to Loyola. "I need you to stay and coordinate with the locals and the house security to get a grid search going. I want the major air routes shut down— shut down, you understand? Along with the ports. I'm trusting you to get it done."

"I'll go with the teep," Loyola said flatly. "You've got more favors out in this city than I do right now, and we need it fast."

Jarrod thought, then nodded.

"You going to be able to handle this?" he asked me, in that tone of voice that cops use to make a question an order.

"Yeah," I said, and pulled to my feet again. I felt like utter and complete crap, but I was functional and the vision—and Tommy's panic from earlier—would not let me go. I would push through the pain. "I'll handle it if it kills me."

As we entered downtown, I was still sorting through the images in my head. Loyola sat next to me, his disapproval tangible in the air of the small car.

I couldn't think about what I'd done to that man, not now, not even as I was rummaging through his memories with everything that was in me. I had to think about

Tommy, not my stupidity and failure at losing him, not his death in the vision, but the possibility of saving him. To stay sane, at any cost I had to think of saving him.

I wanted to run away. I wanted my drug with every ounce of my body. It didn't matter. If there was any chance in hell I could save him, I had to try. I had to believe I could.

The van crossed over some invisible boundary, and the tires started bumping on cobblestones, *bump, bump, bumpity-bumpity-bump*. The driver from the sheriff's department hit the anti-grav then, and we popped up two feet before settling with a lurch that bothered my stomach. The car skimmed barely above the ramp then, occasionally touching down with a tap against a higher stone as it made its way down to the river. Using the anti-grav was an energy-expensive way to do this, but that was what the fusion drive was for, and the gravity fields didn't interfere with Mindspace, so I didn't really care. If anything, though, it made the car move slower down the cobblestone ramp.

Around us were a mix of very old and very new buildings, all either two hundred years old or built within the last thirty. As we got farther into downtown, the new ones gave way almost completely to the older. A few buildings were vacant, abandoned, and the air felt strange around them. I wondered how much pollution they had, and what the impact of the Tech Wars had been around this area. There were some strange toxins that had gotten out in Atlanta—had they had similar or worse here?

The driver brought the nose of the car up with a lurch, and the tires went *bumpity-bump* on a level surface then, buildings on our left, the river on our right. He found a flat parking area next to the river, pulled into a spot, and turned back to me. "Where are we going? I've given you all the time I've got."

"Give me one second," I said, and held up a hand when he was about to tell me off again. "Just one."

Heart beating too quickly, all the pressure of the world on my shoulders, I tried one more time to force Keenan's fractured memories into some semblance of order. He knew they were going to the cobblestone area, on foot. He knew roughly where it would be, but we were already in the rough area he'd specified. I was frustrated, and I felt like crap, and I was genuinely worried about Tommy. I used that to push aside all of the other worries, and focus.

I went back to the fragile connection half-broken in the back of my head, and it turned on like a lightbulb. I backed away, and it disappeared, then approached, and it begged for attention. This was strange. This was so strange. I could feel his fear, and a desire to talk to me or anyone who could help, and more important, those emotions came with a sense of direction.

"Where is he?" Loyola asked me, his disapproval loud and clear between us.

"I don't know," I said, eyes still closed. "But I can tell you direction. Let's play a little game of hot-cold." I pointed in the direction I was feeling.

The driver asked, "How far?"

I thought about it. "He's moving, but not fast. Keenan's buddy said they were going to move by foot at one point. It's . . . up. They're above our level, maybe on one of those ramps down."

Loyola had an affirmative feeling, like he was nodding. "On foot, then."

River Street was a long street squeezed in between a muddy river and a wall of ancient buildings with the occasional covered tunnel; its ground-level shops saw little sunlight in the wake of the height of the buildings on top of them. On the ground floor, boarded-up and abandoned buildings rubbed shoulders with stately restaurants and tawdry tourist shops. A tattoo shop on the ground floor under an overhang advertised bioluminescents in the window, but its door was a supermaterial advertised to be break-in proof. A small stream of tourists dressed brightly walked past a homeless man half in an alley full of cobblestones and trash.

Above, a man leaned out over a metal railing of a hotel balcony, the intricate shapes of the metal nearly lost in the coating of old rust. He smoked a cigarette and looked down on the dark street below. In another window high up, a woman stood in profile wearing very little. In another, a sign advertised accountant services. River Street smelled, of mud and perfume and old sweat, of bright dreams and dead hopelessness, of mold and mildew mixed with the freshly cooling pralines from the candy store at the street's end.

I felt overwhelmed. This was an old place, a place that advertised ghosts for ghost tours, and I could feel them, not spirits left behind—so far as I knew there were no spirits left behind—the debris and remaining emotions of hundreds of years of continuous human habitation, of death and danger and hope and love all baked together like the layers of a lasagna Cherabino's grandmother served at Sunday dinner, layers and layers of one thing after another until they baked into one messy, settled whole. Mindspace was dense here, and full of echoes upon echoes. It was also full near to bursting with people's minds in every direction, which made it hard to keep Tommy's fear in front of me. Years of Guild training made it possible—but only just, like the half-heard memory of a song from two years ago.

Worse, Tommy's fear-sense was getting quieter. He was tired, and there would eventually come a time in which even Guild training wouldn't let me pick up the signal. I kept myself very, very still, straining to hear that signal.

I kept following that sense to a ramp intended for cars, winding up to the street level above, cobblestones threatening to turn my ankles with every step. Loyola followed behind, like a shadow of disapproval. A restaurant was to our right, a cloud of fried smells hitting me as a door opened to their back alley, part of the main cobblestone riser here. A man in a dirty apron emptied a trash can into a dumpster with a *clang*.

The feeling ended here for a moment, but when I stopped and concentrated . . .

"Where is he?" Loyola rumbled.

"You're not helping," I said.

"Sorry," he said, but he wasn't. He wanted this over with. He wanted something to shoot, and it didn't have to not be me.

My brain didn't want to focus. I didn't want to focus. I felt like crap. But there was a kid's life at stake, and I'd already had the strongest warning the universe was capable of giving me. I pulled on brutal training to force myself to do it. And the answer didn't make sense.

Tommy was ahead, directly ahead, on the other side of the dumpster a hundred feet or more. The restaurant ended to the right; there was literally nothing on the other side of the wall. And yet that was where his fear was coming from. I'd better move; it was getting even dimmer as I waited.

I walked forward, holding on to the signal with mental hands turned white from pressure. I walked forward, forward and to the left, up the curved sloping surface of the alleyway. And there—there it was, on the other side of the dumpster. A grate.

The grate was maybe two and a half feet high, old iron bars like the ones you saw in jails in old Westerns, three up and down and one side to side. It was low, but behind the bars the sunlight fell on a dirty few inches of cobblestones even lower, and extended deeper in an impression of darkness, darkness that extended several feet. There was a tunnel there, and by the looks of it, it was a tunnel big enough for a man to stand up in, perhaps hunched over, perhaps not. Three feet wide at least, and maybe five up and down. Who would have put such a tunnel system there?

"You're looking at the grate," Loyola said.

"Yes," I said, and leaned down. I pushed back on the bars, but they didn't budge. Low on the ground were scratch marks, though, scratch marks like someone had put some iron thing down to pry open the bars and then set them back in the stone. I leaned forward farther, and there on the ground was a crowbar. But it was on the other side of the bars.

I'd put on some weight since I'd gone clean. I'd lifted a few weights—normally under protest, in the police gym. But I was still thin, thinner than I'd been as a professor. You burned up a lot of calories with Ability, more with Satin that hit that part of the brain over and over, and it took a long time to add weight back.

I bent over and grabbed one of the bars with one hand, reaching through with the other as far as my hand would go. Still shy of that crowbar.

"What are you doing?" Loyola asked me.

I'm finding where they went. Give me a minute, I said into his head, so nothing would echo down the tunnel I suspected Sibley and the others were walking down even as we spoke. I sighed, pushed up, and took off the long coat. It was chilly out here, and colder at the grate, but nothing was as cold as the knowledge that Tommy's fear—that fear I'd been following for the last hour—wasn't here anymore. The coat hit the ground with a plop I could feel.

Then I squeezed my shoulders through the two central bars. It hurt. The dress shirt wasn't any padding to speak of, and the old iron pulled, a jittery rusty scraping that hurt. I *pushed*—and the widest part of my shoulders was through. I held my breath, and pushed again, and found myself caught. My fingertips were one inch from the crowbar, one small inch from my goal, and the bars kept me from moving any farther.

Then it happened. The bars moved. With a low *errrie,* then a *squee,* and I was falling forward, chest caught in the bars.

A hand caught my foot. I stopped falling, catching myself on my hand in a ridiculous wheelbarrow position from field day at the Guild's school.

The bars were still attached to the top of the tunnel, bowing out now, while my body slid slowly down, the gravity pulling at my shirt until it tore, and the rust abraded my skin, and then I was mostly free—and would be, if I let myself down on the dirt-mold floor.

"You sure they're down there?" Loyola yelled in, his voice echoing.

Shut up, I sent, but it was probably too late. I pulled at my foot, and he let it go, and I tumbled down, getting a faceful of the nasty slime-dirt over old cobblestones. Hard cobblestones. The whole right side of my body hurt. But I pulled myself up to a crouched standing position and looked back.

"Come on," I said in a voice pitched not to carry. "I can't feel them anymore and they've got to be moving fast."

"Get reinforcements," Loyola told the driver. "See if you can cut them off."

I lifted the grate—which, apparently, was on a set of rusty hinges—enough for him to get through. He cursed, low, not liking the nastiness, not liking to crouch. He liked even less having to get so close, only inches away in the shadows as we pushed the grate closed again.

He leaned down and grabbed the crowbar to offer me. "Here." He had a gun, he thought. "Don't hit me with it."

I looked at it. "What do you want me to do with a crowbar?"

"Take it and move," Loyola said. "We're not getting all the way down here just to lose them."

I took the crowbar, its ancient iron heaviness an ominous weight in my hands. I thought I heard, at the edge of my hearing, a distant scream of a kid. Even if it was just my imagination, it made me move.

Loyola took point, his overly prepared belt already bearing a flashlight. Unfortunately the flashlight's organic-cell battery hadn't been charged in over a year and was probably already degrading; the light flickered dully in the space and looked a little green, literally. That was the only light we could see, as the tunnel grew narrower and I bent over deeper, feeling like the ceiling was literally caving in on top of me. And still we kept moving. Still we moved, the only sounds we heard the beating of my heart and the squeak of my now-wet dress shoes on the nasty tunnel floor.

I hadn't had claustrophobia going into this tunnel, but the deeper we went, the more I thought I'd have it when we came out. Mindspace was dead and cold here, still like a century of stillness with one group of focused minds—and a line of terror—leaving a thin, already-fading trail for me to follow. And above, ten feet of dirt at least like a heavy weight ready to drop at any moment. I could hear water running, close and far, and it terrified me. The water table was low here, and tunnels liable to collapse at any moment. They must have scooped these out during the Tech Wars for them to have lasted this long. It didn't mean they wouldn't collapse today.

I heard Tommy's fear again, in the inside of my head, for one split second before it faded again.

"Why in hell would somebody run this way?" I asked, apparently out loud.

"Thought we'd never find them," Loyola said, annoyed. "Not for you or a bloodhound, we wouldn't have." He wasn't happy about this fact. He also didn't know what the hell we were going to do if we caught up to the bad guys, in this small space with limited visibility. Radios wouldn't work. We'd be on our own.

"Which way?" Loyola hissed.

I squinted and looked ahead, my back bent nearly double trying to keep my face out of the ceiling. There were two tunnels ahead, equally big, both of which smelled of mold and old air.

"The one on the right," I said, after a bare moment's contemplation, most of which was spent getting my mind to focus past the pain. The rapidly fading Mindspace signatures went in that direction.

Loyola kept going but took out his gun now, flashlight set on top of gun, both pointing in the direction of the tunnel we were headed down. The gun barrel blocked half of the already-dim and flickering light so that I saw a bright spot at the barrel and the rest of the world got even dimmer in contrast. The air seemed to haze as we went down this new tunnel, and the ceiling opened up another foot. Loyola moved faster.

I followed and worried, dully, about the quality of the air. This was an old, old tunnel, and there were worse things to be found in tunnels than broken sewers and tainted water. I wanted a canary, artificial sensor or real bird. I wanted to know if I was going to die well in advance. I wanted not to be here at all, to be honest, and wouldn't be, except for one important thing: Tommy had been here before me, and I could think of no hell so bad I wouldn't still go after him.

My old brain injury started to act up, in the darkness, tried to make light where there was none. I started to see halos ahead, halos and artifacts of moving air and light and who knows what else. Mindspace and reality lost their clear edges as my brain tried desperately to build a picture of the world; it was disorienting and worse, because I felt my precog, my stupid stubborn future-sense, try to get in on the act too.

The Guild told you to get lots of sleep and eat well. The Guild told you to scout out your surroundings and plan ahead, and know reality. At worst, they told you to build a steady sense of reality in stolen glimpses of other people's vision. There were blind men at the Guild who saw just fine like that, through others' eyes, through Mindspace and overlapping views of the world. But this—this was everything the Guild told you not to do. This was like Satin, like my days on the street, like the days when my senses took over for one another and the world bled joy and pain as two sides of the same coin.

It scared me, and it scared me deeply. I'd spent years—years—trying to get away from this feeling, from this merging. And if there was any way to surface away from this and still save Tommy, I would have taken it in a heartbeat.

"You okay?" Loyola asked. He shone the light directly in my eyes.

I winced and shut my eyes hurriedly.

"You can't just stop here. How much farther are they?" *How much farther did the tunnel have to go?* his mind asked me. He was scared too, under this much dirt. Scared and depending on me to have the answers.

I saw the flashlight clearly then, and realized it was still being held as a unit with the gun. Now pointed at my head.

"Point that thing elsewhere," I hissed. He did.

Then I considered. I was back in reality—for the moment— and he was clearly needing some touchstone to the world right now.

There's a time to tell the truth, and there's a time to lie. When you're in the middle of a horrible tunnel and you can't see and your mind is busily trying to take your senses apart one by one—and you're with a cop of whatever stripe— this is not the time for the truth. Even less so when he's faltering.

It hurt, but I'd been in the interrogation rooms long enough to know when believing in something—even falsely—mattered.

"They're a couple hundred feet ahead around a bend," I said quietly. Totally made up, but details would sell it. I added mind-to-mind, *Only luck they haven't heard us already. How do you want to handle this?*

His heart sped up, but he settled then, in that total-focus mental place I'd seen in nearly every cop I'd ever worked with under pressure. "You get Tommy out of the way somehow—floor, wall, whatever—and I return fire," he said. His face looked like a ghost's in the half-light, features coming in and out of focus.

You return fire? I asked incredulously.

"Do you really think they're going to come all this way and not fight to get away?" Loyola said.

Do you really think the bullets won't ricochet and kill us all? I asked.

"Oh," he said.

"Yeah." Then I felt the weight of that crowbar I'd been carrying all over again. I'd been using it as a walking stick, on and off, something to help me bend deeply enough not to hit my head. But it would work just fine for a weapon, wouldn't it? If I could see enough in the dark to do any good with it.

You get a good shot, you take it, I told him, *but you don't fire wildly. I'll do my best to take out the others.* I hoped I could live up to that. It all came down to what Sibley was carrying. I hadn't seen the evidence, but then again I hadn't believed that he had really been here until it was too late. It was my guilt, mine, that drove all of this, and I would do everything in my power to stop it.

"The others?" he asked.

"No matter what you do, you aim for and take out the bald one," I said. "No matter what." If we both tried, maybe one of us could do it. "Tommy is our priority, but unless Sibley is out of the way there's nothing we can do."

"Do you know something I don't know?"

Down the tunnel, I heard a slam, echoed several times over but close. Wait. Did my brain guess at the right answer without me getting involved? Were they really, truly only a few hundred feet away?

Then there was a spot of light, ahead, ahead, and it was gone. Had someone just exited the tunnels? Had they been there all along? I felt like I was losing track, like the world was running faster than I could keep up.

Loyola was already moving ahead, and I followed, crowbar a heavy weight in my hand, knowledge a heavy weight against my conscience. Should I stop and try the complicated mental blocks Kara had given me, just in case? I pulled together the ones I could do quickly, without preparation, as best I could while moving. But that was B5, C4, B8, a bank of the A's. Nothing specific enough and extreme enough to carry it. Anything more on no notice, under this much stress, and I risked putting myself in that half- or total-blind-and-deaf state. I would do no one any good there, as bad as I was already. I might get worse, much worse.

I buttoned up what I could, as close to the prescribed pattern as I could manage on no notice, running after Loyola, praying I wouldn't hit my head in the dark. And then I prayed—literally prayed—that it would be enough.

Loyola stopped and I hit a corner. Pain—pain!—across my head and neck. Mold smell as I backed away, mold and brick. "What?"

"Damn," Loyola said, and kept cursing under his breath. "They've blocked it off."

"Where are we?" I asked, moving around the corner, hand out to make sure I didn't run into anything else, crowbar still dragging behind me.

"How should I know?"

He'd put his gun in its holster and his flashlight in his teeth. I got a good look at a door of some kind, a bar over it, dull light coming through the seams, before the flashlight finally died.

"Hold up—I have a crowbar," I said, and he moved—at least I thought he moved; his mind seemed to move away, at least with what telepathy was hanging around through the block-sets.

I stumbled, caught myself on the wall. The crowbar got stuck, scrabbled. My heart beat all too fast in the space. Finally I got the head of the crowbar into the vertical slit where the door was, and pulled.

With a truly horrible noise, the door shifted. I pushed again, Loyola helping, and it opened all the way. We fell into an open space of blinding light.

CHAPTER 17

Blinding daylight, and the sound of a kid yelling. Tommy. I saw—more with my telepathy than my eyes—I saw him kicking and screaming and trying to get away.

"Stay still," Sibley said, and Tommy stopped fighting.

I cursed and pushed myself to my feet, my eyes squinting but finally adjusting.

Three men in the alley, one with Tommy, one being Sibley with that horrible sphere in his hand, one moving toward me.

We were in another covered cobblestone alley, this one with heavy, wooden green doors we'd just come through. Boarded-up windows stood across the way, a store long abandoned. A small aircar stood beyond in a dirty street with greenery all around, its engine already whining.

I reached out, trying to get a grip on the mind of the guy coming toward me, but my grip slipped. Too many blocks on my mind. The guy kept coming.

Loyola was up, gun in hand, and I heard the *whoomp, whoomp* of a larger-caliber gun discharge.

Sibley's body shook with two hits, center mass, perfect.

But then he stood, confident, his mind with little pain. His shirt was now rigid in two circular spots, discolored, a supermaterial that had caught the bullets and absorbed them like armor. He was bruised but not seriously hurt. And he had that device in his hand.

He yelled at Loyola, "Stop. Let us go."

Loyola reacted, but I couldn't tell how; the other guy was on me.

I threw up the arm with the crowbar, instinct only, and his fist and then his jaw connected with it; he fell back.

I scrabbled for a hold on his mind again, letting go of the blocks recklessly.

His fist connected with my side then, and I cursed as I lost my concentration. He grabbed the crowbar and—

I finally got my grip on his mind. He slumped, unconscious, down to the ground, crowbar and all. I let him go.

The sound of two gunshots, smaller caliber, *crack, crack*. Pain from Loyola; he was down on the ground then.

Tommy was screaming, screaming, all over the real world and Mindspace both. His fear ran over me like a waterfall. He was reaching, reaching out to me to try to connect again, to try to get away. But he had no teleportation. He had no way of controlling the world, and no training to control the minds around him.

And Sibley was busy now, reestablishing control. They were dragging Tommy toward the car, but he wasn't going down easy.

More pain from Loyola as he tried to get up. The FBI wasn't flush enough to have supermaterials in their agents' clothes, and neither one of us had—or had worn—a vest.

Tommy quieted, all at once, the silence ringing. The car door opened.

Every second we delayed here, every ounce of noise we could make would bring reinforcements. This was a busy tourist area. We had reinforcements in the area too. If I could just slow them down . . .

I reached over to grab onto the other guy's mind then, but I was too late.

Sibley had met my eyes, sphere in hand, now just three feet from me.

"Go to sleep," he said.

I fought the compulsion, I fought with everything in me. I had a block, a little one, but one still.

"Go to sleep," he said one more time, but Tommy's life was on the line. I fought, a bear in a cage clawing, a bear with its foot caught in a trap, fighting no matter what the pain was.

I got the second guy's mind, the guy who had Tommy, and turned off his consciousness. He slumped, trapping Tommy in the car. Damn.

"Go to sleep," Sibley said one more time, and he was so close and I was so open I felt him decide shooting me would just invalidate the device, would just wake me up. And Fiske wanted to torment me. So he walked away, like I didn't matter. The ultimate sign of disrespect.

I remained conscious as Loyola fought to his feet, fought to run after the now-lifting aircar. I staggered to my knees, the effort horrible and painful, that bear with its paw caught in the door. I heard Tommy screaming through Mindspace, as they pulled him away toward the car.

I staggered forward.

Loyola ran.

But the car was lifting off an anti-grav, and neither one of us could make it in time.

Jarrod and the local police arrived on the scene ten minutes later. I got Loyola to the EMTs, gave a quick report, and made sure the police had a clear direction. Then I found a map and started walking, trying to make out which direction they'd gone.

It was useless, and an hour later, the police confirmed that Sibley and Tommy were gone. The guy I'd taken out didn't know where they were going, or was a good enough liar he could fool even me.

I had failed. A dark heaviness sat on my chest as I rode back to the house. I had failed utterly.

Jarrod chewed me out, briefly, like he was too tired and defeated to bother to do it properly.

I stayed, while Loyola, arm in a sling, talked to the Savannah PD and the rest of the feds about setting up a search area.

I stayed, and took my orders and did what they told me. I deserved nothing less. And I tortured myself, wanting Satin and not having it.

My head was pounding with every beat of my heart, but I kept walking. There was an old theater on my left, two doors down, a place that had been renovated so many times you could hardly see the original windowsills beneath the paint. This part of town was old, almost deserted, and the occasional graffiti gang sign stood on signs and walls there above a dozen layers of paint before the locals could paint it again. An empty paper sack skittered along the street in the wind.

I walked up to the theater, feeling three conscious minds inside, and knocked. With any luck, they'd have my drug, I thought. But then made myself focus on the mission, on getting Tommy back.

For the fiftieth time that afternoon, I waited for someone to come to the door. Also for the fiftieth time, I could tell you within seconds that it wasn't any of the people we were looking for.

When the door was opened, though, I got a surprise. The guy had a gun.

"We're in the middle of something," he said flatly. "Theater doesn't open till seven. I'd suggest you come back." He waited, giving me a critical look. He was a lanky twenty-something light-skinned black man who moved with the slightly hunched quickness I associated with basketball. He was wearing a bandanna with a basketball team logo, also, which hopefully was about the team and not about a local gang.

Okay. Well, better that I knock on this door than the other searchers. At least I didn't smell like police. I lifted the two pictures I was carrying. "I'm trying to find a missing kid. You have a second?"

"No," he said, hand on the door. He paused then, looking past me.

I felt a mind coming up behind me then, and I turned. It was Quentin, Tommy's father, in casual clothes and a hat.

"Basie!" he said to the man cheerfully. "How goes it?"

"Quentin." The man with the gun relaxed a little. "Theater's not open till seven today, but you're welcome to wait. We're finishing up the funding drive."

"What are you doing here?" I asked Quentin, guilt hitting me all over again. I was tired, my head hurt, but I'd been pushing through on the slight chance that doing something—anything—the searchers told me to do might help find Tommy. I had to keep moving, or it would all hit me at once.

"You know this guy?" Basie asked.

"A nice man indeed, and generous to a fault." He glanced at me. "He has graciously agreed to help me in my search for my son, currently missing. I trust you will help as well?"

"Who took him?" Basie asked, wary.

Quentin sighed deeply. "His mother tangled with the wrong set of people. I am here to discover who was involved and what they most want in order to get my son back."

Basie's eyes shadowed then, and I felt sadness. "That's rough." He put the gun in his back waistband and opened the door. "As you know, with the funding drive going you have to stay in the front room. I'll ask the guys if they know who is involved."

I got a strong picture of guns and other military-grade things being prepared for sale, their "funding drive" to keep the theater solvent.

"We try to keep our nose clean from some of the more extreme situations, but inevitably people talk to thespians. Probably somebody will know."

"Ah yes," Quentin said. "Nothing like a deeply moving play to make one's tongue wish to wag about one's exploits."

"You know it is," Basie said.

Wait. Military equipment. Was he in contact with whoever had stolen the equipment for the boy's original attack? If so, he might be very useful indeed.

"Thank you for your generosity," Quentin said.

I followed them into a tattered main lobby area, complete with old-style ticket booths from the early days of movies, the glass so old it was starting to run, waves settling into it as the glass fell slowly, over decades. The carpet was newer, but still tattered, the few seats in the area threadbare. Mindspace was quiet here, not disturbed much over the last few days.

Two large double doors led past the ticket booths to the theater itself; a smaller door, to the right, had two minds on the other side of it; I got a general impression of counting merchandise there, doubtlessly the guns.

"Do you work with the Hard Knocks gun shop?" I asked Basie.

He tensed, hand drifting toward the gun. "Quentin, your companion is asking uncomfortable questions." He was thinking that I knew too much. And the cops had just been to the gun shop. "You'll have to leave if he keeps it up."

"My apologies, Basie, truly. Adam here has the great and terrible fault of being curious," Quentin said quickly. Then looked at me. "Feels he must know everything, whether it is or is not his business. Please ignore his little peccadilloes and fetch your associates. I fear that our time is running out."

Basie looked at us both. Then, finally, at Quentin. "You're in a hard spot, and you've been good to the theater. I'll overlook it this once." Then he turned, hand going away from the gun, and went into that side room. He was careful not to open the door wide enough for us to see inside.

"What are you doing?" Quentin hissed at me.

"What are you doing here?" I asked. "I'm on the search grid. They couldn't find the flyer and they think maybe it grounded in this direction. Door to door." The movement, the questions thus far were keeping me from panicking too badly, but seeing him made it worse, made it itchy, made it all real.

I'd lost his son, and he should hate me. I should hate me. My heart sped up again.

"No way in hell am I sitting on the sidelines while my son is in danger," Quentin said, and I realized the suave face he put on for the world had just disappeared. "This is the right place to go to get answers. I should be asking you what you're doing here messing up my tactics."

"I was just—" I went quiet as the door opened again, and two more guys came out, a black guy in his teens who kept looking around like he expected trouble, and an older white guy in glasses. I'd been under the impression that Savannah crime split along racial lines, so unless I was misinformed, the mix here was unusual and therefore interesting.

"Thank you all, sincerely, for the gracious gift of your time during the critical fund-raising season for the theater,"

Quentin said, and his charm and the apparent sincerity was back in all its glory. He was even extending a low-level emotion into Mindspace, more charm and likeability. I didn't know if he was doing it on purpose or simply by accident, but I could see the guys relax. "As I was telling your associate, my only son has been taken. I need to know who, and what they are looking for, to best start a negotiation that will satisfy everyone. I know that the three of you talk to everyone, sooner or later. Have you heard any useful information of any kind on this topic?"

"Getting kids involved is trouble," the older guy said.

"Who you looking for?" the younger guy asked.

I held up the two photos. "Here's Tommy, the boy we're looking for. And this here is the guy we last saw him with. Anything you can tell us about who he works for and with would be very helpful."

"You cops? You working with the ATF?" the younger guy asked suspiciously.

"No," I said, with as much sincerity as I could put in my voice. "I have a few friends, but I have friends with everybody. Today we're just wanting to get Tommy back. I'm not interested in anything else."

Quentin frowned at me, then turned to the others. "Truly, fine gentlemen, we are only here for my son. I beg you to help me. I've done many favors for this theater, and I'd like to call them due at this time, for your generosity."

"Give me that picture," the older guy said.

I handed them both over.

He looked at them for a long time, then handed them back. To Quentin he said, "Your ex is in a world of trouble. That's the big boss's man. The Python."

The other two criminals stared.

"Anything you can tell us?" I asked, stomach sinking.

"People end up dead when they cross him," Basie said. I

realized he was legitimately afraid. "And that's just for start-ers. The gun shop? Well, maybe we work with their phone number. I'm not saying we do. But the rumor is, the hotline arranged a contract on the wrong person, somebody the big boss wanted to take care of himself. Everyone involved is dead. This is why the theater is so careful what we get involved with, you understand. We don't want trouble. We don't hurt anybody. We just provide supplies in exchange for the money we need to keep the theater running."

"Admirable, of course. How best should I negotiate with these gentlemen, in your opinion?" Quentin asked. "How do I set up contact?"

"You don't, man," the younger one said simply. "You do what he says. If he's sending the Python to enforce, he don't want to hear from any of us. It's too late to talk to the Booker."

"Who's the Booker?" I said.

Basie looked uncomfortable then. "We've mentioned too much already. Look, as we said, we don't get involved in this kind of thing. You leave now and we'll forget this happened, okay? You never heard anything from us." He was afraid for his life against this big boss, against the guy I thought was Fiske.

Quentin turned, but I didn't.

I held up a hand. "One more question and I leave."

"You ask too many questions," Basie said.

"It's just a little one."

We need to go, Quentin told me pointedly, mind-to-mind.

Basie crossed his arms.

"The contract they took they weren't supposed to? Was it from Pappadakis?" I asked.

"The rich guy who's on trial?" Basie asked, surprised. "No. Some woman, actually."

"Could she have worked with Pappadakis?" I asked.

"That's two questions," Quentin objected.

Basie shrugged. "Word on the street is that she's an independent. The man's been keeping his nose clean. At least this week. The big boss is watching."

Huh. That was not at all the information I'd been expecting to get. "Thank you, gentleman," I said. "You've been very helpful."

And I let Quentin pull me out of the building and into the street.

Quentin was not happy, and didn't bother to hide it in Mindspace. "What a royal waste of our time. They didn't have any information we didn't already have."

"How do you know what information we already have?" I asked. But I was disappointed too.

"You should know by now I can read people. Supervisory Special Agent Jarrod was all too willing to calm down the grieving father," he said. "Unfortunately for him."

"Why aren't you falling apart?"

"If I sit down and think about it, I will. But if there's anything—anything—I can do to help in the meantime, I will. It's far more helpful to move forward in situations like this than to sit in a corner and grieve."

I understood that. My own guilt was sitting like an anvil suspended over my head, and I knew if I let it fall, I'd be in trouble. "Aren't you pissed at me?" I said, unable to help myself.

A flash of hurt and fear hit him then. "I saw the school bus arrive. I don't think you or I would have been able to stop them at that point. And you went after them. I saw you. We'll get him back. I have to believe that."

"If I just knew where they went . . . ," I said, my stomach filling up with nerves and my own fear. I couldn't feel

Tommy anymore, in the back of my head, and that was the worst of all.

Quentin paused in his walk. "You're going to find him, right?"

"I'll do everything in my power," I said.

"Okay. See that you do."

CHAPTER 18

There was a federal safe house downtown, but I didn't know where it was with any certainty, so Quentin dropped me off not far from the judge's house. I walked my way in, hands in pockets, my fingers running over the hard weight of the judge's house key over and over, over and over, trying not to think about what had happened, and not succeeding.

I felt . . . lost, empty, vacant. A failure. I wanted my drug. I'd broken my own set of ethics, and it hadn't even worked to get Tommy back. I'd hurt people, and abandoned Cherabino, and all of it hadn't even staved off the vision. I'd failed, a hundred ways. It was like an emptiness I couldn't fill.

Swartz said when you failed, you got back up and made it right. The only way I could think of to make it right, barring the door-to-door search that probably was going nowhere, was to use the telepathy. Even though I was exhausted beyond bearing, my hands shaking from need and guilt and everything else, I thought maybe that was the only thing to do. Or, at least, the only one that didn't make me fall off the wagon.

So, as I let myself into the judge's house, I told myself I had to try. I had to. Even if it didn't work, even if my mind was too tired, the connection too fragile, and I did damage to both. I had to try. What else was I going to do?

Mendez sat behind Jarrod's board of electronics, head-phones on while she talked to someone on the other line. A map of the city was folded out in front of her, a map and at least four different-colored markers with their caps off, as she had dotted the map over and over in different colors.

When she saw me, she said to the person on the phone, "Could you hold on?" She dropped the headphones to around her neck. "You finish the door-to-door? What sector?"

I told her where I'd been. My voice must have been as flat as my mood, because she paused before marking down the streets on the map. "I didn't finish," I said, and told her about Quentin.

"Well, you're on the abracadabra duty," she said. "What-ever you can bring to the table that we can't, you should do."

"Yeah," I said. "Yeah." I dug my hands deeper in my pockets. "Listen, I'm going to lock myself in the coat closet, okay? Don't disturb me if you can help it?"

She frowned at me.

"Telepathy stuff," I said. "It may not work, but I've got to try."

Her face cleared, and she nodded. Then a tinny sound came from her earphones and she pulled them back up, fold-ing out the microphone again. "Yeah, sorry. I'm here. Yes, Abercorn? You got it. Be advised Metro PD is covering the area starting at the Burger Spot at the end." And she kept on in that vein while I went to the kitchen, forced myself to eat yogurt from the fridge and drink water, quickly. I'd need the strength for what I was about to do.

For what I had to do.

I locked myself in the closet and fought off horrible thoughts of how I'd failed, how I'd ruined everything. And what might be happening to Tommy right now. I fought them off, and hands shaking, I won. This time. I had to do this.

Last year, when Cherabino had been taken by a serial killer, I'd used our small proto-Link to connect with her, to figure out where she was, and I was hoping I'd be able to do that now, with the boy.

I wasn't sure it would work. We didn't have a Link, or at least any kind of Link I'd ever seen before. I'd never felt the kind of location-based tether I had with this kid; with his latent telepathy, he'd done something that I didn't know how to categorize. Maybe it would act like a Link, though. Maybe, if I was calm enough, and smart enough, I might figure out some clue that would get us to Tommy faster. I couldn't help with Jarrod's coordination of the police officers in the area—they'd pulled out the old AMBER Alert laws to get absolute cooperation from several agencies. Maybe they'd find him that way. But I had to try, had to do my own search, no matter what it cost me.

I turned off the light in the small closet, coats shifting above me with a rustling sound. It smelled of rain pollution and mold from the jackets and the umbrella next to me, and of the powdery, sandy dirt from the two sets of boots on the floor. But the nearest mind felt far away, and in the dark, and the quiet, I could push the failure aside enough to focus.

I did what we taught kids at the Guild to do first, what I hadn't managed to teach Tommy yet in so many words. I took a deep breath and turned inward, diving inward, to the crowded spot in the back of my head that held my Links, the fading one to Cherabino, the old, bricked-up one to my ex-fiancée, Kara, and the tag that connected me to Stone at the Guild. There, like a frayed cord next to them, sat the connection to Tommy, askew, broken, and not at all like the others.

I turned inward, and followed that connection like a
Link, deeper, deeper, with the intention of finding Tommy
and figuring out where he was and how I could help.

The sensation of falling, falling slowly through horizontal space with overwhelming pain, and then the sound of
distant police sirens. The pain eased.

Quiet, the bad man's voice said. *Quiet.* It was a dark
tone, a bad tone, and I shivered from fear of it. I wanted to
go home, I thought, folded into the wheel well like the
other bad day, the day when Tanya died.

Tommy felt me there then. *Adam? Adam, come get me.
I'm scared.*

Where are you? I asked. *What does it look like around you?*

I don't know. I'm sorry I ran ahead.

I know. I'm sorry too. A crushing sense of failure hit
me, but I pushed it away. I was here. It was working. *Can
you see anything around you?* I asked. When I'd done this
with Cherabino, I'd been able to see with her eyes, hear
with her ears, but it didn't look like it was going to work
that way this time. *What do you hear? Are there buildings
or trees?*

He swallowed, scared.

Just try to look, I said. If I could get information this
way, if I could get his location . . . if I could get his location
I could make this right. I could help save him.

Slowly, slowly, he unfolded from the wheel well, lifting
his head up, up to see out the window.

Trees, he said. *Big ones. Lots of them.*

Where is the sun? I asked. *What side of the car?*

He thought about that then—burst of fear. Then pain,
pain as someone hit him across the jaw.

And the connection was broken.

Crap. My head hurt, from the reflected pain, from my
own pain, from the strain of holding a long-distance

connection on the tatters of that connection. Back in the closet, I rubbed the nape of my neck, over and over, the movement soothing. I had to try again. He was scared, and he deserved to at least have someone with him. I was genuinely afraid that this time, the tatters of the connection would break permanently, and I'd be out of luck.

Still, if I could get the direction of the sun and the trees, it would dramatically change the search area. That alone would be worth whatever it cost us; it would get Tommy found and safe much faster than the searchers would be able to do on their own.

I pushed all considerations of failure down and locked them in a strongbox; I'd have to deal with them eventually, or the box would break open at an unexpected time. But for now, at this moment, with these stakes, I couldn't deal with them. I couldn't, no matter how much Swartz said locking things up was a bad idea.

And I dove again, with again that sense of falling.

This time was different, though; this time I lost control and fell, fast, wherever the path took me. I suppressed a shriek—this had never, never happened before. Was I Falling In? Was I . . . ?

And then it was over, and I breathed quietly to myself as I got my bearings.

I sat behind an old wooden table, scratches layered upon its top in endless lines. My dress uniform pinched my neck, the front slightly too small, so that I couldn't lean forward without worrying that the breasts would strain the buttons all too much. They were talking about me again, lies, and my anger was a living thing within me.

Breasts? I separated myself from the stream-of-consciousness thoughts, desperate to figure out where I was, whose mind I found myself in.

Cherabino?

She started a little, surprised to hear a thought that wasn't hers. *Adam?*

I didn't mean to end up here, I told her. I missed her terribly. *How's the trial going?*

Stick around for a few minutes and find out for yourself. Her mood was dark, unhappy, angry, like a wolf with her foot caught in a bear trap, still not quite sure if she could get out with the foot intact.

I looked out through her eyes. At the front of the large conference room was a chair. They'd pulled out the conference table and put in two old wooden tables, one for her, one for the IA investigator. Technically he wasn't supposed to be against her. He was supposed to be finding out the truth. But that wasn't what was happening here. No, that wasn't what was happening here at all.

They'd allowed three reporters in the back of the room, along with the union rep and the police commissioner's representative. The Internal Affairs guy was one of their senior guys, and he'd been paying far, far too much attention to the reporters and the police commissioner's representative. She was getting angry, watching this. It was a travesty. Next to her, Chou, the new lawyer, was as tense as a caged tiger.

Her sensei had just sat down at the chair. He was a wiry man with glasses, Puerto Rican by heritage, in better shape at sixty than Cherabino had been at twenty-five. Those brown eyes saw everything. He nodded at her, and then turned his attention to the IA detective, who had sworn him to tell the truth.

"Why are you here?" the IA traitor asked.

"I'm here to speak for my longtime student Isabella," Sensei Rivera said.

"Why?"

Rivera blinked. "She is accused of something I believe she did not do."

"Why don't you believe she did it?"

"She is a good person who believes in justice and who values her job and its rules above anything else. I do not believe she would treat a man the way she is being accused, and certainly not outside her jurisdiction."

The IA detective nodded. "Were you there? Did you see the events of that night yourself?"

"Well, no."

"Did she tell you about that night?"

"She's too conscientious for that. I've only read about the details in the news, and the basics her lawyer felt comfortable sharing with me. The charge, for example."

"So you don't know what happened. You're only guessing."

"I know Isabella," Rivera said quietly.

"You realize we don't normally allow civilians into Internal Affairs matters. But if you're here to testify as to Detective Cherabino's character . . ."

"I am."

"Then I do have a question." The IA traitor paused for effect, looking back at Cherabino. I wanted to read him in Mindspace, I wanted desperately to figure out what he was up to, but Cherabino's mind had no such capability. "How long have you known the detective?" the guy asked.

"Oh, ten years now. She is an excellent student."

"And by excellent student, you mean she is good at the form of violence you teach."

Rivera stared at the IA guy; he was clearly offended. "She is good at judo, if that is what you mean. It is not a very violent martial art. She is good at its philosophy as well as it forms." He opened his mouth, to explain the nonviolence emphasis in detail, probably, but the IA guy cut him off.

"Have you ever known her to have a temper?"

Rivera set his jaw.

Now the IA guy was fishing for evidence to support the angle he'd already made his mind up about. He was acting far more like a prosecutor than an impartial detective. Cherabino was livid, taking deep breaths so she wouldn't show it. Too much anger would only play into his hands.

"Have you ever known her to have a temper?" he repeated.

Rivera met Cherabino's eyes, almost an apology. Then he said, "Isabella has made great progress in managing her anger in appropriate ways. I have been very pleased."

"So you've known her to show anger in inappropriate ways?"

"On occasion, years ago. She has learned great control."

The IA traitor paused, for a moment. "In your opinion as someone who knows her character, is Detective Cherabino capable of beating a man to death? As her teacher."

"She is capable of the physical stamina and skill it would require," her sensei said immediately. "She has learned her lessons in the dojo well. But under those circumstances I do not believe—"

"That is not what I asked you. Is she capable of beating a man to death? Not only physically, but the mental decision to do so deliberately? In general."

Rivera looked away from Cherabino then.

"Answer the question."

"Yes, I believe she would be capable."

Cherabino closed her eyes.

"You may leave now," the traitor said.

Her sensei stopped by the table to say good-bye, and

Cherabino greeted him, putting a hand on his arm to let him know it was okay. The truth was always okay, even if it hurt. He'd still come to speak to her character, or try. He'd tried to help. Even if she was so angry she couldn't think, her anger wasn't at him.

I was amazed, this close to her, at the depth of warmth she felt for her sensei. He wasn't just a Swartz to her. In a way, he was a father.

Before the door had even shut behind him, the IA detective said, "Detective Cherabino?"

"Yes?" she asked, still standing. She turned and stood at attention, the lines of her body helping her to stand strong against this fool.

"Let's turn our attention to the disciplinary mark on your record from last year. You punched a rookie in the face on no provocation, and your supervisor put you on administrative leave."

"There were extenuating circumstances, sir," she said. "May I explain?"

"Please do." He stood, waiting, and all the weight of all the eyes in the room were on Cherabino.

She felt that weight like a thousand knives. She wanted to concentrate, and she wanted me, at least, not to be here.

Are you sure?

Yes, she was sure. She had to be clear and concise and defend herself, and she didn't need the distraction. She appreciated me trying, though. She appreciated it more than she could express. But I needed to leave now.

With deep regret, I let go of the Link and found myself back in my own body, at the bottom of a darkened coat closet, my head feeling like an ice pick was jammed behind my eyes.

Was Cherabino going to be okay? I hadn't realized

things were so horrible. If they were even turning her sensei's words against her . . . I should be there. Regardless of what she said, I should be there. If her world was falling down around her, I should be there. But I couldn't. The guilt of that twisted around my guts, a parasite draining my energy.

Cherabino was in the worst fight of her life, watching all of her life's work being degraded, her character being called into question, and there was nothing I could do. It hurt. It hurt on a deep level.

I was failing her, just as surely as I was failing Tommy. I didn't know what she'd do if it all fell apart.

I breathed, over and over again, getting the emotions and the pain under control. But when I went to reconnect with Tommy . . . I couldn't. I tried over and over, but the pain only got worse. And I just couldn't, not now. I couldn't help Cherabino, and I couldn't help Tommy. And I'd broken all my ethics to get here—and here was not working.

I picked myself up, eyes watering, head hurting.

For the first time in ten years, I regretted the lack of Guild drugs. They handed out the things like candy, and I'd never approved of how often they were used. If I had a focus drug now, though, I could reconnect with Tommy. Perhaps do myself damage, but I could make my mind work beyond the pain, beyond the warning signals. Maybe help him, so I could get back to Cherabino faster. Maybe I could be there for her.

Maybe the world wouldn't fall apart, if I had drugs.

Then again, it might not work. And I couldn't have drugs of any kind on the program, not unless they were doctor-prescribed for a legitimate medical condition, and sometimes not even then. Oh, and aspirin. If you didn't abuse it. Aspirin sounded wonderful about now. The Twelve Steps said it was all too easy to fall for another, different drug, and today I understood.

I got up, heartsick, opened the door, and went looking for aspirin and food, in that order. As guilty as I felt, I had to do something. Otherwise I would be locked in that closet for the next three weeks, and be no good to anyone.

CHAPTER 19

Sunglasses on and aspirin taken, I took a bowl of rehydrated dehydrated very bad soup to Mendez, along with a cup of freshly brewed coffee.

Thanks, she mouthed as she listened to the headphones, making another notation in a colored marker on the map, which was starting to have more marker splotches than printed areas. She gestured for me to put the food down across the table, beyond the county map she'd set up and was working on.

Finally she pulled down the headphones. Her eyes had dark circles under them, and her hands shook. When I looked at the clock, I saw it had been nearly three hours for both of us, and neither one of us had had it easy. Outside the front porch, the sun was going down, the light getting longer and more orange inside the house. Friday night, and not a happy night for anyone.

"Did it work?" she asked me tiredly. "Whatever it was you wanted to work?"

"Not enough," I told her, my own exhaustion meeting hers in Mindspace. "But I did connect with him a little. He's outside the city, I think, or at least surrounded by an awful lot of trees."

Mendez looked at the maps in front of her. "Yeah, that would have to be the case. We've covered most all of the city block by block. Any idea of direction?"

"Trees. Lots of trees."

"I hear the frustration. Trust me, we're all there. You keep working. Once they've got him settled, his odds go down, so we need to keep moving."

"Yeah," I said. "Eat the soup. I'll get my own bowl and come back, okay?"

"Thanks," she said. "Oh, coffee!"

I turned as she was pulling her headphones back up, microphone circling out. But then I felt the minds approaching the house. Jarrod, and Sridarin, both tired and upset, and then . . . then a mind I thought must be the judge. I didn't know her as well, especially from a distance. She hadn't let me put a tag on her.

"It's time for you to leave," the judge's voice echoed through the porch windows.

Mendez looked up, pausing in what she was doing over the maps.

There was a reply, muffled, a lower man's voice.

"Don't you think you've done enough?" the judge's voice echoed, again too loud.

The door opened, and the judge, Jarrod, and Sridarin entered the house.

Jarrod and the judge stopped. The judge stood just a little too close, her arms extended in a classic "power posture"; Jarrod's body language wasn't budging in response. He wasn't happy.

"Judge Parson, you must realize that—"

"I must realize? I must realize? You . . . you people lost my son! You let him be taken by criminals! I don't see one possible thing that you can do for me here that you can't screw up elsewhere. And I don't want to look at you. You get out of my house, all of you."

"I understand you're upset. But—"

"This is not a discussion, this is me informing you that you are leaving. You have half an hour to get your things out of my house."

"Ma'am," Sridarian said then.

"That includes you. Everyone." She crossed her arms, taking a visible posture of waiting. "Twenty-nine minutes thirty seconds."

I could see Jarrod thinking, see it like bubbles moving in a pot of boiling water. Finally he stepped back, calculation still moving behind his eyes. "Let's pack up, people."

"Really?" I asked. "You're coordinating half the city's police and federal forces from that console there. We can't leave now."

"And you," the judge said to me, "you. You'd better pray they find my son again. Because if they don't, I am holding you personally responsible." And she made a show of turning her back on me.

I felt . . . sliced open, like a cat-o'-nine-tails from the old movies had sliced my face in a thousand cuts. She was right. Even if the words made me bleed, made the guilt rush out like water. It was my fault, and she knew it.

Mendez put her hand on my shoulder, on the fabric of my shirt, in solidarity. Her mind strengthened briefly, but all I felt was that solidarity. Then she was moving, her intention to get out of this place quickly.

Ten minutes later, in the car outside, my stuff in a single bag next to me, I was feeling twitchy. I couldn't take the condemnation in the judge's eyes. I couldn't take the condemnation in my own. I wanted ten cigarettes in a row, and I wanted my drug, but I wasn't going to get either one, maybe. My hands shook anyway.

The trunk opened, then a thud and a reshuffling of the

car, once, twice, three times as heavy equipment was added. Then the slam of the trunk closing, and the front passenger-side door opened.

"That was harsh," Mendez said. She folded into the front seat and shut the door. "She's hurting, and the harsh has nothing to do with you."

"She's right, though," I said, still itching to be somewhere, anywhere but here. "I took Tommy outside the courthouse. I lost him." The knowledge sat on me like a heavy weight, impossible to dislodge, crushing me.

Mendez was quiet for a moment, considering. She realized we hadn't discussed this, that no one had discussed this. There hadn't been time. "So far as it goes, that's true. Sibley and his crew . . . they had an established plan, though. They had the shock grenade. It's impossible to know. Maybe they would have managed it anyway. Neither Loyola nor I was expecting a crew like that. Not then and there."

"You should have," I said then, resentful. "The first attack, if nothing else, should have told you that."

"It's easy to assume we should have known things in retrospect. But the attackers were dead by then," she said. "Another group was working, if any. Sibley—if we believed he was a threat at all—historically has worked alone. We were more concerned about a stealth jaunt at the house, to be honest with you. He surprised us." She paused, and I felt a wave of exhaustion go off her again. "We all fell down on this one. In retrospect, we should not have left you alone for such long periods. But it's more important to find him now than it is to throw blame."

"It was my job!" I fell down on my job.

"You were the first to tell us that Minding isn't your specialty. You adapt to your personnel, or you should. Jarrod's been distracted, but I should have said something."

"It's not your fault," I said automatically. It's something

you'd say in the interview rooms, with a witness who was telling you the truth as she'd seen it.

"It's as much mine as yours. There's plenty of blame to go around," Mendez said. I felt her guilt there, but I felt her determination more.

"What are we waiting for?" I asked.

"Jarrod and I can leave at our discretion, and likely Loyola—if he will. Sridarin is assigned directly to the judge, not her son, and Loyola has taken on that responsibility as well. I imagine Jarrod's sticking around for support, and to make another set of phone calls. It's been a lot, working as the coordination point for the agencies. The ATF, at least, is picking up the ball with the local PD."

"How likely is it that you think we'll find him?" I asked her.

"I just gave out your information to everyone, so they're packing up in city center. Honestly we were about done there as well. They're looking outside the city in the direction of the flight out. I've done these cases before. Sometimes something will pop, and now's the time if they're outside the city. It helps that the PD knows it's a judge on their side of the table. Sibley's organized, but he can't possibly have accounted for us mobilizing as fast as we did. We'll get there."

"Oh," I said.

"Give Jarrod another few minutes and he'll be out here. Most of the gear is already with us. We'll move to a hotel and set up shop there. It won't be the first time."

"You're not upset about Tommy at all," I said. I regretted it immediately; the tone petulant and guilty. But she wasn't, and it bothered me.

Mendez turned all the way around in her seat then. "*Don't* allow your emotions to take you over. There will be a time to be upset, but that time is not today. Today, we do everything. Today, we find him."

"Okay," I said. She was probably right.

"You are new, I understand. But you cannot fall apart. It cannot happen."

"Okay," I said. Took three deep breaths, and forced more of my emotions into that little box, that little strong-box with the iron-reinforced sides.

The hotel was a mile or so out of town, on the interstate, an ancient hotel that was scrupulously maintained. The clerk at the front was a college kid, but he'd been an athlete at one time and had plenty of confidence.

"Room 202, that's on the right," he said as he took my hurriedly scrawled form and deposited a key in its place. Mendez and Jarrod had already been through this process, getting rooms for themselves and a central room from which to run the equipment.

The clerk leaned forward and pointed his arm to the right. "See the staircase there? Up a floor, turn left, fourth door on the left. You want to be on the quiet side of the place, that's where you go."

He turned back to his book without further comment, a dismissal if ever I heard one. But the book was a collection of Robert Frost, and he read loudly to himself in Mind-space thoughts, so that "The Road Less Traveled" followed me out the door and into the night.

The irony was not lost on me. Nope, not even a little.

The room was small and sad, and it echoed with various shades of loneliness, the faded flowered curtains rubbing shoulders with a downtrodden pale carpet. The bed squeaked when I sat down on it, but it held. The nightstand and chest of drawers were covered in scratches and faded with age, but clean. The whole room seemed clean, actu-ally, at least on the surface; an odd, musty smell remained, though. Perhaps somebody smoking in the room, though smoking what, I couldn't tell you. From the smell, perhaps something with mold as a key ingredient.

I checked the shower—a real water-shower, no sonics in sight—and found it clean enough. No visible mold anyway, and wherever the smell was coming from wasn't the sheets either. This would do.

Then I went back out on the balcony for a cigarette of my own, watching the drizzle of the day fall slowly to earth. It still felt strange to smell the faint salt of ocean in the air, and see gnats in clouds. It was strange to feel the ancient oaks, almost minds, settled into Mindspace. And most of all, it was strange to be without Cherabino. I missed her terribly, worse now when she was not here to tell me to stop whining and start working. She would have told me what to do about Tommy. She would have fixed this, or at least kept me from screwing it up worse. My hands shook with all the things I couldn't think about, chief among which was how much I wanted my drug.

I stubbed out the cigarette in an ashtray, unable to get the taste of failure out of my mouth. Both Cherabino and Swartz wouldn't stand for me giving up, not at this point, not when I could be doing something—anything—that might help the kid I'd come here to save.

But I felt the vision barreling toward me, becoming more and more real, and I was beginning to believe I couldn't stop it.

I called the department to leave the new number for Cherabino, and talked to Michael again. Then I called Swartz and got Selah.

"He's having a bad day. He's finally sleeping. Is it an emergency?" she asked me, voice defeated.

I paused, wrestling with the question. It was bad. It was pretty bad. But I didn't think I was going to use right now,

and I'd be around the FBI most of the day, which would
keep me from doing it if I changed my mind. Plus, Swartz
had had a heart attack not too many months ago and it was
a bad day.

"Adam?" she asked.

"No," I said slowly. "No, it's not an emergency."

But as the dial tone rang, I wondered if that was really
right. It was pretty damn bad right now.

I changed shirts and went back downstairs. Jarrod and
the others had probably been waiting for me a long damn
time, and I shouldn't keep them waiting anymore.

I worried still, about Cherabino, about the man whose
memories I'd stolen against all ethical boundaries, and about
Tommy. Above all, I worried about Tommy. What were they
doing to him? Was he even still alive?

CHAPTER 20

The sun was setting as Loyola and I made it to the crime lab, one of the small, flat buildings with tall trees behind them. Inside, it smelled like brick and chemicals, and we had to pass through security again to enter the main hall. Sridarin from the sheriff's office was sitting in a bench about halfway down.

He looked up, circles under his eyes. He'd been sent away from the judge, he was thinking, and was feeling guilty despite his duty to get the shell casings over here after the attack. Jarrod was walking toward us from the other end of the hall.

"Hi," Sridarin said.

"Hello," Loyola said. "Any news on the ballistics?"

He stood from the bench. "Yes. They're running it again to confirm since it was such a rush, but right now it looks like at least two of these are stolen weapons, one used in a robbery a few weeks ago. The gun found in possession of the attacker at the scene is a clear match to one of the shell casing sets, so between that and the witnesses, we have him cold. His is not in the system, but there's a clear registration trail and the ATF is looking into it." He took a breath. "With any luck, the idiots bought all of the guns at the same place and brought a couple of stolen items besides.

Sheriff's department is on protective duty with the judge and assisting Metro PD in the search."

Jarrod reached us, his bootheels thudding against the floor. "Mendez is set up to coordinate out of one of the spare rooms, Metro PD dispatchers on assist. I'm going to need some help with phone calls."

"Whatever you need," I said, feeling like the world was already falling out of place.

Jarrod frowned at me. "I meant Loyola. Sridarin if he has the time. You can help, but if there's something you can do that we can't, now's the time."

I shook my head.

"Another vision with more detail might be useful about now."

I sighed. "I'm pretty burned out right now. Give me some phone calls and I'll see what I can do after that."

Next to me, Loyola's disapproval swelled. I was too tired to really care. There was more than one way to find Tommy, and give it another hour and I'd try the connection again.

I limped up the stairs to my hotel room, anxious and feeling defeated. I could still feel echoes of Tommy's fear in my head occasionally, and I'd called half the city. I'd even begged my stupid difficult precognition to help me figure out the future and how to stop it, but no exercise I could give it produced anything but a reprise of that old, terrible vision. I'd sleep and try again, and pray that Tommy was still alive at the end. If he wasn't, I didn't know how I'd live with myself.

I unlocked the hotel room door with shaking hands, telling myself I could have another cigarette, hell, I could have four if I needed them, but I had to calm down, and I couldn't have my drug. I stopped two steps inside the room. The door shut behind me with a bang.

The room smelled different. Moldy, yes, but something else . . . something like gun oil and cedar. Someone had been here.

I hunted for the lamp's light switch, anxiety spiking. It was probably just the maid, I told myself. I was being an idiot.

When the lamp switched on, no one was there, and I took a breath. I could still feel another presence here like perfume. I went over to drop my coat on the desk—and saw it.

A box. A intricate wooden puzzle-box, something I'd never seen before but that somehow looked familiar. Its dark mahogany surface was vaguely the size and shape of a cigar box, with a more intricate pattern. Deep grooves like the lines of a map were set into its surface, along with small metal balls in the grooves. It was sitting on the freshly made bed, at its foot, with a folded piece of paper that read *Adam*.

The hairs stood up on the back of my neck.

I looked around the entire hotel room, first in Mind-space, then in the real world, pulling the shower curtain aside, opening the closet door with heart beating. No one was here. Not anymore.

I opened the box then, slowly, with a square of the sheet between its side and my hand. It clicked, the metal balls rolling, but it was open; it opened.

When I saw what was inside, I cursed and dropped the lid. Then, with a deep breath, opened it again.

Sitting in the recess of a red satin-top pillow were two things: one, a small vial of what looked like purple liquid against the red fabric, and two, a needle still wrapped in medical-grade packaging, a small needle with marks up the side in exactly the denominations one would need to use the vial.

My hand shook as I picked up the note, no longer caring of potential contaminants. I knew what that box held. I knew it, and it was far worse than any bomb. It was high-grade Satin, by the chemical formula on the label, a bluish drug that hit the sixth sense like a freight train. My drug. My poison. The thing I'd battled long and hard to be free of, and here it was, sitting there, for free, all too available. Blood rushed in my ears; my heart beat all too quickly.

I opened the note.

Imagine my surprise when you became involved in this minor judicial matter in Savannah, it said. *I have adapted. Here is a gift for you, your drug of choice. Rest assured it will not be my last gift via my associate.*

Remember, you were the one who made this personal.

It was not signed, but I knew who it was. I half fell, half walked backward, pulling out the chair in front of that desk and sitting with shaking knees.

Fiske had found me. Not just Sibley, who some of the time I'd assumed had been hired by Pappadakis, but Fiske. Cherabino and I had attacked his house and forced our way in for a reason that seemed to make sense at the time. He'd let us go, but he'd said he'd remember what we'd done.

Apparently he was the kind to hold a grudge, hold it for months, and then play with the source of that grudge. And he'd promised me gifts.

Somehow I doubted any of those gifts would be pleasant. Not when he'd started this way.

I sat there and looked at the box, at the vial, at my drug. I wanted it so badly I couldn't . . . quite . . . think. My palms sweated, my heart beat, and I felt drawn to it, like someone had a piece of string attached to it, reeling me in.

I closed my eyes so I couldn't see it. I turned away, literally turned away like a small child. And I breathed, deep breaths designed to calm my nervous system so I could think. I had to think. If I didn't I'd jump in headfirst, and whatever I decided, I couldn't throw away almost four years of being clean on an impulse. It wasn't allowed.

My hands shook, and the strongbox of all my emotions shuddered, the locks holding, but only just. If I could just fall off the face of the world . . . If I could just take my drug . . .

A breath. Two. My problems would still be there waiting for me when I got back, I heard Swartz's voice tell me. Just because it was here didn't mean I had to use it.

I wanted to! I turned back around, then took a step back. I wanted to so much.

But Fiske wanted me to as well, or he wouldn't have bothered to send it. My worst enemy—the person—had sent my worst enemy—the drug—to torment me. And though I wanted it with everything in me, I couldn't just hand Fiske a victory.

Because for all my want, all my need, it would be a victory for him, a failure for me. A last, permanent failure on top of the dozen he'd already forced down my throat. It was pretty, that vial, but it was poison. Swartz had always said it was my poison.

Tommy could still be alive. Maybe. Somewhere. And if I was in a drug stupor in a corner somewhere when he died, when I could have done something about it . . .

There was no choice, not really.

I breathed for approximately forever, in and out, pushing down my internal demons. It was a battle, a real battle, with real blood and sweat. But I already knew its conclusions, and the part of me that wanted the drug did too.

So I closed the box and tried to think what to do with it.

I was exhausted, now worse than ever. I could break the vial and throw away the glass, destroying the drug—part of me felt actual pain at that thought—but I didn't want to expose the hotel staff to the glass, and I didn't want Jarrod or anyone else finding the vial if I threw it away. The dumpster outside had been overflowing already.

After a few minutes of temptation one way and the other, I wrapped up the box and the note in a pillowcase and stuck it in a desk drawer. Probably no one would look there, and it would give me some more time.

Then I called Swartz. Selah picked up.

"Yes, it's an emergency," I said, and waited while she got him.

A minute later, Swartz's gruff voice picked up. "What's wrong?"

I closed my eyes in relief. Such relief. I didn't have to do this alone. "It . . . it's a bad time, Swartz. I need you to talk me down."

And he did. With no hesitation, for an hour or more, Swartz sat there and talked to me. Reminded me of all the things I believed in now that I wanted more than just a drug, reminded me of Cherabino, and the department, and being an interrogator. Reminded me of the program, and him.

Reminded me that I really wasn't alone.

After it was all done, I stripped off belt and shoes, pants and shirt, and fell into the bed.

I was asleep almost before my head hit the pillow.

I woke to the sound of a ringing phone, high pitched and loud. I groped for the phone, somewhere on the nightstand, and found the lamp instead.

RiiiiiIIIiiiiing, the thing rang, horribly loud, as I switched on the light. There . . . there was the phone.

I picked up the receiver. "Mmmph?"

"A-a-adam?" Cherabino's voice came through, wobbly.

"Isabella?" I asked, sitting up. Every fear I had rolled over me, all at once. "What's going on?"

She took in a wobbly breath, and I could hear the tears she was suppressing. "They did it. They put the whole damn system so much in knots—they found me guilty."

I rubbed my eyes, heart beating far too fast now. "Guilty of what exactly?" I asked, afraid.

"Police brutality and wrongful death. They said I'm lucky the family's not suing and I don't get a murder charge. Lucky!" She laughed, a bitter, broken sound. "I'll have police brutality and wrongful death on my permanent record for the rest of my life."

My stomach knotted. "What? Are you sure?"

Now she did cry, long sobs into the phone, no words. It broke my heart, and I didn't know what to do. Isabella didn't cry. She just . . . she didn't cry.

"You didn't do anything wrong," I said, hurting for her, hurting for me, afraid for her. "I was there. You didn't do anything wrong."

"It's on my record." She sobbed again, the crying taking on an angry, frustrated tone.

"But you didn't do it."

"It doesn't matter! IA determinations can't be appealed. If it wasn't for the union . . ." Another angry sob. "Bastards."

"But I know what really happened. Branen believes you, right?"

It took her another few breaths to be able to speak, and when she did it was heavy with defeat. "It doesn't matter what he believes. It's the determination, and it's in the papers now. His hands are tied."

I felt hollow. "What will they do? You can't—" I couldn't even bring myself to say it out loud. Her job was everything to her, literally everything, her whole life. And her job was a big part of my life too, a part of the system that kept me on the wagon and sane. "Will you still be a detective?" I asked finally, unable to help myself. What would she do if she wasn't?

"I don't know. I don't know. The brass are reviewing the files. They'll have a decision in the next few days. Branen said he wanted to do it out of the media limelight, that it would be better for everyone that way."

"What does that mean?" I asked, worried for her.

"I don't know." She took a breath. "Maybe they bust me back to traffic, maybe I'm Michael's assistant now. I don't know how in hell I'm going to earn my way back, not after this kind of mark, but I'm going to try. I have to try. This is the kind of thing that destroys people's careers."

"You have the highest close rate in the department," I protested, trying to make myself believe they wouldn't fire her. They couldn't. It might destroy her.

"It doesn't matter. The mayor wants to be seen as against brutality, at least that's what he said at the press conference today. I made the mistake of watching it. People forget the commissioner is appointed, but times like this . . ."

"If he doesn't keep the mayor happy, he loses his job."

"Yeah. Branen told me."

She'd stopped crying, but the silence on the other end of the phone—and the other end of our weak, distant Link—was still vacant, devastated.

"If this goes badly for me . . ." She trailed off.

"What?" I asked.

"When you asked about the private eye thing, us opening one on our own, was that a joke?"

I paused. "Not if you don't want it to be."

She took another shuddery breath. "Let's keep that on the back burner for now."

I took a breath. If she was thinking next steps, that was a good sign. Maybe she wouldn't fall apart. Maybe. "I know you'd rather be a cop, even if they bust you down to traffic," I said. "It's okay. I know your job is your life."

"It's not my whole life." Then, after a second: "I feel bad. If I'm not at the department, I don't know if they'll give you the hours."

I tried to figure out what she was really asking. "Branen hasn't let me work with you in six weeks anyway. He already doesn't like me. He decided that I was worth the aggravation, or at least he has so far."

"Let's hope he keeps thinking that," she said.

Now I was afraid. I'd been worried for Cherabino, sure, but with all that had been going on I hadn't even stopped to consider that I might lose my last hours of work at the department as well. I wished she hadn't brought that up. Now I was worried for me too.

Suddenly she said in a rush, "I know it's late, I know you're on a job, I know there're all sorts of reasons why you can't, but could you come here? At least be here when they tell me?"

"I thought you didn't want me in the building even," I said, my heart sinking.

"I . . . I know I said that." She took another breath. "Look, forget I asked, okay? It's just . . . it's just really . . ."

"I wish I could be there right now, I really do, but I can't," I said quietly, and opened up the Link as far as it would go. It wasn't the total presence from earlier, but I could feel her, and I thought she could feel me.

I pictured wrapping her up in my arms and whispering compliments in her ear, I pictured all the warmth and comfort I had in me, and then made some up. I sent it all, all I had, and my fear and heartbreak for her went too.

She sniffled over the phone and gave a little sigh. Just a little one, like maybe it had done some good.

She relaxed in my mental arms, put her head on my chest, and held on. I hung up the phone, gently, and held on too. It was an incredible amount of mental energy to keep up the contact over such a long distance, and it probably strengthened the Link. Right now I didn't care. She wasn't alone either, and she needed to know that.

I held her like that, mind-to-mind, for at least half an hour, until she fell asleep. And then I let it go. My head pounded dully, and what little rest I'd gotten had just been obliterated.

I got up, pulled on my pants, and sat in the office chair, the light from the lamp spilling over on the other side of the room sparring with the red reflected-neon-sign light coming through the blinds. I sat there and thought, my feet getting cold, my back getting cold.

Could I really save Tommy? And if I couldn't, did I have any business at all staying here, when I could go back to Atlanta, back to Cherabino? Showing up for Cherabino was different from the drug, I told myself, but I didn't believe it.

I would be a coward and a failure one way or the other: a kid's life or Cherabino's real need when her world was disintegrating. I tried, rubbing my bleary eyes, to figure out what Swartz would want me to do.

I felt torn, unthinkably torn. It was too early to call Swartz, probably. Five a.m. In another hour, maybe.

There was a knock on the door. It was Jarrod's mind, and it was as buttoned-up and overcontrolled as I'd ever seen it.

I answered the door, still in my undershirt and the wrinkled pants from last night. "What is it?" I asked.

He passed me a photograph, grainy and on thin paper

like it had been photocopied. In it, Tommy sat on a chair, purpling bruise on his face, mouth split, holding up a copy of a newspaper dated this morning.

TELL THE TRUTH OR HE DIES, a note said, cut from newspaper letters, also photocopied.

CHAPTER 21

"**Where did you** get this?" I asked Jarrod. I felt like I was in free fall, helpless. Oddly, though, there was some relief mixed in with everything else.

Tommy looked bad, looked scared and dehydrated and poorly cared for. My heart broke. He was still alive, though. He was still alive, though his eyes looked dead. Whoever had him could have done anything.

And I might have left him for the drug, or for Cherabino. I might have failed him yet again. The certainty felt like a two-edged sword. I had no choice. He was alive, and there was that vision. Cherabino would have to wait, whatever it cost her, whatever it cost us, me. Because somewhere—maybe—Tommy was alive, and maybe I could save him.

So why did I feel like the world had just turned into confetti? Why did I feel like such an aching failure?

"Wh-wh-where did you get this?" I repeated to Jarrod.

"Sridarin saw a teenager delivering it at the judge's house half an hour ago." His eyes were sympathetic.

"I thought we were all supposed to leave," I said. My hands still shook from the emotions, the overwhelming emotions. I struggled to think.

"Sridarin takes his responsibility on protection duty very seriously," Jarrod said. "He stayed behind on stake-out, just in case, and it's a good thing he did. We have the teenager in custody, but he's not talking. Can you take the location from his mind like you did the other?"

I paused, brain literally stuck for a moment. "Um, yeah." I held open the door. "Come in while I get a shirt on."

He did and my brain finally turned on.

"Can I have an opinion?" I said.

"Of course."

I took a breath, wanted a cigarette, wanted Satin, wanted to be anywhere—anywhere—but stuck between these choices. But I was finally thinking. "To be honest, I think we need to lean on the judge. Whatever is going on, she's at the center of it. That's what the note tells me. I know interrogations. I think she cracks first."

Jarrod nodded and stepped in, the door closing behind him. Judging from the deep circles under his eyes, he hadn't slept much more than I had. "I still need a location for where the teenager got the photocopy."

"I have nowhere else to be at this moment," I said. I pulled on a clean shirt, buttoning it. "We'll do what we need to do."

Mendez met us out front, a carrying case of coffees in her hand. For the first time, I felt fear from her, true fear.

In my experience, when the cop gets afraid, you should be terrified.

"Tommy's not going to live, is he?" I asked, once we were in the car.

A short silence while the two of them tried to figure out how to respond. Jarrod put on the anti-grav engine, floating up into traffic, and made a show of being very busy with that. Finally he said, "I have a hostage negotiator driving in from Atlanta. He'll be here in a few hours. If we can get them talking . . ."

"Have they called?" I asked. "Do we have any contact information from them at all?"

"Nothing but the phone call you picked up the other day," Mendez said. "And we don't even have a recording of that one. If they're communicating with the judge some other way, we don't know about it. No letters, even, except the one we showed you."

"So unless we get them talking, you think he dies."

Resounding silence in the car. My heart broke.

A few minutes later, struggling to stay on topic, I said, "In the vision, I'm there with Tommy, at least mentally. And I'm talking to Fiske over the phone. If I get a chance to talk with him, what do I say?"

Mendez turned all the way around in her seat again. "You're sure you talked to Fiske? And Fiske has some influence on the man who took this child?"

I nodded. "Yeah."

"You bargain," Mendez said. "Hostage taking is never about the hostage. It's always about power, or respect, and or some third, difficult-to-obtain goal. If you can calm this guy down and negotiate with him, it's possible we all walk away from this."

"What do I possibly have to offer Fiske?" I asked, thinking of the drug he'd left me. "He's not exactly a fan of mine."

"Everybody wants something. But we'll cross that bridge when we come to it. I'm far more interested in exactly where this man is. If we can get there rather than negotiate, it's better for everyone."

"It's an abandoned barn in the vision, I told you that," I said.

"There are countless abandoned barns within a hundred miles," Jarrod said. "If you can keep him talking and get additional information about his location, we can send in a special unit to talk this out. The FBI has a hostage retrieval unit on standby—they have helicopters, and they're ready to scramble. But there's no point until we know where he is. How soon do you talk to this guy?"

"I have no idea! It's not like I can call this stuff up out of the void." I'd tried for another vision already and failed. At this point, though, I wouldn't want to get another vision. If all of this led to Tommy's death, led to the ending I saw in the vision, I didn't want to know. I had to believe I could change it. I had to. It was the only thing keeping me sane right now.

Jarrod let out a sigh, like he'd been wanting me to do just that, to call up mystical answers. He was going to be disappointed.

"We're all on edge," Mendez said. "Let's see what the judge says."

Jarrod changed skylanes, as cautiously and controlled as everything else he did. "Mendez, I want you to meet up with Sridarin and get a location out of that teenager. I don't care what you have to do. Then go there and see if there's evidence. You can have the car once we're at the house."

"Don't you need backup with the judge?" Mendez asked.

"I will handle the judge with Ward here."

She nodded. "Yes, sir."

Sridarin was waiting for us on the sidewalk of the judge's house, in a long trench coat. Under the streetlight, his face was half in shadow, but from what I could feel in Mindspace, he was grim. "I have bad news."

I stopped midstride.

"What's going on?" Jarrod asked.

"You remember the jury was held over the weekend because they couldn't come to a decision? Anyway, they all received envelopes under their hotel room doors this morning before anyone could waylay them. The security camera we set up surreptitiously was disabled. We have no footage of the perpetrator."

"What was in the envelopes?"

Sridarin shook his head. "It's the same picture the judge received, of her son in obvious distress. Helpfully labeled with who his mother is. The jury is panicking, and I suspect there will now be a mistrial."

Whoa. It seemed impossible to believe that Fiske had won—and won so quickly. An overwhelming sense of guilt and responsibility rode me, and rode me hard. I wanted to be somewhere, anywhere but here, dealing with this.

"Why a mistrial?" Mendez asked.

"With the sequestration, the pictures are going to seem like credible threats. It's all over. Jury tampering is a felony, but that doesn't mean that it won't give the perpetrators what they want in this case."

"That's not our issue right now," Jarrod said. He was overly controlled again, his emotions muffled like a tuning fork against a piece of velvet. "Is the judge awake?"

"She's awake—the light has been on for an hour—but she's not letting anyone in or answering the phone," Sridarin said.

"Thanks for the update," Jarrod said, and moved past him.

Sridarin just looked at the man, reacting to his rudeness.

"It's been a rough morning," Mendez said. "Thanks for sharing. You going to be here for a while?"

"I'd like to actually be in the house if that's a possibility." He still felt driven and a little guilty, but with the forward motion, better. I knew how he felt.

"Come with us," Mendez said, and we followed.

Jarrod talked us into the house and gave the judge a copy of the photo.

I could feel the photo hit her like a blow to the head. She closed her eyes.

Parson sat down on the closest chair, still ten feet away, the strange egg-shaped thing that I'd interviewed the bodyguard on. Her hands were shaking, her mind caught in some horrific processing loop.

I knelt down, my knees hurting, to be more on her level. "What truth are you supposed to tell?" I asked quietly. The others were close enough to hear but not close enough to interfere or feel like they were standing over us.

"I hate you," she said, tears starting to pool in her eyes. "I hate you, you understand? I hate you."

She meant it, but it wasn't the worst thing that had happened to me in the last few days, not by far. "I know," I said, and, as much as it hurt to apologize, "I'm sorry. If there's anything you're holding back, now's the time."

Parson laughed, a bitter, bitter laugh. "After all of that? Really? And you still haven't guessed. Fucking terrible telepath if you ask me."

I suppressed any reaction the same way I would in the interview room. Strong emotion meant I was doing something correctly.

I waited, because it seemed like she wanted to talk.

She looked down at her hands and laughed that horrible laugh again. "After all of that, all of that."

"What did you do?" I pressed, seeing the beginning shapes of it emerge in her mind, surprising and disturbing.

She looked up at me. "The death threats were real. The death threats were real, do you understand? But I got bodyguards for Tommy and me and I rode them out. I'm a good judge. I play by the rules."

"What did they want you to do?"

She took in a breath of air. "First they wanted me to

recuse myself from the case. I wasn't going to play that game. Like I said, I got the bodyguards, and I let the local police know. It was manageable."

"Then what?" I prompted, when she seemed like she wanted to go silent again.

She glanced up at the other agents behind me.

"I'm a telepath. I know already," I said, a standard lie to get suspects to confess in the interview rooms.

She laughed again. "No, no, you don't. After all of that, God help me, but you don't."

I waited. She was confusing the hell out of me. Finally: "What did their demands change to?"

"They wanted me to throw out the testimony of the licensed prostitute, the one who actually saw him beat the woman. And disallow certain evidence that was collected by the police that doesn't have a perfect chain of evidence." The last was accompanied by a sense of deep shame and anger, so intense she shied away from it, refusing to spend any time there.

"Why was that a big deal?"

"The prosecution's entire case turned on those two facts: the hair in the hotel room belonging to Pappadakis, and the testimony of the lady of the night. Everything else was circumstantial." That intense sense of shame again. "But then . . ."

Flashes of images I couldn't quite make sense of, including evidence bags, a cop's face, other things that made no sense. And that shame, that shame and anger and disgust that had driven her to the impossible.

Behind me, Jarrod said, "But you told them no, right?"

She shook her head, pushing all those images away.

Shut up or leave the room. She's on the verge of shutting down. If you want information, you get really quiet right now, please, I told Jarrod specifically mind-to-mind, and repeated the warning for the others in the room, one by one. *I know what I'm doing.*

"I never should have trusted you people," she said. But it was a lie, because she'd not trusted us to begin with. In fact, she'd done the opposite. "You screwed everything up! How was I supposed to fix it? How with you people here?"

"What did you do?" I asked, wanting to back up. I knew that mix of emotions. It was what came out in the interview room when someone had murdered, or worse. When someone had crossed every moral boundary she'd ever had. "What did you do?"

"There was a murderer for hire up on parole. He'd been one of my convictions. I told him I'd get the parole approved if he'd connect me to someone who could do the job. And then I set up the attack. The original one. On the way to Tommy's school, not the attack outside the courthouse. That one was all him, all the man who was blackmailing me."

I had to physically restrain myself from reacting. "You set up the original attack on your son?" I kept my voice as flat as I could, but some of my shock and horror must have leaked through, because she looked up.

Behind me, every agent in the room reacted, a storm in Mindspace. One gasp. I repeated my warnings to be still and quiet or leave.

She looked at them and thought about being silent then, about clamming up and getting a lawyer. She'd said more than enough. But there was that picture . . .

"Tell me," I said, to bring her attention back to me.

"They were just supposed to make it look good. Credible. No one was supposed to get hurt." That laugh again, a sound grating on my nerves like a cockroach skittering across the floor. "No one was supposed to get hurt."

Now the images were coming freely. Her shock and dismay when the court lawyer's call had the FBI showing up at exactly the wrong time. Her plans to take herself and her son out of state in fear for their lives and as a way to remove themselves from the threat. Her determination to keep her secret no matter what it took. Her pride and horror when I hadn't had a clue, despite everything. She'd been avoiding me, yes, been so uncomfortable around me, but I hadn't even noticed. Her son was a better telepath than I had been, and he was ten.

She'd been genuinely horrified when Tommy was taken. She didn't love him, not the way a mother was supposed to love a son, and she regretted this. But he was hers, her responsibility, and he was in danger. He had been taken by the man who had first threatened her, in retaliation for changing the game.

"Garrett Fiske," I said. She hadn't known his name, but I knew the voice who'd called her. I knew the inflections of the man who'd talked to her on the phone at the location the letters had told her to go. And I knew the twisted sense of humor that would imperil the very boy that she'd used as her getaway card.

"If that's his name. He told me yesterday that he didn't usually involve families." Her voice shook then; her hands shook. "But since I'd involved the boy first . . ."

She'd played the card that got Tommy involved, I realized. Fiske's stupid sense of honor. My stomach dropped, and I hated her. I hated her in that moment as much as any human being could hate another.

"That's not the worst of it, is it?" I asked. I forced myself to control my feelings against this woman, who had played a power game she'd thought she could control, and escalated things beyond any control.

She'd gambled with *Tommy's* life. If this went badly, *she* would have been the one who'd gotten him killed. Tommy, a smart kid, a patient kid—all he wanted in the world was to make his mom happy and to be a telepath. "How dare you endanger him?" I spat.

"It was supposed to be for show! It was supposed to be my get-out-of-jail-free card. With that kind of attack, I could have a hiatus on my duties and come back to it with my career intact. With that kind of attack I could figure out how to take down the man for good. And Pappadakis would be somebody else's problem. I had a plan, okay? I had a plan that would have fixed everything."

I took a breath and forced myself to be the interrogator now. I would get every scrap of information buried in this monster's brain and then I would never speak to her again. "You thought that the next judge would probably give in to their commands," I said flatly. "You thought that you were handing the next judge over for the same kind of death threats or worse. Maybe they were killed instead of you. Maybe there's a mistrial. Or five. You didn't care. You fucking didn't care."

"I'm doing the best I can!" she yelled at me.

"Tell me. Tell me what you're hiding," I said. There was more buried there, like a folding fan still half-closed.

She shook her head, but the images were coming into her head faster than she could push them away.

"The evidence," I prompted, the baggies coming back up along with the shame and anger and disgust, shame strong enough to drown in it. "The evidence. Tell me or I will take it from your brain." It was unethical, it was a violation, and I wasn't sure if I crossed that line a second time in two days I would ever be the same person, but right now I almost believed I could. I threatened it; I lied, hoped I was lying. I threatened like hell and hoped I didn't actually have to make the choice.

We waited on the knife's edge, her shame and anger and

contempt and disgust warring with my threat. She held my eyes, considering.

I didn't know what she saw in my face, but she must have believed me.

Parson looked down. "I allowed tampered evidence into a trial. A different trial than this one. It was two years ago." She met me in the eyes. "He was a pedophile. He liked little girls. He'd gotten off on three technicalities prior to this and the trial was going badly." Overwhelming shame from her again, along with anger and a painfully strong sense of self-righteousness. "They couldn't make it stick, so . . ."

"The detective in charge of the case wanted to add evidence, and you knew it was falsified, and you let it happen anyway," I said.

"Yes."

I closed my eyes to hide my contempt.

"A pedophile went to jail for the rest of his life. I did the right thing," she said. "But nobody could ever know about it. I don't know how they knew about it."

"And now they want you to do the same thing for the Pappadakis trial."

"Yes."

I opened my eyes again, sat back on my heels. "You knew you'd lose your career if your previous misdeed came out, but you didn't want to work for Fiske. You didn't want to mess with the evidence in the Pappadakis trial. And you couldn't report it, not either way. You were between a rock and a hard place."

She nodded, hands shaking again, but finally feeling that sense of freedom that comes from telling the truth. I'd seen suspects admit to things totally against their best interests, over and over again, for that cleansing feeling of telling the truth, finally telling the truth to someone who was listening.

She nodded one more time; then she said, "If I wasn't part of the case anymore, if I was in a different state, there was no reason to make the information public. They'd charge me money for blackmail, yes, but I'd pay it. Or they'd ask for something else, maybe something I could find a way to do without helping the criminals. And I had time to take them down. I have friends."

It was critical to her self-image that she was one of the good guys, against the criminals. Ah, how she'd fallen away from that self-image.

"One last question," I said. "The picture. Why take Tommy? And then why tell you if you didn't tell the truth they'd kill him?"

She laughed that bitter laugh. "He told me, if I didn't do what he wanted, I'd lose the thing I cared about most. That's why I needed to get out of the state. So this wouldn't happen."

"Who is he?" I asked. She didn't mean Tommy when she said the thing she cared about the most. She meant her career, as horrible as that was.

"That friend of Pappadakis, the man on the phone. He's a shark, but I didn't think he'd like to play with his food quite so much. I should have just done what he said." She looked at me with complete vulnerability then. "My career is over. No matter what else happens today, that's the case. But Tommy—I couldn't bear it if he died because I screwed up."

Her emotions were strong, terribly strong, but she was so controlled, like an iceberg holding all the things inside in a solid frozen mass. When she melted—and she would melt eventually—what she was holding back would damage, or destroy, her. Fiske had won all right. She would never be the same as a human being after this.

She looked up, beyond me, at Jarrod. "You call the news

agencies and you tell them. I don't want to face people. But if he sees it on the news, maybe he lets Tommy go." She stood up and looked down on me. "I still hate you."

I stood too. "The feeling is mutual."

She nodded and went upstairs to her room, hands wrapping her robe around her, mind shaking from intense emotions of every kind roiling around. Overall, a sense of frozen horror, frozen loss, the kind of loss I'd felt before when a couple had lost their small daughter. Her career—her career she did love like a child.

CHAPTER 22

After I'd gotten absolutely every detail out of the judge that I could think of, I sat down on the back porch steps and smoked. The others were doing police things, things that they could do without me. I was getting an itchy feeling, a bad feeling that wasn't at all impacted by the cigarettes. Something that felt like the precog trying to wake up again.

I reached out to Tommy—and actually connected. But he was asleep, or unconscious, and that connection between us was frail. Jarrod had said that they'd leak the judge's confession to the media and maybe that would be enough, but I didn't think so. Once Fiske started a play like this, he'd carry it through to some larger end. It wasn't just about the judge anymore, I realized with a sinking feeling. It was partially about me. Me. And my connection to Tommy.

Would he kill Tommy just to torture me? I couldn't get the idea out of my head. It would be like Fiske, and he was angry with me.

My hands shaking, I finished the cigarette. I couldn't stay here and do nothing. Sure, I could make more phone calls. But as Jarrod had said, they had people to do that. It was up to me to do the things only I could do. And if Tommy died and I didn't do every fucking thing in my power to stop it . . . well, even if I did, I wasn't sure I could live with myself.

Even if I had to cross another ethical line I'd never be able to undo. Even if it meant I couldn't be there, wouldn't be there for Cherabino. It hurt me, but that was my choice, I realized. I was sober for this, and I'd do the best damn job I could, no matter what it cost me. I stubbed out the cigarette. It might cost me a lot.

I went back inside to tell Jarrod where I was going, and then got my rented car from the side street next to the judge's house. I had an errand to run.

I parked across from the theater and walked in, scanning the world around me with a tired mind, hands jittery from nerves.

The theater folks had protested long and loud they didn't hurt anybody, and the more I'd thought about it, the more it seemed likely that they were connected with a larger organization. They'd even referenced a couple of key players in what I was betting was a lower level of the organized crime group Fiske at least in name controlled. You weren't that sure you didn't hurt people unless there were people you dealt with who kept the messy parts out of your way. Either that or you were an idiot, and these folks—though odd—didn't seem like idiots.

The morning was bright, a blue sky dotted with clouds barely gray with pollution, the air almost clean enough not to make me cough even at a quick trot. The cars on the ground cruising slowly through parks and streets, a beautiful old Jewish temple dominating the skyline a few blocks away, looking down on the rest of the street, including this ancient theater.

I'd convince those guys to tell me how to get in touch with their contact in the organization, and then convince him to refer me to his boss, and his boss. Eventually someone would connect me with someone important. Eventually, like Mendez had recommended, I'd be able to negotiate.

I slowed down near the circular post in front of the theater, the green-and-white stone tile across its bottom glittering in the sunlight. I moved up and knocked on the door. It was locked, and the lights were off.

Crap, what was I going to do now?

Behind me, I felt a mind approach with purpose. I turned, on alert.

A man in a suit and a hat nodded at me, walking slowly, something under his arm.

"Who are you?" I asked.

"Are you Adam Ward?"

"Who wants to know?"

He nodded, and slowly—slowly enough that even the most hair-trigger cop wouldn't have pulled a gun—shifted the package under his arm until it was faceup. It was a puzzle box, I saw, as he stopped walking four feet away and gave me a good look at it. It was a puzzle box exactly like the one that Fiske had left in my hotel room, except half the size.

"My employer has a gift for you," he said.

"Fiske?" I asked.

He smiled. "He pays me well enough that I neither know nor care about his name."

"What is it?" I asked warily.

He smiled again and said nothing, holding out the box. His hands were bare, so there was no contact poison there, probably. But if Fiske's new gift was anything like his old one, there would be plenty of reason not to take that box.

I sighed and took it.

The man tipped his hat and turned around to leave.

"What? Don't you have anything else to say?" I asked.

"My business here is done," he called over his shoulder.

The street felt empty, void of minds all around as I held the ominous box in my hands.

I took two deep breaths and opened the box. It opened as simply and smoothly as the other one, its locking mechanism disengaged. Inside was a smaller space lined in red velvet, and a folded piece of paper. I picked up the paper, shook it to unfold it, and read.

There was only a single number written on its surface.

I have the information you seek, it said.

I found a pay phone in a park a block away, under a magnolia tree that smelled vaguely of powdery rot. A sentry plant glared at me from a few feet away, almost like an old man. The park itself was empty, all too empty.

I took deep breaths, several in a row, trying to get the emotion to damp back down. I'd have to negotiate. I'd have to think to do this correctly.

It started to rain. The rain was light, but it smelled terrible, like baked-in pollution of the most dangerous kind. It wasn't the worst thing I could deal with today, but I winced as a droplet ran off my head and down the back of my neck. Cancer flushes were pricey, and even with the Guild's part insurance, I didn't have the money to be spending indiscriminately.

I dialed slowly, double- and triple-checking the number. I put the box down on the ground and straightened up while the phone rang. And rang. And rang.

Finally he picked up.

"Adam Ward." Fiske's voice popped the syllables of each letter slowly, taking the maximum enjoyment out of the moment. I knew then that this would be bad.

"Fiske," I said. "Is this the part where you tell me there's a sniper to take me out already set up here?"

"An excellent question, Mr. Ward. An excellent question indeed. How gratifying that you take me seriously. As it happens, I have other plans for you today."

I paused, using all my skills as a Minder to identify every mind in the vicinity. A few dog walkers a block away, office workers, and the like. No one near. No one paying attention, and no one with the focus I thought a sniper would need. Assuming they were within my half-mile range. Of course, I'd thought to check only after I'd talked to him. If someone had been there, it was probably already too late.

The only comfort I had against that thought was that Fiske wasn't a straightforward man, at least from what I'd seen and participated in in the task force. Yes, he rewarded loyalty and punished disloyalty. He usually did what he said he was going to do. But he was a chess player, a wheels-within-wheels kind of guy. If he said he had other plans for me today, they would be far worse than a single bullet, but I might, in the end, survive.

"What are we here to talk about?" I asked him.

"Mr. Ward, you should know two very important things. One, that I am the architect of your partner's destruction, and two, that I hold your charge's life in my hands. I imagine you have questions. You may ask them, and then I will offer you a series of choices. I suggest you choose very wisely."

I took a deep breath, putting my emotions aside with great effort. I had one opportunity to take back some control. Mendez and Jarrod had said, if I could keep him talking, that I might be able to get Tommy back. And I'd been on the street too long to think rolling over got you anywhere at all. I breathed again, deeply, once, twice, knowing that I wasn't going to get a second chance at this.

"If you remain silent, I will kill your partner," Fiske said in a matter-of-fact tone that made it all too clear he was serious.

"You will not," I said finally. "I will play your game, so far as it goes. Just realize I'll have some things to say as well."

"Ah, wonderful. I do so love an intelligent opponent. Ask your first question."

"By my partner, you mean Cherabino," I said, stalling. I felt like I was behind, like I was still processing what had happened up to this point, much less what he was saying now.

"I'd suggest you not try my patience with obvious questions."

What was his exact wording? "*Why* did you engineer my partner's destruction, and what exactly does that mean?"

"That's two questions, but I'll let it go for now. The why is simple. You came into my house without my permission and killed one of my associates."

So I had killed him. "That was an accident," I said. I'd turned on the sleep center of the woman's brain, and she had hit her head on the tile on the way down. "I did not intend to harm her permanently."

"You exposed a hole in my security system and so I let you go, but the death . . . I do not take the death of my associates lightly," Fiske said. "You should know by now that I had to answer that."

By his rules, I suppose he did. "And this is your retaliation? Against me?"

"I had a plan, naturally, to discredit you at the highest levels, but you ended up in Savannah before I had a chance to implement it. Fortunately you were there for your partner's destruction, which was an excellent start."

Finally it clicked. "You set up the guy outside the concert? You had someone beat him to death, and then you planted the fingerprints and bribed the witnesses to lie?"

"Ah, finally he asks a good question. Yes, that is exactly what I did. And today, my dear friend the Decatur mayor will inform the police commissioner that your partner must lose her job. So much more apropos than a simple execution, don't you agree? She does so love that job, your partner."

I closed my eyes, feeling vacant, horribly vacant. If I hadn't had that vision of the future, and Cherabino hadn't acted on it . . . "Is there anything I can do to get you to use your influence to reinstate her?" I asked, and then kicked myself. I couldn't deal with this guy. I couldn't.

But negotiation was the only thing that might work, I told myself. That was what Mendez had said.

"Ah, but he wants to jump ahead. Let's finish the question section of the game before you move to the choices. Ask your next question, and make it a good one."

"Why kidnap Tommy?" I asked. "If the judge set up the attack on her own, and your blackmail wasn't working, wouldn't it have been easier just to release the information to discredit her?"

"I can hear the pain in your voice. How wonderful. I must confess, it was delightful to find you popping up here, in the middle of this judicial matter. Especially after my men lost you in Atlanta, which they already regret. I have a policy that no one takes a job against me or mine, or against anyone I am already targeting myself. This is basic courtesy for the boss, and if I don't enforce the policy strenuously, I don't deserve the title. I had already made it clear I had an interest in the Pappadakis case, and the judge was involved. Her freelancers should never have accepted her money, and they have been appropriately disciplined."

"They're dead," I said.

"Yes, Sibley is very efficient, isn't he? The bodies should not have been found for a few weeks yet, but I did force his timeline unnecessarily fast. I have arranged for the critical evidence to be lost and we'll end up in the same place as we started. Plus a mistrial, and an opportunity to deal with you as you deserve. I do so love it when I can kill two birds with one stone."

"How can you be sure the evidence is lost?" I asked.

"I have allies nearly everywhere. You should know this by now, Mr. Ward."

"In the judicial system here in Savannah?"

"Ah. Another intelligent question. The judicial system in Savannah has been strangely reluctant to accept my little favors, it is true, especially as compared to your own home territory. But until this little dustup, it seemed well on the way, and the business community is very open."

"Like your friend Pappadakis."

"He is not a friend, he is a supplier. Surely you know the difference. I provide him with certain . . . connections in exchange for difficult-to-obtain parts that I need for other business ventures."

"You don't seriously think you'll get him off the charges? I mean, it's clear he beat his mistress to death."

"So judgmental. You have your little foibles as well—never, ever forget that, Mr. Ward. In this case I merely have to provide a significant show of resistance. His second-in-command has already been groomed, and if I show myself a strong ally, he'll make the same deals with me as did his predecessor. And to be honest, it's far more fun when they resist. I had had hopes that your dear judge friend might turn into an ally, after an appropriate time. But she did not, sadly."

"Why attack the judge at all?" I asked.

A small, self-satisfied laugh. "And why should I not? If she agrees to my terms, I have a powerful ally in a relatively new territory. Judges are so useful, you understand. If she resists, she is easily made an example to keep my allies here in Atlanta—or really, anywhere in my territory—inclined to keep their end of our little deals. There is no downside."

I shook my head, processing all of that. Fiske was playing a chess game, a long chess game for some final goal I didn't understand, and we all were just pieces to him.

"Why Tommy?" I demanded finally. "Why the photograph? Why kidnap Tommy? You already had what you wanted from the judge." I was unable to keep the desperation out of my voice. It was almost worse, the turmoil going on inside me against the absolute calm in his voice.

"People who get too clever must be dealt with," Fiske said, and I could hear the smile in his voice. "Forcing the judge to destroy her own career seemed ever so much more fun than doing it myself, as I said. Not to mention I get to see the local news commenting on her perfidy as we speak. She is ruined, and I get to watch. And it leaves us here, with this little game between us. You made the mistake of getting attached to the boy. I do so love it when opponents make mistakes. Without you, I likely would have returned him today."

"So he's still in danger, and it's my fault." I closed my eyes. "You want me to destroy myself the way that the judge did. That's why you sent me the vial."

"Very good, Mr. Ward. And thus far you seem to have passed up my little temptation. Good for you, and I mean that. I have every confidence that it won't last, however. Once an addict, always an addict, is that not what your precious Twelve Steps program says? How delightful you've given me a second hold over you now. Tommy is such a delightful little boy, is he not?"

I felt like he'd stabbed me with a serrated knife in the heart, and was twisting it, twisting it. "What do you want?" I asked, barely with it enough to do anything but react. But I had one chance to get through this. "What will it take to get Tommy out of there alive?"

"Ah," he said, the sound of a shark admiring a particularly lovely prey trapped against the reef. "I see it's time to enter the choice portion of our little discussion."

I reached out without thinking about it, to Tommy, just to try to connect one more time. After all the failures, however, somehow this time it worked.

I was suddenly in two places at once, in a moldy barn full of hay, and on the sidewalk, a phone receiver pressed to my ear. My internal eyes struggled to see both at once.

"The lady or the tiger," I heard Fiske say, as if far away. "Shall we see what you will choose?"

I looked around at the barn, as if with a sense of inevitability. Thin, winter-clear sunlight pooled around me in watercolor streaks, the imprecision coming from the odd connection with Tommy.

With a thought, I was outside the kid, looking at him, while at the side Sibley stood near a phone, waiting.

"Are you listening, Mr. Ward?" Fiske asked.

"Yes, yes, I'm listening," I said. I didn't know what I'd missed, and my heart lurched. I was going to lose track of this. I was going to lose Tommy, or Cherabino, or myself, or all three.

"What do you choose?"

"You have to give me more information about the choice," I said, hoping I didn't give away how lost I felt, torn between two realities. Fiske would take full advantage, I knew.

"I know you are stalling. I can reinstate your partner in her job with minor consequences. All it takes is a phone call to our dear mayor, and from him to the commissioner. In exchange, Sibley will visit you some dark night and strangle you to death. You won't know when. You will have at least a few weeks to anticipate the blow."

"Sibley will have to go back to jail," I said, grasping at straws.

"Perhaps. Perhaps. I do have other enforcers, Mr. Ward. So what will it be? You give up your own life in exchange for your partner's career? As you watch the ticking time clock on your life run out? Sibley has said your fear was particularly strong when he strangled you. This time he won't stop. He'll take his time, and perhaps he will take a recording to amuse me."

I thought about agreeing, as horrible as that was. I seriously, truly thought about it. But Sibley . . . I couldn't sign up for that, one of my worst fears, when I didn't know when it was coming. And Cherabino would kill me herself if she ever found out I'd gotten her job back from Fiske. She'd spent years on a task force to take him out, not to play nice.

But how to say it? This was the time at which Swartz would probably say I should pray. So I threw up an intention to whatever Higher Power that was listening, and hoped it might help.

My heart was beating in my chest like a drum.

"Time is ticking, Mr. Ward."

"What will it take to free Tommy?" I spat out, voice thin and breathless. I couldn't believe I was saying no. I couldn't believe I was letting him destroy everything Cherabino loved. But I couldn't just agree, not knowing what it would mean for that kid who'd trusted me to keep him safe. "How does that choice affect the kid?"

Fiske laughed then, and I didn't like the sound. "Very good, Mr. Ward. You cannot have both."

I forced myself to breathe, and thought of Tommy. I had to, or I would fall apart. I would do anything for Cherabino, anything. I would crawl over glass for her . . . but that vision, that vision that had haunted me for months. I couldn't turn my back on that kid either. Then, like a switch, my mind connected with Tommy's again, and I was back in that barn, with the old, moldy hay. I could feel his fear, his fast-beating heart as he stared at Sibley.

Adam? he said, shock in his mind. *Is that you?*

I'm here, Tommy. I'm here. I'm so sorry we haven't found you yet.

I felt him think, and then a rush of words I didn't catch. The Link was light, and I was strained already.

I was back in my own mind listening to Fiske say, "If you go silent again, I will shoot your partner in the head."

"I'm getting tired of threats," I said, tired, stupid in my tiredness and fear, well past any sense of self-preservation. "Let's assume for a moment that I'm doing the best I can to manage a very tired mind. And that I believe you absolutely in what you're promising. What is the second choice?" I asked him. "What is the deal for Tommy's life?"

He paused for a long moment. "I ought to kill you for talking back to me."

"But you'd rather not. You'd rather not kill me, or you would have done so already. Isn't it more fun to torture me with possibilities, to hold things over my head? Where would the fun be if I just rolled over and gave you what you wanted?"

Another long pause.

"I'm right, aren't I? The torture part is working, and it's

working well for you so far. Why not just tell me how the rest of the game goes?"

He made a thoughtful sound, and I tried to reach out to Tommy again, not as deep, just enough so he'd know I was there and help was on the way.

Fiske said then, "You're right. If I wanted you dead, you would be dead already. The rest of the game is simple. I know you have a connection to the boy, psychically. You were Minding him, after all. I'd suggest you connect to him again."

"It will take me a second," I lied.

"Take your time." A tinge of sarcasm in that voice, a tinge of frustration, but still that quality, that confidence that made me think I still had him, or he had me. Either way, he wasn't hanging up the phone.

And I did—I strengthened that connection with Tommy. *I'll stay with you as long as I can,* I said.

"Are you in place, Mr. Ward?"

"I'm here," I said. "Tommy is scared."

"Wonderful. He's not a fool, unlike his mother."

Tommy asked, *What do I need to do?*

"Wh-wh-what was the choice?" I asked Fiske, finding myself very weak in that moment, knowing I was out of time.

"You are a very perceptive man, Mr. Ward. Since you came into my home and destroyed a person in my employ, I too will come into your world and destroy something that you love. You have a choice—this boy here or your loyalty."

"What?"

"It truly doesn't matter to me. You, as I, share this idea of keeping your word, so far as it goes. You promise to do an unspecified favor for me, in the next two months. There will be a watch counting down this time, a watch with a tracking device I can read. If at any time you take off this watch, I will know it and our deal will be over. You will not like what happens if our deal is over."

"What favor?" I asked.

"Ah, ah, ah. Nothing so easy on your end. I will have you do something you very much do not want to do. It won't be against your partner, or your sponsor, but against someone else—anyone else. You will do whatever I tell you to do, promptly, because I asked."

"Why?"

"Because it amuses me to take from you the one thing you value more than your partner values her job—your integrity, Mr. Ward. You've had it a handful of years now and you value it highly. You have thirty seconds to make your decision."

"You have to give me more time. Please, Fiske, you have to give me more time." I moved closer to Tommy, staying there, trying to offer whatever comfort I could. The air was cold, the sunlight thin, and I smelled the old moldy hay and horse droppings like they were right there next to me.

Tommy's mind held on to mine, shivering. *How do I get away?* he asked me, small and scared.

Sibley was leaning against the post now and glanced at the phone. Clearly he was waiting for Fiske to call.

"You have to give me more time," I repeated, my own voice small.

"I have to do nothing I don't want to do." Fiske's tone was smug, amused, everything that made me want to destroy him.

How do I get away? Tommy asked me, and he struggled on the chair.

Be still, I heard Sibley's voice sound, and that over-whelming force of that device I couldn't see came over Tommy. He was still.

I didn't see a way out. I didn't see a way out at all.

"If you do not promise to do what I say, Sibley will kill him," Fiske said, still in that obscenely happy voice. "He will kill him and you will watch. You deserve this, after all. You deserve to be put in your place after you made this personal."

I couldn't bear to leave Tommy here, or to watch him die. Cherabino wouldn't have a job tomorrow, maybe, but he'd said nothing about killing her if I played fair. I took a breath and said, as vulnerable as I was, "Kill me instead." My voice shook. "I can't watch this. He's just a boy. Kill me instead. Leave them both and kill me instead." I closed my eyes. "You get everything you want that way. You know that I signed up for it. You know that I destroyed myself. You even get to watch."

"No, you don't get to be self-sacrificing today," Fiske said to me over the phone, the receiver a heavy weight in my ear as I watched Sibley through the boy's eyes. "I will make you suffer through the results of your actions. I will make you make a choice. Which is it, the boy or our deal?"

"What if I choose Cherabino?" I asked, out of nowhere, not even sure where that question came from.

"Ah, a moral dilemma. How sweet."

"Please, I need to think," I said. He was putting me in an impossible decision, worse than the Guild had done just a few months ago, worse than when they'd threatened me with death—

And that was it. My way out.

"You have no more time, Mr. Ward."

I knew what I needed to do. I knew! But I needed time, and the only way to get it was to play along, to eat my pride. "I beg you, Fiske," I said in the smallest, most pathetic voice I could. It burned to do this, but if it would save Tommy, I'd do it. "I beg you. Please don't make me do this. The choice . . . I need more time. Please give me more time. Please. Please."

"Ah, how the mighty have fallen. I do so love to hear a grown man beg." His voice was smug, self-satisfied. "You have twenty minutes, Mr. Ward. I am very serious. On the first second of the twenty-first minute, if I have not heard a satisfactory decision from you at this number, Sibley will strangle your adorable little charge to death. But of course, do take your time."

CHAPTER 23

I heard a dial tone and I hung up the phone. Knees weak, I sat down—on the stone path of the park. In the distance, I could hear the sound of a fountain running, birds chirping. The old stately oaks waving overhead in the breeze.

My hands shook. I wanted to throw up, to run, to fall off the face of the planet and get away from here. Anywhere but here.

But I had twenty minutes, and I'd better make them count.

I grabbed for the phone receiver.

"Stone?" I said the instant he picked up. "If you've ever in your life wanted to be a hero, now's your chance. I have a ten-year-old boy who is going to die in"—I looked at my watch—"eighteen minutes if we don't do something fast."

Three heartbeats went by. Then Stone said, "What do you need?"

I took a breath of deep relief. "Okay. I need you and a teleporter who can carry at least two additional people at least a hundred miles here as quickly as you humanly can. I'm in Savannah, so that's at least two Jumps."

"Why me?" he asked.

"You saved my bacon once already against this guy. It's the strangler we faced last year. Bring guns," I said. "And be prepared to deal with coercion."

Another few heartbeats and he said, "You're lucky I have your number on a priority flag. I'll be there in less than ten minutes."

I closed my eyes. "Faster if you can do it."

"Already moving. We'll talk about procedure later." And he hung up the phone.

I found a small bench maybe ten feet away from the pay phone and sat, watching the seemingly peaceful park around me. Every second felt like one less second on a ticking time bomb. I pulled out the paper from the puzzle box and put it in my pocket. In my slacks pocket was another piece of paper, this one folded several times.

I pulled it out. That's right—Quentin had given me his number. I stood back up and dialed the number. I couldn't just sit there.

But the phone rang and rang, and no one picked up. I left an awkward message with no return number asking him to be on alert and close by to the phone, and sat back down.

The next seven minutes were the longest of my life.

Finally—finally—I felt Stone connect to the tag in my brain, and a *wrench* as he or someone else used it to triangulate for a Jump.

The world turned upside down, and then the air *popped* out in a small explosion. Standing in front of me were two people, Edgar Stone and a smaller blond woman who looked very much like him. I could feel her effort; she sat on the ground without shame. Stone pulled out a thermos and handed it to her. A milk shake, his mind supplied. Highest-calorie thing one could drink quickly. And she did, gulping it down through the attached straw as quickly as possible.

Teleportation took a hell of a lot of energy, and to make

the four-hour groundcar drive to Savannah in less than ten minutes—at least two to three Jumps—was impressive by itself, much less with another human in tow. If Kara had done that, she'd have lost pounds of body fat and days of function. I'd seen it happen. Adding calories to the mix just seemed wise.

"Thank you for coming," I said.

Stone straightened. "You'd better not be exaggerating. This is my twin sister, Margaret. She can tow me anywhere, but you're going to be another issue."

Margaret waved a hand at me from the ground.

"That's how you've been disappearing all over the place!" I said. "She Jumped you out. That's kind of impossible, you know."

"We know," Margaret said from the floor, taking a break from the milk shake.

"How long left?" Stone asked. "What's the timeline?" He knocked on my brain. If he was really going to do more for me, he needed to know the truth.

"We have eight minutes before the call," I said, and dropped all my shields. He took the information off the surface of my mind but didn't push deeper.

"How the hell did you get in this situation in the first place?" he asked me.

"I'll explain later," I said. "You know I'm telling the truth. That's what matters. You have a gun?"

"Yes," Stone said. He sent some kind of mental communication to Margaret.

"Well, then. Let's save the boy. Give me forty seconds," Margaret said, setting the now-empty cup on the ground. She breathed in, deep calming ritual breaths. "You have a location?"

"It's a very fragile partial mind-link," I said. "But he's

in a wide-open area, so anything in the vicinity should be safe."

Margaret shook her head. "That's going to be tricky. Your timeline is ridiculous."

"We have to try," I said. "I have to try." And if I failed, I'd call Fiske back and agree, and deal with the consequences later.

"Okay," Margaret said, and stood. "I'm pretty mind-deaf, so Edgar's going to need to do the heavy lifting on the Link. If you can get me to the location mentally, I can Jump there. We've done this in drills plenty of times. Oh, and be aware. This many Jumps this quickly, I'm probably out of it when we arrive. If I'm sleeping, let me sleep, okay?"

I nodded and held out hands. Stone grabbed one, Margaret the other, and they held each other's remaining hand, a triangle made of people. I'd do anything—anything—to save Tommy if I could, so I dropped every shield I had.

Stone walked into my mind, focused, and I showed him the Link. A lighter, more feminine presence drifted behind him, caught up in his mental wake. Margaret. A sense of intense focus from her, and exhaustion, and pressure—a sense of bottled pressure, waiting for me.

Now was the time when it would all either work or not work. I tried to connect with Tommy. I tried. . . . And failed.

One more breath. Try again. Two heartbeats, and then it worked, along that fragile thin cord that connected us. We were there. A fuzzy image of that barn and Tommy, looking at Sibley with a thin cord in his hands. We were there.

I latched onto Tommy's mind, that foyer we'd built so carefully, and threw my whole mental weight into the connection.

Stone grabbed onto that Link, bringing his sister with him, and the pressure burst. The world stopped.

I turned inside out like an Escher painting, folding in space until nothing connected, until it was all impossible. Until it all hurt, wrenching horrible pain. The connection in the back of my head fell apart, and I thought for one terrible moment we would be lost in the between.

Then the universe righted itself, and I felt hard-packed dirt under my shoes. Margaret fell back to the floor, shaking, her hands falling out of mine. I felt her mind go under, into unconsciousness. Stone brought out his gun. And I looked up.

We stood in an old stable, rotting hay and dust smells incredibly strong. I sneezed. Sunlight beams came down like in the vision, and old horse stalls lined both walls to the right and left. A huge barn door, currently closed, stood twenty feet ahead.

Tommy was bound to a chair about five feet in front of me, and Sibley farther on, near a large post on which was hung horse tack of some kind. A low table held a phone on its cradle, its cord trailing away, and a small sphere. Crap. He had the device.

"Adam!" Tommy yelled.

"Hang in there," I said.

Sibley darted back, to the table, and Stone was already moving forward, gun pulled up. I had seconds to make a decision.

And I made it.

I took three steps to the right, away from Margaret's unconscious body, so I wouldn't trip on her. "A1, B5, B7 through 9, A13x, and C4 closed," I muttered to myself as I squinted, looking internally, deep. Repeated the chant, made the adjustments one by one, fast. "HL7 spun up . . ."

I pushed that part of my mind as tension, as tight and up as possible. Then, foolishly, threw a mental blanket over Processor 4, with all my strength.

The world went dark. Not the darkness of the inside of a cave, but the darkness of a man who has never known light. I literally could not think, no matter how much I tried, of what things might look like. I was blind, totally blind, inside my skull.

But I could still hear. Two gunshots in quick succession, then a crash.

Sibley's voice, ahead and to the right. "Put the gun down."

A clatter and a misfire, bullet screaming too close to my ear. But it hadn't hit me. I felt oddly calm, focused, like time was moving far more slowly than it ought.

"Sit down," Sibley said, but his words didn't have that weight of command, not to me. I could do this.

I could still feel an echo of Mindspace, though it felt empty, cold, far away. There was Tommy, afraid, on the left. A shadow that must be Sibley ahead and to the right. I moved forward, one step, two. Careful not to step on Margaret. Then faster, once I was sure I was past her.

Another shadow—Stone?—struggling but unable to move.

The phone starting ringing, a loud piercing ring.

Footsteps moving toward me now. It took the human brain minutes to run out of oxygen, and at least twenty seconds to run out of blood even if your throat was cut, your vessels laid open. He'd be coming for me; I could hear the footsteps. I turned up the collar of my coat, buttoned the button to protect my throat.

The phone kept ringing.

"Sit down," Sibley repeated, closer to me specifically.

"No," I said. "No," with all the force of all the months I'd been afraid of him. *"No!"*

"Watch out!" Tommy yelled. "He's coming for you!"

My left hand went up and over the front of my throat, firm, to protect the blood vessels. My right arm down, ready. Then I moved *toward* Sibley, everything in me ready for the push, the risk, the roll of the die that would save me or damn me, no questions asked.

He hit me like a ton of bricks, hard across the face. I went to my knees, stars blooming in my head despite the blindness. I let him, bracing for another hit.

Instead he had a cord up and over my entire neck with punishing speed. The cord made it partially under the coat, starting cutting with that specially serrated edge. It got the back of my hand—bad. Very bad. A bright line of pain there, and a feeling of damage. I let it go.

With all of my focus, all of my will, I forced my right arm up to grab his wrist, slipped, got the grab. He let me, squeezing down on the cord. More pain. More blood, and a feeling of incredible pressure on my neck as the cord pulled tight around the coat, around my neck, around my hand. I had to . . . I had to . . .

My hand hit his skin, and I opened all of the blocks I could in one rush, relaxing my mind. His thoughts moved in—and, between the space of one and the next, I had found the back of his mind, the right spot.

I pressed it.

He collapsed, the cord pulling tight with a snap that almost pushed me over. But he'd fallen, to the ground, asleep. I was still standing. Still alive somehow.

The phone stopped ringing.

Now that the blocks were gone, the emotion rushed in too. I stood there, and shook. And shook. My hand was bleeding. The back of my neck was bleeding. I felt the neck with my right hand all the way around, shallow cuts, it felt like. The coat collar was sliced, but it had protected me somewhat. The cuts in the back were deeper, but not much. I rotated my head, and it worked, but it hurt. Crap.

And my left hand . . . I couldn't move some of the fingers. It hurt, bad. I carefully felt along its back. There was a deep cut on the back of the hand, leaking blood. I could feel the bone. I shuddered.

"Are you okay?" Tommy asked.

"No," I said, voice still shaking a bit.

I had survived. That had been the most foolish thing I'd done in my life, but I had survived.

I pulled off my coat, shaking. It wrenched my hand and I almost screamed. I hissed in breath through my teeth. Finally it was off, and I asked the dark room, "Stone, you there?"

"Yes. Can't move," he said from maybe three feet to the left of me.

"It'll wear off in a few minutes," I said, in pain. Maybe I could find the device and use it to cancel whatever it was, but I didn't know what it would do to him to cancel it early, and I knew it would wear off in time. Plus, I was busy.

I unbuttoned my dress shirt with my right hand, bracing the shirt with the heel of my left. Crap, that hurt. One button, two, more.

"Is Margaret okay?" I asked.

"Is Margaret the woman on the floor?" Tommy asked me. "I'm okay too, by the way."

I closed my unseeing eyes in relief. Opened them, which was worse since I couldn't see. "I'm glad, Tommy, really I am. Is she breathing?"

"She feels okay to me," Stone said. "Just exhausted. We got enough calories in her, I think, to let her recover on her own in an hour."

I struggled with the next button and the next. Finally finished, and pulled the shirt off my right arm carefully.

Pulled the left sleeve over that hand, slowly, slowly, and used the main body of the shirt to wrap the hand, hard. The neck was shallower, I thought, since I'd shielded most of the serious area. Mostly bruises, maybe, and shallow cuts. The hand needed the bandage more. I wrapped it tight, cursing at the pain.

The warm blood dripped from my neck down my chest, one drop, two.

"How bad am I hurt?" I asked Stone.

"You're vertical and you're talking, so that's good." His voice was from a higher elevation now. Oh, good, he'd gotten to his feet. I felt . . . distant again. Blood loss or just a brush with death?

"Um . . . ," Stone said, from right next to me.

I started, moving back a step. Then took a step. "Sorry. I can't see."

"Why can't you see?" Tommy asked, still from the same spot. That's right—he'd been tied up.

"Minor mind Structure mishap," I said to Stone. "You have to pay for immunity somehow, apparently. I'm going to need somebody to unkink my brain when this is over."

"Understood," Stone said. "I take it it's not something I can do?"

"Have you got any deconstruction training?" I asked.

"Not for years."

"I'll wait for the specialist. Thanks." I could talk him through it, but some of the Structures were fragile. He could end up doing me worse damage than I'd done to myself.

After a moment he said, "The cuts on your throat don't look serious to me. They're already starting to clot."

"Good to know," I said. "Could you untie Tommy for me please?"

"Yes, somebody untie me!" Tommy said.

And we'll need to use the rope to tie Sibley, I added to Stone, mind-to-mind.

He acknowledged.

While all of that was happening, I took one small, careful step at a time toward the table I remembered being there. We'd need the phone.

I ran into it with my knee, hitting it with a small bang. Pain, but not serious. I felt around the table for the phone, found the receiver. Picked it up, set it on my shoulder, and dialed 911 by feel with my good hand.

Tommy's mind got brighter all of a sudden, and he started moving my way.

The dispatcher for the local county picked up. "Hi," I said. "We need an ambulance. And probably a prison transport. And the FBI."

"Where are you?" the dispatcher asked.

Where was I? Tommy grabbed me in a hug.

The Happy Go Lucky Stables, he told me. *I saw the sign on the way in.*

I told the dispatcher, asked her to contact Special Agent Jarrod of the FBI with the information, and gave her his number before hanging up. "Ten minutes," I told the other two. "Sooner if they call Jarrod on time. I think he has a helicopter available."

I could hear Stone ahead with the rustling of cloth. Tying up Sibley, most likely. We'd throw him back in jail, but I wasn't entirely sure how he'd gotten out in the first place. I'd ask Paulsen how to make it permanent, if it could be done, later. I hoped it could be done.

You couldn't have told me about the mind-control machine? Stone asked me.

I paused. *I thought I had, honestly. Why didn't you pull it from my brain?*

I was kind of in the middle of something, and you didn't seem to be lying. You'd rather I had spent the time to go rummaging through your mind instead of saving the boy here?

Um . . .

A moan came from his general direction. "Oh, good, she's waking up," Stone said. "Early even. We'll get another meal bar in her and she'll be fine."

Tommy held on, for a long, long moment. I let him, wanting comfort after that day we'd had myself.

"You showed up," he said quietly.

"I told you I would," I said.

And let him hold on for a while.

"You hurt?" I finally asked.

He shook his head and I felt it.

I pulled away. "Why don't you call your dad?" I asked, and got him the slip of paper from my trouser pocket.

"I know the number," Tommy said, in that dismissive tone.

I took a sigh of relief. He was okay, if he could talk like that. I might be blind, and the hand might not quite be working, but he was okay. Hopefully all else would be as easily remedied.

Then came the sound of the receiver being picked up and numbers dialed. After a few seconds, Tommy said, "Dad, it's me."

I heard some loud sound on the end of the line as Quentin went wild on hearing his son's voice.

"Don't yell, okay?" Tommy said, then paused. "Yeah, I'm okay. Adam and this other guy and a girl did the tele-totting thing and, like, showed up in the middle of the room with this crazy loud sound. The bad guy didn't stand a chance." His voice caught a little on the last part, and I knew he wasn't over what had happened.

I sat down on the floor, careful of the hand, and listened

to Tommy talk to his dad. For all the fear of the day, for all the roughness, sitting there listening to the love in Tommy's voice as he talked to his dad made it all worth it. He was okay. He was really, honestly okay.

And I'd done that.

CHAPTER 24

The phone rang in the stable several more times before the cavalry arrived, but I told them to let it ring. Fiske could wait. He'd done enough damage for one day, and not knowing what had happened would be good for him. Even if I suspected that it would make things worse for me some other day. The consequences would be rough, I was sure. They would haunt me for weeks or months or years. But right now, with Tommy alive, it all seemed worth it.

Margaret, now awake and hungry, fussed over Tommy while they both ate meal bars. Stone had sat down near me.

"Thanks for showing up on no notice," I told him.

"Yeah, well, it's nice to be a hero sometimes." He paused while he tried to figure out how to say something.

"My debt's going up from this stunt, isn't it?" I asked quietly. I was resigned to the cost. If they didn't overcharge me.

"It's not that—I'll give you my time for free. I have the discretion. The situation was exactly as you described, and you've earned a few of these. It's just, Margaret—"

"She's one of the elite couriers, isn't she?" I asked. "To send you here and there separately, she has to be good. She's pretty thin for someone who eats that much, and pretty comfortable pushing until she passes out."

"She's special," Stone said, a little wistfully. He'd never

really been special, not like that, but he'd done well enough. He pulled his focus back to me with a snap. "Anyway, they track her every quarter hour, and since she says she's going to be out for a day or so after this, I have to charge you."

"Wait. She pushed herself to passing out and she only needs a day of recovery?"

Stone laughed. "And enough food to feed a small horse. You think I'd have her teleporting me for effect if she couldn't spare the energy?"

I shook my head—and stopped immediately. "Ouch," I said.

"They'll be here soon," he said. "I called the Guild board here and they'll send somebody out to take care of your eyes."

"Good," I said.

The helicopter arrived a minute before the paramedics, the distinctive sound of the rotor blades filling the sky above the roof. The stable door opened with a *screech* a few seconds later.

"Dad!" Tommy yelled, and ran to see him, by the sound of the rapid footfalls.

"They're hugging. It's sweet," Stone said quietly.

"Good," I said. "I'm glad."

At the hospital, they fused my tendons back together with a machine and sewed up the hand with an old-fashioned needle. I whimpered.

"You're under local anesthesia. Don't be a baby," the nurse said from next to me as the doctor sewed.

"It hurts."

"I sincerely doubt it does," she said. I gritted my teeth and held on as another nasty stitch went in.

Everything hurt worse when you couldn't see it coming.

Ow. Another stitch. And another. After an unthinkably long amount of time, the butcher finished the job.

"We'll get you set up with a brace when you leave," the doctor said. "Don't move it for the next three weeks any more than you have to. The binder protein won't set, and your body won't grow a proper cell matrix if you move it."

"Okay," I said. Then jumped into the scary question, made worse by the lack of sight. "What's the long-term damage?"

"If you take care of it properly, you should get most of the use of the hand back," the doctor said. "It may always be stiff, but there are exercises you can do to encourage the strength to come back once it's fully healed. *Don't* move it for three weeks, or the damage will be a great deal worse. You're lucky we got you within an hour and it's a clean cut. Any longer, or any more complicated, and you'd lose a lot more." He thought about mentioning artificial nerve implants, then decided I'd be better off not knowing about other treatment options. Maybe scare me enough not to cut myself again.

He stood up. "Nice to meet you, Mr. Ward. Don't get into trouble again anytime soon, okay?"

"Do my best," I said.

Stone's phone call paid off a short while later, as the Structure Guild specialist arrived at the hospital. I had a long—and embarrassing—conversation with her about exactly what I'd done to myself, with details. Then, after a thorough and professional exam, she reset my mind.

Two things happened at once: I got a blinding headache, worse than the worst of my life, and my vision returned in full color. My eyes watered from the pain.

"Hmm," the specialist said. She was a black woman, taller than I'd thought she was, in the scrubs of someone who worked in a hospital full-time, though probably a mental hospital rather than this place. "Reaction headache is stronger than expected. With your permission?"

I nodded—then stopped. My neck still hurt, and the bandage pulled. "Do what you have to do."

She put her hands on the side of my head to help her focus better. I felt like I was in a blender for one terrible moment, the world wrenching and liquefying, and then it was over. The headache had turned into a dull pound. And my vision, if anything, got sharper. The world and Mind-space resumed their normal patterns.

"Thank you," I said. Took a breath. "How much do I owe you?"

She smiled, a truly beautiful smile. "This one's on the house."

I smiled back then. Today was not such a terrible day after all.

It was two a.m. by the time Jarrod drove me back to the hotel, my arm in a sling to keep me from jarring the thick hand-brace. It was dark outside, very dark, as we drove through south Georgia in an area largely without street-lights. The headlights made pools of light on the asphalt ten feet below, and on the trees on the sides of us. He was in the lowest skylane, and driving sedately, which was fine with me. I was tired, and the hand hurt pretty bad since I'd refused pain pills, and I was distracted by the trees going by outside.

"You realize you broke practically every rule in the book sometime in the last forty-eight hours," he said, after a long silence.

I looked over at him and remembered the ethical bound-aries I'd crossed with reading that unconscious man. That would haunt me for a while. With Tommy okay, though, it seemed worth the cost. "You sure? That procedures man-ual is pretty long."

Jarrod laughed then, a surprised, open laugh that filled the car. I'd never heard him laugh before.

"I'm sorry I got Tommy kidnapped," I said quietly when he was done.

He shook his head then. "That's all of our fault. For not investigating to the end fast enough, and for leaving you on your own. You were the one who got him found first. We were still working through the list of abandoned barns."

They'd have gotten there, but too late. And who knew whether Fiske would really have given Tommy back if I hadn't been here? He liked his cruelties. In the end, though, I'd fended off the vision, or its consequences. Enough, more than enough, for today.

"You're unconventional, even for a telepath," Jarrod said to me then. "But you brought me solutions like I asked for, and you got the job done. They don't always go this well."

"Thanks," I said.

"Thank you. I'd like you to work with us again, if you're willing, when something comes up."

"I'd like that," I said.

He nodded then. "Your check's in the glove box. There's a bonus. I know those Guild guys don't come cheap. I can't hire them directly, but . . ." He trailed off.

I reached forward, careful of my hand, and opened the glove box in the darkened car. I pulled out an envelope, which was going to be hard to open one-handed. Instead I pulled the amount from his mind. It was right on his surface thoughts, after all.

"That's a lot of money," I said.

"I have a discretionary budget," he said. After a few moments of silence, he added, "It's another half hour to the hotel. If you want to sleep, I'll wake you up when we get there."

"Thanks," I said.

Jarrod woke me up as promised when we reached the hotel, pointing out the rental car of mine they'd reparked here.

"This is good-bye?" he said.

"Yeah. I need to get back to the city," I said, yawning. "If there's anything else I need to handle, call me there, okay?"

"Can you drive with your hand like that?" he asked me.

"I drive with my right hand anyway," I said. "And it's mostly interstate."

He nodded. "We'll need a report and some other paperwork. The rest of the details here we'll handle with the locals."

I opened the car door, then paused. "What's going to happen to Tommy?"

Jarrod shrugged. "Up to the locals, but I have the feeling Tommy's going to end up living with his father."

"Maybe just as well," I said, then got out and said my good-byes.

I climbed up the outside stairs, exhausted, but oddly free. I'd stopped the vision. It had cost me, but I'd stopped the vision and I was still alive. It was like some immense weight had been lifted and I could breathe again.

The hotel room had the same musty smell, with a new component. No minds were there—that much I had made sure of before I'd entered the room—but there was a new note, just a note, sitting on the bed.

You won't see it coming, it said. *One day soon—but not too soon—you will die. Let the anticipation take you over.*

It wasn't labeled, signed or anything, but I knew who it was from.

There were advantages to being as tired as I was. I didn't have any energy left to worry about my safety in the future. My precognition was typically pretty good at giving me a warning, and by his own stupid design I knew death wasn't coming all that soon.

So I put the note in a plastic bag with some tweezers—just in case somebody could get prints from it later—and packed it up along with everything else.

When I got to the puzzle box in the drawer, I paused.

I wrestled back and forth with the decision, but in the end I took it with me. I slung my bag over my uninjured shoulder and checked out of the hotel, talking to the same poetry-thinking clerk. The FBI had already paid up my bill. That felt good.

There was an all-night coffee shop on the interstate just a few miles up the road. The car was working, and the bill was paid. I could leave at any time. But I had something to do first.

I stood in front of the hotel dumpster, a car-sized rectangle that smelled of rotting eggs, dirty laundry, and overly strong cleaning products bought on an industrial scale. It had been emptied since I'd last seen it, the pale resin covers shut over the top, all but one, still open, on the right.

I set down the bag on the ground, with a thud I felt should be louder. And all the old cravings, all the old justifications played in my head, but they seemed quieter somehow. I pulled out the puzzle box from the bag, struggling with the zipper one-handed. Then I straightened, and just held it in my uninjured hand while I stared at the dumpster.

I'd kept a vial of my drug in a secret compartment in my apartment for years without touching it, like a security blanket, like a promise to myself that I could use if I wanted to. That being clean was only today, and only tomorrow, not forever. This box would fit nicely in that little compartment. It would fit nicely in my life. No one would know. Even Cherabino wouldn't know, and I didn't have to take the drug tests anymore, not like I had. I even had my own money, to buy more of the drug.

But that was the thing. I didn't have Swartz here, to barge into my apartment, and his health was such that he might not do that for me again for a long while. No, it was just me, facing myself, and at home I wouldn't have all the distractions I had had here. I wouldn't have a ten-year-old prototelepath who I literally couldn't think about the drug around. I'd be there, me, nothing else.

I wanted the vial. I did. I wanted to fall off the planet, to make the world disappear, just one more time. Maybe I always would. But I wanted other things more.

Tommy was alive because of me, and Fiske hadn't won. Both of those things had required that I stay clean, and I was proud of them both, injured hand, injured mind, and all. I was legitimately proud of them. And those things— and the world that made them—could not live in the same world as using.

So, though it hurt something inside me, I lifted up the box and threw it—threw it—into the open side of the dumpster. It hit the back rim with a *crunch* that splintered the box. All the pieces fell, and I heard the sound of breaking glass.

My heart broke then too. But I was also proud, proud in a sad way. I picked up my bag and headed toward the car. I'd have a long time to figure out what I had to say about this in the next NA meeting. Several hours, at least, fueled by coffee, to think and wonder and plan. I hoped with everything in me that Isabella was okay, that her sanity and her hope had held even if the worst had happened, and that she'd give me a chance to be there for her now.

I'd given up my drug for the chance.

I arrived at Isabella's small brick house in north Decatur about seven a.m. The sun was just coming up, making pretty stripes in the pollution-covered sky. I was so wired on coffee that my right hand shook, but I was strangely happy. Worried and happy and everything, all at once.

She answered her door in a nightgown and robe. She seemed upset, but not destroyed, not from the quick look at her mind. One critical part of me relaxed.

"Can I come in?" I asked.

She pulled her robe closer around her, and I could feel the tiredness that matched my own. "Nice that you finally showed up," she said, but I felt her regret at my earlier absence, stronger than pleasure to see me.

"I've been up all night," I said. "Please let me in."

So she did.

"What happened?" I asked, inside. "With your job, what happened?"

She looked up, pain in her eyes obvious to even a non-telepath. "They fired me. For excessive force and police brutality. I'm gone from the force. I can't appeal. I can't appeal, Adam. And you weren't here!"

"What?" I said. I was tired, and not quite tracking.

"You heard what I said. You weren't here."

"You told me that I could work," I said, not knowing how to react. I felt guilty enough without her making a huge thing of this, especially if she was okay. She seemed okay. "I saved a kid's life yesterday."

She literally took a step back. "I didn't say you couldn't save the kid."

I could feel her anger and frustration bubbling up, though.

"But you couldn't be here, and then you show up out of the blue, without so much as a call. You could have been dead. You could have been sleeping with some tramp."

Now I was hurt. "You know me better than that. If I'm sleeping with anybody, it's going to be you."

"You couldn't tell."

I took in a deep breath, getting angry myself. "You're the one who doesn't want the *permanent commitment*. I'm keeping my damn promise! You want things different, you say the word."

She looked down first. Crap. This wasn't about the no-sex policy, was it? As tired as I was, my body was all too interested in the sex. I took a breath, then another, to get it under control. Exhaustion helped.

"What is this really about?" I asked her, taking control of my body and emotions by sheer will. This was the worst possible time to do this, but it was what I had.

Her thoughts settled, from chaos to a single thought. I hadn't been there. And if I wasn't showing up for her in some ways—though the thought of sex that meant something terrified her—she felt like I should be there for her otherwise.

"It's nothing," she said.

"Don't be a liar," I said, my voice too hard. I was frustrated myself, it looked like. "I'm sorry I wasn't here—I really am—but I'm here now and there's a kid still alive because I was gone. You have to work with me here. I work with you plenty." She hadn't fallen apart, had she? I'd made the right choice!

"Don't call me a liar," she said, and I felt the anger rise in her again. But the anger scared her—I got a picture of the trial, and people calling her all sorts of names, calling her anger the enemy. She breathed, feeling trapped, angry, and ashamed of being angry all at once.

"I'm here now," I said, feeling very, very guilty all on my own.

"Take the couch," she said finally, words bitter and broken. "You drove all this way. I'm not sending you back out. But you're not sleeping in my bed."

I flinched. "Does this mean we're over?" I asked, knowing

it was the wrong thing to say, unable to keep myself from saying it. I was exhausted, and I'd been afraid of this the whole drive up. Eager to see her and worried she'd be destroyed and afraid she'd turn me away. Again.

She breathed, stared at me, swallowed an agreement to the question. She finally settled on "I need space, okay? I don't know what else. I don't know. I just don't." Her world was falling apart.

I closed my eyes. That wasn't a yes, but it wasn't any certainty either. "If you're just trying to drop me politely . . . ," I said. I was disappointed, horribly, horribly disappointed, but I'd known this might happen for months.

"You want me to do that?" she yelled, stepping closer to me. "You want me to end this and walk away? Would that make you happy?"

"No." I shook my head, too much emphasis, but I didn't care. "No, that's not it at all."

The tension sat between us for one long moment, and then she broke.

"Then give me my damn space," she said. "Let me figure out my whole damn life before you go screwing with me, okay?"

"You can have the space, but—"

She cut me off. "I mean, you can't just not show up, not be here, and still expect me to totally trust you when it comes to the PI business. You have to earn this shit."

I just looked at her. "Wait. We're opening a PI business?" I'd thought that was off the table. I'd thought everything was off the table, and it had hurt. To hear different now . . .

"Yeah," she said. "And I need some space to figure this out. It's my whole life, Adam. My whole life . . . my whole life was that police force, and *you weren't there.* It doesn't matter why. It doesn't. That's what's the truth right now. And I'm not sure I can do business and personal both right now."

I took a breath. I'd have her in my life however she'd let me. I had no pride when it came to Cherabino, no damn pride at all. "So the personal . . . ?" I needed to hear her say it. I needed the hope to be gone if it was going to be. I needed the hope to be completely gone, if I had any chance of getting past this.

"Not now," she said, and laughed, a dark, angry sound. "Give me until we figure out this PI thing, okay?"

"I don't know what that means," I said, hating the sound of my own voice then. I was so tired, but even this tired, even this guilty, I wouldn't beg.

She frowned at me. "You're being an idiot. I'm not breaking up with you. I just need space, okay?"

A sense of relief washed over me, a tangible thing, relief and disappointment mixed. "Sure," I said. "Sure, take all the space you need."

CHAPTER 25

Two weeks later

"It's too small," Isabella said, looking around.

"It's what we can afford. This could really work," I insisted.

We stood in a vacant office space about the size of my tiny apartment, a single room with a dividing half wall, ancient stained carpet, and concrete walls. But the ceilings were high, the exposed pipes industrial in an interesting way—even if they were old and clearly functional—and there were huge windows behind us pooling sunlight into the space. The overwhelming smell was sunlight, with a hint of old stains. It was just right for what we needed.

Isabella turned. "What, are we supposed to entertain clients in the main room where everybody can hear?"

"What everybody?" I said. "It's you and me. Maybe a receptionist on a good day to take phone calls, you know, once we get enough cases. But it's not like we'll be fighting for space. We can actually afford this one."

She made a *hmrph* sound. "What's the bathroom like anyway?"

The building manager, a plain woman with a very tall hairdo with a flower in it, pointed out the small door on the far wall. There were two doors, and the bathroom was the one on the right, apparently.

"I thought that was a closet," Isabella said. But she followed the Realtor to the bathroom. After a moment, she came out. "It's disgusting. But at least it has a shower." A necessity for the workaholic Isabella, who had been known to sleep at the department more than once during heavy workloads. And she could clean the dirt.

"How much is it?" she demanded of the building manager.

I took a breath of relief. She'd made up her mind. Finally.

The manager named a price just barely within the budget we'd talked about. Isabella objected loudly. They started negotiating, Isabella's mind quietly happy in the process.

I took a deep breath, feeling the open sky above the office, the quiet minds of the accountants below us, an artist's studio on the right with blobby emotions like splotches of paint. I could work here, and work well. The sunlight hit my back, warming my bones. This would do well for the PI office. And she was happy. I'd cut off my hand to make her happy, even if it didn't get me what I wanted in return.

I adjusted my stance, settling the left arm in the sling better, the right hand in my pocket. Then I felt it. The paper that Fiske had given me, crumpled within the pocket. His death threat was still outstanding, still out there, and I hadn't told Isabella.

I hadn't even told Swartz.

Isabella and the manager reached an agreement, and Isabella turned to me with a smile. "We'll take it," she said.

I forced a smile to echo hers. "We'll take it."

We took care of the paperwork together, her shoulder brushing mine, her happy mind warming me like a fire in some clever cabin, almost enough. But when we got the keys and walked into the empty space, I felt it.

An overwhelming sense of loss, from her.

"You okay?" I asked.

"I'm fine." Her voice cut me off. She'd cut me off all too much these past weeks.

I turned to her and put my right hand on her shoulder. She let it stay, let it stay for the first time since that day, that day I'd shown up at her door after she'd been fired.

I half hugged her then, hope blooming like an insidious flower, a thing of heartbreak and possibility. Maybe she'd let me in again, eventually. Maybe. "This'll work out," I told her. "Even Swartz says this will work out."

I'd have her in my life however she'd let me, I told myself.

"It had better," she said. And she didn't pull away, even though she didn't move closer either.

With the sunlight falling on the empty space, I thought, it had to work out. Even with that crumpled piece of paper in my pocket, and all that she'd lost. All that I'd lost.

This was a brand-new, empty space, and we could fill it with what we wanted.

ABOUT THE AUTHOR

Alex Hughes has written since early childhood, and loves great stories in any form, including sci-fi, fantasy, and mystery. Over the years, Alex has lived in many neighborhoods of the sprawling metro Atlanta area. Alex Huges grew up in Savannah, where *Vacant* takes place.

ALSO AVAILABLE FROM

Alex Hughes

CLEAN
A Mindspace Investigations Novel

Adam used to work for the Telepath's Guild before they
kicked him out for a drug habit that wasn't entirely his
fault. Now he works for the cops, helping put killers
behind bars. His ability to get inside the twisted minds of
suspects makes him the best interrogator in the
department. But the cops don't trust the telepaths, the
Guild doesn't trust Adam, a serial killer is stalking the
city—and Adam is aching for a fix. But he needs to solve
this case. Adam's just had a vision of the future:
he's the next to die.

**"Reminds me very much (and very fondly) of
Jim Butcher's Dresden Files."
—SF Signal**

Available wherever books are sold or at
penguin.com

facebook.com/acerocbooks

R0153

ALSO AVAILABLE FROM

Alex Hughes

SHARP
A Mindspace Investigations Novel

Parts for illegal Tech are being hijacked all over the city,
the same parts used to bring the world to its knees in the
Tech Wars sixty years ago. Plus a cop-killer is on the loose
with a vengeance. It falls to a telepath to close both cases
and prove his worth, once and for all…

"A fun blend of *Chinatown* and *Blade Runner*."
—James Knapp, author of *State of Decay*

Available wherever books are sold or at
penguin.com

facebook.com/acerocbooks

R0177

ALSO AVAILABLE FROM

Alex Hughes

MARKED
A Mindspace Investigations Novel

After being kicked out of the Telepath's Guild, Adam
never expected to set foot inside their headquarters again.
But they need his help. A strange madness is slowly
spreading through the Guild. And when an army of
powerful telepaths loses their marbles, the entire world
is at risk...

"Fans of Jim Butcher will enjoy this series."
—*USA Today*

Available wherever books are sold or at
penguin.com

facebook.com/acerocbooks